FEEL ME

BOOK 2 IN THE NOVUS PACK SERIES

M. JAYNE

Publisher's Note

This book is a work of fiction. Names, characters, places and incidents either are the product of the author's imagination or are used fictitiously, and any resemblance to actual persons, living or dead, business establishments, events, or locales is entirely coincidental. Any mistakes are the author's own and may be intentional and fictional. All rights reserved. Except for use in review, the reproduction or use of this work in any part is forbidden without the express written permission of the author.

Feel Me – Copyright May 2019 by M. Jayne for Big Dog Publishing

Cover Design by Fiona Jayde

Editing by Delilah Devlin

Proofreaders: Susan Panak, David Panak, Susan Cambra, Wanda Adams

Medical Advisor: Joy Smoll-Adams

Author's Assistant: David Panak a/k/a The Manny

First Edition

ISBN E-Book: 978-0999642153

ISBN Print: 978-1094983394

CONTENTS

FOR

Those of you are that hurting.
Please know that you are not alone.
You matter.
Ask for help.
If you are in crisis, PLEASE CALL
1-800-273-TALK (8255)
Or Text the Word—TALK
to 741741

PLAYLIST FOR FEEL ME

Listen Anytime:

You Say by Lauren Daigle
In My Blood by Shawn Mendes
Shadow of the Day by Linkin Park

Please look for a song recommendation at the top of each chapter.

AUTHOR'S NOTE

HELLO,

Welcome to the world of the Novus Pack. I've been a part of Novus since 2009. The story has changed over time but the theme has stayed the same: a human female thrown into the dangerous Lycan world. This was not an easy book to write. The subject matter is rough. **If you are sensitive or have triggers then please know that parts of this story might not be for you.** I wrote this book so that there is a build-up to those scenes. You **will** know what is coming.

The most troubling chapters are marked as such, for example:

[Character Name]

Violence is part of the Lycan World. Every action has a reaction and in this story there are painful scenes. However, there is hope.

It is a Romance-there is always hope.

#IAMNovus

Remember...
Cum Nobis aut Contra Nobis
With us or Against Us

ONE

THEODORA MORRISSEY

Impossible by Shontelle

WE WALKED QUICKLY DOWN THE HALLWAY OF THE executive floor in the Novus office building in Wolfsbane, Nebraska. I knew better than to speak where so many could hear even a whispered thought. Lorenzo Barducci, one of my personal guards, was on my right. He chose that position because his right arm was dominant, and if there was an attack, he would be unimpeded. After we entered my office, he closed the door while I kicked off my heels and dropped onto the sofa and moaned, "This sucks."

"I do not understand your distress." Lore lowered his body on the other end of the sofa, calmly watching me...like the wolf that he was.

I felt cornered and uncertain of what I should do... unsure whether I wanted to do anything. Nope, that option was off the table, removed by our Packleader, my lover and, at times, my tormentor, Raider Black.

This definitely was one of those times.

Dejectedly, I said, "I'm not sure what is expected." *Or more accurately, what he expects.* My fingers twisted the heavy ring, round and round my finger. It was the only piece of jewelry to adorn my hands because Black had given it to me.

"The Laird, with the Board's approval, has invited you to confront the man who did injury to you."

I crossed my leg over my other knee and started to swing it. "Black should take care of him. He has the bigger beef."

He tilted his head. "What is beef? We are not speaking of cows."

Lore was well over two thousand years old and didn't always understand my use of slang. "'Beef' is a problem. I meant that Black's issues are much greater than mine."

His dark eyebrows lowered. "You are not angry that he ordered a punch on the Laird?"

I barely kept myself from rolling my eyes. "It's called a 'hit'." I stopped swinging my leg and instead wiggled my foot back and worth. Lore knew that by getting me to talk about my feelings that I'd decompress. *The Godddamn tricky wolf.* "Of course, that infuriates me." I'd seen the ambush in a vision. Once I'd shared what I'd witnessed, Black had intentionally put himself in harm's way. We'd had a massive fight over it. The wait for news had made me a nervous wreck. I'd been terrified for the male I loved, worried that my vision hadn't been accurate, and they'd miscalculate leaving him unprotected. I'd also feared for my future if something had happened to The Laird.

"Then use that anger."

"To do what, Lore?" I allowed my frustration, which was fueled by fear, to seep into my tone. "Do I go out into the middle of the field and slap Romero Peters a few times. What's that going to prove? Who's that going to impress?" I never forget that I am always the weakest in the room. Some might treat me with reverence, but I was still prey.

Carrying the mark of The Lady, the Goddess of the Lycan race, made me a rarity and a prized possession. The general belief was that the Marked are to be protected and treated with reverence. However, I wasn't naive enough to believe that. I'd been attacked, and another attempt would come, my gift had told me so.

Because of my vulnerability, my guards rarely left my side when I was away from Black. Many feared Lorenzo Barducci, and with good reason. He'd been the son of a Packleader and his chosen Consort, a renowned Seer, and also a master spy, intelligent, wily, and a notorious mass-murderer. Some believed he should've been executed, that he was unstable. Black had welcomed the loner into Novus when the pack was forming. He didn't fear the legends, and in turn, Lore was loyal to Black, and to a lesser degree, Novus. When we'd met, and he'd realized what I was, he'd taken over my training after I'd almost been killed.

We worked well with one another. I think he was incredibly lonely. He accepted his position as an outsider. I, too, was an outsider, no matter how many surrounded me. His mother had shared much about her gift with her son. He'd inherited a bit of her talent, although I was cautious about mentioning that subject. He was a very dangerous male with secrets, and I didn't push. I enjoyed his teaching style, and I think he's become comfortable with me, but if I would overstep, I couldn't be sure about the consequences.

"You will not slap the man." His voice came out low with a bit of a rumble. "You will use the gifts The Lady bestowed upon you."

I held up my palm in a stopping motion. "Just hear me out."

When he didn't speak, I swung my leg a few more times while I searched for a way to verbalize my concerns. "If I show what I can do...could that be a problem on down the line?"

"Go on." He said the words slowly as if he was running different scenarios in his mind.

"Would it be an invitation for somebody to attack me?" I ran out of air at the end of the question. I'd learned how to use my gift to sense movement before my eyes could register any motion, but I was no real match in a fight against a Lycan in either form.

There were few detailed records of what Seers could do. I'd already demonstrated publicly that I could communicate with their wolves while they were in human form. What if I proved I could do more? Would that be perceived as a threat?

"You are well-guarded." He pursed his lips slightly. "Even the small one is dangerous."

I rolled my eyes. "Don't call Issa that. You know she hates it, and every time you do, you two end up fighting, and then somebody has to clean up the blood," I grumbled.

"I will admit I did not think she would stab me in the eye." The smile he displayed was unsettling because it was genuine.

"I don't ever want to see anything like that again." I was never going to get used to the violence that always lingered right below the surface. Black called it "claws and jaws negotiations." For now, I allowed my guards to work out their differences in their own way, but my patience was wearing thin. Removing blood from my clothes was becoming tiresome, as were the extra showers.

"She is a decent fighter for her size."

"Could we focus on me?" God, I couldn't believe that I was saying that, but I didn't want to listen to another rant about Issa.

"You will do damage to the one who wronged you." At times, Lore sounded very much like the prince he really was.

"But what..." I didn't want to say this out loud, "what if word spreads, and *she* hears I can do more?" I felt ashamed of my fixation with the female who was contracted to mate with Black. There had been a strong attraction between The Laird and I from the beginning. He'd fought it, curbing his wolf's wish to pursue. I understood he was promised to another, and yet, we were together. I lived with him in the Packhouse and slept in his bed every night. I was in love with him.

Black was a very popular leader, but there were Novus members who disagreed with his choice. Onyx, who sat on the Board, had made no secret he thought our living together was a huge mistake. His problem was not that Black had taken a mistress, but that I was human, and therefore, not worthy of a Packleader's attention. Plus, my former tutor disliked me. He thought my skills a disappointment.

7

"You should be honored the Laird has chosen to lie with you."

"I am honored." I bowed my head slightly.

"Then why are you concerned with the Dolan princess or any other female?"

My anger flared. "Because if I was contracted to a male like Black and I found out that he...he had taken another, then I would want to kill her." I stumbled because my grandmother had taught me that jealousy was a sin and unbecoming.

Lore chuckled. "Of course, you would."

I waited for him to continue but got nothing. Truthfully, this issue wasn't something I should discuss. My worries concerning Siobhan Dolan were my own to bear. The few times I'd tried to talk to Black, he'd given me his kingly stare and stated that he could do whatever he chose. When would I learn that I shouldn't expect a Lycan leader to have the same morals and beliefs as a human?

"Theodora?" Lore was sniffing the air, probably reading my emotions.

I uncrossed my legs and sat straighter. I needed to face my responsibility. "How much damage do I have to do to please the Pack?"

"Blood will be necessary."

I nodded once, slowly. I had to accept this; it was my duty.

"I think the thin blade will do nicely."

"I need to go home to change." I scooted off the sofa. I liked this top. When this was done, I would throw away whatever I wore and bury the memories.

. . .

Three hours later, Novus members and the humans who wore the brand of the pack, gathered in the large field behind the community center. The sun was starting to set. Somebody had set up and lit torches to mark the outline of the circle.

My guards stood beside me, and I could feel the excitement and anticipation in the air. I tried to block it out, but it was a constant electrical current that ran through my body. We assembled to the left and five steps behind the Laird. Conal MacGregor, the pack's Second, was on his right with the other Board members.

The cart carrying the prisoner approached. I could feel the buzz increase and glanced at Black. In profile, he looked so calm, standing shirtless, waiting to sentence the man who'd tried to interfere with Novus.

"You do not need to worry," Issa said quietly.

I turned to her and gave a small frown. I wasn't worried about Black. He was created for moments like this, so passionate and protective of his people, the show-man, and the punisher.

"It is only right to extact vengeance. It is our way, Seer, and you are one of us."

One of us, one of us, the chant played in my head. I had worked very hard to learn my new role. Solle MacGregor, my closest friend, had confessed that, in the beginning, there had been concern that I would fight or try to escape. Instead, I'd surprised them. The adjustment hadn't been easy. There were still many parts of this life that made me squeamish and others that I chose to ignore or risk my sanity. Black endlessly teased me about my mandate that he brush his teeth thoroughly after he ran in wolf form. I didn't want to know what he'd chased and most likely caught while out.

The cart appeared, pulled by two black draft horses. Asher and Wale dragged the human from his bench seat into the center of the circle.

I studied the human with interest because his clothing was not torn, nor did I see any bruising. Black had flown to Los Angeles to capture the man, personally. I expected a visible sign of a struggle. For me, the most surprising thing was that Peters wasn't bound. Had they broken him so easily?

Asher stepped forward and bowed grandly to the Laird.

"Ass," Issa hissed.

I couldn't smile, but I enjoyed watching the self-assured male's pursuit of my guard. By silent mutual agreement, Issa and I did not share much about our relationships. I didn't think it would be proper to talk about Black because of his position, and I don't think Issa knew what to do with the handsome male who was actively trying to woo her.

Black's walk contained a bit of a swagger as he moved further into the circle. He would never admit it, but he enjoyed putting on a show. I think all Lycans secretly did. Every event was a production, and to get an answer to seemingly simple questions sometimes took hours. He stopped a few feet in front of the prisoner.

I felt Black's energy swell or, perhaps, it was magic that caused Peters to drop to his knees. Since the first time we'd visited The Lady's Plain, I could sense The Laird's power without trying. It was yet another way that I was tied to him.

"Romero Peters, you are an enemy of Novus." His voice thundered on this quiet evening. "What say you?"

Peters glared at The Laird. "Go to hell."

Black's lips stretched, but the smile wasn't jovial; it was anticipatory. "Onyx, read the charges."

The dark-skinned man's voice was easy to listen to. Like a well-trained stage actor, he knew when to stress a word and how to use pacing to build drama.

I watched the prisoner's face as the list was recited. Peters stared boldly at Black. Perhaps, he still didn't understand he was going to die and that his death was going to be painful. I'd seen first-hand the damage Black was capable of committing, but this time, the transgressions were very personal.

I turned my head slightly to my right. "Lore?"

"My Lady?"

"Don't let me...you'll stop me from...doing anything...?" I meant stupid or unseemly. I feared that if things got too intense I might try to run.

"Of course." He dipped his chin.

"All of us are your victims, Romero," Black told the man. "You tried to weaken us, but look around. We are strong. We live." Black's odd gray eyes rested on me for a moment, signaling that I should prepare.

A part of me thought him magnificent, while the rest was terrified. He was totally in control and waiting to strike. His wolf was ready to render injuries in the most painful manner.

"Theodora Morrissey." The Laird didn't turn away from the prisoner. He expected me to enter the circle and join him on his command.

My guards didn't whisper any last minute instructions or words of encouragement. They followed one step behind me as I moved forward. I'd chosen a pair of jeans, a thermal shirt for warmth, and a hoodie that fit tightly to my body.

As I neared Black's left side, I paused and slid my sleeves up my forearm to display my Novus brand. "Laird." I bowed my head. "How may I serve Novus and you?"

"Come." With great ceremony, he held out his hand.

Our palms touched, and his energy surged through my body. Immediately, I felt stronger and more focused. My blood pounded in my ears, and I might have smiled, showing my teeth.

I looked into his eyes hoping for a message, an indication of his confidence in me. This wasn't only about righting a wrong. I needed to send a message to my Pack that I was worthy of The Laird.

He flashed a smile I knew was for me, alone. He then broke our eye contact and spoke to the prisoner. "You trespassed on Novus land and left this woman to die." Black's voice rumbled with outrage.

"Doesn't look like it hurt her too badly," Peters sneered as he studied me from head to toe.

"The human world's loss is our gain," Black said, pitching his voice lower. "It was by chance that she was found and survived."

Again, Peters studied me. Maybe he noted my expression because I did nothing to hide my growing anger. "What's she going to do?"

Not only had this man left me to die in the elements that snowy night, but he'd ordered that Black be killed. I concentrated on that. My anger at his daring and at the unease his actions had caused. I'd endured a vision of Black's head being blown apart and then experienced the ensuing wait while he'd tried to draw out his treasonous conspirators.

"On your feet," I ordered using a tiny bit of my gift that would "push" him to act.

He was taller than me, and I knew from personal experience he had no problem hitting a woman. I felt Black drop my hand and move away. I was alone with our enemy. "Would you like to take another swing at me, Mr. Peters?" All the attention was on me, and I made sure that my voice didn't shake.

He threw back his head and laughed. "So that someone can step in and beat my ass?" He looked around the circle. "You didn't put up much of a fight before."

I felt my heart rate increase as I studied him, deciding where to strike. "Times have changed. I've changed." I think I smiled as I threw my first punch at his jaw.

He blocked me as I'd expected.

I allowed momentum to carry my body so that I spun around on one foot and kicked him in the head, connecting with his ear and cheek and knocking him to the ground.

He landed on his ass and shook his head several times to clear it.

I smiled. He was bleeding from his nose and mouth.

He then rolled to his knees, and when he was on all fours, I kicked him in his ribs. At the moment of impact, I heard bones crunch. He ended up on his back.

I stood over him. "You were saying?" I could feel my fury boiling. Hitting him wasn't depleting my power. Instead, it was growing stronger.

He was breathing heavily, which had to hurt. I knew from experience; my ribs had been broken when I was thrown down his private plane's steps. He dropped his arm so that it was lying perpendicular to his body with his palm facing up.

I stomped my foot on that hand. I ground my heel into his palm, snapping every tiny bone and grinding them to dust. I called to my gift, holding him in place while he screamed in agony. "See me, human—I am Novus. Feel me, for I am The Lady's gift to the world. Today, I am vengeance." I stepped off his hand and released my psychic hold on him. Purposely, I turned my back on him and started to walk to Black.

I sensed movement. My gift communicated that he was running toward me. I turned and barely raised my voice when I ordered, "Stop."

He looked shocked and perplexed as I held him frozen.

I turned again and continued to Black. I pushed up my sleeve again to present my brand. "Laird." I lowered my chin, showing my gratitude.

"Seer," his voice rumbled.

I raised my head as he reached for me and pulled me into his arms, kissing me thoroughly in front of the pack. "You please me greatly."

"Thank you, Laird," I whispered breathlessly.

TWO

NOVUS

RAIDER BLACK

Love and Happiness by Al Green

MY SEER WAS AMAZING. SURPRISINGLY VICIOUS, AND YET, so soft as she melted into my body while I kissed her. This human woman had done the impossible; she'd captured my heart. I slowly released her and wondered if I would grow tired of putting that slightly dazed look on her face.

I glanced at Peters who was still frozen in place, and said quietly to her, "Can you release him?"

Her eyes went huge as she stammered, "I...I don't know how I did that."

I chuckled deeply at her confusion. "You used my magic."

Now, her mouth formed a perfect "O". "How?"

I took her hand in mine. I could feel our connection. "Concentrate."

She nodded once, then turned to look at our prisoner.

Through our connection, I felt her search for the right path that would lead to the man. Like a snap of fingers, the man was free.

Theo stepped to the side as her guards flanked her, and I moved to meet the man who'd attempted to take from my Pack.

"Make it quick," Romero Peters demanded.

Idiot. He had no right to ask for a favor. I was going to make him suffer. "That wouldn't be any fun." My people expected a show, and I wanted to give them one. If one of us was attacked, we all were. Our saying was, "With us or against us."

I was very careful not to do too much damage too soon. I'd held back, and yet Peters was no longer able to stand. I'd let him land a few punches, to give him some hope that he might have a chance against me.

His blood coated my body as I considered my next move while I stood over his inert form. "Romero Peters, I sentence you to death for attacking Novus." I called to my power and felt the energy spread from the tips of my fingers down my wrist and to my elbow. It was as if a hundred bees were stinging me. My hand changed to a paw with six-inch claws. I bent over and thrust it through the man's chest. I lifted his body into the air so that he was three feet off the ground.

Peters had screamed as he saw my paw, with its long claws, approach his body. Now, his cries had weakened to yips.

I squeezed my hand around his beating heart until it could pulsate no more. I shook his body from my now human hand, and I turned my back on him. I left the circle, ignoring the roar of the crowd.

Asher jogged to meet me. "What do you want me to do with the body?"

"Leave it in the forest for the scavengers." I wanted to check on Theo.

She stood between Lore and Issa. She was pale, and I could feel her unease. My human did not like to witness our brutality or her own. "You okay?"

"Yes, Laird," she answered immediately, but her voice shook.

I continued to study her posture and her tightly fisted hands at her side.

"I, uh, I think I did okay."

"She did not hide her face," Lore informed me with a touch of pride in his voice.

"Theo." I held out my bloody hand.

She didn't hesitate, gripping it, and then she threw herself against my chest, hugging me tightly.

She told me to go for a run while Lore and Issa drove her back to my home. I knew she would shower to clean the blood from her body. I walked her to the SUV and kissed her again.

"You know somebody is going to have to clean the seats before anybody can ride in this again." One side of her mouth tipped downward.

"That won't be a problem." It amused me that she worried about things like blood on the furniture. I opened the door for her to climb in, and then closed it securely. Lore and Issa were still standing beside the SUV, waiting for my dismissal. "Stay with her."

"Of course, Laird," Issa said with a crisp nod.

After my run, I took the most direct route to the Packhouse where I had a suite of rooms on the second floor. There I found Issa, sitting on the floor outside of the bathroom with the door cracked. I raised my brow, enquiring about my Seer.

"Lore dropped us at the back door, she stripped and left her clothes outside. Then she went directly to the shower."

"How long?"

The guard knew what I meant. "She cried for ten minutes." The first time Theo had witnessed an interrogation, she'd spent several hours in the shower crying. I think she believed the sound of the water masked her sobs.

I nodded to signify that I understood. "Thank you and good night," I said, excusing her.

I left my clothes outside the door. As I walked into the bathroom, I greeted Theo, allowing her time to prepare. "I hope the water is hot." I opened the door and found my woman sitting on the bench along the far wall.

She looked up. "Hey."

I thoroughly brushed my teeth before stepping under the jets, and after I soaped my body and rinsed, I joined her on the bench. "Time for the truth."

She scooted closer so that our hips and thighs touched. "I don't know what happened out there." She looked at me with eyes filled with worry. "I...I wanted to hurt him." She let out a labored breath. "I wanted to grind his hand down until it was dust."

I thought about her concern. I leaned back and placed my arm around her hunched shoulders, pulling her to my side. "It is our way, to make the transgressor pay."

She was trying not to cry. Her breathing was labored. "I didn't feel like myself. I mean, it was me, but I've never wanted to do harm like that."

"Theo, you know that you are human, but The Lady has given you more."

"It's scary…to feel that much need to hurt another."

"You were magnificent." I dropped a kiss onto the crown of her head.

Her body relaxed a little. "I'm glad I didn't embarrass you."

My wolf howled with happiness. He approved that she put us first. "You were very brave."

"I have to be." She wrapped her arm around my belly. "I need to show that I'm worthy of…of you."

"Theo," I said her name softly and waited until she looked at me. "You are." I kissed her lips.

Her cheek rested against my chest, and her right leg covered my thighs. A smug smile tugged at my lips. Perhaps, she was too exhausted to move. After a kill, I always searched for sexual release.

As soon as we found our way into bed, she'd rolled me onto my back and climbed onto my belly. "I loved watching you by the torchlight. You were so strong, so vicious. You were primal." She ran her lips along my jawline.

"As the weather cools, we can live with candles and the fireplace," I'd teased as my hands caressed the soft skin along her spine.

"An evening in front of the fire sounds good," she'd purred as she'd kissed a line down the middle of my chest.

"Do you know what else sounds good?"

She'd chuckled deeply. "I can guess." Rising on her thighs, she'd captured my hard cock in her hand and positioned it. Then she'd lowered her body onto mine.

I'd wrapped my hands around her hips. She was so beautiful like this. Her head tilted back, her mouth slightly open, eyes closed, and her big tits bouncing enticingly with each stroke. I took her hard nipple into my mouth.

"Sooo good," she'd purred.

We were.

Fully awake now, I lightly ran my hand over her upper arm. "Babe, are you asleep?"

"No, just resting." She pressed a kiss against my skin.

"We need to discuss what happened earlier when you froze Ramon Peters' body."

Her body tensed, and she raised her head to look at me. "I don't know how that happened."

I frowned. "Have you and Lore been working on that skill?"

Abruptly, she moved off my body, sitting up, then crossed one leg in front of her body and pulled the other knee tightly to her chest. "No. I didn't know I could do that. I don't even know how I did it."

My senses told me she was telling the truth. Words could speak lies but the scent of emotions could not. "You pulled the energy from me."

"I did what?" Her voice went up an octave.

"I've felt us connect before when you've communicated with our wolves, but this ability is new." If I was being honest, I found this new ability rather startling.

"I didn't know that I was doing it," she said, her voice rushed. "I didn't plan on doing it, Black."

I rested my palm on her exposed knee. "I'm not angry, Theo. I'm curious."

She studied me intently.

I could feel how hard she was thinking. Her emotions were churning with a combination of nervousness, analysis, and trepidation.

I used a gentle voice because I didn't want to frighten her. "Do you think you could do it again...against Lycans."

Her eyes widened for a moment. "No."

I should always remember that my human was very good at seeing the big picture. I waited for her to elaborate.

"It was probably a combination of our connection and my...my anger." She licked her lips nervously. "To control a human would take very little energy as opposed to controlling a Lycan."

She'd once described herself as my gift and my weapon. It was no wonder why she was afraid. If she could learn to use our energy to control a Lycan, then she would truly be my weapon.

"Black?" It was a plea.

My heart stilled. If she could learn to control a Lycan on her own...I would have to destroy her. "Shhh." I pulled on her arm signaling that this discussion was over for now.

She uncurled her leg and twisted her body so that once again she was lying against my side. I thought she'd succumbed to sleep when she whispered, "Sometimes, I hate what I am."

I knew that, and I admired her greatly for working so hard to adjust to this new life. "Do you mean being mine?" My hand momentarily tightened around her hip.

"No," she burrowed closer to my body, "that's the best part of my life."

THREE

NOVUS

THEODORA MORRISSEY

Cowboy by Kid Rock

"I THINK THIS IS THE GREATEST IDEA YOU'VE EVER HAD."
I hadn't heard the female's approach, not that I ever did unless the Lycan wanted me to. It still surprised me that people so large could move so quietly. "So, you're having fun?" I turned away from the porch rail to face her. She towered over my five-and-a-half feet by a good six inches and was muscular. The word "Valkyrie" always came to mind when I thought of her. Glass was in charge of the Pack's guards and a respected member of the Board. I also considered her a friend.

"The food is plentiful and the music good."

She was very to the point in her speaking. "Everybody outdid themselves," I murmured. The Novus Pack liked to socialize. When I'd suggested that we organize a monthly get-together, where all ages could mingle, I'd been a little surprised at how easily the Laird had agreed.

"You see things we didn't know we were missing." My guard for the evening, Issa, ventured out from the shadows.

I gave her praise a small nod of acknowledgment. "The support from the Pack exceeded my hopes."

"You're doing well," Glass decreed.

I understood that she meant in my role as the woman in Black's life.

"I've been looking for you," Black said as he stepped out onto the Community Center's back porch. The last time I had seen him, he was deep in conversation with his Second and two shop owners. Tonight, he wore a maroon long sleeve shirt, which looked great with his long dark hair.

My hand stretched toward him before I even realized it. We both knew he could easily track me by my scent.

I enjoyed watching his approach. Black was over six feet and thickly muscled, and yet he moved with so much grace. He grasped my hand and pulled, applying pressure until I was pressed against his side. "What are you doing?"

I tried not to fight my body's instinctive reaction and tense. I knew he was asking as my date and not as the big boss. "I was taking a minute to regroup." I tried to smile reassuringly as I looked up at him.

"Are you tired?"

I read concern in his fantastic gray eyes. The unique shade darkened when he was emotional, angered, or aroused. "No," I shook my head, "I just wanted a moment of quiet." Recently, I'd needed to take a break from all the activity from time to time. I was too anxious, and it was exhausting. My gift told me that something was going to happen, but as hard as I tried, I had no more information. I felt like I was always on guard, waiting and searching for that answer.

"The band's going to start in a few minutes."

I made a tiny move to pull away from him. "I don't want to miss that." The community dinner, which my helpers had turned into a huge social event, had needed music. During the planning, I'd learned that many famous bands had members who were Articles. These humans served the Lycan race and wore a brand of their pack. When Tex had mentioned some examples, my jaw had dropped in recognition and amazement.

There was still so much I didn't know, and I needed to learn as quickly as possible. My inner sense cautioned me not to mention the need to rush. Whatever was coming was going to impact my life tremendously.

My first guess concerning the nature of the coming revelation was that it involved my relationship with Black. He'd seduced me, not with his sexual skill, but rather with his intelligence and a few moments of tenderness. However, I hadn't been fooled by the rare glimpses of his softer side. Raider Black was decisive and violent. I'd witnessed him separate a head from a body several times. In my presence, he'd beaten a man with his own severed arm, but he'd also cradled me against his chest when I'd been injured, unwilling to let anyone touch me.

We rarely spoke of our future. Still, I worried. Siobahn Dolan was a princess, and her father was very powerful. Of course, I could be dead by the time they mated. Lycans lived forever, so my human life-span would be just a tiny blip on their timeline. Another possibility was that the Dolan princess would have me killed, or what worried me most, was the thought that Black would have to kill me if I became a threat.

The ancient records hinted that many Seers went insane. Lore's theory was that they couldn't handle their gift, and as it grew more powerful, they lost their grip on reality, unable to differentiate visions from real life. I didn't want to hurt anybody, and I didn't want Black to have to kill me. He would do it for the good of Novus and his race, but I never wanted him forced to make that decision.

As we walked around the exterior of the Community Center, the crowd parted for the Laird. Asher and Wale, two of his full-time guards, led the way. I tried to slip from his hold. I wasn't entirely comfortable in my role at his side. Sometimes, I could hear my grandmother's voice snarling "Jezebel" or "whore," in my head.

His arm tightened around me. I smiled at the members I recognized and pretended that I was comfortable. I was both the princess and the prey. Strong, because I was paired with the Laird and I carried The Lady's mark, yet I was physically weak compared to those around me. I buried that worry as I heard the band hit the first chords of one of their most popular anthems. Many of the attendees wore cowboy hats in honor of one of their hits, and they tossed their hats high into the night sky.

Black positioned me in front of him and wrapped his arms around me. I leaned into his warmth. Unlike the wolves, I felt the cold, so I'd dressed in a silk thermal undershirt, a waffle-knit shirt that matched my blue eyes, and a burnt-orange denim jacket that reminded me of the gorgeous leaves that had fallen to the ground.

"You good?" He sensed my unease, which was a blessing and a curse. I couldn't hide from him.

I snuggled closer into his big body. "Perfect." And this moment was. I was surrounded by my Pack and the one I loved most in the world.

He hugged me tighter, and his hand cupped my breast.

We sang and danced throughout the concert. I was happy that he was relaxed and enjoying himself. Black never complained, but I knew it is difficult work being the Laird. He felt responsible for every Pack member and Article. He and the Board were constantly making plans and revising those in existence regarding how to improve their position in the human and Lycan worlds.

A great deal of their planning was tied to money. In the human world, Novus was employed by those who had particular security needs. The Pack made a good deal of money escorting precious cargo from the Midwest to the west coast and back. They made even more by not asking what was being transported. I didn't agree with that business, but I was realistic. If Novus didn't do this work, then someone else would.

While adjusting to this new life, I'd had to accept many ugly truths in order to survive. I lived amongst predators who were superior to humans in many ways. I couldn't apply my "human" rules and expectations to them. In my personal life, I was still trying to comprehend that I would never be an equal partner to Black. He was the Laird, and any proclamation he made was acted upon as law.

"You are very quiet today."

Issa and I were sitting out on the back deck of the Packhouse because it was a sunny afternoon and I was tired of being cooped up inside my office.

"I didn't get much sleep last night," I said off-handedly.

"Having fun times with the Laird?" She gave me a tiny smile.

I felt my cheeks heat. Black was inventive and demanding in all things. Not that I minded. In fact, I loved that he could push me to the edge of reason. Early in our relationship, The Lady had changed my body. It had been an incredibly painful process, and those who'd witnessed those first few hours, had worried whether I would survive. My body could handle more physical pain and damage. There was a limit to what I could take, and I was by no means unbreakable, but now I could keep up with my Lycan lover. He only needed to be gentle with my body when he chose to be. I think we'd fucked seven times the previous night, and my knees were still a little tender to the touch from the rug burns.

I didn't answer right away. Issa and I rarely spoke about the men in our lives. "Some times are more fun than others."

She took a sip from the hot pink cup she'd filled with a highly caffeinated and sweet soft drink earlier. "I know what you mean."

Now, this was interesting. I tried not to pry into her personal life, particularly Asher's pursuit. "But the good times can be very good," I murmured, hoping she'd continue the conversation.

"I don't know about that." She frowned but still looked adorable. She was petite and favored pastel colors and, to many of the males' dismay, Hello Kitty graphics. "He's so bossy. How do you deal with that?"

Was she talking about Black or Asher? "It isn't always easy. Sometimes, I have to bite my tongue because I want to snap back."

"He thinks he is always right," she groused.

I chuckled. "I think that comes with having a penis."

"Ahhh yes, the penis." She wiggled her eyebrows.

Now, I was blushing again and giggling. "Don't get me wrong; I really like his penis."

"I am happy for you." But she didn't look like she was. She opened her mouth to speak but closed it quickly.

I tilted my head. "Issa, what's going on?"

"I'm not sure you will want to know."

My heart began to thud against my ribs. "Is Asher still alive?" I tried to recall if I'd seen him today. "You didn't do something permanent to him, did you?"

She laughed. "I could."

"I know." I'd seen several skirmishes between Issa and Lore, and that had been enough to convince me that she was a skilled fighter.

"I do my best to stay out of his way, but he...he is around all of the time." She sounded upset and yet proud that he continued his pursuit.

"Been there." For a period of two months, Black had tutored me nightly in the MacGregors' basement. He'd been a fantastic teacher, but I'd had a terrible time concentrating because I constantly wanted to run my tongue along his strong jawline.

Issa's face screwed up into a fierce frown. "I want things to stay the same. I am happy like this, with my work and my house."

29

"Have you had this conversation with him?" I didn't know all the particulars of how the Lycan mating process worked. Solle had said that Conal saw her across a crowded bar and knew immediately that she was his mate. Within four months, she'd moved here to Wolfsbane from California, and they were mated in a formal ceremony.

"A conversation?" she snorted. "He wouldn't listen."

"You don't have to answer if you don't want to, but it would help me understand things better if you would…" I waited for her response. She might be my guard, but if she felt disrespected, she could kill me before I even saw her coming.

"You may ask," she said, her tone wary.

"Is it that you're worried that Asher is too bossy and opinionated, or do you really feel no attraction to him?"

She didn't answer immediately, and when she did, it was in a quiet voice. "He is not unattractive."

Understatement of the year. The male was tall, and his body was cut. He wore his black hair long, almost to his waist, and his almond-shaped eyes hinted at mysteries. Plus, the man could flirt and tease with ease. "No, he is not." I smiled in a non-challenging way.

"Many say that he is skilled at sex."

"That is a part of a relationship, but you do need more." Since when was I an expert on relationships? I did an internal eye-roll at myself. We needed Solle for this conversation. She was the blissfully happy one.

Her lower lip protruded. "I have worked hard to become what I am. I won't give that up."

"Did you come to Novus so that you could train to be a guard?" I knew very little about many of the Lycans' backgrounds. I attributed some of this to their immortality. Many had forgotten years of their long lives. My reticence in asking for more details was due to the fact I feared that being too nosey wouldn't be appreciated.

"Yes. In my birth pack, women were not allowed to train." Her eyes turned cold. "That way...the males could stay in power."

"So, in that pack, women couldn't challenge or hold any positions of authority?"

"They could, through their family lines or by mating, but that was tied to the males' bloodlines."

This was fascinating. I wondered if humans learned this behavior from the Lycans or the other way around? "What about property and businesses?"

"No. The Pack owned everything, and the leader was in charge," she said, bitterness in her tone.

"I...I'm sorry. It's tough for me to imagine a life like that." My love of learning was battling my empathy for my friend. "I can understand why Asher's actions have upset you."

Issa's eyes shone with unshed tears. "It's not that I don't want...things, but I can't give up what I have. I sacrificed everything to get here. Does that make sense?"

"Yes," I rushed to assure her. "I wish I could tell you that loving another is not filled with having to give up things, but I can't. It's...hard, sometimes. I won't lie to you. I think that one of the partners is always going to have to give up more than the other." I had to swallow hard because I felt like I was going to cry.

"I might be able to love him...someday," she admitted slowly.

"Iss, you've been through a lot recently. If you aren't ready, you shouldn't rush into any major decisions." For months she'd laid in the hospital bed not moving while her body healed in the "human" way. She'd been injured protecting me from a newly-changed, feral wolf. She'd almost died.

She nodded in agreement.

"Asher was so worried about you when you were injured. It showed another side of him. I think that he realized he might lose you."

Using what I called "Lycan logic", she proclaimed, "I cannot be lost. I am too smart to be sent away."

We were quiet for a bit. The sun was starting to set, and I was growing chilled when Issa said, "You love him. The Laird. You used the word love when you talked about your feelings."

"Iss," I cautioned her, "it's too dangerous to talk about."

"But you do," she pushed.

I looked down at my feet and then closed my eyes tightly as I let out a long sigh. "How could I not? He's... he's everything." I couldn't find the words to explain all that Black meant to me.

"That is good. You will make him a fine mate."

"Don't say that," my voice harsh. "Don't ever say that again."

"But..."

I cut her off in a sharp tone, "I forbid it, Issa. Never...again." I couldn't stand to hear that because it would give me hope, and our relationship had an expiration date.

I got to my feet and walked into the house. It was like a punch to the stomach hearing those words, because I wanted so much for them to be true.

FOUR

NOVUS

RAIDER BLACK

Work Song by Hozier

MANY WEEKS HAD PASSED SINCE I HAD KILLED THE TWO traitors in my pack, along with the human outsider who had purchased their loyalty. We had recovered from the deaths, and there were no more issues during our escorts. Still, I'd issued the order for everyone to stay vigilant. It went unsaid that any more perpetrators would be dealt with swiftly and without mercy. I made sure that word spread about Romero Peters' long and drawn-out death. I wanted a certain number of our business contacts and other packs to know that Novus and I wouldn't be toyed with.

My life had settled into a routine, one that pleased me greatly. The Seer's belongings had made their way into my rooms. Although we still traveled to Conal's home every Sunday for breakfast, she was living with me and sleeping in my bed every night. The only ring that she wore was the one I gave her, the first night that I had her. It was an easy transition. She gave me space, and yet, I would find myself alone in my office wondering what she was doing. I now understood why Conal sometimes wore a small smile. I was besotted with my human. My blood heated with lust every time I glimpsed the faint scars on her hips and back from my claws. *Mine.*

The intercom buzzed. "Yeah?"

The voice of my personal secretary, Basil, sounded tinny through the speaker. "Laird, Packleader Dolan is on the phone."

Great, I frowned. "Put him through."

I heard the click. "Roy." My greeting was one word. This was an unscheduled call and therefore unwelcome.

"Black, how the hell are you?" He lulled many with his easy charm. However, he had led his Pack for close to four centuries, and "soft" did not stay in power.

"Doing well, and you?"

"The Lady smiles upon us," Dolan answered in the standard reply. "The reason I'm calling is that I'm hearing some things…"

I didn't take the bait. The man would tell me the reason for the call.

"They are troubling…"

"What kinds of things, Roy?" I found the need to play these games unnecessary. The older the wolf, the more difficult they were when it came to sharing information.

"You are involved with a female."

The muscles in my middle tightened. I had known that word would travel. I chose not to respond.

"A *human* female." He spat the word as if it was vile.

34

Careful, wolf. I responded coolly, "Are you calling to tell me my own business, or is there a point?"

"You are contracted to my sixth daughter."

"I have done nothing to dishonor that promise." I did not break my vows.

"I won't have Siobhan made a spectacle," the powerful leader and father ranted. "You are to be her mate. I won't have you doing anything to embarrass her or my name."

"Roy," I said calmly, "Neither Siobhan or I are in any hurry to mate. I last saw her four years ago and we exchanged no more than five words." At the time, Conal had felt it was a snub, and had taken offense on my and the Pack's behalf. "Am I to do nothing until the time comes that your daughter is ready to move here and take her rightful position?"

His voice's volume lowered. "But a human? Isn't she...weak?"

Interesting, his spy hadn't mentioned that she was marked by The Lady. "She suits," I answered carefully.

"Are you sure it has been four years? Perhaps Siobhan should travel to your Pack Lands for a visit...?" Roy turned thoughtful.

"We have plenty of time. Allow your daughter her fun and freedom from responsibility. You and I both know how much time our duties occupy."

"That is generous of you." He didn't sound grateful, but I did not care.

Siobhan Dolan enjoyed the jet set life. She traveled across Europe, had a place in New York City, and partied in Hollywood. Life in Nebraska would be very different for her. "She isn't ready to settle. I don't want to force that upon her." I didn't savor the idea of having to wrangle Roy Dolan's daughter, my contracted mate for all of eternity.

"I'm going to mention it to her…a visit to your land. She should become familiar with your holdings and you."

Roy would make it happen, eventually. "Novus will welcome the daughter of Packleader Dolan," I promised with a feeling of dread. I knew my duty to Novus, but I loved another. Theo was my heart. My wolf wanted to claim her as our true mate. However, I honored my promises. Novus would come first, always.

We said our goodbyes. I then leaned back in my office chair. I couldn't imagine that the Dolan princess would be in any hurry to visit our land. Lycan time ran differently. For Roy, a planned visit could be ten years away, I reasoned.

Life with Theo had spoiled me. She was easy-going, and when we did disagree, things were settled quickly and usually naked. I'd caught on early that if she said something was important to her, then she would fight for it. Otherwise she went along with my decisions.

She'd organized the social event last week. I'd played a bigger part than ever before, and she'd been by my side most of the evening, welcoming Pack members, or getting me something to eat or drink. When conversation had become stilted, she'd known what to say to smooth over the silences. She was helping to make me a better Leader, selflessly and with ease.

I should reward her. She'd asked to celebrate the human's Thanksgiving holiday. Lycans did not acknowledge the day, but I knew that our friends would not turn down a meal planned by Theo.

Lore had designated himself her personal guard. I'd

always thought the man to be odd, but he and Theo got along well. She loved listening to his tales of Lycan history, and he enjoyed hearing about her life in the human world. I'd never heard the wolf laugh until he'd stood in my kitchen drinking a beer, watching her attempt to make pasta from scratch while under his supervision.

Lately, Onyx, my legal advisor, had become difficult. He wasn't happy that Lore had usurped him as a tutor, and he took every opportunity to point out that the Seer wasn't doing enough. His subtle insults were becoming more vocal and daring. Eventually, I would shut him up, perhaps permanently.

The Pack's Second and my closest friend, Conal, knocked on my door and didn't wait for my answer before coming in. The only time he waited was when Theo was with me. "Couple of things that we need to go over..." He started talking before he'd taken his usual chair and placed his huge feet on the table in front of him.

"Lay it on me." I picked up my ballpoint pen and spun it on my desk.

"I got a call from Benedict Rhys. The Council wants him to interview Theo." Conal leaned back in his favorite chair and waited for my reply.

My senses alerted to danger. "When?"

"He's in northern California. He could be here tomorrow."

My wolf stirred. "That's interesting timing. Roy Dolan called me an hour ago."

"I wonder if he was sitting in front of Dolan as he made the call?" Conal and I did not believe in coincidences.

37

"Roy wanted to let me know that word about my relationship with Theo had reached his ears."

"I wonder who's been talking?" Conal's frown did not bode well if that person was revealed.

"He said something about his daughter coming for a visit."

"I hope you nixed that idea."

"I don't have to. Siobhan doesn't want to come to Nebraska. What would she do?" I spun my pen again.

"You can't have your intended visit when Theo is installed in your bed."

The man was my Second, but he cared for Theo. In the beginning, it had been Conal to whom she'd turned for reassurance. "The Seer is protected."

"The Seer is also your lover. She lives with you and acts as your Consort. Siobhan Dolan will not be pleased having the human in her presence," Conal argued.

"She is mine," I growled as my wolf fought to break free.

"You are exposing her to danger," Conal said in that calm, quiet voice that masked his anger so well. "You need to tell Dolan that *you* will be the one to extend the invitation to Novus land, not some fat old fuck who made this deal long ago."

"When, *and if*, he brings up the subject again, I will put him off," I promised.

"This request by Rhys, I don't like it," Conal grumbled. "Theo hasn't been with us a year, and he's ready to come in and try to take her back to Edinburgh."

"She won't go."

"Black, she's good," Conal said, his expression worried. "Lore has helped, and her power is growing. I've felt it and witnessed her in action. He isn't going to overlook that," Conal reasoned. "The Council would reward him greatly for bringing a talented Seer for them to use."

"She wears my brand," I said flatly. "She won't go because I won't allow it."

"The Council will ask for her to visit, and then they won't give her back," Conal opined. "They will summon you both."

"We won't go."

"This feels like a trap or a test of Novus's right to her." He sat up abruptly and placed both boots on the floor.

I agreed. "Nobody is taking her away from me." I stared at him for a full minute. After he dropped his gaze, I continued, "Theodora wears the Novus brand, and she willingly serves the Pack and me."

"So, with Rhys here, will you continue with her publicly?"

"I won't fuck her in the middle of Zumba night at the Community Center, but I won't change my life because the Council's messenger is here."

"We could set up parameters regarding his time with her."

I studied his expression. Conal had something in mind. "He will not see her alone," I decided—for her safety and to make a point.

Conal smirked. "You are going to put Lore in a tiny room with the man, aren't you?"

"Of course." I returned his look, giving him a small smirk. "Lorenzo is her personal guard and tutor; it only makes sense."

"And he would die for her." Conal watched me closely. "But you know that."

"Their connection pleases me. She has improved and is happier under his tutelage. I believe the spy is enjoying his time here with us." Lore had been a loner for centuries and even after he had joined Novus, he rarely was in Wolfsbane.

Conal shook his head. "I don't understand it, but they seem to work well together."

"Theo says he is a great teacher."

"Maybe when he tires of the spy game, he might help at the farm?" Conal suggested.

I chuckled. "That would terrify the parents. Imagine a mass-murderer tending to their newly-changed? I would get so many complaints." I shook my head, although the idea did hold merit. I'd file it away for the future.

"So, do we tell Theo and Lore together or fill him in first?"

"Together." I enjoyed their dynamic. My wolf knew that Lore wasn't interested in Theo sexually and she was committed to us.

I pressed the button on my phone for Theo's office.

Two minutes later, Theo, followed closely by Lore, entered my office. I'd felt her approach, but it was Basil's deep booming laugh that gave her away. She was a favorite of my prickly assistant.

"Laird," she greeted me with a respectful nod of her head. Although we were among friends, she insisted on following the formal etiquette.

I motioned for her to sit down.

Lore nodded and took his place standing behind Theo's chair.

"What are you studying today?" Conal asked. With these two, it could be almost anything.

"Lore is teaching me about what this area was like when you moved here, and the early days of the Pack." Her eyes sparkled with excitement.

I'd have to answer a hundred questions later tonight.

Lore spoke, and I swear he was almost smiling, "I made sure to include how you threatened me, Scot."

Conal smirked and gave a slow one-shouldered shrug. "The infamous Lorenzo Barducci petitions to join Novus? Of course, I would be suspicious."

"I wasn't." I winked at Theo, who was turning her head back and forth, absorbing the story.

She'd bent forward a little and looked over her shoulder so that she could see Lore's expression. "So, they didn't welcome you?"

"Hell, we didn't even know that The Lore was real," Conal remembered. "I'd always thought he was a myth. A tale created and passed down to frighten our young."

"Maybe you should kill off twenty or thirty every few years to keep the story alive," Theo suggested teasingly.

"Who says that I do not?" Lore looked nonplussed by the suggestion.

"Seriously?" Her voice went up an octave.

Her tutor didn't answer, and his silence told her all that she needed to know. She slunk down in her chair and looked at me. "I'm doing it again, aren't I? Trying to apply human rules and expectations."

It was like we were the only two in the room. "You're learning."

She then turned around to face Lore. "I apologize if I short-changed your reputation as a psycho killer, Lore."

He gave her a quick grin and nodded before making his face blank.

She then turned back to me and flashed a sassy look and a tiny smile.

I cleared my throat because in a few minutes she would have us all charmed, and then we'd end up at the gun range or on our bikes going for a long ride. "Conal has some news."

"The Council?" Lorenzo interrupted.

"Why would you think that?" I narrowed my eyes. His mother was a Seer, and Theo believed that he'd inherited some of her gift.

Lore stood with his hands loose at his sides looking relaxed, yet I knew that he was ready to turn violent at any minute. "There is an energy here. I believe it originates from our Seer's strong connection to The Lady. A visitor might have noticed and mentioned it to their Leader, and then someone probably made a call to the Council. Jealousy comes in many forms, Laird."

I shot a glance at my Second. "Conal?"

"Now that I think about it, there is something more in the air."

We then all looked at our Seer for her explanation.

She shifted in her chair and tucked a leg under her thigh. "I ask The Lady for her blessing every night."

"The Lady favors you," Lore said.

She widened her eyes at me.

"You've seen this or felt this kind of energy before?" I asked my spy.

"My mother would spend time on The Plain with The Lady. I believe they grew quite close. That was the main reason that Her retribution was so swift when Lady Octavia was murdered," Lore said. "So, who are they sending?"

"Benedict Rhys," Conal told him.

Lore's snort of disdain made his feelings quite clear. "You know of him?" I asked.

"He is a hanger-on. The Council sends him to the new world, and he stays with a pack eating their food, enjoying their women, but he does little himself."

No member of the Council had traveled to North America. They considered it to be too primitive for their sophisticated tastes. "What does he know about the Marked?"

"I'm sure he has done his research and has listened to the tales, but he did not descend from a line," Lore said dismissively.

Conal continued, "He claims he needs to conduct testing on our Seer."

Theo paled at the news. She shifted, pulling a knee to her chest.

Lore narrowed his eyes as he considered this information. "I think that is for show. He desires a reason to visit Novus."

I didn't like official visits. We always had to go through the social niceties, and it was a huge time suck.

"What kind of testing?" Theo asked quietly. Her midnight blue eyes had gone big, and I felt her nervousness.

"You have no need to worry," Conal assured her instantly.

"You are never to be alone with the man," I told her and Lore.

She handled that order well. "Do I pass his tests?"

My wolf approved of her question immediately. I, too, admired my woman's agile mind.

She dropped her chin. "I owe my allegiance to Novus only."

"My first inclination is to say no," I murmured.

Conal added, "I concur. We don't know what his end game is."

She shot me a quick look. She sensed there was something else that hadn't been stated.

"Black won't let you go," Lore summarized succinctly. "So, you only show him a little of your talent, Theodora. Very little."

"Go?" She focused solely on me. "What does he mean?"

I was never gentle with my Seer; she needed to know what she was facing. "There is a chance the Council might wish your attendance in Edinburgh."

Theo only nodded. She did not ask any other questions.

Rhys arrived five days later. He was a small male with close-set eyes. From the start, I labeled him as difficult with a cruel temperament. It had been reported that he'd snarled at the maids and sent back food to the kitchen while complaining loudly. Today, he would begin a series of meetings with our Seer.

Conal had installed them in one of our midsize conference rooms, with Asher standing outside the door. The guard had been given explicit rules about the length of time Rhys spent in that room with Theo.

A knock sounded on my door. "Enter."

Tex sauntered in. The Board Member was easy to underestimate due to his laconic ways. "Do you want me to put this on your big screen or your monitor?"

"Big screen," I told him. We would be watching the direct feed from the conference room down the hall.

He tapped on his tablet, and within moments, the conference room showed from two different angles. Rhys was unpacking a briefcase, methodically placing yellow legal pads and pens in front of him.

The hallway door opened, and Lore entered followed by Theo. She had been anxious this morning. I'd done my best to ease her nerves, but I could tell by her expression that she was apprehensive, worried about what was in store. She wore an ivory-colored dress that skimmed the floor. She thought it was more "Seer-like".

Rhys pointed to the chair in front of her. "Please, sit down."

Lore pulled the chair out for Theo, and she thanked him with a smile.

Rhys eyed Lore with disdain. "You sir, are excused."

Lore did not move. He stilled and stared at the smaller male.

"The testing needs to be conducted with no inter-ruptions."

Lore crossed his arms over his chest.

Rhys turned his attention to Theo. "Human, dismiss your guard immediately."

Tex sputtered, "What the fuck?"

I didn't like this, but I wanted to see what she would do.

"Laird?" Tex was waiting for my instruction.

"Let it go...for now." I leaned my forearms on my desk.

She sat up straighter and gave the stranger her most haughty look, "Do not address me as human. I am certain you know my name and my title."

The man held up a hand in a "hang on" motion.

"Ms. Morrissey, you are new to our world. I have been charged with official Council business."

She blinked once slowly. Definitely not impressed.

"You will accommodate my demands or be deemed uncooperative, and I will report that to Raider Black," he told her. "So, I would suggest that you make no trouble for yourself."

"I am ready to begin." She leaned back in her chair.

He glanced again at Lore. "Your guard…"

"No," she answered calmly.

"You refuse an order from your…your better?" he spoke louder.

Tex scoffed, "Better?"

"Lore stays." She kept her tone even, but I could see her eyes flash.

"I will forgive you for your ignorance. I'm certain that you don't know who you entrust with your life."

I gritted my teeth. He sounded so condescending.

Lore acted as if he hadn't heard the insult.

"I know exactly who owns me, and that is Raider Black, Leader of Novus. This Lycan," she said, tilting her head in Lore's direction, but never taking her gaze off Rhys, "is legendary, and he is Novus."

"He is a psychopath who murdered an entire pack. He should have been put down." Rhys's voice thundered through my speakers.

Theo's eyes narrowed for a second then flashed, and then she said in a low, angry voice, "How dare you."

"What?" The man must have sensed something.

"How dare you stand on Novus land, in our building, and besmirch a member of our Pack." She shoved her chair back and got to her feet. "You disgust me." Her lip curled in disdain.

"Sit down," Rhys ordered.

"You do not have the standing to order me to do anything. I carry the Mark of The Lady. I answer to only one—Raider Black. Your commands mean nothing to me." She turned on her heel, and Asher opened the door so that she didn't break stride as she exited the room.

Lore showed his teeth as an insult before he followed Theo from the room.

"Well, that went well." Tex turned off the big screen.

"She'll be here in a moment." This should be fun. A worked-up Theo was always entertaining.

The door to my office swung open, and Theo stomped in. "Do you know what that fucktard just did?"

I was curious about how she would rank her irritations. I didn't have to respond because she continued as Lore quietly closed the door.

"He insulted Lore." She turned around sharply to face the offended party and put her hands on her hips. She studied the wolf as if to make sure he wasn't upset, and then she turned to face me. "Here, on our Pack's land." Her hands were fisted, and she was shaking with rage. "He can't do that."

I glanced at Lore.

He was now casually leaning against the door, watching The Theo Show. "He is rather full of himself," he murmured.

"You should throw him out," she told me. Her chest was heaving with her ragged breaths. "Who the fuck does he think he is? Coming here, demanding to see me, and then insulting Lore. You should send him away after…after I don't know, spitting on him or something…" She ended weakly, and then grimaced and began to pace.

"I should?" I tried not to smile, and I didn't dare look at the others. She was infuriated that her pack mate had been disrespected. It pleased me greatly, but I couldn't ignore the irony that it was Lore whom she was protecting. One of the most dangerous wolves in existence.

She stopped in front of me and I felt her use her gift. She shook her head. "You watched everything, didn't you?"

I grinned. "Guilty."

"He was very disrespectful." She was calming down.

"He was."

"He can't talk about a member of Novus like that here and…and in front of me." Her eyes flashed hurt and frustration.

"He also called you human," I reminded her.

She rolled her eyes. "I sorta expected that. You all seem to think that's really hurtful."

"Do you want to continue with the testing—after an apology, of course, by the Council's Representative…?"

She turned to look at Lore. "What do you say?"

He pushed off from the door and stepped further into the room. "I would first like to thank you for your support, Seer. It means very much to me." He bowed formally to Theo.

She gave a single slow nod in reply, as was appropriate.

He continued, "It is your decision, Laird."

"You saw his tools; what kinds of tests do you think he could do?" I was certain he had missed nothing.

"He'll ask about her background, interactions with The Lady. He might do something basic like writing a number and asking Theo to tell him what number he chose." Lore frowned, clearly unimpressed. "He knows nothing about Theodora. If he had gathered any intel or held an innate skill, he would never have addressed her as 'human'. It takes but a few seconds to sense that she is more."

Her gift was growing steadily, and although she still behaved very much like a human, her scent had changed subtly. I studied my Seer and quickly made my decision. "You two, go out today."

"Yes, Laird," they said in unison.

"Tex, find Rhys. I want to speak with him."

"Will do." He left, and so did the other two.

I prepared for the representative by taking in slow deep breaths. I heard Rhys's blathering before he entered my office. "This treatment is outrageous."

He followed Tex into the room and strode to my desk, stopping directly in front of me. "I have been treated terribly."

I simply raised my eyebrow at the man.

"I represent the Council, and I was shown utter disrespect. I am making a formal report to you and Edinburgh."

I motioned for him to take a seat. "Let's talk about that for a moment."

He sat and was preparing to continue his diatribe when I cut him off by continuing. "I watched your meeting with my Seer."

"What?" His eyes widened in surprise.

"Our conference rooms are wired for sound and video, so as is my right as Laird, I watched."

"But the testing is confidential," he sputtered. "I was not informed."

"She belongs to Novus. Nothing in her life is confidential."

"That will also go into my report."

I had had enough of this odious man. He would not upset Theo again. "There will be no more meetings with my Seer. You are to pack your bags and remove yourself from Novus land."

"You can't do that. I am an official representative of The Council," he thundered.

"The Council can reprimand me later. I want you gone." I pressed the intercom button on my phone's base. "Please send in the guards."

"You think you are so powerful," he sneered. "There are plenty of others who'd like to take you and Novus down. You have no idea what I can do."

"Come on." Tex stood over his chair and wrapped his hand around Rhys's upper arm.

The male got to his feet and glared at me. "I will bring you down."

When he got to the door, I called his name, "Rhys."

He turned around.

"I don't take kindly to threats."

"You think I don't have any power. You'll see," he spat venomously.

I didn't give him another thought as I walked out of the building on my way to find Theo.

FIVE

NOVUS

THEODORA MORRISSEY

Million Reasons by Lady Gaga

I T   H A D   O C C U R R E D   T O   M E   T H A T   T H E   R E A S O N   B LACK
agreed to let me host Thanksgiving dinner was that he
got turned on when he saw me in the kitchen. Not that
we hadn't had sex in every room of his quarters, his
office, and his SUV, but something about me in the
kitchen, with my sleeves rolled up around my elbows and
a bandana holding back my hair, got him hot.

A week ago, I'd realized that I'd taken on too much.
Cooking for one Lycan meant making five times the
usual amount for a man, but then I'd invited ten more to
dinner, and, well, I couldn't keep up. The staff at Packhouse offered to assist. I think the cooks were thrilled to
prepare for so many.

I took a final look around the huge dining room table
that was decorated in fall colors. I approved—correction,

I was proud of how it had turned out. I wanted this meal to be special. Closing the double doors behind me, I ran through my mental checklist. I really needed to get showered and dressed before our first guest arrived.

I met Black on the first landing of the staircase.

"I wondered where you were," he said, looking scrumptious in jeans and no shirt.

"I was doing my final check."

"This was supposed to be fun, not stressful." He draped an arm over my shoulders and guided me up the steps.

"It is fun."

"You aren't sleeping," he stated plainly.

"They're just dreams." Bits and pieces of scenes that made no sense, but I would wake in a cold sweat with my heart hammering in my chest.

"I don't like it."

"Well, it's not fun for me either, but I don't know how to stop them." He usually fucked me to exhaustion before I fell asleep, but even all the sex couldn't stop my unease.

"You've never seen the male before?"

"No." We'd been over and over this. I had no idea who the wolf was. His features were blurred. "And I'm not on Novus land." I sighed in frustration. "I can't explain how I know that, but I do."

We'd made it to his living room when he stopped and pulled me closer so that we faced one another. "There's more that you aren't telling me." He studied my eyes and expression.

I dropped my gaze to his bare chest. "This is where it gets weird. I don't know if these feelings are part of my gift or a manifestation of my fears. That's why I'm hesitant to say anything. I don't know how to tell the difference."

"I don't care if it is your imagination gone wild. I want to know." His hand dropped to my butt, and he pulled me closer.

"Something is going to happen. It's like I feel the energy building." I glanced up at his face. A part of me still feared that he wouldn't believe me or in my gift.

His expression turned stoic. He'd lived a long time, been through so much. I guess the threat of bad news wasn't alarming. "We can handle anything."

"I hope so," I said, choking out the words.

His eyes turned sharp. "You needn't worry about her."

"We've been over this before. If I have nothing to worry about, then why did it take you four days to tell me that her father had called?" I broke free of his hold, but it was only because he allowed it.

"I didn't tell you because I knew you would be upset."

"You alphas and your egos," I growled and then let out a long frustrated breath. "He's powerful, and it's his daughter. He isn't going to let it go," I argued as I paced. I was sure the man was furious with Black.

"You know this or are you guessing?"

"I know this because I see that kind of behavior every day. I'm surrounded by alpha wolves. I know how you all deal with a slight." I crossed my arms under my breasts.

"You manage all of us." He approached me and tucked my hair behind my ear. "If Dolan demands a formal visit for Siobhan, it's no big deal. She'll come, be bored out of her mind, and go back to her life. She is not impressed by Novus or me."

Was she insane? Black was powerful, protective, and sexy as hell. I was frustrated with myself. I'd agreed to this gilded cage and knew of no way to change my circumstance. "Then she's an idiot."

He wrapped his arms around me again. "I like it when you get jealous." His voice was low, and that timbre always made my stomach flip.

I grimaced. "In this case, it's a pointless emotion."

"But it makes you wild, and I benefit." He kissed me.

The damn wolf was right.

He led me to the bedroom we shared and undressed me.

My Lycan loved to torment me by moving slowly to build the anticipation. His hands were everywhere, stroking, plumping, smoothing. "Please, Raider," I begged using his first name. "I-I need…."

He wrapped his arm around my waist, lifting me and moving us so I could crawl forward on my knees to grasp the headboard. "What do you need?" His teeth closed on the spot where my neck met my shoulder.

I widened my knees and sighed. "You. I need you."

He buried himself deep in my body. I panted a few times. "More, Raid."

He pulled back his hips and added a slight twist as he rocked forward. "Like this?"

God, yes. "Please. More." I moved to meet his thrusts.

I heard and felt his chuckle against my back. "My beautiful Theo, so greedy."

"For you. Always," I promised. He was my everything.

His answer was a deep growl.

The meal was a success. Everybody had had eaten their fill. Even Onyx complimented the food. My relationship with my former tutor and Board Member was uneasy. I was much happier with Lore supervising my learning, and I'd wager that Onyx didn't miss seeing me and enduring my so-called idiotic questions.

Black cleared his throat, and we all quieted immediately. "Thank you all for coming to share this occasion, and now, Theo would like to say a few words."

I sat to his left as Conal was on his right. The Laird had never made a formal announcement about the change in seating arrangements. One day he had taken my hand and seated me on his left where his Mate or Consort would one day preside at Pack events. I could feel their gazes on me. "Thank you, Laird, for allowing me to plan this gathering." I then glanced down the length of the table. "I know that Novus does not celebrate this holiday, but I wanted to do this because you all have helped me so much over the last year."

Conal nodded formally. "It has been a pleasure, Seer."

I smiled my thanks to my close friend and continued, "Thanksgiving has always been a special time for me. Growing up, it was my favorite holiday because it seemed like everybody put aside their disagreements as we gathered together for a few hours. My grandmother would have us go around the table and state what we were most thankful for." I looked down at my empty dessert plate as I prepared to go on. "My answer was the same every year. It was family. Sometimes, it was because my mom and I weren't living out on the street and I had a warm bed, and other times, it was because I felt that I was loved."

Black put his hand on top of mine that was gripping the edge of the table. He knew I had a complicated history with my relatives in Ohio.

"Since you found me, I have tried your patience and good humor with my questions and, well, my human failings." I flashed Onyx a sideways look, and he gave me a small nod. "But you all have given me what I've always wanted most...a place where I felt comfortable and content." I lifted my wine glass. "To Novus," I toasted my friends.

Black lifted my hand to his lips.

I saw him mouth, "Mine," before he brushed a kiss over my knuckles.

"To Theo," Conal proposed the toast.

"To Theo." They raised their glasses in unison, which made me blush.

"Who needs more to eat?" Quickly, I tried to divert their attention.

I could see that Tex was considering his options when Clifton, the male in charge of the house, entered the room. He bowed his head as he stood by the door.

Black asked, "Clifton?"

"Laird, there is a male at the door. He does not have an appointment nor was he invited, but he is most insistent."

Conal's relaxed posture disappeared immediately. "What kind of visitor?"

"It is Mr. Rhys. He claims to be on Council business, Second." Clifton dipped his chin.

I watched the different expressions flash across our

friends' faces. Conal was angry, Tex curious, and Lore... resigned. I didn't need to use my gift to know that this unexpected visit was not welcome.

Benedict Rhys strode through the open door, "I told your servant I needed to see you immediately," he said, his gaze locking on Black.

Clifton sputtered, "And I told you to wait in the foyer."

Black still held my hand, looking relaxed, although I could feel his fury. "I'm sure that you did," he assured his majordomo. Clifton was a proud male and a stickler about the house rules.

Conal was now on his feet. "What is this about?" he demanded.

I watched the stranger take a long look down the dining room table. "Good, you're all here. That will cut down my work."

Black raised one eyebrow. "Your work?"

"I've just returned from the Dolan Pack, and Roy asked that I deliver his message personally." The man gave a smirk that told us he enjoyed being the center of attention.

Tex leaned forward, frowning. "You, a representative of Council business, are now acting as a runner between packs?"

"Roy was most interested to learn what I'd witnessed here during my visit. Many of my findings distressed him greatly." He gave me a hate-filled look. "When he decided that a message must be sent, I, of course, volunteered for the job."

Lore growled, "You vile little wolf..."

Black held up his hand to silence his spy. "Just share

the message." He used a bored tone, but I knew his wolf had awakened and was ready to attack.

"It is in the form of a video. Don't you think that is much more personal? Packleader Dolan wasn't sure about the technology, but I set it up for him," Rhys sneered.

"Tex, big screen," Black directed his tech expert.

Tex got to his feet, went to the wall, and pressed a button that I didn't even know was there. A screen descended from the ceiling against the far wall.

Rhys handed him the flash drive, and Tex produced a tablet from God knows where. In a minute or two, he stated, "All ready, Laird."

Black nodded once.

A male appeared on the screen. He looked to be in his fifties with reddish-blond hair and a ruddy complexion. He sat at a huge desk, which reminded me of a film set. There was a family crest hanging over his left shoulder and a suit of armor to his right. "Greetings, Raider Black, Leader of the Novus pack, contracted mate to my sixth daughter, Siobhan." His accent had not dissipated with age or location. Perhaps he liked it that way...? "I've received troubling news from the Council's messenger. Your actions will not tarnish my family and my daughter's reputation. I have reviewed the terms of our contract, and I am invoking the contempt clause."

I glanced at Black, but his face was impassive.

My gut tightened, and my heart beat even faster.

"Consorting publicly with a human woman? Moving her into your lodgings? Treating her as if she has standing?" His volume increased with each charge. "I will not tolerate it. My daughter is not to be made to endure ridicule for your foolish choices. She is to be mated to a male of standing and honor." He glared at the camera.

He's breaking the contract. The thought echoed in my head, and my heart leaped with joy.

"I know you are young and do not understand your actions' impact, how they will be interpreted by those who sit on the Council and with other Pack Leaders." The man went on, "It weakens your position. There are some who believe the witch has bespelled you."

I stared at the screen in bewilderment. If anything, it was the other way around. From the moment I first saw Black, I was a goner. I'd fought the attraction, but how could I say no to him?

"So, to save you from yourself, I demand that the terms of the Mating Agreement be met, immediately. Siobhan has been summoned home to prepare." He lifted his chin, and he looked like a man that had just won a chess match. "The Contracted Mating will benefit both the Dolan and Novus Packs for centuries." Then he gave what he must have believed to be a superior look. "I expect for you to deal with your human. I will not have my daughter's reputation sullied by *that* embarrassment."

The screen faded to black.

There was a ringing in my ears as I bowed my head and held my eyes shut. I knew there were murmured conversations going on around the table, but I couldn't hear a thing. My heart beat too loudly and so hard that my chest ached. I tried to make sense of what had happened, but I couldn't make my brain work.

Conal growled, "How dare he tell you what to do!"

Others joined in with their angry opinions as their attention focused on our end of the huge table.

I couldn't look up. I felt trapped inside my body. The

only thing I could do was shout inside my head. *No, no, no.*

Onyx spoke loudly, "He can." He sounded almost sorry. "When we drew up the contract, Dolan insisted on that clause. I thought it was a provision in case his Pack experienced a downturn and needed the help of Novus."

Rhys chose this moment to add his thoughts. "I've reviewed the contract, and Roy Dolan has every right to demand the mating."

It's too soon. I want more time. Dear God, I thought we'd have more time I silently cried.

Tex cautiously asked Black, "Laird, what are you going to do?"

The room filled with anxiety and dread. I could feel their emotions as they all watched their Leader. I knew the answer. I'd always known the answer, but a tiny part of my heart hoped he would disavow the contract. However, that was not Raider Black's way. Novus was his priority. His pack depended on him, and his word was his bond. He would sacrifice himself for the greater good of Novus.

I made sure my head was raised, and that I was staring straight ahead. I couldn't look at Black, but I was not going to cower at this critical moment.

"I will welcome Siobhan Dolan to our lands," Black answered simply. His tone held no anger or joy.

My eyes squeezed shut. I couldn't stop my reaction. I'd told myself this would happen, but sweet Jesus, it hurt. I felt my heart ripping apart.

"Black, you can't." Solle's voice was filled with accusation and pain.

Conal pulled her chair closer to his and began whispering in her ear, trying to calm her.

Black leaned his forearms on the table and explained, "I signed the contract, and I must uphold the terms. It is my duty." His voice was a little rougher, but it might have been my imagination. "I did it for Novus, to help ensure our future."

"But what about Theo?" Solle looked outraged and concerned. She was a protector, and now all that energy was directed at me.

Rhys spoke before the Laird, "Yes, Black, what do you plan to do about your pet?" Again, the look he gave me was venomous.

I think it was Lore who growled at the outsider.

"Don't think for one moment that you'll be able to hide her away. Dolan's daughter will bring her staff, and they will watch everything closely and report to her father," he promised the room.

"A Dolan will not dictate what is done on Novus land," Glass thundered.

"He does have some say," Onyx said, using his "teaching" tone. "His daughter will be the mate of our Leader. Her position is esteemed, and anyone," he glanced at me, "who challenges her standing would be considered a threat. They would be dealt with as an enemy of Novus."

"I make the rules." Black's voice thundered and echoed off the walls.

"You would put her in danger?" Onyx countered.

Was Onyx defending me?

Black tapped his fingers on the table as the muscle at the corner of his jaw became evident. He was trapped by a deal of his own making. He looked directly at the messenger, "Get out."

The small male flashed a satisfied grin, "As you wish, Sire."

Clifton followed the male from the room, closing the door silently behind him.

I was having trouble breathing. Black was furious, and I could feel his anguish. We both—no, everyone at this table—knew that Siobhan Dolan would kill me or worse, deem me a threat and make Black execute me in retaliation. I glanced at Black. He was grinding his teeth so hard that the muscles at the side of his jaws were pulsating, angry with the circumstances and with himself for a sound decision made long ago. He couldn't pull out of the contract without causing financial damage to the pack along with a loss of esteem. There was no way he couldn't see the final outcome, me facing charges for treason against the Pack because I loved him. He would have to kill me.

That is not what I wanted for him; it never was. He was the most honorable and strong person or Lycan that I had ever met. I knew he loved me. However, as Pack-leader he would try to find a way to honor his agreement and to keep me. I didn't even want to consider what would happen to Novus if The Lady became involved when he was forced to execute her gift.

She would terrorize or decimate my Pack, my friends, my family.

Keeping me would never work. I would become a liability, divisive to our friends and his Board. They would choose sides, and then when I was killed, they would all suffer.

My lips were so dry. My hand shook as I reached for the crystal glass holding my water. I took two sips as I tried to figure out what to do to save the ones I loved.

A painful idea started to form. This was for the good of the Novus. He couldn't or wouldn't make this decision for me, so I had to be the strong one. Black would search for a way to protect me while keeping me. Oh God, Lore. He...he would kill anyone that tried to hurt me. I knew that to be true, even his Packleader. Jesus, I couldn't allow this, putting the people that I loved most in danger.

I took in a huge lungful of air as I sat straighter in my chair. I had to do this. I opened my mouth. The enormity of the moment caused my words to come out hoarse, "Sell me."

The room went absolutely silent.

Black bellowed, "What?"

Solle and others shrieked, "No!"

Asher shoved his chair back from the table.

I knew this was the right thing to do. They couldn't see it, but years from now, they would. I had to sacrifice everything for them. That was what you did for the ones you loved.

"Sell Me." This time, it came out stronger, imploring. I had never broken eye contact with Black. His eyes blazed with fury, and his muscles flexed, stretching his shirt across his thick chest.

I slowly pushed back my chair and stood on shaking legs. I took a step to my right and fell to my knees beside the Laird's chair. I bowed my head as I displayed my brand. "I, Theodora Morrissey, Seer to the Novus Pack, respectfully petition the Laird, Raider Black, to sell me, your loyal servant..." my voice cracked, "for the good of Novus. For our pack's future." The tears fell down my cheeks.

He jumped to his feet, sending his chair flying, and

loomed over me. "I make the rules."

I could feel the wetness on my cheeks as I lifted my chin just enough so that he could see my face. "Raid," I begged in a voice so quiet I might have mouthed the word. We'd known this day would come.

"I will not be told what to do with my woman." His fisted hands were shaking at his sides.

Onyx spoke in a calm, reasonable voice, "Laird, the Seer, she makes good sense. Allow Theodora, who has been so generous to Novus, to make this sacrifice. It will be her legacy to us."

I heard Solle sobbing in the background.

Black was breathing hard. I could see his chest rise and fall. We both knew we were trapped, and this was an out. He closed his eyes briefly, and then looked at me again. "Is this your wish, Theodora Morrissey?" Black asked formally.

"I can't stay." I had to pause because the thought of leaving him caused a bolt of agony to shoot through my chest. It made me feel dizzy. "It will only cause you pain and problems. Let me...my decision...bring more riches to Novus."

When he looked at his boots, I knew that he agreed. He took in a deep breath and let it out slowly as he again stared into my eyes. "Then I must agree to your sacrifice." He said it quietly as if it was meant for me alone. "Theodora Morrissey, your petition is granted."

Solle moaned.

I felt hands slide under my arms to gently lift me to my feet. Lore was behind me, still holding onto me, sheltering me.

"Conference room," Black ordered, and the members of the board rushed to follow him.

64

Lore used his hand to urge me forward and out the door. He led me down the hallway in the opposite direction to a small receiving room. He closed the door behind us, and I walked shakily to the window. It was an overcast day, the sun shielded by clouds. It was how my heart felt. I finally turned to my tutor, my guard, my trusted friend. "Tell me that what I did was right." A sob escaped, and I covered my mouth with my hand, trying to muffle the sound.

"My Lady." He walked to me so gracefully that I was distracted by the beauty of his movement. He dropped to one knee. "You are brave, and I'm honored to serve you." He bowed his head.

For a warrior to drop to his knee and display his vulnerable neck to another was the greatest compliment a Lycan could give. I placed my fingertips on the back of his head and then stroked his hair gently. I cared for him greatly. "Please, Lore, tell me," I could barely get the question out, "did I do right or make a horrible mistake?"

He stood smoothly, and I leaned into his chest. Slowly, he wrapped his arms around me although I could tell he wasn't comfortable doing so. "It was the only way to benefit us all."

"I love him," I admitted aloud.

"I know." He patted my back. "We all know, and for any Lycan who doesn't, they will. This story will be remembered forever."

"I'm scared," I admitted, knowing he would never share my confidences with anyone.

"I can feel your fear." He slowly dropped his arms. "Wherever you go, I will teach you all that I know. Help you any way that I can."

From the spy, that would be a huge gift. "Thank you, Lorenzo," I answered formally.

There was a knock. Lore motioned for me to take a seat on the sofa, and once I was settled, he went to the door.

Asher entered. "My Lady," he'd never addressed me in this formal manner before, "The guests have departed, and Conal's mate is overseeing the clean-up. The board is convening in the conference room and should be there for some time."

"And Rhys?" Lore asked.

The handsome wolf snarled for a moment. "I escorted him to his car, and then sent five guards to see him off Novus land."

"Thank you, Warrior." I never wanted to see that male again.

"I will be outside the door if you should need anything." He walked stiffly to the door.

An hour had passed when Solle rushed into the room. "Oh God, Theo." She threw herself into my arms. "Why did you do that?" She started to cry.

"I didn't want to," I whispered. "I don't want to go." I started to cry with her. "But Solle, it's the only way."

"Black wouldn't let anything happen to you. He cares, he really does," she assured me.

"Oh, honey," I hugged her tighter, "I don't doubt his feelings."

"Then...then why?"

"He can't be mated and have me," I tried to explain.

"Conal wouldn't let anything happen to you." She was grasping at straws, hoping to find a way so that I could stay. "Or Lore."

"I know Conal would die for me." I pressed my forehead against hers for a second. "I can't...I can't put Black, Conal, or anyone in a position where they have to choose between me and Novus, or Black's...," I had to clear my throat before I could say it, "mate."

"He would choose you," Solle said with heat. "We all would."

"But you shouldn't." I gave her a pleading look. This was exactly what I didn't want to happen. "She should come first."

"I don't want you to go. You're my only real friend." She began to cry again.

"I'll always be your friend," I promised.

Lore cleared his throat, drawing our attention. "You can make demands, you know?"

I turned away from Solle to look at him in surprise. "What do you mean?"

"You are Marked, a Seer with great talent," he said, his tone calm. "You can make certain demands, conditions that must be met as part of the sale."

"Like? Like Solle and I could talk?" I wondered aloud.

"Really, Lorenzo?" She had stopped crying.

"There would have to be certain parameters set, like no discussion of Pack business, but I don't see why not," he said.

"Can you go tell them, er, The Board, that I will have a list of demands?" I asked my guard.

He gave me a slight, sly grin. "Of course, My Lady."

Solle watched the wolf as he left the room. "You two do have an interesting dynamic."

"I will miss him and his teachings."

"He respects and cares for you," she said. "I wonder if he will want to go with you?"

67

"Black wouldn't allow it," I said, shaking my head. "He's too valuable to Novus, and Black needs him as much as Lore needs Novus. I think he's finally starting to feel that he has a home here."

"She'll never be able to take your place," Solle said with heat.

"Don't do that, Solle," I cautioned her.

"No, I mean it. You think about your friends. Hell, you think about everybody. You've given us so much." She gripped my hand. "You are special."

"I love you," I told her.

"I hate this." Her eyes filled with tears.

"Me, too."

Hours passed. Asher offered to bring us food and drink. I didn't want anything, but Lore and Solle did. She eventually fell asleep, and Lore settled into a chair and stared off into space. I wondered what they were discussing in the conference room. Oh God, I would miss so much. I'd never hold Conal and Solle's young or watch Issa and Asher find their way.

I sighed and looked out the window at the moon. I prayed to The Lady asking for strength, and to watch over my friends, my Pack.

Much later, Conal entered the room. I glanced at Solle, who I was certain was aware her mate was near, but she was keeping her eyes closed. I got to my feet and met him halfway across the room.

He dropped to his knee. "My Queen."

"Conal," I whispered in surprise. As the pack's Second, addressing me by that title meant a great deal.

He stood in one smooth motion and hugged me to

his chest. "You will always be my Queen." His voice shook with emotion.

I felt the tears build. "My most trusted friend."

He loosened his hold. "The board has discussed and agreed on the procedure for your sale. Of course, the Council must give their approval, but that is all for show. Tomorrow, we will need to discuss your list of conditions, and we have several of our own."

I nodded.

"I'm anticipating the auction to start in two days, and it could go on for a day or two," he told me.

"Then what happens?"

"We prepare for your departure." He frowned. "I'm sure you will want time to learn about your new home and to say good-bye."

I knew he was giving me a message. I squeezed my eyes shut because the tears were threatening again.

He continued, "Do you want to come home with us?"

I opened my eyes. "Did…" I had to start over because my voice shook. "Did he say that I should?"

He looked away. "Uh, no."

I waited until he looked at me again.

"As soon as we were done with the meeting, Black changed and took off."

I understood. He was devastated by the events. First, he'd been out-maneuvered by another Packleader, and then I'd made my petition. He'd been blind-sided and surprised. I hoped that his run would help him find some kind of resolution. "Thank you for the offer, but I will wait for him."

Conal smiled his approval.

SIX

NOVUS

RAIDER BLACK

Hurts by Johnny Cash

MY NOSE TOLD ME THAT THEO WAITED IN OUR ROOMS. *Our*...but that was ending. She was leaving me. As soon as I opened the door, she twisted her body on the sofa and placed her feet on the floor. "Hey," she said quietly as if she was testing my mood.

I closed the door harder than I had intended and crossed into the room. "You should have gone to sleep." I leaned on the back of the large wingchair.

She stayed standing, facing me, but her tense body language indicated she was unsure. Her hands were linked in front of her. "I practiced some things to say, but right now, they don't seem right."

"Then I'll start." I gripped the top of the chair. "Why?"

She blinked twice as she thought about her response. "Because I am selfish." She then dropped her head.

Her ability to disarm me with her utter honesty still caught me off guard at times. I responded slowly, "Go on."

"We might believe that if I stayed here, we could come up with an adequate plan."

"I..."

She talked over me, "Raider, put aside the fact that you're the boss of everything for a moment. Please hear me out."

I tried to tamp down my frustration and anger. I *was* the Laird.

She studied me and then continued. "You deserve to find happiness with her. You two should have every opportunity and make every effort to find a kind of love that makes your lives better." She looked away and moistened her lips, and I noticed that she gripped her hands so tightly that her nails dug into the backs. "And from that love, you should have many young." She nodded her head twice. "If I stayed here, you'd be torn, at first." Then her face filled with such an aching sadness I started around the chair to her.

She held up her hand. "Or I'd hope that you'd be torn," she took in a ragged breath, "and that would be very wrong. But the worst part is that...that you could be forced to kill me because I would be in the way."

"Theo..." I fucking abhorred that she was correct. I took my seat in the chair and noticed that my chest hurt as I considered her words. "I hate this," I ground out.

She walked to my chair, climbed onto the cushion, and bracketed my thighs with her knees, facing me. "I wanted to grow old here, with you. I prayed every day,

72

hoping that would be my future, but it can't be." She placed her cold hands on my chest, one positioned over my heart.

I gripped them. "It could," I started to say.

"No, you can't give me that." A few tears fell down her cheeks. "One of the reasons that I...I love you is because that is who you are. The Leader, the Lycan who sacrifices himself for the greater good of his people."

"It seems you are doing the same." She should be by my side as I ruled Novus. My wolf howled at the lost opportunity.

"This is my home, the place where I really belong. I have a purpose, friends, a family. You are my love. It feels so natural to give all that I can." Her blue eyes were shining with tears.

"I will never forget you. I swear, Theo, never," I vowed and kissed her.

She grasped my shoulders as if I were her only lifeline.

The kiss went from gentle and exploring to hot and rough in a matter of seconds.

I stood while holding her as her legs wrapped around my waist.

As I carried her to the bedroom, she pulled her shirt over her head.

We stripped, and then our hands explored.

I had to be inside her. As I entered her body, I sighed, "Mine."

"Always," she vowed, and I believed her.

It was only noon, and if it were possible for me to get a headache, I would have the giant, brain-exploding kind.

Word had spread about the auction, and I had to close off our floor because people were flooding our offices.

I hit the intercom button. "Basil, can you locate Theo?"

"She and Lore are in her office with two guards on the door."

I walked with a "don't fuck with me" purpose down the corridor. When I arrived, the guard opened the door with a respectful nod. Theo sat cross-legged on the sofa while Lore wrote on a legal pad.

"Laird," he greeted me.

"I wanted to see how you were coming with your list?" And I wanted to see her. I sat beside her and wrapped my arm around her shoulders.

She snuggled closer. "According to Lore, I don't know what I'm doing."

"She will need to explain that she needs her meat cooked and for vegetables to be provided." He flipped the pages of the pad.

"Will you listen to my list and tell me what you think?" She sounded tired. "You know my ways... What am I missing?"

"Of course." I knew that she liked to sleep in a cool room but under a thick blanket, that she loved strawberries, and that she thought using a fresh towel every time she showered was a waste of water and my staff's effort.

Lore began to read the list.

Her requests were simple and straightforward. "So, you want your own quarters and doors?" I grinned at her.

"I loved my time with Conal and Solle, but I doubt that I could ever find hosts like that again." She rubbed the space between her eyebrows.

"I agree."

"The request for communication with Solle might be a problem because Conal is my Second," I cautioned. "I know that others might not understand this, but I walked away from my human life without a fight. I can't give up everything again. It's…it's too soon. I don't think asking for a thirty-minute call once a month is too much." She watched my expression. "They can monitor my call if that is the only way that I can have contact."

"I will make it happen," I told her quietly.

She squeezed my hand that rested over her shoulder.

Lore continued, "We should discuss the safety precautions."

She looked from her tutor to me.

"They cannot allow her to be injured in any manner —physically, mentally, or emotionally," I said.

"I'd add psychically," Lore suggested. "Especially if the Council becomes involved. There are stories that they have…experimented."

"I thought Lycans aren't supposed to hurt me?" She pulled away from me.

"They are not," I told her, enunciating each word clearly.

"But…" Lore shut up when I flashed him a look.

"I will do everything that I can to make sure that you'll be protected," I told them. "If there is cause or suspicion of an incident, then Novus will once again take possession."

"Immediate possession," Lore added. "A Pack might not understand the need for immediate medical treatment for a human."

"And, uhm," she shifted so that she was facing me, "I was going to ask you if it would be okay that when I…"

She closed her eyes for a moment and chewed on her bottom lip. "When I die, can I be buried here on Novus land?"

Fuck, she tore my heart out of my chest. It was bad enough that she'd live away from me, but I hadn't considered our world without her.

"I'd like to know that one day I can come back home." Her voice was ragged with emotion.

"Of course." I pulled her onto my lap as she cried.

Lore left us without a word as I held my beautiful love.

Five days later, it was done. For the price of three hundred seventy-five million, the Seer would be transferred to the Burke Pack in rural Texas. It was the pack that Tex had left years ago. I had no idea where Travis Burke was going to find the money, but the wire transfer was to arrive within the hour. Oddly, the return of her remains was a major area of contention, and I found it all silly, so I stated that Novus would pay for her body's transport when that day came.

Tex did not look happy. "I'll get with Lore and tell him all that I know."

"I'm sure he will have quite a bit to add."

Conal growled, "I don't trust any of the Burkes."

I waited for my Second to continue. Conal had stayed in the conference room for the entire length of the auction. He needed to see his mate and to run. "We've always believed them to be one of the poorest packs, and then somehow he manages to find that kind of money..." I clenched my fists. "It doesn't make sense."

Onyx did that slow blink thing that always reminded me of a cat. "He's out in that Godforsaken place. Perhaps he presents that he has nothing so that his pack is left alone...? We appear to be rough, uncultured, and only caring about our bikes and muscle cars." He shrugged one elegant shoulder. "It is all about perception."

"Tex?" I asked. He was our real expert on the Burke Pack.

"It was a very different time, and when I was made, we were homesteaders, barely getting by." He narrowed his eyes as he recalled. "I don't think they wanted luxury or knew to want it. There was always food, but we hunted for our own. Honestly, it's hard to compare my life then, as a human. I remember always being hungry and exhausted, and then when I was changed, I was wild for a while. I didn't know to notice those kinds of things. It was only about survival."

"We know they are insular, and few join or leave the pack. Some of the families have moved to surrounding towns to find work to support their own," Onyx shared from the intelligence gathered by my spies. "I doubt they are keeping up with tech or other fast-changing trends."

"Well, if they are behind in tech, then that is to our advantage." I was proud that many of our young went out into the human world for college and training. I had an entire team, led by Tex that did nothing but study tech breakthroughs.

"You really want him to set up her place? Right under their noses?" Conal asked.

"We protect her," Glass said with heat. "She can't take a guard with her, so she's going to be alone... amongst them."

I'd made that decision prior to the auction's end. "We wire and set up cameras, and if they catch us, then we take them down. But she is ours to watch over."

"Are you going to tell her?" Glass asked slowly.

"No." It would be safer for her not to know.

"So, she is to be delivered in fourteen days," Onyx said, trying to wrap things up. We were exhausted.

"Pull it all together. Use whatever resources you need. I want to have a plan in place by this time tomorrow," I told them, and then I waited until they left.

I sent a text to Lore: **My Office**.

Lore: **As you wish**.

He knocked and then entered within ten minutes. "Burke's Pack?"

"Yes." I watched him take the chair across from my desk. "I'm going to need everything you have on them."

"I will have the file to you tomorrow morning," he said solemnly.

"They wouldn't budge on the accompanying guard." Not that I was surprised; I would have done the same.

"They would have never allowed me to accompany her." He knew his reputation.

"You could still cross their border, get in and out, right?" I meant with Theo if need be.

"Of course." He stiffened momentarily, looking offended. "If there was a need, I could steal her away from the Council."

Of that, I had no doubt.

SEVEN

NOVUS

THEODORA MORRISSEY

Fields of Gold by Sting

TWO WEEKS WAS A SHORT AMOUNT OF TIME TO SAY goodbye to your current way of life, but it was also far too long. After day four, it was decided there would be a huge gathering the night before I was to leave. It seemed that I spent all my time saying goodbye, mostly to Pack members that I'd never met. They interrupted my classes and even knocked on Conal's front door at seven in the morning, thinking that I still lived there.

Lore, Glass, and I were working out on the mats in the gym. They both thought it very important that I keep up my training. I didn't have the nerve to ask outright if they were worried about my safety, my gut knew the answer.

I was getting better. The key to hand-to-hand was not to trust my eyes but to go with my instincts. A Lycan would still be able to kick my ass, but the hope was that I could do enough to stall until help arrived.

"Take five," Lore ordered after I had rolled Glass onto her back and off the mat.

"Seer, Lore…" The Warrior got to her feet. "I must go. I'm to check in at The Farm."

I held out my hand, and she pulled me to my feet. I tried not to cringe as I put weight on my left leg. My hip had taken my all weight when I'd gone down. "Thanks for making time to help, Glass."

"Of course." She squeezed my hand then jogged to the locker room.

I tried to stretch my sore leg.

"I will place weapons around your quarters," Lore told me. "On your person, you should have two blades at all times."

"Won't that be a problem in the shower?" I quipped, trying to lighten the mood.

He simply stared at me.

I sat down across from him on the mat. "I know." I rubbed my hand against my forehead. It seemed like I was constantly on the verge of getting a tension headache. "I think I'm at that point where I'm about to break down and..," my voice sounded rough to my ears, "and I don't want to do that because then everybody will go crazy with concern. I'm trying to be strong, but…it's a lot." Since the decision, I'd confided more about my emotions to Lore. He was an incredible listener, and I think in some odd way that it helped him. He'd been alone for so long. I think he needed to remember how others felt. After I was gone, I wanted him to continue interacting with the Pack. I'd made Solle promise that she would make sure he came around, even if she had to ask Conal to force him. He needed his Pack.

"The Burke Pack is a bit of an unknown. We did not expect them to enter into the bidding, nor to win."

"If I ask you for your honest opinion, will you give it to me? Not as a member of Novus, or my tutor, but as an elder, can you do that?" From day one—okay, it might have been day five—I'd given him my complete trust.

I liked that he didn't answer immediately. When he did, it was with caution. "It will depend on your question, Theodora."

That was fair. "Is this a huge mistake? Did I act too fast? Was I too afraid that I couldn't handle him with her?" When I swallowed, it hurt my throat. "Did I not have enough faith in Black and what he could have done to make things work with her and keep me?" I dug my nails into my thighs as I waited for his answer.

"I can't answer the part about it being a mistake. Only time will tell."

I frowned. *Fuckin' logical wolf.*

"Is it selfish that you don't want to die?" He smirked. "You do realize that as an ancient Lycan, I am almost impossible to kill so I can't comprehend your fear."

"Oh." I dropped my gaze, disappointed. I was looking for affirmation or information from this wise wolf.

"But I respect your will to survive. As a group, we underestimate you because you are human, but you have shown that you are strong. You have a connection to The Lady, and you understand that you have a purpose. Some of the Marked never come to terms with that, yet you have accepted your role with dignity."

I'd had to.

"Siobhan Dolan would see you dead within a week."

My heart skipped a beat at the surety in his tone.

"The Laird cares for you deeply. That is clear to all. She would not like you around her intended mate. The outcome would cause many problems within Novus for the Laird, and if he chose to punish Siobhan, there could be war between the packs."

"I told him all of that," I explained. "Plus, it isn't fair to her either." I squared my shoulders. "She is being sent here to a new place. I can empathize with her. I wouldn't want a lover around."

"And the Laird wouldn't stay away from you," Lore added, not in a joking tone or with a leer, just in his honest way.

"I would have told him that we'd have to stop our affair. I wouldn't do that to another female," I said hotly. "More than anything, I want him to find happiness, and I don't think being torn between two women would help."

That made him grin. "Do you really think that the two of you could stop?"

No. "I'd try," I vowed, but the tears that quickly filled my eyes spoke the truth. I looked away, stunned by the depth of my feelings for my lover.

Lore allowed me to regain control. "My Queen, you've chosen a difficult path, but you did it for very honorable reasons."

"He cares about the Pack's stability. Money buys stability." I tried to brush off his compliment and to remind myself of the reasons why I was giving up everything.

"And you saved him from having to make some tough choices," Lore added quietly.

He understood.

I let out a ragged breath. I pulled my knee to my chest and rested my cheek against it. This was so painful, but it was the best option in the long run.

"I will visit you."

I lifted my head to see that his eyes were filled with mischief.

"I didn't think that I could have visitors. They won't allow me to bring even an attendant."

He jogged an eyebrow up and down. "They can't keep me out."

My heart filled with warmth at knowing this, and it gave me some peace. "Well, if you promise that you won't get caught..."

"I promise, my Queen."

I knew certain things about some of my friends' futures. They hadn't come in debilitating visions, but more like simple scenes that were thrust into my head. I hadn't shared this because the time hadn't seemed right. Maybe I would leave letters for the others...?

"I saw a part of your future," I disclosed.

"I am sure that you get glimpses into many."

He would never ask, so I decided to share a little. "You must take care of yourself. She isn't ready to meet you, but when it does happen, she will recognize you immediately for what you are." I did not know the woman, nor could I see her clearly, but in my vision, I could feel her strength. She wasn't Lycan. She left me with an impression of fire. I was sorry I wouldn't see this courtship. I couldn't begin to imagine how Lore would go about that.

"Thank you, Seer." He bowed his head.

"I will miss you, Lorenzo. You have enriched my life greatly. Your mother would be very pleased with your generosity and the male that you've become."

"It has been an honor and a pleasure."

Solle and I were alone, packing my clothes into a huge box. It was taking longer than it should. I think we both knew that when we sealed the boxes, we'd have to talk. So far, we had stuck to light topics, the party tomorrow night and harmless gossip about our friends.

She carefully folded my jeans. "I know it's pointless, but I don't want you to go."

"I know... but you do understand why I can't stay, right?" I gave her a pleading look.

"If you asked, he'd break the contract." She placed the jeans in the box.

I sat down on the bed and patted the spot next to me. "You know I can't do that, Solle."

She dropped down beside me and put her head on my shoulder. "I know, but I still wanted you to try or for him to offer."

"I love you. You are my closest friend and my sister. Please remember that."

She started to cry.

I held her. When she slowed, I whispered, "I've learned so much from you about how to be strong and to take my place in the Pack. I will forever use those lessons."

"It won't be the same without you."

"You'll have Conal. You can turn to him for comfort, and I need you to...watch over Black." I asked her for what I couldn't do. "Sometimes, he's very alone."

"I'll try."

"Thank you."

We continued sitting on the bed, side by side, holding one another.

I heard Conal's boots on the hardwood floor, and then he leaned against the doorframe. "You about done?"

I dropped my arm from around his mate. "Yeah," I said, trying to smile bravely.

"It's not too cold out. I thought we'd take a short ride on my bike, like old times."

"I'll even wear my helmet." I tried to keep things light.

"Let me find you a warmer coat." Solle hurried from the room.

Conal looked at the boxes. "I'll make sure these are loaded onto the plane."

"Thank you." I had enough clothes for a couple of days, but everything else was packed. My entire life fit into five boxes.

We rode for miles. Conal's wide body blocked most of the wind. I wasn't complaining. I knew this was his gift to me. He understood how much I needed the quiet and to feel a bit of freedom.

He pulled off to the side and signaled for me to dismount. He did the same, and I followed him as we made our way to a fallen tree. I sat down on the trunk.

"You've made a difference," he said.

"I could say the same, my friend."

"I mean to Novus, and I'm not talking about your gift. I mean, you brought us closer together."

I smiled and nodded.

"And you are good for him."

I knew that he meant Black. "I love him."

"Has he told you the same?"

"Not in words," I answered honestly. "I'm not sure that he can." He might have been saving that word for his mate.

He watched me closely. "But you know that he does."

"Yes."

He ran his hand through his hair. "I don't know how to…help. There are so many emotions."

"I don't think you can," I said slowly. "You can hold Solle if she cries, but Black, he won't ask for any emotional propping up." I snickered at the thought. "Maybe you can have a good fight, fuck each other up. That might help."

He flashed a smirk, approving my suggestion.

"I want you all to move forward." I swallowed because this next part hurt to say. "She will come, and you must welcome her. You have to be the first, so the others will follow. Then there will be their mating to celebrate and…" I couldn't finish.

He took the spot beside me and wrapped his arm around my back. "You know if you ever need me…"

"I know, and I appreciate your offer…" But to ask that of him would be a diplomatic nightmare.

"I don't care about that shit. I mean it, Theo, if you need me, I'll come."

"You are brave and loyal, with a heart as huge as your body. I'm lucky to call you friend, Conal."

He hugged me. "I will miss you, my sweet, sweet girl."

EIGHT

NOVUS

RAIDER BLACK

Shadow of the Day by Linkin Park

IT WAS SUPPOSED TO BE A PARTY. THE ATTENDEES WERE trying to be festive, but the taint of sadness hung in the air. The females had done an outstanding job setting up and decorating the grounds around the community center. There was a balloon-covered arch erected at the entrance, and Theo had been positioned there with Solle and Conal, along with Lore lurking close by. My spy's behavior worried me. He was too genial and appeared not to be concerned with Theo's exit. My gut told me that would be a problem. He was very attached to the Seer.

The food was plentiful, and I had taken a seat off to the side at a table with a few members of the guard. I held a beer, but I watched Theo. She was dressed for the weather. Although mild for December in Nebraska, she wore a fleece jacket in a medium blue that matched her eyes with a knit band covering her ears. She smiled as she spoke to Mr. and Mrs. Yu, and then accepted a hug from the female, Kenta's mother. All the damage that their son, who'd turned feral, had caused was forgiven. I think every member of Novus had hugged her at least once.

"How you doin'?" Tex took the chair across from me.

"Great turnout," I observed.

"It's for her. Of course, they would come." He glanced in Theo's direction.

"Look, if tomorrow is going to be a problem for you, I understand." I didn't want to focus on my feelings.

"Oh." He narrowed his eyes and looked away for a moment. "I appreciate that, but I want to be there to check things out," he said, his tone even.

"She's worried that going back will upset you," I said quietly. We would all miss how Theo cared for each Pack member. She had taken the time to get to know all those who came around.

"She had that talk with me too, and I told her I would be fine. It was a long time ago."

His eyes still held a haunted look. Reliving that history had to be upsetting. A hunting party from the Burkes had invaded his human settlement. One of the males took Tex as his prisoner. Tex had endured much in order to survive. When he'd been changed, he'd killed his captor. Being newly changed without supervision, he'd turned feral. When the Burke Pack had recaptured him, they'd kept him imprisoned and tortured him for years. "Some scars never heal," I said, keeping my gaze on Theo. "We can pretend, but they are still with us."

"Even if I didn't want to go back there, I would for Theo." He nodded, got up, and disappeared into the crowd.

My woman had made her mark upon my Pack.

I had no idea what the future would bring. Theo and I had stayed outside until the early hours of the morning the day after the auction. We were not summoned nor transported to The Lady's Plain, but Theo spoke to the moon. She explained her decision and prayed to the Goddess to watch over Novus and those closest to her. She asked for strength as she started this new path with the Burkes. I had watched over her as she spoke that night to The Lady, memorizing every moment. She was a gift to our race, but Theo was mine. I didn't care what a piece of parchment proclaimed; she owned my heart.

Theo had moved away from the entrance, and now was standing by the bar, whispering something to Lore. He shook his head once and grinned.

Solle placed a fresh beer in front of me. "You know you could stand beside her instead of watching her from across the field." She took the seat Tex had vacated.

"If I join her, then the attention will be split between us, and tonight, it should be hers." I took a long drink.

"I'm trying not to be angry," she shared, "but I am a little bit with you."

"I understand." I, too, was angry with myself and the decisions I'd made many years ago.

"She told me that we should help each other through this, but I suppose you'll be busy with your intended." She looked down at the table.

"Solle, I will always have time for you." She'd mated with Conal, and they had absorbed me into their family.

"I wanted to explain, you know if I become a little

distant," she said softly. "I'm going to need some time to get used to the changes."

"I do understand." She loved Theo, and I suddenly realized that Solle had been lonely before Theo had arrived. Although she had a mate, she needed other friendships, and our human had given her that.

The sounds of the band warming up caught everyone's attention.

"I can't believe that Gordon came back for this. I'm going to stake out my place." She pushed up from the table and headed toward the stage.

Gordon was a member of Novus, but he was a wanderer. In his human form, he looked like the kind of guy who could take care of himself in a fight. He was only a few hundred years old and had spent a good deal of his time living on some small lake in Minnesota. He'd petitioned to join Novus because I didn't require that he live on Pack lands. He paid his dues and caused no problems. I don't know how Tex had lured him back, but it was a joyous occasion when he took the stage. The man could sing.

I moved around the back of the gathering, enjoying the show. Lore was with Theo, and she'd managed to get something to eat. The first notes of the next song sounded, and I watched her head rise as she looked at the stage. She hurriedly whispered to Lore, and he pulled back her chair. I watched as he cleared a path to the stage. Then he motioned to Gordon and pointed at Theo.

Gordon held out his hand, and Lore lifted Theo up so that she could climb onto the stage. "Please, welcome Theodora to the stage."

The crowd went wild while Tex rushed from the side of the stage and gave her a microphone.

When she was set, she walked back to stand beside Gordon. "I'm not a very good singer, but this song... Well, it means something special to me, and tonight, it says it all."

The band had been playing filler chords, but they went back into the opening to Linkin Park's "Shadow of the Day." The crowd settled as Gordon sang the first verse and Theo joined him during the chorus. I'd always thought it was a song about dying, but tonight, it was about closing a chapter. She was asking the Pack to let her go.

I knew Gordon was going to extend the song; he was an entertainer, and the crowd was hanging onto their every word. I couldn't take it anymore. I could feel her pain. To watch her be so transparent with my Pack, I needed to touch her, to hold her. I pushed through the crowd to get to the stage...to her. I shoved people out of my way as she wiped tears from her cheeks. I vaulted onto the stage and yanked the mic from her hand, letting it fall to the floor. I pulled her into my arms and kissed her.

Time stopped. There was no sound. The only thing I was aware of was the soft woman in my arms. My world for a few hours more.

When I let her come up for air, she sighed, "Raid."

I lifted her into my arms, and she hid her damp face in the crook of my neck as I jumped from the stage. I carried her through the crowd. People clapped me on the back, but I didn't stop until I got to my bike. I put her on her feet. "Ride with me."

She smiled, and it felt like the sun had come out at midnight. "Anywhere."

We took off fast. I needed to feel the speed as she held on tightly to my waist.

We rode until I finally stopped at the same spot we'd visited back in August. I knew she recognized it as well.

We climbed off the bike, and I led her to the picnic table. I helped her up onto the bench so she could sit on the table. I positioned myself between her thighs.

She was watching my face. "Raid?"

"I love you," I said, rushing the words.

Her eyes flared wide.

"I should have said it every day," I admitted.

"You didn't need to, because you showed me in a thousand different ways." Her eyes filled with tears as she smiled. "You know how I feel about you. I've loved you practically from the start."

I held her face in my hands as my wolf howled that she was our mate. "I should have said the words. I don't know why I held them back." I kissed her softly.

"You didn't want to make a promise, and no matter how practical I am, it would've given me hope." She'd burrowed her hands under my sweatshirt.

"I wish—"

"Don't. We can't." She stroked my back. "Let's enjoy these hours because we have to go on. We're better for having loved one another, but we have to go on, Raider."

Keep her, my wolf howled.

I kissed her again.

"I want to show you tonight, Raider, how much you mean to me. Take me home," she whispered.

I lifted her into my arms and carried her back to my bike.

. . .

I knew she was exhausted, but I still wanted her.

Theo was draped over my chest breathing hard. "I swear I'll move in a minute," she said, her voice was muffled against my pec.

"You don't have to." I ran my hand over her ass.

"Good, because I was only saying it to be polite."

I smacked her ass once, lightly.

She giggled.

"Babe, we need to be serious for a minute." I rubbed my hand along her spine.

She propped up her head on her hand. "Okay...?"

"You and Solle can talk once a month. Burke didn't object to that request. I can't guarantee that your communications won't be monitored." I paused to see how she took the news.

"By the Burkes or by Novus?"

"Both."

She didn't seem too upset by that information. She understood some of the inner-workings of the business of running a pack.

"Now, this is the important part, Theo. If you need my help, we need to come up with a phrase that seems natural, but I'll know that it means you're in trouble."

I felt her body stiffen. "What are you expecting?"

I told her honestly, "I don't know."

"But...?"

"I'm trying to think of every angle. I can't be there; I can't talk to you. So, I'm depending on others, and that makes me uneasy." I continued stroking her soft skin. My gut clenched because I would never be able to do this again.

"So, if I need Novus's help, I'm to insert something into the conversation..." she said the words slowly as she pondered her choices.

"My help." I'd give up Novus if she needed me.

She breathed my name, "Raid?" She understood.

"Or you could tell The Lady," I reminded her.

"Jesus, when Lore asked for her help, she made it so that he could kill an entire pack in a few hours." She bit her bottom lip.

"Well, then she's your last resort."

"Ya think?" She smiled. "Okay, how about if I talk about getting a dog."

I know that I gave her a horrified look. Our canine brothers did not feel comfortable around most Lycans, so we rarely kept pet dogs. "That's good."

Her eyes turned a deeper blue. "I've tried to be very brave."

I wrapped my arms around her and held her tight. "I know."

"I'm scared," she whispered. "Really scared, but...I know my duty. I don't want to embarrass you or Novus."

"I know." I ran my fingers up the back of her skull, letting her silky hair fall between my fingers. I felt the same way, too.

"I want it to work out," she continued. "I'm not expecting my life to be as good as it is here, but it doesn't have to be terrible. I can adjust." She dropped her face onto my shoulder to muffle the sob she'd been holding back.

"You are strong. Baby, you are so strong. You've amazed me time and time again," I crooned, hoping I could give her more strength.

"But if I really need your help, you'll come." She

said it as if she was memorizing the statement, holding onto it.

"I will move mountains to get to you," I promised her and myself. "No matter what, Theo."

"That helps." She raised her head again. "I promise that I'll only...talk about dogs...if...if it's really, really bad."

She was killing me. I kissed her again, and then we made love. I didn't care if she was exhausted for the plane ride. I couldn't stop myself. I needed her.

Finally, we slept for an hour. The knock on my quarter's door woke us. I pulled her to me and whispered against her hair, "Please do the thing with your brand. That's how I will always remember you in the morning, riding my cock, while presenting your wrist."

"Anything," she said as she climbed over my hips.

Had any man, human or Lycan ever had a woman who was so generous?

I traced the marks from my claws that she carried on her skin. They were a permanent reminder of our love.

Soon she lifted her hips and slid down my cock. She then presented her brand for the last time. "Good morning, Laird," she said in a quiet voice.

"My Lady."

Glass had reported to me that, after she'd explained that she would cover Theo's Novus brand with a flat brand before the Burke's marked her, Theo's response had been, "Make sure it hurts. I want them to think I'm crying because of the pain, and not because I'm losing my family."

I made love to her one final time in the shower. From that point on, I couldn't touch her. I didn't want my scent on her. Rumors of our affair could circulate, but no outsider would know of our true feelings.

Lore met us in my living room, and I went into my office so that they could have a few private moments. He wouldn't be traveling with us because he wasn't welcome on the Burkes' land, and I didn't want to call attention to their close relationship.

Fifteen minutes later, I returned. They were embracing. I watched Lore drop to his knee. "I will carry you forever in my heart, my Queen, next to my mother."

"And I will never forget any of your lessons, Lorenzo. Please stay safe, my brave friend."

"It is time," I told them.

She looked around the living room where we had spent hours talking, laughing, and fucking. After squaring her shoulders, she said, "I am ready, Laird."

NINE

THEODORA MORRISSEY

Dust in the Wind by Kansas

THE BURKE PACK WAS VERY DIFFERENT. I STOOD IN front of my refrigerator and tried to figure out what to eat for dinner. I lived alone in a small one-bedroom apartment in a five story building that had a beauty salon and barbershop on the first floor. I was the only residential tenant. I'd been told that visiting dignitaries stayed in this building, so basically, I was alone.

I pulled out the carton of eggs and checked the cheese situation. An omelet would be easy and a better choice than the cereal I'd had last night. Two weeks had passed, and I was having trouble adjusting. The rules were different, and yet, the same. No computer, no cell phone, no driving, but since I'd had the first seizure, I worried about being behind the wheel anyway. So, that wasn't any different, but what was so different was the fact I'd met only four members of the Pack. I didn't have a guard. There was one at the tenant's entrance, but that was it. The Pack Leader's sister, Anna Maria, was my tutor, er, Watcher. She arrived every morning at nine, and we basically hung out. I didn't have studies. I didn't even know if there was a library of texts that might be available to me.

Anna Maria had never met a Marked before and didn't seem to know what to do with me. She liked to watch daytime TV, so that's what we did every day. I was bored out of my mind.

On the day that I'd arrived, everybody from the Burke side had seemed tentative. I'd assumed they were keeping things short so that Novus would leave as quickly as possible. I hadn't slept on the flight to Texas, and I felt numb. My role once we landed in Texas was to be docile. I'd worn a knee-length navy dress that had a high neckline and a pair of dark gray, low-heeled suede boots. It wasn't bitterly cold, so I had on a dark gray cape made from heavy fleece. Travis Burke had eyed me up and down, and then dismissed me. Black, Onyx, and Conal stayed at their Packhouse where I assumed meetings were held. Tex, Glass, and Solle accompanied me to see my new quarters.

When the Leaders' meeting had finished, they joined us at my apartment, and that was when Mr. Burke introduced his two sons, Edward and Charles. Neither was his Second, but Anna Maria had mentioned they were vying for the soon-to-be-available position. Edward appeared to be in his late forties and reminded me of the stereotypical accountant. I knew immediately that I needed to avoid Charles. He was giving Tex a hate-filled look. When he turned his dark, almost-black eyes on me,

I felt a shiver of dread shoot up my spine. His hair was wild. I don't think that he'd combed it in weeks and his clothes looked dirty. I decided that I didn't want to have anything to do with either brother.

I'd kept my emotions in check until it was time to cover my Novus brand. Glass and I had discussed this, so I was aware of the process. I'd forgotten that branding hurt like a bitch, so the tears were real and a welcome release.

Travis Burke had asked loudly, "Is she defective?"

"Sire," Anna Maria turned to her brother, "humans are weak."

No one from Novus defended me. It wasn't their place. I didn't belong to them anymore.

Glass put her instruments of torture away, but I saw that the warrior's hands were unsteady. She then turned to address the Burke Pack, "After the Burke brand is applied, I will cover the affected area."

Edward stepped forward. "Thank you."

He wasn't as confident with this procedure as Glass. He even sent her a questioning look when trying to decide the placement.

My entire body shook as the Burke brand burned into my upper forearm. Tears fell down my cheeks as I gritted my teeth so that I didn't make a sound. I felt empty, but I would not cry out.

I shook my head to rid myself of the memories, then slid the egg concoction from the frying pan onto the plate and sat at the small table. I made myself gloss over the memory of the good-byes. One day, I would go back and review them, but it was still too painful. The next morning, Anna Maria had shown up promptly at nine, and we'd talked about general things. I wasn't expecting us to become best friends, but so far, it seemed like she tolerated me, and that was all.

This morning, I was dressed and having my third cup of coffee when Anna Maria arrived. "Good morning," I said, standing. "Would you like a cup of coffee?"

"No."

"Are you hungry? I can make you something."

"No."

I'd had enough. "Anna Maria, please take a seat." I pointed to the chair opposite me.

The look she gave me was almost fearful. She moved to the chair.

"I think we need to discuss what we're going to do with one another."

"What do you mean?" Her eyes narrowed in suspicion.

What did I mean? I wasn't sure how hard to press. "I'm not sure what your role is. Are you my guard, or are you here to teach me about the Lycan world and the Burke Pack?"

"I am no guard." She sat straighter in the chair.

"If I need something, can I ask you or can you tell me who should I talk to?"

She narrowed her eyes. "What could you possibly need?"

"Well, for starters, I'd like a tour of the area."

She stared at me as if she might not understand my desire.

"And I need to go out at night, preferably someplace with trees and grass, and with a clear view of the moon."

"Is that because of your mark?" Now, she sounded interested.

"Yes. Being outside, it recharges me," I said, giving her a vague explanation.

"I will make the request."

"I really need to go out three or four times a week."

She frowned. "That seems excessive."

I gave her my best "Gift from a Goddess" look, lifting my chin and my eyebrows.

She let out a sigh. "I'll see what I can do."

"Also, I'm going to need more groceries. Can we plan a trip to the store?"

"What do you need?"

"Do you want me to make a list?" I was trying to stay pleasant. Was she being difficult on purpose?

"You need to make a list?" She sounded shocked that I ate so much. It wasn't like the cupboard had been well-stocked when I'd arrived.

"I eat, and I need coffee." Some of my frustration seeped through.

"As if we haven't spent enough on you?" she muttered bitterly.

"What's that supposed to mean?" This was the most emotion she'd ever shown. I leaned in, feeling very curious.

Her eyebrows lowered as she aimed a glare at me. "Because of you, our taxes are being raised. Some families can't afford it. There's talk that they might have to close the school early because there is no money."

"Your pack couldn't afford the cost?" I couldn't hide my surprise. I'd assumed that a pack as old as the Burkes' would have money. I'd picked up odds and ends of talk around the Novus offices, and I knew they had millions in their accounts. Many, many millions.

"Our membership has decreased, fewer young are born."

"I had nothing to do with the auction or the terms of payment."

"I figured as much. A human would not have a say." She gave me that patented, superior Lycan stare. "So now, we are all paying for you."

I now had my first bit of information about the Burkes. "Look, Anna Maria, if you're going to be stuck with me, then we need to come to some sort of understanding," I said. "I can't sit around all day doing nothing. I, well, I like to learn things. I need to have something to do."

"I thought you had visions. You are a Seer."

Great, another Onyx-like watcher to disappoint. "They don't come every day." Then I added quickly, "Maybe if I can have some time outside, one might come."

"Something helpful to the Pack? Perhaps, you'll have good news?" For the first time since we'd met, she looked interested.

"Perhaps," I waffled. I didn't want to lie, but I needed to make things happen.

"Tonight, we will go outside," she announced.

I tried to add some sincerity to my smile. "Thank you."

My first phone call with Solle began with stops and starts. Neither one of us knew exactly how much to say. We were cautious because Anna Maria was standing out in the hall, most likely listening. Still, it helped to hear my friend's voice. I was homesick.

During the beginning of my second month, I'd had a vision. I had convinced Anna Maria to try yoga with me. I think she secretly liked it but was too stubborn to admit it. I was sitting on my mat after the cool-down, and the vision hit me without any build-up. It was terrifying. I was in wolf form, and I was chasing a child. When I came back to myself, I vomited on the rug.

My Watcher called Travis Burke. The seizure had frightened her.

At first, I couldn't describe the vision. It took me almost another day before I could verbalize what I'd experienced. Then I was driven, along with four male guards, to the Packhouse and admitted to a conference room that was on the shabby side. The cushion of the chair I sat on had been repaired with duct tape. The Leader, his sons, and another man, who I believed to be the pack's retiring Second, were in the room. Nobody bothered to introduce me to the stranger, a stark reminder that things were very different here. Novus had considered me to be theirs from the start. Here, I was treated like a temporary worker, an outsider.

I haltingly told them what I had seen: the excitement of the chase, and then the satisfaction of tearing the child apart and the need to do it again. By the time I finished, I'd broken out in a cold sweat and felt nauseous.

Travis Burke then asked me a series of questions that had more to do with my seizures than what I'd experienced. Edward listened attentively, while his brother stared straight ahead with an eerie smile on his face.

I tried to reiterate that the wolf wanted to do this again.

The Burke Leader said, "That is the natural order of things, human. The weak perish."

Charles began to laugh in a crazed way.

The Second silenced him with a look.

"But what if it is a Lycan child?" I asked, trying to appeal to what the Leader might deem important. Anna Maria had said the Pack had few young.

The Second asked, "Was the child one of ours?"

"I-I don't know," I admitted. "How would I be able to tell?"

He shrugged. "I thought that with your gift you would know."

"I was around several Lycan children before, and I couldn't tell the difference from a human child."

"Parents allowed *you* to see their young?" Edward focused on me.

I blinked in surprise. "Yes. I worked the front desk at a medical practice," I informed them.

"A human working around the young?" Edward shook his head. "Black must have great power over his people."

The Second explained, "Here, we would never allow a human, especially one who did not grow up here, near our children."

"We don't like your kind," Charles said in a sing-song voice, "unless we're hungry."

I didn't flinch or show in any way how much he freaked me out. This Pack's attitude explained why I hadn't met any other members, and why I was locked away.

The Texas spring had arrived signifying that I had been

here several months. I didn't keep a calendar. I had no milestones to celebrate. Every morning, I pledged that I would make the best of my situation, but I was struggling with loneliness. Some mornings, I stayed in bed until eleven, and then took an afternoon nap. I was a prisoner without chains. I now understood why other Seers had gone insane. Spending so much time alone with my thoughts was making me anxious, so I slept to escape those feelings. I looked forward to my evenings outside. I rambled to the moon, hoping that The Lady felt my presence and my need for support. I hadn't been called to her Plain. A part of me felt like my gift was weakening. It was like I was a plant that never received the proper care. I wasn't wilting, but I also wasn't standing strong.

Tonight, sleep would not come. I rolled over and hugged the pillow to my chest. I wanted to cry, but I feared that if I started, I might not be able to stop. What I'd witnessed three days ago haunted me every time I closed my eyes. I could hear the male's agonizing screams and feel the fear of his wolf.

I shifted again, trying to find a comfortable position. I could lie to myself and try to believe that I needed more time to learn the ways of the Burke Pack, to comprehend what was happening. The Burke Pack was flawed. They hid it by keeping to themselves and doing their business quietly. I couldn't offer evidence that could be traced; my opinion came from my dreams and what I felt when I was with the Pack's top-level leaders.

That afternoon, Anna Maria had received a call instructing her that a car was coming for me. I was escorted through the huge Packhouse to a field behind it. There, chained to the ground, was a male.

He was terrified and crying. For a Lycan, he was too thin, as if he was half-starved. I knew that condition was dangerous to all. The need to eat was a driving force to a Lycan's survival. I recalled that the Burke Pack had kept Tex in a half-starved state during his imprisonment.

The Second, who I had learned was named, Odin Springer, demanded, "Is this the one from your vision."

"No," I answered immediately. This Lycan was sane.

"You didn't use your gift." Travis Burke accused.

Careful, the word thundered in my mind. "I could tell immediately. The two Lycans are completely different," I said, keeping my tone even and confident.

The Leader watched me closely. "Use your gift. I want to see how it works."

I nodded and took in several cleansing breaths, trying to center myself. I then kicked off my shoes, hoping that a connection with the earth might help. I was nervous and unsure of my safety. I had no protectors here. I moved to the prisoner.

He cried out as I neared, "Help me. Please help me."

"I won't hurt you," I said.

"Please," he begged.

I went down on my knees beside him and placed my hand on his heaving torso. His wolf howled in fear. I gritted my teeth to keep the connection. I tried to calm the terrified male, but I think I made things worse because he could feel me.

"Why is this taking so long?' Burke demanded.

I held out my other hand, and the Leader grasped it roughly. "Now, ask your questions," I told him in a low voice.

When the Leader was done and the connection broken, I sat back on my heels, exhausted. The prisoner had done nothing more than be in the wrong place when a band of guards appeared, led by the Leader's younger son. I got to my feet and stepped away slowly. I knew not to make any sudden moves.

"So, this," the Second pointed at the male, "has been a huge waste of time." He glared at his Second.

"Not totally," Edward said. "We know that she can force us to talk."

Charles rocked back on his heels. "Doesn't matter. This is all bullshit." He then sent a stream of spit in my direction.

"Go on." The Leader looked at his son inquiringly.

"How do you know she isn't making all of that up?" He shot me a glance filled with hate.

"Because I'd know." The Leader sounded as if his patience had run its course.

"Fuck this shit." Charles moved so quickly I couldn't track him for a moment. He stood over the prisoner.

I think I screamed when I realized his intent.

He tore the male's head from his body.

I just watched him kill an innocent male, a member of his Pack, and nobody lifted a finger to stop him. Nor did anyone offer a towel to wipe the man's blood from my skin. Before I got into the car that would take me back to the apartment, I stubbornly stood my ground and demanded, "A towel, I need a towel." I hated what I had witnessed. I hated them all for doing nothing.

The guard went into the Packhouse and returned with a roll of paper towels.

When I was finished with each square, I tossed them on the ground. I didn't care that I littered. I wanted to dirty the landscape like the events I'd just witnessed had dirtied my soul.

. . .

I rolled onto my back and stared at the ceiling. This situation was bad, but maybe things would get better. Perhaps, I could help.

Pounding sounded on my front door.

I checked the bedside clock, and it read one-fourteen. I got out of bed and rushed to the door. Surely, for all the ruckus, it must be an important summons.

TEN

SOLLE MACGREGOR

Set Fire to the Rain by Adele

TONIGHT, I'D WORKED LATE AGAIN. I DIDN'T LIKE coming home to an empty house. Conal had called a half hour ago, saying that he was heading home. My mate was stressed and putting in many hours at the Novus headquarters. The recent changes had affected us all greatly.

We missed Theo. Sometimes, I thought our monthly phone calls made things worse. Maybe she did too because she hadn't called yesterday. I'd eagerly waited for the text alerting me that the call would be coming. Near midnight, Conal had forced me to come to bed.

And Siobhan Dolan was a bitch. I'd expected her to be difficult, haughty, acting like a spoiled princess, but she was two hundred times worse. She used a tone when addressing my mate that was so disrespectful, I wanted to kill her. From the beginning, she'd made it clear, with words and actions, that she didn't want to mix with Pack members because we were all beneath her.

Black tried to put on a brave face in public, but I knew, and Conal saw first-hand every day how miserable our Laird was. Some nights, I would rest in Conal's arms and plan how I would murder her so that things could go back to normal. The normal before the Seer had entered our lives. Killing the Dolan princess would not bring Theo back.

An incoming message beeped on my phone. It was a number I didn't recognize. I pressed the button that would record the call as our security protocol dictated. "Hello?"

"Is this So...uhm...Soul-lah Mac-Greg-gor?" The voice was feminine and clearly unfamiliar with my name.

"Yes. Who is this?" My instincts rocketed to high alert.

"Look, I don't want any trouble." She began so quietly that even with my Lycan hearing I strained to follow. "If they find out, they'll kill me, but somebody needs to know."

I recognized the fear in her voice. "Why are you calling me?"

"Your friend... He...he hurt her."

"Who?" My voice shook, but I knew the answer. I felt my wolf wake and she was on guard, listening... absorbing every word.

I heard shuffling sounds, and then a muffled voice, "Solle."

"Theo?" I think I forgot to breathe.

"Oh God, Solle." Her voice was slurred and hoarse like she was drunk and about to pass out.

I spoke very calmly, enunciating each word. "Honey hit the camera button."

"Solle…" By her tone, it sounded like she was refusing.

"Have the female turn on the camera, right now," I said, my tone dead even.

The face that appeared on the screen was not my friend's. It was misshapen and severely damaged. One eye was swollen shut, and the other was only partially open. "Solle?" She couldn't move her jaw. Her lips were split, in several places.

My doctor's brain was making a list of her injuries as I tried to stay calm. "Who did this to you?" I was so angered that my voice went cold and business-like.

"Solle…" This time, her voice was weaker.

I heard Conal's truck pull into the drive and the garage door go up. He'd smell my emotions. He'd know what to do because I wasn't thinking clearly. At this moment, I wanted to kill every member of the Burke Pack. "Honey, who…did…this?"

Conal's boots pounded through the kitchen. He came to a sliding stop beside me and took the phone from my shaking hands. "Oh God, Theo," he said the words with a gut-wrenching tone of shock.

Her working eye closed, and a tear fell down her cheek.

Conal carried the phone in his hands as he moved to the coffee table and switched the transmission to our big screen TV. With greater detail, she was grotesque.

As a doctor, I'd seen plenty of injuries, but this was among the worst beatings I'd ever witnessed. "What happened, baby?" My voice shook.

"I fought him," she said softly. "I didn't want…"

I glanced at Conal, and I knew that he, too, was furious.

"I need a name, Seer," he said in a soft voice, but even that didn't hide his fury.

"I said no," she cried, and I knew that if her face was this mangled, that her body would be worse. The deep wracking sobs had to be killing her.

"Name, Theo." Conal's emotions came through that time.

"Charles."

My lungs burned from my sharp intake of air. "Did he rape you?" My voice was so harsh that I hardly recognized it.

She turned her face away from the camera.

The other woman's voice sounded. "He did, repeatedly. He violated a Marked...a gift from The Lady." Her voice was filled with fury.

Theo wouldn't look at the camera as she spoke, "Tell him, tell him that I want a dog. I'm going to get a dog." Then she opened her eye and begged, "Solle, please tell him about the dog."

Conal asked, "Is she concussed?" Then he looked at me perplexed. "Why is she talking about a dog?"

I had no idea, but to her, mentioning a dog was very important.

"Solle...you have to...tell him."

I didn't have to ask who she meant. "I will honey," I promised.

"How bad is she?" Conal asked the woman.

"Look, I should hang up. I don't want to get caught," she said, sounding panicked.

"I am Conal MacGregor, the Second to the Leader of the Novus Pack. We will protect you. In fact, for your good deed, I will send you payment so that you can travel to safety."

"I-I don't know…" The woman was terrified. Sharing this news could be considered treason by the Burkes.

"I will text you within the hour how to collect your fee. It will be twenty-five thousand dollars. If you stay with the Seer and stand guard, I will personally deposit a quarter of a million dollars in an account for you," Conal said. "You are the only one who can help the Marked. The Novus Pack and The Lady will forever be grateful to you."

"Okay," she said, as though slowly coming to a decision. "He raped her…repeatedly. He broke her jaw, cheek, and eye socket. Three ribs, her left hand, and right ankle are shattered. There are internal injuries." She paused to take a breath. "Do you want me to list those?"

Conal spoke first. "No, can you…can you send the file to this number? My wife is a doctor. We need to know what we're dealing with."

I was pacing. I couldn't stay quiet another minute. "Theo?"

The female said, "She's asleep."

"Tell her we're coming." I looked at my husband, and he nodded once. "Tell her we'll be there as soon as we can."

"How?" The female stuttered.

"It's better that you don't know. I need your word that you will guard the Seer. Tell me your name, and vow to keep her safe."

"Olivia Stern."

"Olivia Stern, member of the Burke Pack," Conal

spoke formally, "I ask for your promise that you will guard Theodora Morrissey with your life. You have my word as Second in the Novus pack that you will be compensated, and I personally will be in your debt."

Oliva looked terrified. She wore no make-up, but her golden skin paled. "Charles, he's not right. He's the Leader's son."

I didn't want to listen to these negotiations any longer. I wanted to do violence, to make another hurt for what had been done. I ran to the front door, threw it open, and changed on our doorstep. I headed for the Novus Packhouse. Raider Black had a lot to answer for.

It was reckless, but I didn't care. My friend...my sweet, beautiful friend...had been raped by the son of the Leader of the Pack where we'd sent her. I changed back into human form on the doorstep of the Pack-house. I punched the doorbell with my finger, hitting it repeatedly. When nobody appeared within a few seconds, I raised my fist and pounded on the door.

The door opened. "What the fu... Solle?" The Laird glared at me.

I pushed past him and stalked into the foyer. "You fucking son-of-a-bitch," I yelled at him.

"What is wrong with you?" he asked, his voice rising, angry and confused.

"He raped her," I screamed. "He...raped...her." I swung at his face.

Of course, he didn't fight me. He took the slap.

"What the hell is going on?" Siobhan rushed down the steps. "We are having dinner."

I glared at the woman, and then back at Black.

"Solle has just received some upsetting news," Black explained calmly.

"Well, it can't be that important." The woman sniffed, dismissing me.

"Fuck you," I growled.

"What did you say?" She forced her shoulders back and moved closer to me.

I wanted to fight, to injure, to kill her.

"Solle," Black said sharply.

I didn't have time for her. Not now.

I turned back to Black, which was an insult to her, but I didn't give a shit. "A female just called me from the *hospital*." The last word came out in a shriek.

The front door opened and Conal entered. "We need to talk." He looked in Siobhan's direction. "This is official Novus business madam, so if you'll excuse us…?"

With a sneer at Conal, she said "Fine." Then she turned around and stomped up the stairs.

After we all heard a door slam, Black turned his angry eyes upon me. "Now, mate to my Second, what is the meaning of this?"

"He raped her, Black." My voice cracked. "He hurt her." Then I burst into tears.

Instantly, Conal was by my side, his arm around my waist, hugging me to his side.

Black's face tightened as he turned to Conal. "What is this about?"

"We received a report that Charles Burke raped Theo. She's in a hospital. We got a call. She's in bad shape, Black." Conal's voice was rough with emotion by the time he finished.

The room went silent for a very long moment. "What the hell are you talking about?" The Laird's thunderous roar made the walls shake.

"We were supposed to have our call yesterday," I

started slowly. "It never happened." I knew he was well aware of the missed call, but I needed to start slowly so I could rein in my emotions. "Just a little while ago, a call came in from a Texas number I didn't recognize. I thought maybe I'd overlooked the alert. I didn't want to miss her call." I felt Conal's arm tighten around my waist, and then he let go. He understood that I needed to move. I started to pace. "It was a female's voice. One I didn't recognize, but then I heard Theo. Well, it didn't sound very much like her. It was hard to understand her."

Black was standing motionless as he listened with every part of his body.

"I told her to turn on the camera. I wanted to see what was going on." I swallowed hard because I felt like I was going to cry again.

"And you saw her." Black's voice was low and dangerous.

Conal had been tapping on the screen of his phone. "I sent you the file."

"He did it multiple times," I rasped.

Our Laird looked enraged. I swear his body did a full tremor. The sound that broke free from his chest was an agonized roar.

I felt my wolf whine; she was afraid. I don't remember my wolf ever being afraid when Conal was near.

Black's jaws ground hard. "Call an emergency meeting, Conal. I want everyone in my conference room in one hour." Then he turned to go up the steps.

"Laird," I timidly called after him.

He shot a glance over his shoulder.

"Theo said something odd, but she said it three

times," I recounted. "She kept talking about getting a dog. She wanted you to know she was getting a dog." I shrugged in confusion.

He closed his eyes for a second. When he opened them again, rage burned there. "Conal," he growled, "I want the plane on standby. Get both planes ready to go."

"Yes, Laird." Conal gave me a look that told me to keep quiet as he started tapping the screen of his phone.

"Healer," Black's tone was straight-up authoritarian, "you'll need to organize staff. Bring two or three, whoever you think is best. I want to be in the air within two hours. Gather whatever you might need. Use the guards to transport."

Thank The Lady we were bringing our girl home.

ELEVEN

NOVUS

RAIDER BLACK

Make You Feel My Love by Adele

I FELT NUMB AS I ROBOTICALLY ISSUED THE ASSIGNMENTS.
I needed a cool head because if I gave in to my emotions
even a little bit, everything would go to shit. We, and
most importantly, Theo, didn't have time for me to react
on blind emotion. Conal and Solle left and I took the
steps three at a time. Siobhan was pacing the hallway
outside of my office.

She had one hand on her hip. "What the hell was
that all about? My father would never have tolerated an
interruption during his dining hours."

I'd grown tired of hearing how her father handled
things. "This is not the Dolan Pack, and it would serve
you well to remember that," I snapped.

"If you want respect then you must have rules and
boundaries." She continued talking as she followed me

to the door to my office. "That way, *those* people will understand they should be happy you give any them attention at all."

I turned to face her so quickly that she almost ran into me. "Siobhan now is not the time for your blabbering."

"How dare you. You should be happy I agreed to associate with you." She lifted her lip in an ugly sneer. "There was a time when your kind wouldn't have been allowed to sit at the same table as me."

"I don't give a fuck," I ground out, my voice rumbling in my chest. "Clearly, this isn't working, so why don't you spend tonight packing your things. I'll arrange for a plane to take you and your staff back to your father."

"You wouldn't dare," she said, sounding aghast.

"You don't like me. You have shown nothing but disdain for Novus—so, yes, I would."

"You can't get rid of me like….like you did your whore," she screeched.

I wanted to tear her head from her body. I lunged toward her and then pulled up. I swear I felt every muscle cramp as I tamped down that need. "Spend some time reading the agreement. It states that I can." I stepped into my office and slammed the door in her face. Even the Dolan Princess wouldn't have the nerve to open the door to my private office.

I dropped into my office chair. I needed to focus. I brushed my finger over my tablet and pulled up the most recent file sent by Conal. I tapped the icon and turned up the volume.

After leaving Theo in Texas, I hadn't watched any of the recordings of her daily life. I couldn't. Conal received a report, and once a week, on Sunday afternoons, he would give me a summary. I did listen to the recordings of Solle and Theo's monthly calls. It seemed like Theo was sad, but I'd tried to convince myself that I was allowing my feelings to color my impressions.

After weeks of listening to another report of Theo's day-to-day activities that sounded boring as fuck, I told Conal to only brief me if something major happened. The feed was reviewed when one of the techs had time, they weren't being monitored live anymore.

I'd made a grave error.

I ran my hand over my face for the second time as I watched the call again. The first time, I couldn't hear her words. I could only stare in horror at her face. Her beautiful face was mangled. I would have Solle find the best plastic surgeons. It would be repaired. I would see to it. She would be beautiful once again.

The next time, I listened to her answers. She was... afraid and defeated until she mentioned our code. The brave woman had remembered. I would not let her down again.

I got to my feet, and after stopping in Clifton's quarters to update him on my plans, I made it clear that if Ms. Dolan's group wished to leave, he was to make the arrangements. The wolf brightened visibly at the news.

I changed and ran to Novus. The exertion didn't dissipate my anger, but it did take off the edge so that I didn't feel like I wanted to kill the next person I encountered. After changing back into human form, I stuck my head into the tech's room, "I want the—"

"It's been sent to your secure email, Laird," a female said as she shot to her feet.

I noticed that she looked pale. "Were you the one to

view…?" I didn't know what to call it, "…the events that transpired?"

"I was," she said, her voice shaking. "Is the Seer alive?"

My wolf howled in desperation. "Solle spoke with her an hour ago, so yes," I said, softening my tone.

"I'll pray for her."

"If you need to take a break or leave, you may."

"Thank you, but I want to stay and to help." Her eyes flashed with anger.

I nodded and headed to my office.

Basil was just taking his chair and turning on his computer. He looked up. "I saw the alert. I await your orders." He looked resolute.

I nodded as I entered my office.

I took my chair and pulled up my secure e-mail. I stared at the message for a minute, dreading what I was about to see. I tapped two keys so that the recording would display on the big screen.

The tech had every right to be affected by what she'd seen. I was watching it for the fourth time, memorizing every second so that when I caught Charles Burke, I would make sure to copy his movements as I broke his bones, tore his skin, and invaded his body without his permission.

"Enough," Basil cried. "Laird, enough." He was beside my desk. "I can't take her screams another second." The wolf's face was tense, his body shaking. "Please, I can't stand it."

I tapped the screen and stopped the replay.

He cleared his throat and straightened his shoulders. "The Board has assembled in the conference room. Solle and a team of three are also in attendance."

I got to my feet and walked to the door, "With me, Basil." I wanted him to see what had happened, and how I was going to deal with it. The word needed to spread to every member of Novus.

I walked into the silent room. The atmosphere was tense.

I didn't wait. I started talking. "It has come to my attention that there was an attack against Theodora Morrissey. The Seer spoke with Solle two hours ago. She is hospitalized on Burke land. Onyx, I want you to go over the contract and be ready to recite the exact page and paragraph of these violations." I didn't wait for his answer; I continued. "Tex, arrange the transportation, and Glass, I want your best guards with us." I knew that arrangements were being made by the light tapping on keyboards on phones and tablets. "Conal?"

"Yes, Laird?" His hands were in fists by his sides.

"Where is Lore?" When he learned of this attack, I wanted him under my control.

"As of two hours ago, he was in Spokane."

"Call him back. Tell him to fly private, and to be waiting for our return," I instructed my Second. "Make sure he understands that, if he chooses to disobey my orders, there will be consequences."

"She'll need him," Solle said quietly.

"Conal..." I paused to tighten the grip on my emotions, "stress that point, for Theo."

"I will."

"I fucked up," I admitted. "We were monitoring the video feed from Theo's quarters, but she rarely left or had visitors. I decided ten days ago to stop the live monitoring."

"You couldn't have stopped him," Conal told me.

"You couldn't have done anything without giving away the fact we'd bugged her place on Burke land," Tex pointed out.

"Do you think that would have bothered me?" My gaze roved over the table. "That I could have shortened this…this nightmare, even if only by one minute, is something I will regret forever," I shouted in a thundering voice.

"Show us," Glass urged in a strangled voice.

I glanced at my Warrior. I had forgotten that she'd been violated as a child by an invading pack. I thought to excuse her, but she flashed me a look that dared me to try. "Basil, lights."

The lights were dimmed, and Tex started the video.

From the camera's angle, one could clearly see the front door to Theo's apartment. There was a pounding on the door. A few beats later, the lights came on. We watched Theo move from her bedroom to the door. She was wearing one of my T-shirts with the Jack Daniels logo on it.

She stopped at the door. "Who's there?"

A male's voice boomed, "Open the damn door."

"Go away." She moved to the side as if he could see her on the other side.

"Seer, invite me in," the male continued in a strange sing-song way.

"Leave me, or I will make a call." She moved to the phone that was positioned on the table by her sofa.

The door broke apart. Charles Burke strode through laughing. "Stupid human, nobody can stop me."

"This is my home. I want you to go." She was moving cautiously to the side of the sofa where I knew she kept one of her blades. She sat down, and I

124

watched her slide her hand along the far side under the cushion.

"You do not matter," he yelled, spittle forming at the edges of his mouth. "You are nothing, human."

If he'd been in my pack, I would have put him down.

She waited until he reached for her, and she sliced open his arm. In a smooth move, climbed and rolled over the back of the sofa then headed to the kitchen, where she kept one of the Glocks I'd left for her. I'd placed it in the drawer, myself.

She didn't make it that far.

Charles leaped across the room. He landed on her back, trapping her arms as he took her to the floor. Her nose, or perhaps her chin, made a terrible noise as it met the tile.

She must have been stunned, but she still fought.

He tore her clothes from her body. Then slapped her face with his palm and then the back of his hand. Each crack caused her head to snap from side to side.

She raked her nails down his cheek then poked his eye.

Glass had taught her that maneuver.

She was bleeding, and her face had started to swell by the time he took her. She'd screamed, "No," over and over, and then, "I don't want this…"

My woman was a fighter even when she must have known she wasn't going to win. I was proud of her, but at the same time, her will and refusal to give in broke my heart.

Charles was relentless.

At one point, she was making whimpering sounds, and he held open her mouth to spit into it, screaming, "Take me, take all of me, scum."

125

The next time he took her, she screamed, "Black, please."

I felt all of the wolves' gazes on me. I'd sent her there, and he'd brutalized her while she'd cried out for my help.

"Nobody will want you when I'm done with you."

He rolled her over onto her stomach.

Her last words were a prayer to The Lady. "Mother, please, please take me."

I hoped that it was to only take her out of the reality of the moment, but I wouldn't have been surprised if she'd wished for death.

She lost consciousness, but that didn't deter the Burke spawn.

We watched until finally he changed, lifted his hind leg, and urinated on her inert body on the kitchen floor.

Five hours later, a female approached the apartment. She stared at the broken door and entered the apartment slowly. She then sniffed the air and rushed to the kitchen area.

"Theodora," she said in a panicked voice.

"Get up." The woman dropped to her knees beside the Seer. She looked helplessly around the room then got to her feet and grabbed a paper towel square and wiped the blood from her hands. She then spent five minutes pacing in the living room, never once looking back at Theo.

"Why doesn't she do something?" Brian, the male nurse, cried.

It seemed like everyone shifted in their chairs, anticipating the woman's next move.

Finally, she went to the purse she'd discarded by the front door and pulled out her flip phone.

She talked on and on to the person on the other end of the call. "No, I don't know when it happened. I can smell his stench all over the room and on her."

She listened to the reply.

"I'll have to check." She walked back to Theo. "Yes, she's still breathing."

More talk.

"Well, I don't want you to draw any attention. Yes, it might be better if you use your personal vehicle. Maybe by then, she'll be dead."

"You, cunt," Solle screamed at the screen. She slid from her chair and rushed from the room.

We continued watching the feed as I fast-forward when twenty minutes later, two men arrived.

I knew the rest of the scene. They carried her out on a folded sheet, not bothering to cover her battered and bleeding body.

Glass had followed Solle out into the hallway. When I got out there, they were embracing.

Solle sobbed, "I can't believe that anybody would do that to her."

"She fought him. Even after he'd snapped her arm, she fought him." Glass was speaking as her trainer and as a Warrior.

I cleared my throat, feeling like an intruder. "Solle?"

"Yes, sir?" She separated from Glass and leaned against the wall as if she needed the extra strength to stay upright.

"From what you saw, can you make any determination about her injuries?" Was she going to be alive by the time we got there?

Switching mental gears seemed to help her. She pushed off the wall and stood straight and tall. "From what I observed during our call, she has significant damage to her face." She counted on her fingers. "We saw him snap her left arm and stomp on her hand. He punched her in the stomach, so there could be internal injuries and fractured ribs. Do you want me to go into the vaginal tearing?" She made a frustrated sound.

"But she's in a hospital, right?" Glass interrupted.

"I've been trying to find out about the hospital in that area. It isn't great, so I'm concerned about the care." Solle ran a hand through her hair. "The nurse who called was supposed to send me her file, but I haven't received anything."

"Can she fly? Or should I be thinking of over-the-road transport?" I wanted to have every contingency covered.

"I won't know until I look at the records and examine her myself." Solle frowned. "Are we bringing her back here?" She eyed me warily.

"Our agreement stated that she was to be kept safe," I said.

"So, we are bringing her home…?" she pressed.

"Solle…" I sighed. "Since she was sold, there is some verbiage that comes into play. The Council will now become involved. We have a Pack that has allowed a Marked to be brutalized. This situation is a diplomatic nightmare."

"Is this because of that bitch, Siobhan?" Solle's cheeks were flushed. "We can't leave Theo all alone. We are her family; she needs us." She glared at me. "*You* can't do that to her."

"We will do what is best for the Seer," Glass cut in smoothly. "I will protect her with my life." She glanced at me.

"My immediate plan is to get down there and take her somewhere safe, where she can be treated for her injuries. If that means that she can fly back here, then that's Option A, but if she isn't stable enough to travel, then I want her off Burke's land and in the closest, reputable hospital."

"My staff is prepared for whatever is needed," the doctor assured me.

"Babe?" Conal joined us. "You okay?' He went to his mate and hugged her.

"No," she said into his chest.

"Yeah, I don't think any of us are." My Second gave me an appraising look.

"Calm and controlled, Conal—until we have her in a safe place," I said.

"Unless Lore goes rogue," he muttered.

A part of me wished he would, but first, we needed to remove the Seer.

Three hours later, we were in the air. Onyx had made the call to the Council in Scotland. After sending them the video of Theo's call, Alexander DeFlavio called the elder Burke. It took an hour for Burke to be located. During that time, two more Council members joined the call.

Burke tried his best to tap dance around the fact that a Seer who wore his Pack's brand was beaten and violated by a member of his Pack. At first, the Leader claimed that no such event had happened. However, when video evidence was presented, he stated that he had no knowledge of the event. At that claim, Alexander told him that his son was named as her attacker and, again, there was video evidence.

We had to listen to him grouse about spies and honor among Leaders. Alexander halted that rant by stating it was his land and that the quarters he'd provided for the woman had been his business to monitor.

Bottom line, the Burke Pack had violated the agreement. Novus would take possession of the Seer. There would also be an investigation by the Council into the assault, and there would be repercussions. The Burke pack would bear the burden of all her medical bills, as well as forfeit the purchase price. Alexander ended the call with a strong warning to the Burke Pack, basically telling them if any Novus member so much as got a scratch, they'd answer to the Council.

The smaller jet took off first, with Glass and her guards and Onyx, who was to be escorted immediately to begin the meeting with Burke. We took the larger plane that had a bedroom outfitted in the rear. Solle and her medical team were seated near that space. Tex was communicating with the pack closest to Burke's land, requesting information about hospitals and permission to travel through their lands if need be.

Conal sat across from me. His long legs stretched out in front of him. To a stranger, he might appear relaxed, but I knew he was boiling with rage.

"Did you reach Lore?" I looked up from my tablet. I kept watching Theo cry out for me.

"Yes. I spoke with him," Conal answered vaguely.

I gave him a hard stare. "And?"

"He knows."

"What do you mean, he knows?" I asked in a shitty tone.

Conal held out his huge hands, palms-up. "His first words were, 'Does she live?'"

"Theo mentioned he'd inherited some talent from his mother," I muttered.

"I told him the Burkes had violated the agreement, and we were going to get her back."

I nodded.

"I told him three times that he was expected in Wolfsbane. That he was to head straight to Nebraska." Conal's eyes flashed. "Although, I wouldn't cry if he disobeyed and murdered all of them."

"Then we'd lose our spy, and Theo would lose a good friend," I said resignedly.

"She's going to need us, her family and friends." Conal looked around.

"You are assuming that the Council will not swoop in and take her," I said, voicing my fear.

"Would you allow that, Laird?" Conal gave me a hard look as he sat taller in his seat. "Take what is yours, the woman who carries your claw marks carved into her skin? The gift that The Lady gave to us? You, Raider Black, will allow them to come onto our lands and take our girl?" His voice went lower with every question, every charge, and challenge, finishing with, "The one you love?"

I didn't answer right away.

Conal narrowed his eyes as he waited for my answer.

My voice came out as a growl, "Hell, no."

He smiled and allowed a deep chuckle to escape his chest. "Damn right."

Tex moved easily to the open seat next to Conal. "Okay, we have safe passage assured by the Volares. They hate the Burkes and have offered the assistance of their guard if we need them. I have a list of four hospitals outside of Burke land, and I was assured that two are top-notch."

"Get that info to Solle," I told him.

"Also, they are looking for Charles Burke," Tex continued. "It seems he has been doing some hunting in their area, and they've had to handle the clean-up."

"What are the chances he will be there when we land?" Conal asked.

"Zero," Tex said, his eyes glinting with grim determination.

I shook my head. "Love for his son has made Travis blind."

"Charles has never been punished—I mean, really punished—for his misdeeds. He should have been put down three hundred years ago, and yet, he is still here preying on the weak." Tex gripped his knees tightly.

"Once we are off Burke land, put out the word, up the reward to the point where nobody can refuse, but we want him alive. He will die by my hand," I said.

"Or mine," Conal added.

"Or mine," Tex added to the list.

Then the thought occurred to me. "But I will offer his death to Theo, first. She was wronged. She should take her revenge."

"That is if The Lady doesn't get to him first." Tex let out a long breath. "I want to punch something, and that it's them...it's getting to me. They've done so much damage."

"Tex, we handle this diplomatically," Conal told the male who was abducted and changed against his will many years ago by a member of the Burkes.

"What about the nurse who placed the call?" I asked, hoping to redirect their attention.

Tex said, "She was born on Burke land. Age seventy, works at the county hospital. She is unmated."

"Do you think she will run?" I asked them.

Tex frowned. "If she doesn't, then she is dead. Burke will punish anyone who has any knowledge of this."

"The second you get there, make sure she has cash to get out of town. Tell her not to take her own car. Hell, help her steal one but get her out. Reiterate that she will always be welcome on Novus land," I told the male who would be escorting Solle and her team to the hospital.

I didn't like having my people separated, but I needed Solle to see to Theo. The news that the hospital was sub-par concerned me greatly. I knew Conal hated being separated from his mate in enemy territory. I hoped that Onyx would have everything in order by the time Conal and I arrived. I'd chosen to arrive later to cut back on the posturing time. I wanted the official paperwork signed.

TWELVE

NOVUS

THEODORA MORRISSEY

Burning House by Cam

I TOLD MY NURSE, NOW GUARD, OLIVA, THAT I DIDN'T
want any more pain medicine. I needed to be aware. A
part of my brain knew I was in pain, but all of my focus
was on the door. As soon as I'd finished the call with
Solle, and then Conal, I'd fallen into an exhausted sleep.
Now, it was eight hours later, and I knew that they were
near.

"Those people...Novus, they won't hurt you, will
they?" the nurse asked in a quiet voice.

"No, of course not."

"I didn't mean to offend." She dropped her gaze.
"But you are weakened."

"Novus is... They are different. You should go to
them," I urged. "There, you would have freedom."

"There will be a price on my head," the woman said, chewing her lower lip.

"All the more reason to come to Nebraska." I closed my working eye because I was tiring. During my stay here, I'd lost the ability to heal quickly. I'd first noticed it when I'd slit my thumb open attempting to cut into an avocado. Perhaps, The Lady had forgotten about me, or was the gift somehow tied to my being with Black? I didn't know, and I hadn't been invited to ask. Too many questions were whirling around in my brain. I needed to save my energy. The next hours would be the difference between living and dying. I had to use my head and be careful. My position with Novus had changed. Perhaps, their feelings toward me had, too?

The sound of multiple heavy footfalls on the tile hallway sounded, as though they wanted everyone to know they were in the building.

Olivia moved to the door in protective mode.

"It's Novus," I said.

She didn't look back, but she did nod her head to acknowledge my comment. She stood in the middle of the doorway, blocking their entry.

A familiar female's voice sounded. "Stand down, nurse."

Olivia didn't move.

"I am Solle MacGregor, mated to Conal, the Second of the Novus Pack. I am a doctor, and Theodora Morrissey is my friend." Solle's voice carried so that I could hear each word clearly.

"Olivia," I said softly, "it's Novus. Let them in."

She slowly moved away from the door and returned to my bedside. However, she was still wary.

Tex entered behind a woman dressed in a navy business suit, followed by Solle and Brian. Suddenly, I could only make out faint shapes because I was crying.

Solle leaned over me so that her face was inches from mine. "Shhh, Theo, shhh." She brushed my bangs back from my forehead.

I tried to speak, to tell them how happy I was to see them, but I couldn't form the words.

"Seer." Tex stood behind Solle. "I am here as the official representative of the Novus Pack. Do you wish to see us?"

"Yes," I whispered, "God, yes."

"Very good." Tex tried to give me a reassuring smile, but his eyes were hard. "We would like for our doctor to examine her and any records pertaining to the injuries." He directed his request which sounded like a command to the woman in the suit, but his gaze never left my face. He was memorizing every bruise and cut.

The suit held out two manila envelopes as if she couldn't wait to rid herself of them.

Brian relieved her of her burden and immediately went to the small sofa at the far side of the room and opened them. Kira and Brenna from Solle's office joined him on the sofa.

Solle whispered, "You're going to be fine."

Tex turned to the woman in the suit. "You are excused."

The executive blinked. "But I can answer your questions."

Solle turned her attention to the woman. "Have you treated this patient?"

The woman gave one shake of her neatly cut auburn hair.

"Then you will be of no help." Solle dismissed her with a wave.

Asher escorted her from the room and closed the door with a loud click as soon as she crossed the threshold.

"Nurse," Tex addressed Olivia, "we will need you for a while, in case there are any questions."

Solle spoke softly, but I knew that Olivia heard her, "We will get you out of here and on the road." She nodded in my nurse's direction. "Very soon."

"Do you drive?" Asher asked from his place at the door.

Olivia opened her mouth, but no sound emerged. She blinked twice before answering, "Yes, but I don't have a car."

Tex gave her a kinder look. "That's even better." He pulled a roll of bills from his front pocket, "From Novus...to get you started. When you hit the road... don't look back. This should give you a good start, and this," he handed her a business card, "is the account information. I believe that Conal, our Second, discussed the details earlier?"

Warily, Olivia looked at Tex's hand. "Is this a trick?"

"No," I told her. "You helped me and my...," I stumbled over what to call them, "the Novus Pack is grateful."

She took the card and roll of bills so fast I couldn't track it.

Tex continued, "Asher will arrange transportation for you."

Asher smiled as if he would enjoy the task. "Do you prefer fast or unnoticeable?"

"Novus thanks you, and we are in your debt," Tex said solemnly. "Do you know what that means?"

Olivia nodded quickly. "Yes, sir."

"Olivia," I said, my voice sounding hoarse, "I owe you so much."

She grasped my right hand gently. "You are a gift from The Lady. It was my privilege to serve you."

My voice shook as I said, "I will ask that she watch over you."

"Thank you, Seer." She nodded at Tex and followed Asher from the room.

As soon as the door clicked shut, Solle started talking. "We brought two planes. Onyx was on the first to arrive and began the meeting with the Burkes. Conal and the Laird went there as soon as we touched down. Glass is in the hallway. I'm not sure that she is ready to come in." She gave Tex an uncertain look. "This has upset her greatly."

I wasn't sure if Solle meant the attack, or Novus coming to Texas, or any decision that Black had made regarding my future. My head was spinning. It was all too much to think about.

"On a scale from one to ten, with ten being the worst imaginable, how is your pain?" Solle went into healer mode.

"I told Olivia not to give me very much for the pain. I wanted to have a clear head."

"So, she is in great pain," Tex answered for me.

Solle didn't glance at her medical staff. She was looking at the drip hanging above me. "Report, Brian."

I didn't understand all that was summarized. I was too busy watching Solle's expression. I knew she was very professional while performing her duties. Today, I saw anger, frustration, misery, and hate flash over her features.

When Brian finished answering her questions, she stood still and stared off into space for a couple of moments before letting out a long breath. She straightened her shoulders and did a slow blink as if she was preparing and organizing her thoughts. "Okay, babe," she glanced down at me, "I'm going to do my own exam. I'm going to have to move you from time to time. It's going to hurt. Do you want me to increase the drip and knock you out?"

Although others were in the room, I spoke only to Solle. "I have to be coherent, when he…if he… I need to be able to think."

Tex had moved to the area at the foot of the hospital bed. "I would guess it will be at least an hour."

I gave Solle a single nod. I didn't want to moan or cry out in front of them.

She punched numbers on the keypad. "Now, Tex, could you and your guards maybe give us some space and turn your backs?"

"The guards can wait outside, but I will be here," he said. "I want to remember the damage because I will give the same."

I had to remind myself that the anger I felt inside the room was directed at Charles, not at me.

Brian gave me a kind smile. "Theo, we are going to take good care of you. We are your friends." Something about his assurance worried me.

My throat was so dry. "Can I ask two things before we start?"

"Of course," Solle rushed to answer.

"Could I have something to drink and can you tell

140

me before you touch me? My, well my flight instinct is really high. I don't want to upset your wolves."

Kira spoke softly, "I'm going to raise your top half just a little, so prepare for the movement."

It fucking hurt.

But the cold water was worth it.

"If you want, I can have Brian stand back," Solle said.

I paused before answering.

"I'll take the notes," he said quickly.

I didn't want a male to touch me, even if I knew he meant no harm.

"Those feelings are normal," Solle murmured.

She must have read my mind.

The hallway door opened, and Glass entered.

Tex tried to intercept her. "They are going to do the examination."

The Warrior stepped around Tex. "Then I should be here."

She didn't maneuver with her usual quick and confident gait. Today, she moved more slowly, perhaps even tentatively. She stopped at the far side of my bed. "Theodora Morrissey."

"Hey, Glass." Lines of stress were etched around her firm mouth.

"I am glad that you live," she said in her formal way.

I wanted to tell her that I'd remembered what she and Lore had taught me. I'd done some damage to Charles.

She spoke softly, "I want to hold your hand. It will help."

I moved my hand towards her, and she gripped it gently.

The exam went on and on. I zoned out when I could no longer handle their gentleness and their touching. Their voices became a low rumble in the background until Solle told me she needed to do the gyno exam.

I started to sob. I knew she needed to do it, but I didn't want to think about that part of my body. What he had done to me.

Solle's eyes were shiny with tears, also. "Honey, I have to do this. He...you... There is tearing."

I nodded, although the tears continued to fall down my cheeks.

"Glass, why don't you tell her about Lore's wolf?" Solle suggested.

"Theodora, will you listen to my story?" Glass asked in a soft voice.

I tried to stop crying as I nodded, anything to take my mind off what was happening.

Glass began to speak.

I knew that Kira and one of the female guards were holding my legs up and open. I tried not to think about it. I closed my working eye and focused on Glass's voice.

"She is a medium-size she-wolf, and he calls her Luna."

"Wait, you mean a real wolf?" I asked slowly.

"Yes. He returned from an assignment, and she was with him."

"Is that normal?" I asked. This was helping. Whatever Solle was doing, it stung, but I focused on Glass.

"Some have claimed a wolf as their familiar, but Lore maintains that Luna is his Guard." She looked perplexed.

For a moment, I had to grit my teeth against the

pain. God, it felt like I was being pinched in my most private place.

"Easy honey. I'm so sorry. I'm trying not to hurt you," Solle's said, her voice rough.

I took in a long breath and let it out slowly, then did it one more time. When I could concentrate again, I asked, "Can he communicate with the wolf? I mean do they talk to one another in wolf tongue?" I asked, suddenly curious.

"Lycans are superior to our wolf cousins," Glass explained.

"So, it's like how a human and a dog communicate —through tone and maybe certain words?"

Glass nodded.

"When did you decide you wanted a dog?" Solle asked me with her head buried between my thighs.

"A dog?" I didn't know what she was talking about.

She straightened and walked around to my side. "During our call, you wanted me to tell Black about the dog thing."

I had to know. "Did you tell him?"

"Of course." She pulled off her gloves as she talked. My legs were lowered again to the bed. "He went from a five to an eleven on the anger chart. You know that most canines don't get along with us? It will take a really special dog to be around us."

"You want a dog?" Glass asked sounding confused.

"It was code," I admitted.

"Code?" Solle gave me a puzzled look.

"I never planned on using it." I had known there could be horrendous repercussions if ever I did.

Glass's laugh was sharp. "The Laird is smart."

That seemed to take care of that subject.

"We need to roll you over," Solle said, once again using her "doctor" voice. "It's going to hurt."

"Give me a moment to prepare."

Glass must have sensed my emotions. "You are strong, Seer. I have watched you develop, and I know you can get through this. Your friends are here. We will protect you. You may lean upon us."

I swallowed hard and told Solle, "Just do it fast."

When I felt her fingers near my crack, I freaked out. I started screaming. I couldn't stop myself.

Tex somehow squeezed behind my bed and leaned over the frame, so that he could whisper in my ear. "I won't touch you, never without your permission. But I can't take your screams, Theo."

"Help me," I cried.

He placed his huge hand on the top of my head and began to comb through my hair. Then he began to sing. Everybody had heard him rap, but I don't think many knew the man could sing. I didn't recognize the song, at first, but the words seemed familiar.

When I finally caught on, I whispered, "You don't look like a Disney fan." He was singing "Beautiful" made famous by Christina Aguilera, a former child star on the mouse channel.

"Lean on us, Seer," Glass added.

I tried to see if my gift would manifest, but I couldn't find it.

"Almost done," Solle promised, but her voice seemed very far away.

Solle and her team were in the corner looking at their

tablets and the x-rays that the administrator had provided.

Asher had returned and stood quietly by the door. Glass and Tex flanked my sides, sitting on hard wooden chairs. I must have dozed for a bit. I knew that time had passed because the sun coming through the window was lower in the sky.

"Hey, you're back." Tex gave me a lopsided smile.

"Thirsty," I croaked.

"Doc, can she have more to drink?" he asked.

Suddenly, Solle was by my side. "How's the pain? I'd like to increase the meds."

"Not yet," I told her firmly. Everything hurt, but I wanted a clear head. I knew that I had to be in control.

THIRTEEN

NOVUS

RAIDER BLACK

I Can't Make You Love Me by Adele (Live)

TRAVIS BURKE HAD PUT UP A BLUSTER-FILLED FRONT, BUT clearly he'd been shaken. He knew he was going to lose everything. He'd allowed his loyalty to his blood to over-rule his common sense.

Odin Springer, his Second, told him that to his face.

Our motorcade made the thirty-minute drive to the hospital in less than twenty. I wanted to see Theo, and I wanted out of this godforsaken place.

Springer had ridden in the same car as Conal and I. He started to accompany us into the hospital's main entrance.

"You will wait in the lobby," Conal bit out the words and then crossed his arms over his broad chest.

Springer gave my Second a hard look then turned to

me. My silence gave the male his answer. "As you wish." He dropped his chin.

Glass had selected ten female guards to accompany us, knowing that males might make Theodora uneasy. Sarita pushed away from the wall where she'd been observing our exchange. "This way Laird, Second." She then turned her back on Springer.

We made our way to the third floor. I hated hospitals. The smell of illness and misery unsettled my wolf and me. I searched for Theo's scent and found it immediately. We turned left, and halfway down the hall, I saw four of our guards.

Conal grasped my forearm as I reached for the door. "Hold up."

I paused and slowly turned to my oldest friend. "Problem?"

"I need a second, and I know that if I need it, so do you." He closed his eyes briefly. "It's going to be bad."

"Did Solle tell you that?" He'd said nothing about the texts that had come in to his phone.

"No." He frowned. "That's how I know." He let out an audible sigh. "When she can't figure out a way to tell me something upsetting, she puts it off."

"I'm in control," I told him and myself.

"I can't get those screams out of my head." Conal's haunted eyes showed the pain he was feeling.

"We will be strong for her. She will need us and expect it," I said as I reached for the handle.

I took four steps into the room and paused in shock. Holy Fuck, she looked worse in person. The scent of her agony was strong. "Why is she in so much pain?" I asked without thinking.

All of Novus came to their feet.

Solle moved toward Conal. After he wrapped his arm around her and pulled her into his side, she answered, "The Seer refuses to allow me to increase the dosage of pain medication."

Still fighting. I approved. I focused on the human lying in the hospital bed. Her upper half was elevated so that she lay at a slight angle. Her face was swollen and purple. Her lips were split open. There was a deep gash along one side of her jaw that ran to her cheekbone. One of her beautiful, expressive eyes was swollen shut. I approached the bed as Tex and Glass stepped away. "Theodora Morrissey, I regret seeing you under these circumstances."

The hand that wasn't in a cast fluttered back and forth over the blanket covering her body. I could almost feel her evaluating my words, looking for a hidden meaning. "Laird," she responded in a hoarse voice.

Suddenly, I didn't know what to say. I wanted to tell her that she was coming home with me and that I was never going to let her go, again.

"Laird," she repeated my title again. "I...I..." She struggled to breathe. I moved closer to her. "Sanctuary," she whispered, and then looked at me with one pleading eye. "Please, Sire, grant me sanctuary...?"

"Granted," I answered immediately. She wanted to come home to us.

She started to cry.

Conal moved to her other side. "Sweetheart... Baby, don't, please don't." That was the closest to pleading I'd ever heard him utter.

"Conal," she sobbed.

"I'm going to increase your meds now." Solle's tone

told me that even if Theo disagreed, she would do it anyway.

"I tried to fight," she told me. "Honest, I tried." She looked afraid of me, and I hated it. Theo had never been afraid of me even when I'd first revealed what we were.

"I know that you did," I said gruffly.

"I didn't want him," she told me. "I swear I didn't."

"I know." I wanted to touch her, but Solle had cautioned us on the plane. "Seer, take my hand if you wonder."

She didn't respond right away. Finally, she moved her hand toward mine. Once our touch connected, I felt the impact immediately. It was like a missing part of my soul took its rightful place. I wasn't empty anymore.

"I'm sorry," she cried.

Fuck me she was in agony. My wolf howled in anguish. "Shhh." I didn't know what to say, how to assure her that nothing about this was her fault. There were too many people in the room who would witness my words of comfort. I fell back into being the leader. "Now, may I tell you what is going to happen?"

"Yes, Laird." She seemed to calm a bit. I didn't know if it was our connection or the meds.

"If you are able to withstand it, I would like the Burke brand removed from your arm. They no longer have any right to you," I told her gently.

She twisted the hand I held in mine to show the mark. "Do it."

"I don't want to add to your pain," I cautioned her.

"I want it off," she rasped. "And replace it with yours."

I glanced at Conal. I really didn't want to go into this now.

She studied me carefully and then dropped my hand. "Oh...I understand."

Oh, hell no. "Theo, I'm sure that you don't." I used a gentle tone. "I, we, every member of Novus wants you back with our Pack. That you asked for our brand, it means the world to me." I paused to catch my breath. "Because the Burkes violated the agreement with Novus, you don't automatically revert back to us."

Her eye closed, and a single tear fell.

"When we negotiated the contract, I thought...well, I believed that no one would dare harm you," I admitted. "We put in the caveat that if there was a breach, then the Council would intervene on your behalf. You would be under their protection until...until other arrangements were made."

"Theo," Conal said, taking over, "he fought for you. The Council was going to send a party to Texas to retrieve you. Black convinced them that since you had ties to Novus that, in your condition, you should come to Nebraska until you have healed."

Her breathing quickened. "I don't want to go to them." She gripped my hand again. "Please don't make me," she begged.

I leaned closer to her. "Trust me."

She stilled immediately and looked into my eyes.

"Theo, I know it is too much to ask, especially now, but I need you to give me your trust."

She didn't hesitate. "Always. You'll always have it."

A plan had been forming in my head since Solle had told me about the dog comment. Now, I knew what I needed to do. "Thank you, Theodora." I tried to smile, to reassure her. "Glass, get your tools,"

I kept talking, hoping to keep her from thinking about the pain that was coming. "I want to send a team to your quarters. We can pack everything as we did before with your things from California and later you can go through it."

"No," she said, slurring the word a little. "I want my books, my papers, my tech, and your T-shirts. Leave everything else."

I glanced at Conal, and he raised an eyebrow.

"Are you sure? Later, you might think of something you left behind."

"The photos, but leave everything else. I don't want them."

Solle motioned to Conal. I let the couple decide what would be best.

Glass cleared her throat. "I will be ready in three minutes, Laird."

"Asher," I said, looking toward the guard lounging against the door. "Go to the lobby and ask the Burke Second to come up. His name is Odin Springer."

"Yes, Laird." He took off.

"He," Theo's heart rate increased, and she looked around the door wildly. "I don't…"

I cut her off. "Theo, the Second has to be here while Glass removes their brand. But he will only stand in the doorway. I won't let him anywhere near you."

Her good eye closed. "I know that you won't." She sounded sleepy. "I'm so tired."

"Solle," I interrupted her whispered conversation with her mate, "can she fly?"

"Yes, but as soon as we land, it's straight to our hospital." She gave me a serious look.

I nodded. I knew she had more to say, but it would wait until we were airborne. "Theo, you with me?" I thought she might have fallen asleep.

"Always," she murmured.

My wolf shouted, *Mine.* I spoke softly, "After we get this step done, we will load you up and get you on the plane."

She didn't open her eye, but she mumbled, "Going home."

"Right, baby, going home."

She slept as the Burke brand was removed, and I think we all were grateful. Nobody wanted to see her endure any more pain as Glass heated what looked like a metal cookie cutter and applied it over the Burke brand. Solle had adjusted the medications, and Theo was out while they transferred her onto a gurney and into an ambulance. Conal and Tex carried the gurney up the steps onto the plane. Once she was set up in the bedroom, we were in the air.

I'd left Asher behind to oversee the packing up of her quarters with their Second. So, I huddled with my board members at the front of the plane.

Conal was typing on his phone. "Lore has arrived and checked in."

"Solle's going to need to explain this report in regular language," I told Conal.

"I think she'll know more after she gets all the results to the tests she wants to run at home. She mentioned they might have to reset her fingers." Conal frowned.

"She is to call in the most knowledgeable doctors, get the best treatments available," I ordered. "I want her to have whatever she needs."

"What about your intended, Ms. Dolan?" Onyx inquired

"That was why I called you together. I want to schedule a call to her father for some time tomorrow. I need you to review the contract and send me a summary of what I have to pay to get out of the deal."

Onyx looked outraged. "You want to break the contract?"

"It isn't working," I said flatly.

"Do you believe that you gave it enough time?" he asked slowly. I must have given him a sharp look because he began to tap dance immediately. "I mean, with all of the changes, were you able to fully focus?" Onyx corrected himself.

"If the chemistry isn't there, then it would be wrong to tie yourself to her for eternity," Tex stated.

"But there's more," Conal said slowly while giving me a narrowed-eyed stare.

"I want Theo," I announced.

"What?" All except for Conal exclaimed at once.

Onyx spoke first. "I know you cared for her once, but she is no longer a part of Novus."

"She will be my mate." I practically growled the words.

Glass recovered first. "You mean, you want her to be. Once she heals, you'll court her, and then ask The Lady."

"No." I shifted in my seat and crossed my leg over my knee. "My wolf recognized her right away. However, because of my agreement with the Dolans, I ignored my true mate."

"Shit," Onyx hissed.

"How is that possible?" Glass asked.

"I don't know," I told them honestly.

"I have never heard of such a thing," Onyx told us all.

"There has never been a Seer like Theodora," Conal proclaimed.

"I will court her. When she is ready, we will go through the Mating Ceremony," I informed them.

"So, how do we handle the Council?" Tex leaned in as he waited for my plan.

"If we held the ceremony soon, while she is healing, that would solve the Council issue," Onyx advised.

"She will not be forced into anything." Glass's eyes flashed in anger. "Theodora should have a say in this decision."

"Calm down," Conal ordered. "Nobody is going to rush anybody or force Theo into something she doesn't want."

"She might hate all Lycans after she stops being drugged and realizes all that was done to her," Glass warned.

"Then we must prove to her that we are good, that she is treasured and will always be protected," I said, looking around at each of them in turn.

"You are making enemies at every turn because of that woman," Onyx accused.

Tex growled. "The Laird is going to find happiness. He tried to sacrifice his true love for Novus. I don't care if we go to war with every Pack in the land. I will stand by you."

"There will be no wars," Conal said in a calm voice. "Siobhan is unhappy with Novus. She tells anyone who will listen. We pay Dolan what he asks, and then we keep the Mating Ceremony on the down low. We won't invite every leader and the Council. The celebration will be kept small. By then, everyone will know Theo's story. They will understand." He leaned back in his seat. "We use this debacle to springboard through the next one."

"Good thinking," Glass told him.

"I will take that under consideration."

"This is going to cause problems," Onyx warned.

I didn't give a shit. "I want Lore at the airstrip when we land," I said. "Theo will want to see him. I hope that will tie him to her so that he doesn't rid the earth of the Burkes."

"Only because you want to do that, yourself." Conal flashed a grin.

Glass spoke so that I didn't have to answer. "Don't we all want to rid our world of that filth?"

"First, Charles," I said. "Then the Pack."

FOURTEEN

NOVUS

THEODORA MORRISSEY

Have a Little Faith in Me by Jake Worthington

I WAS FLOATING. WELL IN TRUTH, WE WERE IN THE AIR, and I was buzzing on pain medication. My body's pain was masked, but my brain was aware as were my instincts that I was seriously injured. At the moment, I was safe, but my body was in bad shape. My internal warning system was on high alert. Technically, I was under the protection of Novus, but that wasn't the same as being a part of the Pack. A small whimper escaped as I held back a sob. What was going to happen to me?

Kira stood and hovered over me. "How bad is the pain?"

I tried to smile, which only made my lips crack and burn. "My brain won't shut off."

"I can call somebody in if you wish to talk." She looked toward the door.

"No, but thank you." I felt like I'd said those two words a thousand times since Novus had arrived. I wished I could fall into a deep sleep, but the feeling that I needed to stay aware kept me alert.

I wanted to roll onto my side. I usually slept on my side, but it was too uncomfortable to change positions. Worse, after a few minutes, I'd want to switch sides again, which would cause more pain. Maybe I should ask Solle to knock me out until next week, so I could sleep through this part of the healing process.

As if she heard her name in my thoughts, the doctor appeared in the doorway to the small bedroom at the back of the jet. "Do you want me to go over the tests I want to run when we get home?"

I was tired of thinking about my injuries. "I'd rather talk about anything else."

She tried to smile, but it didn't mask the fact she looked exhausted. "Lucky for you that I have a great bedside manner." She sat on the side of the bed. "And no problem chatting."

I'd guessed that it was a regular-size mattress. It took up most of the space in the room. "Thank you for taking my call."

Her eyes turned serious. "Of course, I would take your call."

"I couldn't tell you everything that was going on there. I figured... Well, I was pretty sure they were listening, I never felt... Well, it wasn't like Novus."

"You never felt safe?" she asked quietly.

"They didn't have a plan. It was like they didn't know what to do with me." I let out a deep sigh, which hurt.

"So, they kept you cooped up in that apartment until they needed you?"

"Yes."

Solle looked up at the ceiling for a moment. "Christ, that must have been terrible." She looked at me. "You didn't even have a yard."

"I had to ask to go outside." I wanted to sit outside when I got back to Nebraska. "Can I float in your pool or sit at the picnic table for hours?"

"Of course, honey. I am so sorry, so damn sorry for all of this." Her voice cracked.

"Uhm, where's Issa? Did she not want to come?" I was disappointed that neither she nor Lore were with the Novus group. "I understand why Lore didn't. He's not allowed on Burke land."

"They both have been away on jobs. Lore has been called home. Conal spoke with him earlier. I think Issa needed to put space between herself and Asher, so she hasn't been around. I imagine that when she hears about what happened to you...she will return." Solle shook her head. "Those two will probably want to decimate all of South Texas."

"I want to see them...I missed them, and I wish things could go back to normal."

"It will be better once we land." Her eyes darkened. "I bet you can't wait to get his scent off of you."

"What?" I cried, my voice shrill and even though my jaw was wired shut, I was loud. "Do I smell like him? Now? Can you smell him on me?" I couldn't stand the thought. I started to shriek uncontrollably.

Solle stood and leaned over me, shouting in my face, "It's okay, it's okay."

I couldn't stop screaming. God, I wanted to tear off my skin. I started to scratch at my chest and arms.

The tiny space filled with bodies. Hands were holding me down while I couldn't stop screeching in pain and humiliation. How could I still be carrying his scent? *He was still with me.*

"What is happening?" Black filled the doorway, his voice thundered.

I couldn't stop repeating, "No."

"I mentioned that we could still smell him....on her." Solle dropped her head.

"Out." His voice was quiet, yet they all obeyed, even Solle.

He ran a hand through his hair. He seemed tentative, not stepping further into the room. "If you don't want to be alone with me, I understand. I'll talk to you from here."

I hated this, all of this. "I didn't want...I don't want any part of him...please..." I wanted him to understand that I hadn't wanted to leave him or to live that life with the Burkes.

He nodded his head slowly. "I know."

It took me a few minutes to even out my breathing. Black stayed in the doorway, never did he give me a look like I was taking too long. "You can come in."

"If you get nervous or feel uncomfortable, I'll leave."

Would he leave? He was the Laird. He didn't have to do anything. I felt my heart beat faster as he turned to close the door.

He then paused and studied me again. When I didn't say anything, he took one step into the room. "I don't know where to start." He looked down at the floor.

"Doesn't happen very often," he muttered then flashed a sheepish, closed-lipped grin.

The few times that I'd witnessed the unsure side of Black, it had totally disarmed me. I'd wanted to comfort him and usually rushed to do so. "You can come closer." God, I sounded unsure to my own ears. "Just...move slowly. Okay?"

"Only if you are sure, Theodora."

"Slowly." I tried to nod while I prepared myself.

"When I look at you, do you know what I see?"

"No." I hadn't bothered to ask for a mirror. I could tell from the horrified expressions on the faces of the medical staff and my rescuers that I was a mess.

He cleared his throat. "I see that once again you have gone toe-to-toe with a Lycan and survived."

"He should have killed me." I'd thought he would.

"And yet, he did not. You will live to take your revenge." His eyes were furious, and the muscle at the corner of his jaw pulsed.

"I don't think I'm that strong," I admitted quietly. I used to feel appreciated, treasured, and loved, but now... I was used up and dirty.

"You are very resilient."

I wasn't. I was weak and polluted. I feared that The Lady had forgotten me. I had nothing left to give to Novus.

He took a step closer and paused. "I swear to you, and to The Lady that I never imagined anything like this would happen."

"I know," I said softly. He believed that by carrying the Mark, I would be safe.

"Admitting I was wrong doesn't help things," he said,

his voice going low and rough as he took another step and waited.

I licked my sore bottom lip. "It helps that you came, that I didn't have to stay there."

He shifted his weight to one side then the other. "About that," he gave me another appraising look, "I don't want to burden you when you're like this. Hurting and…"

Things had changed between us. Before, he'd never shielded me. Did he think me incapable since I had been violated? "Just tell me whatever you must." I sounded angry and tired. "But can you sit down, because it's weird…" Plus I wasn't used to seeing him uneasy, and that made me apprehensive. Raider Black was always confident and in control.

He closed the space slowly, giving me the opportunity to stop him.

I looked pointedly at the corner of the bed where I wanted him to sit.

He did so, facing me. He seemed very far away. It made me ache for the days when we would lie in each other's arms and talk in the dark.

"I've missed you," he said softly.

This, I didn't expect. I had to lift my chin to read his expression. "And me, you…very much." My heart broke all over again. Jesus, now I would have to see him with his mate. I felt tears fall down my cheek as I silently started to cry. I tried to wipe the tears away quickly. They could change nothing.

"I've made some decisions."

I had to swallow once before asking, "Concerning me?" Oh God, he was sending me to Scotland. He'd said that he would wait until I was well, but had something changed so…so soon?

"Yes." His hand slid out like he wanted to touch me, but he stopped.

He was going to tell me that we couldn't talk or be seen together. I knew it was only right. "I'm not sure I want to hear it right now." I could barely get the words out.

He lowered his chin but maintained eye contact. "I understand."

I closed my eye. I was so tired, and yet, I wanted to remember this private moment with him. Christ, I still loved him so much, and this might be my last encounter with him.

"I wronged you and us." His hand was still extended resting on the covers as if he wanted me to make a move to reach for it.

"I…I don't understand." I tried to make my brain work faster to prepare for whatever he was going to say.

"I love you." He leaned closer to me.

"What?" He shouldn't, *couldn't* be saying this. It was too dangerous when he had to mate with the Dolan princess.

"Still…always."

"I don't understand." I was trying to figure out what he was saying and what it meant for my current situation. I felt the weight of his words. My casted hand reached out to grasp his, although I could feel nothing through the wrapping. "Black?" I whispered unsure of what all of this meant.

His gaze burned into me. "I lied to you. I let you go and now….*this*."

I squeezed my eye shut and tried to pull my hand

from his. He didn't want me anymore…because of what Charles Burke had done to me. "I understand."

His voice turned low and fierce. "You don't understand a damn thing, Theodora."

"I know that he used me and did things to me…." I choked on the truth.

"Do you think that matters to me?"

I didn't answer because what Charles had done must matter. How could it not?

"Everything that has happened to you is my fault. Do you hear me? My fault." His eyes had gone so dark that they were almost black.

"But…" I couldn't breathe. It was all too much. Too much pain. Too much anguish.

"I swear to your God, The Lady, and to you, Theo, that I will make it up to you." He was now breathing heavily. "I will make this right."

"I'm not sure you can." None of this was making sense; he wasn't making any sense.

"I need time. Please give me just a little bit of time," he pleaded. Raider Black, the Laird, was beseeching for…what?

"It's not like it was before…I'm not…" I shook my head negatively a few times. "My gift is gone."

"We'll have to ask The Lady about that on our next visit. She's helped us in the past."

I had to tell him. "I think she has forgotten me." I watched his reaction closely.

His eyebrows drew together in thought. "Why do you say this?"

"They, I… Well, I couldn't go outside whenever I wanted, and she didn't call. Not one time." I waited to see if he would respond. "When I was allowed out, I tried to talk to her, but it was different. I felt different."

"What about your other skills?"

"I was asked a few times to use them." I swallowed hard. "An innocent man was killed because I couldn't make them believe. I didn't keep him safe, and Charles killed him."

"You would not harm an innocent. I know your heart." He took my hand again. "The Burkes have much to answer for."

"I'm not sure about anything." I meant my gift, my abilities, my life.

He frowned. "You are in shock, traumatized. I understand why you have doubts."

He didn't. "No!" The word came out sharply. "I chose to leave because…" I had to stop and clear my throat, "because I didn't… No, I knew that I *couldn't* stand to see you mated to another. It would've killed me."

"And it almost did."

"Raider," I choked on his name as I tried to find the words to make him understand that all of this had changed me.

He scooted forward so that he was now higher on the bed. He laid his hand on my upper arm, gently. "I am responsible for so much of this. Novus has always come first, and this time my single-mindedness almost cost us your life."

It felt like I was choking from the intensity of the moment. I could barely whisper the words, "So, what does all of this mean?"

Somehow, he understood me. "It all depends on you, Theodora Morrissey." His hand tightened a little on my arm. "You deserve more from me. This time, I want to do this right." His eyes showed uncertainty. "And if you will allow me what I asked…?"

What was he saying? Promising? I swallowed. "I will give you time."

I was so tired and so much had happened, I needed time as well. I also needed him, his strength and assurance that he would keep me safe. "Can you, would you stay here with me?" I was unsure about so much, and my world had just tilted, again.

"Of course."

"I'm scared," I admitted.

"Of me?" His gray gaze swept over my face and looked deeply into mine as if he was trying to read my mind.

"No, of me." I closed my eye. I didn't want to talk about this, but he needed to know before he made any more decisions and exposed his Pack to the risks.

He moved in closer.

"What happened?" Again, I felt breathless. He laced his fingers with mine. "What he did to me…"

"Shhh, you don't have to talk about it."

"I think he broke me."

"No, Theodora, don't say that," his words came out softly, but I could hear the fierceness of his belief. "Don't think that for a moment."

I nodded my head several times, or at least I think that I did. I was so tired that I couldn't keep my eyes open any longer.

For the first time since the attack, I could relax enough to rest. I was almost asleep when I asked, "With Siobhan…did you try?"

"Yes."

I had asked him to try to make it work, so I was unsure how I felt about his answer.

"She is unlikeable," he said grumpily.

"Oh." I was glad to have the information. I was fading, but I wanted him to know. "I never stopped loving you. I still do."

FIFTEEN

RAIDER BLACK

Home Sweet Home by Motely Crue

THEO WAS WITH ME, AGAIN. I WATCHED HER SLEEP, BUT more importantly, I used my senses to feel her sleep. She wasn't dreaming, and her pain level was manageable.

A light knock sounded on the door. In a low voice, I answered, "Enter."

The door swung open. "Landing in ten." Conal studied us on the bed.

Theo woke immediately with a start and made a strangled sound.

"You're safe," I assured her in a gentle voice.

"What's happening?" She had to turn her head to see the room, searching for a threat.

"We will be landing soon." I started to stand.

She gripped my hand, her hold was surprisingly strong, "It's going to be all right, isn't it?"

"Yes," I told her. "You are home, and you are protected. I give you my word that you will be safe on Novus land."

"Never again," Conal told her.

"Focus on healing," I said. "Allow us, your closest friends and supporters, to take care of things until you are stronger."

She sighed. "Thank you, Laird."

Solle joined her mate. "We need to make sure that you are secure for the landing."

"Goody," Theo groaned.

I stayed in the back with Theo. I could feel her pain skyrocket as we descended to the tarmac. When the pilot applied the brakes, I told her, "We're on Novus ground."

"Home," she agreed in a rough whisper.

I knew she was trying not to make any noise, but we all could feel her discomfort. Even though she was hurting, she tried to appear brave. She was magnificent.

The plane was taxiing to the building where the ambulance waited when I heard Conal's voice rumble, "Fuck me."

I was on my feet immediately. "What?" As I exited the room, I saw everybody on the left side of the plane looking out the windows.

I shouldered my way between the two nurses to see people holding burning torches. Hundreds of people gathered along the tarmac.

"It's for her," Brian said quietly.

At that moment, I had never been prouder to be the leader of Novus.

Conal allowed Glass and Tex to carry the gurney down the steps. When the crowd saw her, they cheered.

I walked beside the gurney as they wheeled her to the waiting ambulance.

Lore approached. His expression was enraged. His eyes were flashing.

"Lore," I cautioned, giving him a warning glare. I didn't want her upset by his reaction.

He buried his anger and moved to Theo's other side. "My Queen returns." He lifted her casted hand to his lips.

Without any hesitation or fear, she told him, "I missed you, my friend."

The smile he gave her was genuine. I thought I saw him betray a hint of relief. My spy had missed his friend.

"I want to meet your wolf," she said, turning her face so that she could clearly see him with her good eye.

"You will," he promised.

"Walk with us?" she invited.

"Of course." He stayed beside her, not letting go of her hand.

The crowd was shouting their welcome and her name. We were nearing the ambulance when Theo let out a loud moan, "Ohhh... Oh, God."

"Babe? What is it?" Something was wrong.

"Black, I...I." Her body went limp.

"Solle," I yelled.

She appeared immediately and started checking Theo by touching her throat. Her breath caught. "No pulse."

"What?" Her heart wasn't beating?

Solle jumped onto the gurney and began chest compressions.

I watched in horror, feeling helpless. We were losing her.

Someone in the crowd shouted. "Help your child, Goddess."

Others joined in the entreaty.

We scrambled to the ambulance. Solle worked on Theo as the other members of the medical team shouted orders to one another as they loaded the gurney into the ambulance.

Stunned, I watched as Conal slammed the rear doors closed, and it took off. How could this be happening? She was with me…safe…on Novus land.

My Second yelled, "Laird with me! Lore, you too!"

I'd paced for three hours straight. Theo was alive. Her heart was beating on its own. Solle had been out to report four times. The pressure from the landing had caused a miniscule tear in the iliac artery to rupture.

Lore stood quietly in the corner of the waiting room. "I will stay until we know she will survive," he'd stated earlier to no one in particular.

"You will stay until the Laird excuses you," Conal told him, frowning.

"I want to find him," Lore snarled. "It is my duty."

"We will," I told them all. "But Theo is our first priority."

"I *need*—" Lore started.

"She needs you," I told him in a thundering voice. "She needs your strength to bolster her confidence. She needs to be surrounded by those she trusts. Lore, she trusts you and will depend on you to help her rebuild her life."

I could tell he wanted to argue. His eyes flashed as a low growl erupted from his chest.

"She used the moves you taught her against Charles. She tore his eye from its socket," I said.

He nodded once. "I'm glad that she did some damage."

"She might not want to be around men or strangers, or maybe some of us," Glass said loudly, speaking for the first time in hours. "You have to understand, she doesn't feel safe. Her common sense might tell her there is no danger, but her body and her instincts will disagree. It is confusing and exhausting. She will question herself. If she wants you around, then please, Lorenzo, stay."

I tried not to show my surprise at her outburst. For my Warrior, that was an incredibly emotional entreaty. "What say you?" I looked at my spy.

Lore vibrated with anger, but then he drew a deep breath. "I will stay." He bowed his head.

Solle hurried through the double doors. She was still in scrubs and looked near to collapse. Instantly, Conal moved to his mate and gripped her upper arm.

Solle gave him a tired smile, then turned to face the rest of us. "She's stable."

We moved closer, creating a semi-circle around her.

"The iliac artery is repaired. We also repaired two other weakened points." She took the bottle of water Conal handed her. "Her kidneys are badly bruised, as is her liver. We are going to monitor those closely. Madison took a look at the x-rays of her hand and recommended that we contact a surgeon in Alabama. He is a renowned hand specialist." She frowned. "He'll have to reset at least three of her fingers."

"That won't be for a few days, will it?" Tex asked.

"I'd say three at the most," the doctor told us. "She will need to regain some more strength."

"What about her healing gift?" I asked.

"I've seen no signs that her healing is accelerated." Solle's eyebrows drew together. "The next twenty-four hours will tell us more."

"When can I see her?" I asked.

She glanced at the watch on her wrist. "An hour? But she's going to be out for the rest of the day and most of the night."

"I'm not leaving her."

"Laird, what about the calls you need to make?" Onyx asked, his words clipped by impatience.

"Her heart stopped beating," I roared at the wolf. I wanted to punch him. No, I wanted to tear his head from his body. "Three fucking times, it stopped."

"The call can be made tomorrow," Conal said calmly. "The outcome will be the same."

"Goodbye to bad trash," Solle said quietly, but she couldn't hide a victorious smirk.

"I don't like this," Onyx spat the words. "Even though you two did not work out, Siobhan should still be treated with respect."

"Like she treated us?" Solle pulled away from her mate and confronted the mercurial wolf. "Tell me one nice thing she said about Novus."

"She hates it here," Tex chimed in. "She's used to better *everything*."

"Novus isn't for everyone," Conal said, playing diplomat. "We will never be the fancy Pack, eating off fine china and having formal events. She did not prepare for our way of life."

"She thought she could change you." Solle flashed me a look that all but screamed "stupid."

I didn't bother reprimanding her. She was right. I

174

was tired of dealing with Siobhan. "I'll speak to Dolan tomorrow. Conal, make the arrangements for the call."

"Yes, Laird." Conal continued, giving Onyx an angry look.

"You know your assignments. Get those taken care of, and then get some rest," I said, dismissing them.

Solle and Conal stayed. Conal wouldn't leave my side until I sent him away with a stern order.

Solle yawned then put her hands on her hips and arched her back, stretching the muscles. "I'm exhausted."

"I thank you Solle for all that you've done, and for your service to Novus."

She waved off my gratitude. "Let's enjoy the moment. She's alive, and she's with us."

"I hear a 'but.'" I felt uneasy waiting to hear what she had to say.

"She's been through a terrible trauma. She's going to need a lot of help, counseling. I don't think anybody here can do the job."

"Then find a good candidate and pay them triple what they ask to get them here, immediately."

She frowned at me. "It's not that simple. She needs to find the right fit with a therapist."

"Whatever she needs, get it."

"She's going to be different," she said calmly. "You all have to accept that. To be brutalized like that, when she's always been aware that, in her words, she's 'the weakest in the room,' it's going to fuck with her head."

Conal cleared his throat. "I'll talk to those closest to her and those guarding her."

"I know that she let you sit beside her, and that's a huge thing, but… anything more…like sex," she gave me a look that was a combination of sadness and pity, "she might not want you to touch her in that way for a very long time."

"I understand that," I snapped.

"No, I don't think you do." She let out a long sigh. "You two have pushed past plenty of boundaries."

I narrowed my eyes at her. Did I hear judgment in her tone?

"Black, I know you two played certain games," she said gently. "She might never be able to go to those lengths again."

"I will give her whatever she needs." I stared at the healer willing for her to feel the strength of my vow.

"After you rest," Conal said to his mate, "send us articles to read. Order books but make sure they aren't five thousand pages long with terms we can't understand. We will need to prepare for many changes in the coming weeks."

"This isn't like a scratch," she said. "Her psyche might never heal, and the scars...? We won't be able to see them, but they will always be there. She isn't going to be fixed in a month, or even a year."

My wolf howled for Charles Burke's blood.

"Thank you. Solle. I will do my best to keep everything you've said in mind." I placed my hand on her shoulder and gave it a gentle squeeze. "Get some rest before your mate turns surlier," I smirked. Conal was the most even-tempered wolf I had ever met.

"Shall I make arrangements for the sofa-bed in her room to be made up for you?"

I nodded. "Thank you."

Seventy-eight minutes later, Solle told Conal and I that we could see Theo.

She was hooked up to so many machines. She was still out, according to the healer, but I knew she was aware that I was near.

I approached her bedside and took her good hand in mine. "You gave me quite a scare," I told her. "I would appreciate it if you would not do it again."

Conal snorted. "That's your opening?"

I shot him a questioning look. In fact, I had forgotten that they had followed me into the room.

Solle smiled. "Conal, you're going to have to give him lessons on how to sweet talk his mate."

I gave a low chuckle. "Most likely I will need them." I looked at Theo again. "I'm going to sleep here, in your room, so that you are protected as I vowed." I didn't want her to worry.

Conal neared the foot of the hospital bed. "Glad to see you will live another day to give us hell, Seer." His voice was lower this time. "Missed you, Theo. I hate the reason, but I'm damn glad that you're back."

Solle took her mate's hand. "Let's go." Then she looked at me. "Remember to rest."

"I will." Once I knew that Theo was comfortable.

"I have four nurses and two doctors assigned to her. If she so much as sighs, they will know," Solle assured me. "She's the only patient on this hall. The staff is relocating the others so that she is the only patient on the floor."

"Thank you. I don't mean to sound ungrateful, but you two can go." I wanted to be alone with her.

"Good to know that love hasn't softened you at all," Conal groused with a grin.

No, it had made me more ferocious. Now, I had someone to fight for and to protect.

SIXTEEN

NOVUS

THEODORA MORRISSEY

One by U2

I PRESSED THE BUTTON ON THE RECLINER'S SIDE, LIFTING my feet so that I was almost prone. I snuggled back into the pillows behind my back and head with only a dull ache as I picked up my e-reader from the table beside it. Black didn't understand my choice, but I was comfortable in my new living space. When I'd made my request, he'd given me a long measuring stare. I'd known he was having an internal argument. But after a long moment, he'd agreed without voicing an objection. Not only was I locked in, but they were locked out, or at least it felt that way. I had a window high up the wall that let in natural light and way-over-the-top luxurious linens for my small bed. Some saw it as only a cell in the basement of the Packhouse, but I saw it as a safe place. With Black nearby, I could sleep for several hours at a time. Often, he slept on the floor beside me in his wolf form.

My guards remained outside of the bars. Black was the only Lycan I invited inside. Many of my injuries were well on the way to being healed, and some of my scars had been erased from view, but I still felt broken and ugly. Even if the mirror didn't show the wounds that Charles had inflicted, I could feel them.

Lore was around almost all the time, and he agreed with everything. That worried me greatly; he was not one to be so affable. I wanted him nearby, but this version of my guard made me uneasy.

The Lady's gift of accelerated healing had not returned. Two days ago, I was released after four weeks in the hospital. My bones were knitting together slowly. As soon as the doctors said that I was able, I spent time outside. An hour in the afternoon, with at least three guards, and then another in the evening with Black. Something about sinking my toes into the grass and feeling the breeze against my face helped me feel more like my old self, not the woman I currently was.

I was anxious all the time and emotional. I would burst into tears for seemingly no reason, and I cowered at every unidentifiable sound. Plus, there were graphic nightmares. Sometimes, I couldn't wake up as I endured the violation of my body over and over. When I did wake, I cried hysterically in Black's arms, feeling angry, terrified, and hopeless.

When called upon by the Council to produce him, the Burke Pack couldn't locate Charles. The rational part of my brain knew I was safe from him. There was no way he could get onto Novus land, let alone into this house, but I wasn't sensible all the time. A part of me worried that he would find me and use my body again.

Glass had spent time with me, talking about those feelings. At first, it was strange because the Warrior had never been what I would label a "talker". However, she broke things down simply and succinctly. I knew she was making an effort to share that intensely private and painful part of her life. She couldn't tell me how many years ago a warring pack had her village. Her family had lived in a settlement of artists in a desolate part of northern Russia. All the adults had been killed and the children brutalized over the course of a long arctic winter. Her message was that I shouldn't be afraid of my feelings of anger, distaste, and helplessness. Hopefully, in time, I would be able to use those emotions to become stronger and fiercer as she had done.

Right now, those feelings were too overwhelming. Sometimes, I wanted it all to end. I yearned for a good night's rest and to silence the voices in my head. Not that I ever said those thoughts out loud. Hearing that would send everyone into a frenzy. However, I think Black knew.

A few times, I had caught him giving me a look that was full of pain and helplessness. The Laird didn't handle being unable to fix things well. With me now, he was always extremely gentle, but I'd overheard him being short with the medical staff and with Onyx. He was a demanding leader, but it seemed his nerves were fraying.

In addition, there was the Siobhan issue. She was still here, waiting for her father to send some representative to collect her and her staff. Black had been close-mouthed about his communications with the Dolan

Packleader. I sensed that the conversation had not gone well. He would be a powerful enemy, but as a father, did he really want his daughter miserable for eternity?

Since I'd moved into the basement cell, Black handled business from his office upstairs. This had to be a huge inconvenience for all, and yet, I'd heard no complaints. Basil stationed himself in the small parlor on the first floor, and no one got past him who wasn't invited and approved. Today, I knew that Black, Conal, and Tex were in the house.

I shifted my shoulders a little deeper into the pillows. Lore and his wolf, Luna, were taking a break. The entrance to the basement was guarded. Very few members of Novus were allowed downstairs and never without identifying themselves before treading heavily on the steps.

I tried to focus on the book I was reading. It was a comedy taking place in postwar London, not heavy, so I didn't need to concentrate very hard to follow the story-line's silliness.

Suddenly, I knew that I wasn't alone. I didn't raise my head or jump to my feet, not that I could move so nimbly. I tried to use my senses and my powers. I hadn't realized how much they'd diminished during my time in Texas until I had returned to Novus. Someone was near, and since they hadn't called out a greeting, I knew they were unwelcome.

I put down my e-reader and pressed the button so I could get out of the chair. Once on my feet, I called out, "Make yourself known, wolf." I sounded confident but it was an educated guess.

There was a rather deep, feminine laugh, and then a tall red-head appeared outside my bars. "The reports were not wrong. You are talented," she looked me up and down and then sneered, "for a human."

I knew who she was. "Hello, Ms. Dolan," I said evenly.

She sniffed the air, lifting her nose high and drawing in a few deep breaths. "What are you?"

"I'm Marked by The Lady," I said slowly, fighting to remain calm. "They say I am a gift to the Lycan race."

Her green eyes narrowed. "And yet, you are weak."

That felt like a punch to the gut. It was a direct bullseye to my shattered confidence. Immediately, I was terrified. I glanced at my casted arm and leg. "That is true." Grandma had always said, *When your back is against the wall, tell the truth.*

Her eyes flared wide for a second. My admission surprised her. "He's sending me back to my Pack." Her green eyes turned hard. "Like a purse, you don't like once you get it home."

I gave no response.

"It is because of you," she accused.

"Are you happy here?" I recklessly asked her.

She gave me an enraged look, even turning up her top lip to show her teeth, "Of course, not. It is boring as hell."

My fear made me ramble. "You can spin this as a terrible experience. Play yourself off as the victim of male politics. The grabby upstart tried to tie himself to the blueblood princess." I snuck a glance to my right toward the steps. Where the fuck was my guard? How had she gotten past him?

She laughed harshly, and it made me almost lose control of my bladder. "You don't know my father. He will blame this on me."

183

"Then he will be wrong," I told her because I did feel bad for her never having a choice.

"How dare you criticize my father!" She moved closer to the bars.

"Novus and Nebraska, they aren't for you. You need culture and excitement," I reminded her, trying to grasp the emotional triggers she had displayed and hoping not to touch upon them. Again, I looked to my right. Had she done something to my guard? Could she?

Siobhan flipped back her hair. "He won't see it that way. He will punish me for displeasing the Leader." She pulled a large brass key from the pocket of her jeans and unlocked the door to my cell.

"Wh-what are you doing?" I started to back away slowly because my ease of movement was greatly reduced. My heart pounded, and a roaring filled my ears. "You can't come in here," I said it in a ragged voice that held no authority.

"*You* are the reason I'm being sent away." She closed in on me. "It's my right to take some retribution for the Dolans." Her greenish eyes shone, and her lips pulled back, displaying her very white teeth.

Think, think damnit. "Please reconsider, princess. If you touch me, The Lady will punish you in a far worse way than your father ever will," I warned, hoping that it would halt this madness.

"I don't care."

My back was against the wall. I started to creep to my left, hoping that by some freak chance I could circle around her and escape. "Come on, Siobhan, think about this. Stop this now," I said slowly.

She whispered in a broken voice, "You don't know

my father. He will do things." She closed her eyes for a moment and shivered.

I took the opportunity and darted away. I cleared the barred barrier before she grabbed the back of my T-shirt, and then my hair. I roared, "No!" And I battled. I slammed my casted arm into her face. Blood poured from her nose as I kicked at her. "Not today." *Not again.*

Always, when faced with death, I fought. I hammered my casted forearm against the side of her skull, hoping to injure a sensitive ear. I focused my energy to try to pry her hand from around my throat. She didn't have a good grip, but I didn't have any endurance. I was going to tire very soon.

An arm snaked around my waist, and I was being pulled back, away from the redhead. "I got you," Conal's voice sounded next to my ear.

It was like everything gave out at the same time. I wilted against his body.

Black had the Dolan Princess against the far wall. His hand had changed and dug into her chest cavity. He held her so high her feet off the floor. "What the fuck are you doing?" he raged.

Siobhan made choking noises, but uttered no discernable words.

"Conal?" His voice was filled with rage.

"She's alive," the Second told his Leader.

The slight hold that Black had on his fury gave way. "You dared touch my female? One who carries The Lady's Mark?"

Siobhan stopped thrashing in his hold. A single moan escaped her throat.

"I witnessed you, Siobhan Dolan, attack the Seer. For that act, I decide the penalty, and it is death," Black told the woman, each word distinct. He then threw her to the ground. "Beg me, beg for your life," he taunted her.

"Sh-she wants to die," I croaked. It hurt to speak.

"Then I will give her what she desires." He leaned over her body and tore off her head. Then he then straightened, still holding her head by its red hair. "We do not touch a Marked. We, as Lycans, do not do that." He then dropped the head. "And you," Black stalked toward me, "I protect what is mine. I gave you that promise, and today, I proved it."

I moved without thinking. I rushed to him. When our bodies collided, I wrapped my arms around him.

He grasped my hair, which caused me to look up at him. "Mine, Theodora, forever."

SEVENTEEN

NOVUS

RAIDER BLACK

Heroes by David Bowie

As I started up the staircase to my private quarters with Theo in my arms, Lore rushed to my side with his wolf at his heels.

"What happened?" His eyes were wild.

My response was a low growl as I continued up the stairs. I would say this only once. We would wait until Conal joined us. "With me," I barked. I needed to keep up the appearance I was furious instead of secretly relieved that Siobhan was gone from our lives.

When we reached my door, I threw it open and continued to my living room. I placed Theo gently on the sofa cushion. Solle had reminded me often that Theo was not healed and needed to be handled with great care. "Need a blanket?" She was shivering so hard I could hear her teeth clicking together.

She nodded once.

I walked to the closet and pulled one out and returned to the living room. Before I covered her, I asked, "Did she hurt you? Do I need to call Solle?"

She shook her head one time.

I would have felt better if she had used words. I unfolded the blanket and tucked it around her. I heard Conal knock once, then enter. He'd tracked us by our scents.

"What the fuck happened down there?" He glared at Lore, and then at Theo.

I watched her grimace, nestle farther into the sofa, and pull the blanket tightly around her as if she wanted to disappear.

He was upsetting Theo. "Conal, stop shouting."

Luna, Lore's wolf, let out a low growl.

Conal turned his attention to Lore. "Where were you?"

"He gets a break, Conal," Theo spoke firmly, but her voice was shaking. "He can't stay down there all of the time because of me."

Lore waited a few beats before answering. "I had a pre-arranged break for Luna to go outside and for me to eat at one-thirty. The guard on the door knew the Seer was alone and that I would return in thirty minutes."

"It's my fault," Theo's voice was shaking. "By staying in a cell, I made it easy for her to corner me and attack." She pushed her hair back from her face.

"Your guards know that only a select few are allowed down those steps…" Conal growled.

"Where was Sullivan?" Lore asked quietly.

"Gutted," Conal said sharply. "She took care of him. It was the smell of his blood that caught our attention."

"Is he...d-d-dead?" Theo asked me.

I glanced at Conal.

His response was to look away before answering. "I'm waiting for the report."

Shit.

She swallowed loudly. "That doesn't sound good."

I locked my gaze with Theo's. I took control of the conversation. "What did Siobhan say?"

"I think she feared what her father would do to her for failing here. Killing me would force you to take care of her. In her own twisted way of thinking, she would get a form of revenge for her family. She considered it retribution."

Conal admitted, "We never asked her if she wanted to go back to her Pack."

"What would he do to his own daughter that was so bad she would choose death?" Theo's hand holding onto the blanket tremored.

"You don't want to know," Lore told her quietly.

"This is on us, Black." She covered her face and started to cry.

I moved to her.

Lore approached Theo at the same time and sat on the coffee table across from her. "Seer, do not allow your generous heart to obscure the reality of Siobhan's life."

She wiped the tears from her cheeks. "What do you mean?"

"Her father, the leader of the Dolan Pack, has traded his progeny for centuries. She had no choice but to fulfill the contract her father signed. If she failed, then she would be punished because, to her Packleader, she had failed in the task she was bred to perform."

"That-that's barbaric," Theo said softly.

"That is our way, or I should say the Dolans' way," Lore told her gently.

"Honey, you know our ways are not always like the human worlds," Conal corrected her gently. "She didn't want to answer for her failing, and that was her choice. She could have approached Black, or any one of us, and expressed her concern. Instead, she chose to seek revenge."

She glanced at me, and I could clearly read the anguish on her face. "I'm not sure I'll ever understand this world."

I kept my gaze steady. "You have time."

"What if I never do?" she asked.

I knew what she was getting at. "You will," I told her. She had been born to be my mate and to help me rule Novus.

"I feel sad for Siobhan. It hurts me to think she never really had a choice about her life." Theo raised her gaze to mine. "You can't be like that."

"We aren't." Theo meant Novus, but I meant for our young and us.

"I mean it, Black." Her eyes turned hard.

"I know, and I gave you my answer."

She nodded, and then glanced down at her uncasted hand. It gripped the other so tightly her knuckles were white.

"You will need to call Dolan," Conal reminded me.

"I will when we finish here." I glanced away from my Second. I wanted to hear the full story from Theo. "So, she was going to kill you, and then hope that she would be killed?"

"Our conversation didn't get that far." She continued to look at her joined hands. "But that is my impression."

"She would never have made it out of the Pack-house," Lore murmured.

The scent of Theo's fear filled the air.

"I'm sorry," she said. "I know this makes more problems for you, but...I didn't mean for this to happen." She looked at the other two men, and then back at me. "Please..." she whispered as she scooted forward on the sofa. "Please, don't send me away."

"Nobody said anything about sending you away," I said, keeping my voice soft. Her fears were sometimes illogical. My job was to reassure her.

Again, she looked at the others. "I didn't mean for it to happen. I'm sorry." She started to rock back and forth, chanting, "I'm sorry."

I glanced at Conal, and he pulled his phone from his pocket to call Solle.

"Theo, nobody is sending you away," I repeated. "I made you that vow."

Lore leaned closer to her. "Seer, no one believes you have any culpability in this unfortunate event. We all believed that you were safe in your cell...er, room." He glanced at me because we needed to consider not only her physical safety but her fragile psyche. "Novus must do a better job protecting you."

Her expression showed so much pain. Her forehead wrinkled, and her teeth pinched her bottom lip. "I'm trying to be good."

"Theo, baby, nobody could ever say you aren't a fighter." I wanted to take her into my arms and cuddle her close to my chest, but only very rarely did she want contact from me.

"I hate that I'm causing more problems for you," she looked at me and rushed to add, "and Novus."

"We are fine," I assured her. I would do anything to protect her. I felt a light buzzing vibration against my skin. She was attempting to use her gift to read my emotions.

I'd been shocked to find how greatly diminished her powers had become. Lore, Conal, and I had discussed it several times. Her weakness could have been due to her vast injuries, the Burkes not allowing her outside, from lack of use—or any combination of those reasons. She feared that The Lady was punishing her, but I didn't believe that. When she grew stronger, we would request an audience with the Goddess and learn more.

She closed her eyes and rested her head against the sofa.

"Do you need to rest?" She grew tired so easily. I knew it was part of the human healing process, but I worried about the dreams that would eventually intrude and cause her to wake, screaming in terror.

"Maybe a nap...?" She looked around my living room. "Can I...stay here for now?"

"Of course." She could stay here forever. I wanted her in my rooms. "I'll get you set up." I moved to my bedroom to grab a pillow.

She was lying on her side on my sofa with Luna on the floor in front of her while she stroked her back. "Can you call Solle back and tell her that...I'm okay...?"

Conal waited for my nod. Then, again pulled out his phone.

"I need to make a few calls, and then I'll be back. It should be no more than two hours." I'd figured out that giving her timeframes helped ease her anxiety. "Lore and Luna will stay with you."

"Thank you, Laird..." she said, her voice trailing off.

EIGHTEEN

NOVUS

THEODORA MORRISSEY

i hate you, i love you by Gnash

When I woke, Issa and Lore were deep into a hushed conversation at the far corner of Black's living room. I stretched and felt the now familiar aches as I shifted positions. One of the worst effects of falling into a deep exhausted sleep was that I rarely moved, so I woke up stiff.

I sat up and started to swing my casted leg to the floor. "Luna, watch out."

The wolf was already on her feet and shaking out her fur.

My guards made their way closer to me.

Issa spoke first. "I can't believe I missed everything. She would never have made an attempt if I were there."

"I don't believe she felt she had a choice," I said. "She was very determined."

"Lore and I would have stopped her." Issa stood taller and smoothed her hands over her pink tunic that she'd paired with Hello Kitty leggings.

"I'm very lucky to have you both, but I know you can't be with me every second. It isn't fair to you." I stood with the intent to use the bathroom down the hall.

"Mistress," Lore said, "I am going to take my leave and return in the morning."

I gave him a nod. "I'll see you then."

He bowed solemnly and, with his wolf, left the Laird's quarters.

Of course, Issa followed me into the bathroom. Before, her inability to read my discomfort with this practice had rankled. I'd fought her over the right to pee with the door shut. Now, I didn't care. I took care of my personal needs while she stood in the doorway.

"I can feel you thinking, Iss. What's on your mind?" I didn't have to use my gift. She was bending and straightening one knee.

"So, what now, Seer?"

I moved to the sink to wash my hands, making sure not to look in the mirror. I didn't need to see the scars on my face to know they were there. "I'm supposed to wait here. Black said it would be a couple of hours."

"I mean, are you going to move here, into his quarters, like before?"

I bit down on my bottom lip. "I hadn't thought about it."

"I understood the reason you liked the basement was because you felt safe there….and it was private."

She was right. I let out a long sigh. "I don't know."

"She didn't stay here with him if that is your concern," Issa said, rushing the words.

Of course, that had been a concern. "Issa, what happened between Black and Siobhan…" I couldn't finish the sentence. "I can't lie. It matters."

She motioned for me to follow her, and we ended up at the dining room table with cold drinks. "Of course, it matters. You two are meant to be together."

I whispered because it hurt my throat to ask, "Do you think so?"

She rolled her expressive eyes. "Well, duh." The woman across from me appeared to be twenty, but she was centuries old and deadly.

At that moment, I adored her. She made me giggle, and the constriction around my chest loosened.

She flashed me a mischievous grin. "Anybody with two eyes, or even one, could see it, or smell your attraction."

"He never lied about Siobhan." I defended Black although she had yet to accuse him of anything.

"Do you still care for him?" She tilted her head in that very wolf-like way as she waited for my answer.

I met her stare. "Yes."

The door opened.

Black was always really good about making noise, so I knew when he was near. "I apologize," he said, "the calls took a little longer than I had anticipated."

"I've only been up for a little bit," I said because I knew he would ask. "Would you like something to drink?"

"I can grab my own beer, babe." He did so and joined us at the table. After removing the cap from the bottle, he took a long drink. "Solle will be by in about forty-five minutes. I suggested that she and Conal stay for dinner."

I nodded my agreement. I should do normal things, even if I had to force myself. That would mean there would be the four of us and the staff serving our meal. I felt my heart accelerate at the thought of so many Lycans surrounding me.

"Or we can have pizza up here and keep things casual...?" He was watching me closely.

Of course, he could hear my heart race, so he knew. I gave him a weak smile because I was reminded, again, that he was making concessions so I'd be more comfortable.

Issa pushed back her chair. "It sounds like you have everything under control. If you should need my services, shoot me a text."

"Iss, you can stay for dinner." I stood. This was very unlike her. She usually stayed for her entire shift with me until Black was ready for sleep.

"The Laird will see to you. If you need me, I will come." She allowed me to walk her to the door.

"Iss?" This was confusing.

She leaned close. "Let him," she whispered. "Allow him to care for you."

I felt my body tense at her closeness. I hated that I reacted to her nearness. I trusted her with my life. She was a good friend.

"You'll be fine." She flashed a conspiratorial smile, and then gave me a finger wave and left.

I returned to my seat and tried not to fidget as I felt him study me.

"Did you sleep well?"

"Yes." We both knew he was asking if I'd had any dreams.

He took another drink.

"How did the phone call go?" I couldn't imagine how one told a father his child was dead.

He twirled his bottle around once, twice, and frowned. "I don't think he was surprised or saddened. He only asked for the facts."

My eyes flared wide. "And that means what?"

"It is a small problem for Novus. I'm sure he will ask the Council to assess a penalty, and we will have to pay."

"How much?" The words came out shakily.

He shrugged one shoulder. "Doesn't matter. We will pay, and then this will be done."

I didn't believe him. I thought his answer was more wishful thinking than the reality of the death of a spurned daughter of a powerful Packleader. "How long until you know?"

"The Council will notify us when Dolan files his complaint. We will go from there." He took another drink. "I want to know how you are doing, my Theo?"

"My hand hurts a little." I held up my casted hand. "I kept hitting the side of her head." I tried to smile.

"Her ear?"

"Yes." I sat a little straighter because I could see he was pleased.

"Solle will see to you before we eat."

"I was thinking…" I hated that I sounded so tentative. There had been a time when we'd sat at this table, and I'd felt like I could say almost anything.

"This should be interesting," he teased. His beautiful gray eyes were bright, and the lines crinkled at the sides. He was trying to help me.

I can do this. "I thought that by staying downstairs in a cell, it would help."

"I understand, Theo." His voice had gone low and gravelly.

"But I still felt anxious and jumped at every sound."

"Honey, it's okay. It's understandable."

"I don't think I can go back down there."

He gave me an assessing look. I knew he was using all his senses. "Theo, you can stay wherever you want. Whatever you need, I will make happen."

I knew he meant every word. "I want to..." I had to clear my throat and start over. "I love you, and I want..."

He reached out his hand, and I gave him mine. "What is your wish?"

"I was thinking that I might try to stay...here...with you...?" I wished that it sounded more like a statement. "That way you don't have to sleep on the floor."

"My wolf didn't mind," he assured me.

"And he didn't always stay on the floor." I smiled because last night, I'd awoken to find his wolf form curled up at the end of my bed.

He pressed my hand. "Whatever you want."

"I'd like to try, I mean for you to...to stay in your human form...like this." My eyes traveled over his body.

"You are sure?"

Again, Black was using his senses. I felt the tingling. I licked my dry lips. "I realized when you carried me upstairs that I missed..." Christ, this was so hard. "I missed you...you know, holding me." My ribs hurt from breathing so hard.

"Then we will try tonight." Then he lifted our joined hands to his mouth and brushed his lips over my knuckles.

I felt a flutter of happiness deep in my belly.

Knocking sounded, and I jumped.

"That will be Conal and Solle," he said casually, as though he hadn't seen me flinch. "I'll get the door."

That allowed me a moment to take control of my emotions and prepare.

Solle burst into the room. "They said that you were okay." She stopped right beside me.

I rose. "I might have done something to my hand." I held out my arm. "I used it to hit her in the head," I admitted with a tiny smile because I knew my friend hadn't liked Siobhan at all.

"I can't believe she tried to kill you." Solle frowned as she took my casted hand and pulled me toward Black's bedroom. "We'll be right back."

I followed her into Black's bedroom. I hadn't been there since the day I'd left Novus. It looked the same, and yet, it felt different. I was different. I ran my uncasted hand over the duvet before I perched on the corner of the enormous bed.

"I'm not going to be able to tell if you did any new damage to your hand. We'll need x-rays." Solle was using her doctor's voice. It was brisker than her usual teasing tone.

"Lore is with me tomorrow morning. We can come to your office or the hospital."

She opened her bag and pulled out a penlight. "Did she knock you out?" She motioned with her hand for me to stay still as she used the light to look into my eyes.

"No. She tried to choke me." I touched my throat and realized that it was tender.

"Then open up."

Solle checked my throat, listened to my heart, and

took my blood pressure. "Anything else causing you pain?"

"Nothing new."

"What about sleeping?"

"I do fine until the dreams come, and then…well, it gets ugly." I looked away. I didn't want to discuss what happened in my dreams. I couldn't find the words to describe the feelings of terror that came from knowing something was stalking me. I wasn't entirely sure that someone who was so powerful could comprehend how helpless I felt.

"I was on the phone earlier with a therapist. He comes highly recommended. His specialty is dealing with people who've been through a traumatic experience."

"A man?" I didn't know how I felt about that. Hell, I didn't know how I felt about talking about what had happened and was still was happening.

"Only if you're ready," Solle said, sensing my concerns.

I looked away and stared at the tall dresser. "I know I'm not right." I glanced at her to see how she would react.

"Nobody who lived through that kind of an attack would be. That's why we're bringing in an expert."

I nodded. She was right. While I'd been in the hospital, Black had shared the fact that they'd watched the video of the attack. It was unsettling to know so many had seen me violated and helpless. Conal had told me that when Lore saw the tape, he'd torn a door from its hinges then went for an eight-hour run. Like many, my guard had sworn vengeance. If and when they found Charles, would I be able to face him? Would it help me heal if I did?

Solle studied me. "Conal said you let Black hold you."

"I was scared, so yeah, I did."

She arched an eyebrow. "How did that go?"

"I'm going to sleep here," I looked at the bed, "with him, tonight."

"Was that his idea?" she asked, her voice getting a little brittle toward the end.

Solle was a protector. "No," I shook my head. "I want to try it. Black doesn't pressure me." If anything, he was being too understanding, too patient, and I knew it was because I wasn't in good shape.

"If he or anybody makes you uncomfortable, just tell me, and I'll handle it."

"I know." I'd heard the same from Lore, Issa, and Glass. "Thank you."

"Conal's going to knock." Solle had just finished the last word when I heard a tap.

"Coming," I called.

"They must be hungry." Solle followed me from the room.

"Or they're worried that we're plotting against them," I teased. This felt very much like old times.

So, we entered the living room giggling, and I felt the mood of the room lift. I walked to where Black sat in a huge reclining chair. I perched on the arm.

Conal patted the spot next to him on the sofa for his mate. "Should we be worried?" He eyed Solle then me curiously and then winked.

"Perhaps," Solle said.

"How is she, Doc?" Black asked Solle.

I spoke before she could. "Lore will have to take me in for x-rays in the morning." I held out my casted hand.

He gently took it in his large hand. "Does it hurt, because I can take you now…?"

"I might have done something to it, but it isn't bad. It can wait." I wanted to spend time tonight with our friends and Black.

"Promise that you'll tell me if it changes."

I stared into his eyes. I'd never met anybody with eyes that color, like a dark cold winter's day. "I will tell you."

"Are you hungry?" Conal asked.

I thought about that for a moment, because since the attack, I hadn't had much of an appetite. "I am," I said, surprised it was true.

"My Warrior," Black said quietly.

Over dinner, Conal told stories of when he and Black were young and serving the council in Edinburgh. We laughed, and I knew that they were all secretly watching me for any sign of tiredness or discomfort. When Solle and Conal left, Black turned to me and asked, "Do you want to change first?"

"I don't have anything to change into." I felt a moment of panic. Why? I didn't know. This was easily fixable.

"I'll get you a T-shirt," he offered.

I told myself to stop being so foolish. Things were going so well.

I followed him into the bedroom. He started digging in his T-shirt drawer. "Do you want sleeves or no?"

Another side-effect of the attack was that I never got warm. "Long sleeves."

He tossed a black tee onto the bed. "You change and do your thing while I lock up."

I knew he would give me plenty of time, but I hurried to undress and pull his huge shirt over my head. I kept my panties on, and for a moment, I realized that except for the hospital gown, these were the fewest clothes I'd worn in weeks. I hurried to the luxurious bathroom and found an extra toothbrush. I brushed and rinsed my face with warm water. I felt some trepidation as I approached his bed. I stood to the side and stared at it for a full minute.

We had shared so much here.

"Babe," he called out so that I would know he was approaching. "Hey," he walked in. "Do you need anything else?"

Black was being so sweet. This was a side I rarely saw, but whenever he did show it to me, I melted. "I was waiting for you."

"Just give me a sec to throw on some shorts."

Before, we always slept naked. "You don't have to," I rushed to tell him.

"It's not a problem." He grabbed the hem of his shirt and lifted it over his head.

I'd forgotten how gorgeous his body was. All Lycan males were strong and their muscles apparent, so the way the light played with the sinews was magical.

"Be right back. Go on, climb in," he urged.

I pulled back my side of the covers and crawled onto the mattress. Next came the hard question. How far did I travel? I used to sleep in the middle, curled against his body.

"Sweetheart, you don't have to sleep in my arms, if it that makes you uncomfortable." He was done in the bathroom.

"Can you leave the hall light on?" He'd have to add

more lights for me because his room was pitch black when he turned off the main lights.

"I'm going to leave on the light over the sink in the bathroom, and the door open to the hall." He turned off the bedroom lights and waited beside the bed. "Need more light, Theo?"

I didn't answer right away. I was with Black. I was safe. "No, I think I'm good."

"I can always turn more on...later if you need." He got into the bed and moved closer to me but didn't pull me into his arms.

That made the tears burn the backs of my eyes. It shouldn't be like this.

"Babe?"

Of course, he could smell my emotions. "I missed this, and now, I want you to hold me, but I don't know.... I don't know if I can handle it. And I fucking hate being like this," I sobbed. Charles Burke had done this to me. I hated him for it.

"Try this, okay? I will lie still, and you can move closer to me." He sounded so calm as if I hadn't just dissolved into tears.

I slowly counted backward from ten, trying to calm my sobs. I rolled closer to Black and reached out to stroke his arm with my fingertips. His skin was always so warm to my touch. My fingers skimmed over his strong shoulder and to his chest. I whispered, "I missed you so much."

"You've scared me before, but when your heart stopped on the airstrip..." He drew a ragged breath. "I...I thought I might burn the world to the ground. I had you again, and then you were gone."

I moved closer to his body, staying on my side, my

thighs almost touching his. I laid my head on my casted arm and touched the side of my face to his arm. This felt so good. I rested my hand on his chest, lightly stroking his skin. "Touch me," I urged in a whisper.

He didn't rush. He moved his outside arm so that his palm rested on his chest. Every time my hand brushed his, he entangled our fingers for a moment. It was almost like a game, but I knew it wouldn't end in sex. Not tonight, maybe not ever. *No*, that couldn't be true. I loved him, and I needed him. I had to get better for him.

"Can I move my right arm?"

I shifted so he could move the arm I was lying on. He then very gently stroked my waist. "Okay?"

"Yes," I whispered.

We stayed like this for a bit.

"I wish I could do more," I said, my voice catching.

"You are healing. This is fine. You are here with me."

A few hours later, I was running. It was dark, and I ran down an endless hallway. I followed the different turns as I tried to escape my tormentor. I knew he was getting closer, but I thought he was playing with me, allowing me to run out of energy until I finally stopped. But I wouldn't give up. I could hear my wheezing breath and feel the burn in my leg muscles as I continued looking for a door, for some kind of help.

He grabbed me, and I started to cry, "Please. Don't." I fought as he held me down.

"Theo, baby, it's a dream."

The words didn't make any sense.

"Theodora, wake up." He sounded angry.

205

I opened my eyes and found myself staring directly into Black's face as it hovered over mine.

"Baby, it was a dream. You're safe."

We were in his bedroom in his bed, just Black and me. "I...I was..." I tried to explain.

"You scared the piss out of me," he said.

I scooched up and leaned my back against the headboard. I was still breathing hard and my ribs hurt. "I'm sorry." I pulled my sweat-soaked shirt from my chest.

"I know that. It caught me by surprise that's all." He sat up next to me.

"He was chasing me."

"Charles?"

"I didn't see his face; it was a feeling." Jesus, it could be others. I'd never considered that.

"So, you were running?"

"Down a hallway, a never-ending hallway." I dropped my head onto his shoulder.

He immediately took my hand in his.

His touch did not set off any warning bells, this time.

"I used to have dreams about my time in captivity. I would hear the guards' steps coming down the hall for me and the smell..." He rubbed the tip of his nose, "Every once in a while I can still get a whiff."

My stomach muscles tightened at his tone. "How long did your nightmares last?"

"At the time, it seemed like forever, but it was probably thirty years."

I squeezed my eyes closed. That could be the rest of my life.

"I was imprisoned for decades."

I was in shock that Black was talking about his

imprisonment. I'd learned of it during my time on The Lady's Plane. "Did they torture you?" I asked quietly.

"Yes." He moved our hands so that they rested on his thigh. "For a Lycan, being locked away is torture."

"Were you alone?"

"Sometimes." His hand involuntarily squeezed my hand for a moment. "Imprisoned Lycans tend to kill one another."

"Oh," I breathed the word. I'd witnessed his violent side. It had scared the shit out of me.

"My captors pitted us against one another for entertainment. So a great deal of damage was done."

Jesus, that hurt to think about. "You chose to be captured. Did you know that it would be like that?"

"The prince, he wasn't strong. It was my duty to take his place, to impersonate him."

And because he did and had survived, he'd been given the charter for Novus. "Did you know it was going to be that bad?"

"No." He let out a long sigh. "I was young... Well, young for a wolf, and as I said, it was my duty. But I had no idea what it does to your psyche to be cut open every day, to watch your organs being pulled from your body, over and over, because I could change and heal. They wanted to break me and force me to choose not to change."

I didn't want to hear about that. I hated that he'd been hurt. "When you were found, how did you...what were you like?"

"I was weak, physically weak, and somewhat mad. Like you, I didn't want to sleep. I stayed in my wolf-form and ran. Conal stuck with me, and we covered miles and miles. Sometimes, I felt like I was being pursued, and others, I just wanted to be on the move. My spirit was too restless."

"I'm the opposite. I feel safe in one place."

"Whatever you need." He dropped a kiss on top of my head.

I closed my eyes and smiled.

NINETEEN

NOVUS

RAIDER BLACK

Losing My Religion by REM

"WELL, THAT DIDN'T LAST LONG." CONAL STRETCHED his long legs out in front of him in my office in the Novus building.

"I told you, it has to be the right fit." Solle practically stomped from the bar to the sofa.

"You did say that." I hoped my tone communicated that I respected the doctor's opinion.

"I didn't like the guy from the start. He asked too many questions about everything." Conal took the beer his wife handed him.

"I didn't like the way he looked at Theo," I admitted.

Solle started to chuckle but stopped when I gave her a sharp look. "I think his interest in Theo was based upon the degree of damage. Dr. Nichols probably didn't even notice that she is beautiful; he just saw the list of symptoms and got a hard-on."

There was a brief knock on the door and I knew that it was Theo. "Come in."

She did so, and I noticed that her shoulders were slumped.

"Hey." She said the word quietly.

"Grab something to drink and sit," Solle said.

She didn't head to my bar. Instead, she moved toward the other wing chair.

"By me, babe."

Before she'd gone to Texas, she hadn't been unsure of where to sit. When with our friends, she always sat beside me or on my lap.

"How do you like the new office?" Conal asked as if he hadn't noticed anything odd.

She bent one leg under the other and answered. "I like it. I know that Basil had a big hand decorating it."

The suite was next to mine and painted a light blue with white trim. The desk was a cherry wood parson's table. I'd told my assistant to spare no expense, and I feared that he'd taken me at my word.

She continued, "It was very thoughtful to make a space for Lore."

"When you feel able, he can resume your lessons," I said. Solle had suggested that we try to set up a schedule for Theo so that she had things to do.

"I'm sorry about Dr. Nichols." She was looking down at her hands.

"Nothing to be sorry about." I draped my arm around the back of the sofa.

She shifted her body forward a little, so I could place my arm along her shoulders. "I didn't, I tried but…"

"Theo, it's okay," Solle said. "We need to find the right fit. If you didn't feel comfortable with the guy, then he wouldn't be able to help you."

"That first day, when he asked me what kind of clothes I liked to wear... It just seemed like a really wrong question." She frowned.

"He worded it *entirely* wrong," Solle said, frowning. "I think he was trying to figure out where you are now. Clothing choice can be an indicator of mood. I think he was trying to learn more about your current state as compared to before."

"Then I got it all wrong?" Theo sounded devastated.

"No," Solle rushed to tell her. "If his manner of communicating caused you to be uncomfortable, then it's a good thing that you figured it out early. We can move on and look for somebody you might do better with."

Theo glanced at me, and I nodded, agreeing with Solle.

There was another knock on my door. I called, "Enter." It had to be important, or Basil would have dealt with it.

Onyx entered the room. He gave me a nod then glanced at Conal. "Good, I'm glad to see that you are here, Second."

"What's going on?" The man was holding his tablet in his hand.

"The Council has responded to the Dolans' Petition." Onyx loved this shit, crafting long documents, jumping through the necessary hoops that the Council required for Pack business.

"What do we have to do to make them go away?" Conal asked lazily.

Theo made a move to slide forward to get to her feet. "Come on, Doc. Let's leave them to discuss business."

I knew it hurt her that, technically, she wasn't a part of Novus, although she was. I'd followed Solle's advice and not pressed the mating, but I needed to have that discussion with her very soon.

"I think you should stay because the Council responded to the Burke petition as well," Onyx said, giving Theo a sideways glance.

She slid back and a little closer to me.

I knew she and Onyx had had their share of problems when he'd been her tutor. I'd first learned of the issues from Solle, and then I'd paid closer attention. To this day, Onyx was very vocal in his criticism regarding Theo, and I hoped he would choose his words carefully. My wolf could feel her sense of unease as soon as the male had entered the room. He was hoping for an excuse to tear his head off. "You have the floor."

"Both issues will be heard in California at the Gathering." He started tapping the screen. "The Dolan Pack has asked for recompense in the amount of seventy."

Theo looked at me to explain. "Million," I told her quietly.

Onyx continued, "We have requested an accounting of how they came to that number. Our research shows Siobhan has never worked, so the only money she has generated for her Pack was from the Mating Contract with you."

"Get it lowered to fiftyish and pay it," I told him.

I saw Conal nod once in agreement.

"But Laird, that amount is outrageous," Onyx sputtered.

"We keep the rights to the routes and we'll pay it."

Onyx studied his tablet for a few moments. "Well, you did toss aside the Packleader's daughter, and then slaughter her."

"She tried to kill Theo!" Solle raised her voice, going into protector mode.

"She felt like she didn't have a choice," Theo said quietly.

"Of course, she had a choice," Solle railed. "She could have packed up her twelve trunks and gone away."

Theo turned to me and whispered, "Is that going to take all of Novus' money?" Her eyes had grown huge.

I so fucking loved her. She was worried about Novus and me. "I'll cover it. Novus will be fine."

"You can take my money," she offered. "Not that it's very much, but I'd like to help."

I shook my head, fighting off a grin. She was too perfect. "Thank you, but we can pay this restitution and still be able to cover the bills."

The others had heard our conversation. How could they not? Even Onyx gave Theo an approving nod.

Conal asked, "What does Burke say?"

"I sent an update two days ago," Onyx explained, "outlining that although many packs were cooperating in our search for Charles, a few were not."

"We have it narrowed to three in the Americas," Conal explained for Solle and Theo's benefit, "one in Chile, another in Paraguay, and one in northern Canada." He wanted her to know they were far away.

"Burke has asked that the Seer be produced so that an independent doctor can examine her, and for questioning by the Council." Onyx watched me closely when he finished relaying this outrageous demand.

"What?" Solle and Conal spoke as one.

I waited until they quieted. "We haven't received their payment." I shrugged. "They are stalling."

"But why do they want an additional medical examination?" Solle asked.

"Who cares? The records speak for themselves. We have those from the hospital in Texas and our own here. If the new doctor wants to take more x-rays, they will see where the bones have knitted back together." I glanced at Onyx. "Demand that we use the daughter of the Edmonton Leader." I glanced at Solle. "You've met her, Sophia, from a few years ago."

Solle had narrowed her eyes. "Didn't you and she...?"

Theo rolled her eyes. "Don't tell me that you want one of your lovers to check me out?"

I trusted Sophia. "You'll do fine with her. She has spent quite a bit of time in the human world."

"My question is, how much did you like her?" She smiled, and I realized how rarely she did that now.

"Feeling jealous?" I teased.

She glanced away.

"Why would your mate worry about a female you had years ago?" Onyx asked, his eyebrows rising.

A growl formed deep in my chest.

"Thank you, Onyx," Conal excused the male hurriedly.

"But they want the Seer to testify," he pushed.

"What does that mean?" she asked.

"It means nothing," I told her and them.

"The Council will have questions," Onyx persisted.

"And we will answer them," I said, using my "don't fuck with me" tone.

"They saw the video. What more could they want?" Conal asked.

"They...they saw everything?" Theo pushed away from me. "So they...they..?"

She sounded mortified as she covered her mouth.

"You can refuse them access to your *mate*, Laird. It is your right," Onyx's voice thundered.

She dropped her hand from her face. "Why does he keep saying that?" Theo asked me.

I didn't want to have this conversation here...now.

"Black?" Her voice shook. "What's going on? What aren't you telling me?"

"We need to go." Solle hopped to her feet and shot Conal a look. "Right now."

The three left my office and closed the door. I tried to think of how to explain all of this.

"Raid?"

I hated that she sounded so uneasy. Theo was a fighter. "I have a lot to tell you, but I wanted to wait until you were stronger."

She nodded once, although her eyes were troubled and her scent was a mixture of sadness and nervousness.

"You've gone through so much that I...I wanted time...time for you to heal so that you would be ready," I finished weakly.

She didn't respond, but I could tell she was rehashing my words in her head. After about two minutes she said, "Black?"

"Hmmm?" I focused on her. I'd been busy trying to come up with the best way to explain my actions and omissions.

"Could we get out of here? Maybe go for a ride?"

As always, she surprised me. "Are you sure?"

"I miss your bike."

"We can do that." I smiled. "Go grab a sweatshirt, and I think there's a helmet in the guard's station."

"Or we could be rule breakers and forget the helmet...?" She flashed a little smile. "Like we did that first time...?"

"I won't tell Solle if you won't." I stood and held out my hand to her. "She can get scary when riled." Her slap had not been gentle.

"I need this...to get out and not have to think."

"Then let's go."

TWENTY

NOVUS

THEODORA MORRISSEY

I Want to Know What Love Is by Foreigner

I LOVED THE FEEL OF THE WIND WHIPPING THROUGH MY hair as we rode about the Novus land. I kept my mind blank, not even wanting to imagine what a meeting with Council Members would mean to me and my life. I purposely ignored the Mating talk. I wouldn't allow myself to hope that would happen. I was in no shape to be a good match for the Laird. A male like Black deserved a strong mate.

Black was laughing; I could feel his body shake under the cheek that rested against his back.

"What?" I didn't know if he could hear me.

He shook his head. Too soon, he slowed and pulled off the road onto a paved area. I climbed off the back of his bike and almost landed on my ass. He grabbed my arm to help me stay on my feet.

"Thanks."

He climbed off, and again, I was reminded how much I loved watching him move. Once, when we'd been psychically linked, I'd run with him in his wolf form. He was so powerful and yet fluid.

"We won't walk far," he said.

My walking boot wasn't made for a nature walk. "Do you know all of these little nooks?" I took his hand. After our first night together, he'd taken me for a bike ride, and we'd stopped at a pull-off that overlooked a field. It was very picturesque and romantic. I think it was there that I'd first admitted to myself that I loved him.

"Every single one and I plan on showing them all to you."

We walked into a wooded area, not really a forest, more like a large grouping of trees. There he found or knew about a fallen tree, and he motioned for me to sit. "I wanted to do this conversation in a different way."

"Nobody likes having their hand forced." Especially the feared and revered Raider Black.

"You've shaken up my life."

I didn't know if he considered that a good thing, so I waited for him to continue.

"I wasn't like Conal, who knew that he had a mate somewhere in the world. From a very early age, he was confident that he would find her. I, on the other hand, didn't believe in love."

"You didn't?"

"Never." He shook his head once. "I liked to fuck. There were a few times that I stuck with a female for a short period, but I never wanted more." He looked away and moistened his lips. "You know that I'm not good at the romantic shit."

"That's not true, Black." It might not come naturally to him, but he'd done so many things to show me that he cared.

"When we figured out that we could make money running escorts, Dolan hinted that he had an available daughter. If I contracted with her, Novus would secure access."

"It was a no brainer," I finished the thought for him.

He shrugged. "I'd never loved a female. I didn't know what it meant. How it changes everything."

"Raider, we've been over this. I understand why you signed that contract, and as much as I hated it, I accepted it. I had to. You didn't lie about any of it."

"But I did lie to you."

"I don't understand what you're saying." I started to feel the panic grow in my belly.

"I don't even know how to explain it…." He tore out the band that had held his long hair in a ponytail.

"Try," I choked out the word through my constricted throat. I pulled my good leg up to my chest and wrapped my arms around it. This position was hard on my healing ribs. I felt better like this as if by making myself smaller and by protecting my chest, I was less of a target.

"I lied to you and to myself." He let out a ragged sigh. "I did it for selfish reasons." He started to pace. "I don't want to admit this, but I must. At first, feeling the way I did about you, with all its implications, it…it terrified me."

"This doesn't make any sense…" I was beyond confused. "Why?" What could scare the Laird?

His gaze locked with mine. "You are my true mate, Theo."

"What?" I think I inhaled a huge lungful of air as I

said the word and then cringed as the pain radiated through my body.

He stopped right in front of me. "I've had to battle my wolf constantly. After you moved in, it was easier, but he wanted to claim you, to make it official."

"So, when you would say 'mine,' you really meant it?" Why that popped into my head as my first thought, I had no clue.

"Did you ever doubt it?" He watched me, but I knew —no, I felt his wolf watching me.

I blinked several times while I thought about those months. Really from the beginning, he'd always been possessive, and I'd known there was more behind his possessiveness than just my Marked status. "No," I said, not sure how I felt about his admission and his misleading me all this time. "I never doubted you felt like you owned me."

"There were so many times I wanted to take off for Texas, to steal you away and…and disappear."

That news stunned me. "I don't know what to say…" I didn't know how to continue. He'd considered giving up Novus for me?

He sat beside me. "This is our second chance. I don't know why The Lady has given us this, but I want to take it."

"This is…I don't know what to think." I was stalling because this is what I'd always wanted, but now I was suspicious, on guard. Another thing that Charles Burke had taken away from me was the ability to trust others and myself.

"You were put on Earth for me. You are my other half," he said, his voice becoming hoarse. "Together, we will rule Novus. This is how it is supposed to be, Theodora."

"And you know this is to be true?" God, I wanted it so badly, but I wasn't the same woman he'd fallen in love with.

"You will realize it too when you have the courage to look to the future." He sounded so sure of me, of us. "I love you, and I want this, my wolf wants this. You by my side, our young growing up and playing with Solle and Conal's. It is our destiny."

My stomach cramped. "Black..." I needed to inject some reality into his dream. "Black, I don't know if I can...if we can...I'm not sure that I'll ever be able to be a real partner to you." What was he thinking? I was sleeping beside him, but the touching was barely there, and when it did happen, it took a great deal of time and patience to ease into it.

"Of course, we will. We'll find a therapist who can help you, so you can grow strong and take your place by my side."

He used his "kingly tone." I knew that if I argued it would fall onto deaf ears. The Laird had decided my future. "I need time," I said quietly.

"I know." This was said in a quiet voice as if he was considering it.

"I hope that you do." I felt like I was going to cry. What if I could never be intimate again? That wouldn't be fair to Black.

His eyebrows drew together, and his gaze locked with mine. "Theo, are you mine? You claim to love me." His eyes had turned a darker gray.

"I have always been yours, Raider Black. You know

that. Your wolf certainly knows it." My scent couldn't lie; he knew how I felt.

"Then why do I sense your reticence?"

"Because there is so much that I can't do." My voice cracked. I took such a big lungful of air that my ribs hurt. "I jump at every noise. I don't want to be in a crowd, and...and I can't...we can't...do..." I started to cry.

"Shh," He lifted me onto his lap like he had a hundred times before the attack, and I wrapped my arms around his shoulders.

"What if I can't?" I said into his neck as he cradled me to his chest. "Every time I think about sex, I freeze. I don't know if I'll ever be able to...and that's not fair to you."

"You will because you are my Warrior. You can do anything, my love."

I prayed that he was right. Our sex life before had been hot. Before it had only taken a look from the Laird and I was wet. Now, even the thought of his hand on my bare breast made me want to retch.

Preparing for the trip to California was so much work. I had to learn about the special and in my opinion—antiquated etiquette. Because of the attack, it was decided that I did not have to accompany Black to the formal evening meals, so I didn't need five gowns made and even more lessons. However, Issa was enjoying every minute of the preparations. I'd put her in charge of dressing me for this trip.

I didn't relish the idea of being in a room full of powerful Lycans, but I had no choice. The arrangements were made. We would arrive outside of San Diego on Monday and leave early Friday morning. Our group was so large that we'd been assigned a house on the expansive estate where this meeting was to be held. The rules for me were simple. I was to go nowhere unattended by guards. If Black was near, then I was to stand on his left side.

My packing had taken over an entire room at the house. I looked around at the chaos. "I don't want to wear black."

Issa stopped unpacking the latest box that had arrived thirty minutes earlier by a courier service. "But I love the jacket."

"It is too severe and dramatic."

"Then try the blue." She dropped the reject and pulled out a deep marine blue dress.

"Hold it up." I studied the simple tank-style dress. "What would I wear over it?" I didn't want the scars that Charles left on my body to show. They made me feel vulnerable.

"We have that crocheted duster." Issa pointed at the rolling rack that was against the far wall.

"Onyx said I would be questioned in front of the Council." My voice shook a little displaying my nervousness. "I need to look conservative, but I'd like to be comfortable."

"That will be via video. They won't travel here. It could go on for hours." Issa shook out the dress one more time and held it out to me. "Try this on."

I blew out a breath that filled my cheeks, but I did as instructed. I'd undressed in front of her for weeks, but it still made the burn of anxiety spread through my body.

"Now this." Issa handed me the duster.

I looked down at my body. "I like it." I rarely glanced in the mirror, and when I did, it was only to get a general idea.

"Good." The fashion expert straightened the skirt. "Your gown will arrive tomorrow for the final fitting."

"I know that you hate the dress…" I would be attending a party on the last evening as Black's date. I knew I had to do this, but I felt sick every time it was mentioned.

"You should have something beautiful, not so boring," she said with heat.

"Next time," I promised.

The dress was violet in color and had three-quarter sleeves and no cleavage. The back would be secured by lacing—my only concession to a decoration. I think my "boring" dress broke Issa and Basil's hearts.

I added them to the list of people I was disappointing. I'd had three sessions with another therapist last week. She had decided it was not going to work out. I wasn't giving enough energy to the process, she claimed.

I didn't want to spend hours listing all my weaknesses since birth. I wanted the nightmares to stop. I wanted to sleep, a really good, deep, healing sleep. Once I was rested, only then could I combat the negative voices that seemed to speak to me all the time.

We did have some good news. Solle was pregnant. I had seen this in a vision before I'd left for Texas, so I wasn't surprised. Conal was beaming from ear to ear. I was happy for them both. They would be fantastic parents. When I'd first arrived, they'd "parented" me.

Today, we'd arrived safely in San Diego and had settled into the house. Basil had presented me with a schedule for the day about an hour ago. Solle and I were to meet in a few minutes for tea with the doctor who would do the required medical examination.

I knew this casual meeting was set up so that I could get to know Dr. Sophia Richards. I'd reviewed her list of degrees and publications with Solle. She sounded very learned. However, I still viewed her as the enemy because she was not one of my trusted circle.

I glanced at my schedule. First the tea, and then later tonight, the Second of the host pack was coming to dinner. Black was meeting with his Board in the upstairs study. Issa was sitting in the corner on her tablet, and our other guards were patrolling and learning the physical layout of the house and surrounding land. Lore and Luna were... I had no idea where they were. Since the announcement that I would be testifying here, he'd seemed thrilled, and that was concerning because I couldn't figure out the reason, and I'd learned that Lore always had a reason.

Issa didn't even look up. "Solle's coming."

I looked expectantly at the doorway as Solle strolled in. Although she was only a few weeks pregnant, I swear she was glowing. "I hope we have plenty of food because I'm starving." She'd changed into a bright pink sundress and matching sandals.

"Well, you are eating for two," I reminded her.

She sat on the sofa next to me. "If this kid grows as big as Conal, I'll be huge."

"Stop your bitchin', you love the guy, and this baby will be so spoiled."

She rolled her eyes dramatically because we both knew that it was true. "How are you doing?"

I wanted to shrug and leave it at that, but Lore had

schooled me in the last few weeks that I must answer in words. "I'm nervous."

"You do not have to worry. I will keep you safe." Issa put her tablet down and moved to the doorway.

"It will be fine, and if it's not, leave it to me," Solle gave Issa a look that said, "Behave." She then focused on me. "I believe that she will be sensitive to your needs."

I heard Issa's hushed tones. She then reappeared in the doorway with a tall, cool, blonde standing by her shoulder. "My Lady, Dr. Richards is here."

Solle and I got to our feet.

"Please, come in," I said.

Issa stepped out of the way, and the female entered.

"Please call me Sophia."

Solle took the lead. "We met a few years ago."

"Solle, I do remember. I enjoyed our talk." Sophia smiled and then turned her attention to me.

"This is Theodora Morrissey, Seer, and the Intended Mate to Leader Raider Black of the Novus Pack," Solle said, formally introducing me by my full title.

I lowered my chin slightly as instructed. "Thank you for accepting my invitation."

"Seer," the doctor bowed her head, "I am honored."

"Please, let's sit," I suggested.

A member of the Novus staff entered and took our drink requests.

Things were going according to what I'd been taught. Now we would make small talk while consuming our first drinks until the food arrived.

"How do you find our ways, Seer?" Sophia asked.

"I've had excellent tutors," I answered cautiously.

"I've spent many years in the human world, and I would imagine that it has been a difficult transition to our world." Sophia made eye contact, but her gaze wasn't challenging.

"I ask a lot of questions, and I lived with Solle and Conal in the beginning, it helped." I smiled at Solle, and then returned my attention to Sophia.

"I find it odd that you chose to leave."

Issa spoke sharply from the doorway. "The Seer chose to sacrifice her happiness for the betterment of Novus."

Sophia glanced over her shoulder at the guard, then at Solle, and finally at me. "I meant no offense."

"The Seer was attacked by the son of that Pack-leader. You've seen the video?" Solle's pause was a subtle challenge.

"I did."

"Then you understand why we are upset. It was me she called from her hospital bed. When I saw what had been done to her face, I forgot all my medical training. I wasn't objective. That was my friend who'd been beaten. So, Doctor, you will find that all of Novus feels the effects of Charles Burke's attack."

Sophia looked down and didn't respond.

"My friends are very protective because of what he did... It changed me," I told the female. "They see it daily." I licked my dry lips. "I chose to be auctioned because I was in love with Raider Black."

Sophia's blue eyes flared wide for a moment. I had surprised her with my honesty.

"He was contracted to another. I knew that one day, his intended would come."

"So, you chose to go," Sophia said softly.

"I chose to be sold so that Novus could be enriched."

"Instead of waiting for his intended to take offense and kill you," Issa finished the story.

"She sacrificed much for us," Solle said with finality.

Sophia nodded once and settled back into her chair. "I am impressed by your choices and actions."

My inner sense wasn't going haywire with a stranger so near, which allowed me to concentrate fully on her words. "When I'm not being noble and self-sacrificing, I like to eat ice cream and listen to music." I finished with a grin so that she would know I was kidding. I hoped that we could be less formal now that we'd survived the initial meeting niceties.

"I like ice cream, too. What flavor?" Sophia asked.

"Do I have to pick only one?"

By the time the tiny sandwiches arrived, Issa had joined our circle, and we were sharing stories.

Sophia cleared her throat. "About tomorrow, I hope to make you as comfortable as possible. You will bring your guard or as many as you wish."

"I thank you for that. I can't say that I look forward to it, but I understand that I must cooperate."

"Theo is very brave," Solle told her.

"You have my word that I do not wish to cause you any more pain."

"Thank you, Dr. Richards."

TWENTY-ONE

NOVUS

RAIDER BLACK

Life During Wartime by Talking Heads

IT WAS OFFICIALLY DAY TWO OF OUR ANNUAL Gathering. The meeting room, which was more like a mini-auditorium, was packed. There were other meetings taking place, but it seemed that everyone wanted to hear this case. I glanced at Theo, who was sitting on my left. I didn't have to sniff the air to know that she was nervous. She had made her face blank and was too still. I hated that, but I knew this was a defense that she was using more and more.

We had listened for two hours as the Council in Edinburgh, via a video feed, questioned Travis Burke. He didn't hint that he believed a flirtation or relationship had formed between his son and Theo. That had been one of the possible defenses we'd discussed and prepared for. Our greatest concern was that the Council members could ask any questions they chose, so preparation was a guessing game.

"So, you wish us to believe that you have no idea where your son is hiding?" Antoine Desjardins asked in a snide voice.

"I do not know."

"I believe that is a lie," the Council member continued.

Burke bowed his head. He was a defeated male.

Theo leaned closer and whispered, "Am I next?"

"Yes."

She sat taller in her chair as I studied her profile. She was pale today. The shadows under her eyes were noticeable. Yesterday, she had spent six hours with Dr. Richards and then had retired to our room. She'd said little, and I didn't press. However, there were more nightmares than usual throughout the night.

Travis Burke was excused. The Sargent at Arms called, "Theodora Morrissey."

We stood as one, Theo, Onyx, Conal, Lore, and I.

TWENTY-TWO

NOVUS

THEODORA MORRISSEY

You Say by Lauren Daigle

THE PORTION WHERE I ANSWERED QUESTIONS WAS reasonably short. I think the Novus team had bored the Council Members to death by submitting hours of videos showing my everyday life with the Burke Pack. Onyx and his people had assembled pages of reports that were kept in huge binders that three Novus members had personally delivered to Edinburgh last week.

We came prepared, and for that I was grateful. My wrist did not carry the Novus brand, but I felt their support.

After my name was called, I walked to the small chair that was erected to face the Council Members who were shown on a large video screen in front of me. I didn't like having my back to the room. Onyx had prepared me for this fact, but as I moved to the chair, I felt rivulets of sweat run down my back.

The female identified herself as Carlotta Fromme. She appeared to be in her early fifties, but from Onyx's teachings, I knew that she was one of the youngest Lycans on the Council. She gave me what I would consider a friendly look as she spoke. "Seer, thank you for attending today's hearing. On behalf of the Council, I wish to issue a formal apology for what has transpired."

I knew this was to make me less nervous. I looked directly at the camera, "Thank you." Suddenly, I wasn't afraid. I had nothing to be worried about. My closest supporters would never allow anyone to approach. Although it was my duty to answer the Council's questions, I could always pretend to faint and further their belief that I was weak. Lore had assured me that it had been years since they'd had interactions with a human.

"Miss Morrissey, are we to believe that this attack was unprovoked?" The question came from a Council Member who was so old that the legend was he needed to choose a name when he'd joined the Council.

"That is correct." I had been instructed to keep my answers short.

"Please detail your prior interactions with Charles Burke." Miss Fromme glanced down at the paper in front of her.

"He was in attendance the day I was turned over to the Burke Pack." I shifted and crossed my legs. "I then saw him on three other occasions when my skills were needed."

"Were you ever alone with Charles Burke?" she continued.

"Never…not until that night." My voice quivered as I said the last word.

"We have reviewed the video of what transpired," she stated for the record. "Charles Burke was on a mission to do injury to you."

I didn't respond, but I was breathing heavily, trying to anticipate where she was going with this.

"Were you interested in having a liaison with Charles at all?"

"No." I couldn't control the challenging look I flashed the camera. I immediately dropped my gaze.

The aged male took over at this point. "He did great damage to your body?"

I wanted to smirk. They had the reports, and they'd seen the video. Clearly, that was true. "Yes. Three months have passed, and I am still recovering." I heard shuffling and whispers behind me, that amount of time must seem incredible to the quick-healing wolves.

"Will you recover?" Another female asked.

My heart was pounding. I wanted to check to see if my chest wall still contained the muscle. "I don't know." I swallowed so hard; it felt like I'd ingested shards of glass. "My bones will knit, and some of the scars can be made less noticeable." I paused because my voice was shaking. "The results of the trauma might never go away. The mental damage is…it affects me greatly." My eyes filled with tears. I hated admitting that. My friends expected me to be strong, or as strong as a human can be.

There was a long pause in the questioning.

Miss Fromme asked, "How should Charles Burke pay for this transgression?"

I honestly didn't know. The easy answer was with his

life, but I knew that was a given. However, that wasn't enough because I suffered daily, as did those who cared for me. Black... Jesus, he was tied to me, and I was a mess. I resorted to what was becoming my new normal. I told them what they wanted to hear. "That is not my decision. It is yours and The Lady's."

"The Lady's? What has she told you?" I now had their full interest. One male even leaned in closer.

I wished that I could see Lore. He would have given me a sign. I tried to feel him, but I wasn't sure that I did or if I was lying to myself. "The Lady has given me no indication of what she has planned."

"What has she told you?"

Careful. In truth, she had not communicated in any way although Black spent almost every evening outside with me. I wasn't going to disclose my fear that she had forgotten me. I licked my dry lips as I considered my response. "It is something that I know..."

They started to all speak at once.

I continued, "It is so deeply ingrained in my soul that I can only compare it to my ability to take a breath. I can't explain how my body knows to do it, but I am certain that it will." I tried to set my facial features into a serene expression. *The Seer has spoken.*

"I have some questions regarding your talent," Alyssa Duchene spoke.

What talent? One of the recriminating voices sounded in my mind. I forced it to be quiet, now was not the time to doubt myself. I worked to clear my head so that I could answer the powerful Council Member succinctly as my team had coached.

TWENTY-THREE

NOVUS

RAIDER BLACK

Better Days by the Goo Goo Dolls

"THAT WILL BE ALL, MS. MORRISSEY. THE COUNCIL thanks you for your service." Alyssa Duchene excused the Seer.

Theo didn't get to her feet right away.

The Sargent at Arms spoke loudly, "We shall take a twenty-minute break. Please return promptly."

She glanced up as I approached the podium where she had endured the questioning. "Am I really finished here?"

She looked exhausted. "Your part is complete."

She rested back in the chair and let out a long sigh.

"Do you want to stay to hear Dr. Richards' report?" Conal had joined me where I stood. "I'd say no."

"What do you think?" she asked me. "I know appearances matter."

"I think it would do you well to hear her thoughts on where you stand," I said, "but only if you won't attach negativity to it. You must keep in mind that she only met with you yesterday." There was no way that Sophia could comprehend all that Theo had been through and survived.

"You mean the weak human, blah-blah stuff?" One side of her mouth tipped upward.

I was happy to hear her use a mildly teasing tone. "There will be plenty of that. She will include that to appease the Council and the others; it is what they would expect to hear."

"I will stay." She held out her hand to me, and I helped her to her feet.

"I'm stiff," she said quietly.

"Honey, you barely moved for three hours. Of course, you are stiff," Conal told her.

We returned to our seats after Glass and Solle hugged Theo.

Once we were seated, I lifted her hand that once again wore my ring and placed a kiss above the circle. When she began to heal, she had been desperate to know if we had found her ring. I was prepared to send Lore to Texas to sneak onto Burke land to find it. Within forty-eight hours of our call to the hospital, it arrived at my office.

She gave me a brief smile, but her shoulders were tense. We had instructed her not to ask how her testimony had been received. There were too many ears close by. The look she gave declared that she understood.

She had done very well.

. . .

"So, what did you think about Sophia's report?" Theo asked me later as we prepared for sleep.

"It was thorough. I thought she had a good grasp on where you are." The doctor had given a detailed report regarding the physical injuries but had stressed the psychological trauma and how it could derail Theo's ability to live amongst us. She also hinted that it could affect her psychic gift.

"I like her." Theo rolled onto her side, facing me.

She'd used a casual tone when expressing that statement. "Why do I feel like you want something?"

"When I had to answer her questions, it was hard, but she was…easy to talk to. Does that make any sense? She didn't rush me or push."

"It does. Would you like for me to see if she would come to Novus for a few months?"

She shifted her body and then settled closer to me. "Would that be possible?" She frowned, "Would it be weird for you?"

"To learn that you found somebody with training that you are comfortable with? No, not at all." I was thrilled.

"But…how would it make you feel?"

I knew she was circling around something, but it wasn't clear. "Not weird." I used her word to tease her.

She let out a loud sigh. "You are going to make me say it, aren't you?"

"I don't know where you're going with this."

"Because you two had a thing."

I started to laugh. "That was…" I started to do the math, "over a hundred years ago." Her jealousy, no matter how she tried to hide it, thrilled my wolf and me.

She didn't say anything.

237

"At the time, it didn't mean anything. If you asked Sophia, she would tell you the same." Damn it, Solle never should have mentioned the very brief liaison.

"I didn't mean to offend." She cleared her throat lightly. "If you're sure that you would be okay...then I'd like for you or Solle to see if she would want to visit."

"I'll talk to Solle tomorrow. We will make it happen."

"I want to get better, Raid." She sounded hopeful and terrified.

Sophia's report had given me a lot to consider. What she didn't know from the exam was that Theo was a fighter, and how hard she would battle to survive.

"We get through tonight and tomorrow's parties, and then we are done." Conal had his boots up on the edge of the conference table.

"Are the nightly parties too much for you as you show off your beautiful mate?" I teased.

"She tires easily," my Second reported.

"I do not," his mate argued. "I said that because I was bored listening to all of those snobs. My cheeks still hurt from the fake smiling. Being polite is what is making me tired."

I turned serious. "I do thank you both for taking on those dinners."

"How is Theo doing today?" Solle asked.

"Two nightmares." I didn't add that she hadn't bothered even trying to fall back asleep after the second. "She is anxious about today's proceedings." I felt my wolf growl in frustration.

"I wish she didn't feel that she carries some responsibility for Siobhan's death." Solle's shoulders slumped.

"She grieves for the woman because she believes that she had no choice," I told them.

"Siobahn could have spoken up at any time," Conal's eyes narrowed in anger.

"She was her father's daughter, stubborn and too proud."

TWENTY-FOUR

NOVUS

THEODORA MORRISSEY

Bodies by Drowning Pool

I THOUGHT TODAY WOULD GO MUCH LIKE YESTERDAY'S hearing. Time spent in the large room where Roy Dolan would speak of the loss of his daughter at the hands of Raider Black and the Council would set the amount that the Dolan Pack would be paid for their loss.

Black had insisted that I sit on his left, over Onyx's objection. "She is mine, and I have no problem with the world knowing it."

The first hour went as expected. The Dolan Pack representative read parts of the Mating Contract into the record, and then listed Siobhan's attributes. I found it sad that her lineage far outweighed her personal qualities. Those thoughts I kept to myself as I sat very still on the hard wooden chair.

When it came time for Novus to speak, Black did so.

This seemed to cause a stir with the much smaller crowd than yesterdays.

He was dressed in a white button-down shirt tucked into black jeans. He addressed the Council in a strong voice as he recounted that Siobhan had been unhappy with the Novus Pack. She hadn't mixed with his Board or Pack and was critical of all things.

"I told her many times that she could leave. I would inform her father that I would accept responsibility for our failed mating." He didn't duck his head as he recounted the past conversations. "She chose to stay but did nothing to modify her standards or behavior." He paused, and I felt the room waited expectantly for his next words. "After I was made aware of the events that transpired with the Burke Pack, I told her that a plane was available to take her wherever she wished. I was formally breaking the contract. She was free to go."

"And yet she stayed." Alyssa Duchene was involved again in today's hearing.

"It was her choice."

"And you killed her."

"She attacked the Seer. Siobhan murdered one of my guards, and then assaulted a Marked human who was in my care." I assumed that everyone noticed the subtle change in his tone; it carried a hint of malice.

"And your lover." Alyssa did not sound challenging, but the comment was enough.

"My true mate," he countered in his kingly tone.

I felt every attendee's attention turn to me as I labored to control my breathing. To Black, this was nothing but a fact, but to my heart, it was a lifeline and the reason why I continued to fight every day.

I kept trying to use my gift. Something wasn't right,

or at least I felt that to be true. The Council had asked for ten minutes to review what they'd heard and to decide the compensation.

Roy Dolan got to his feet. "I would like to ask that I be allowed to offer an option."

And here it is.... I heard the words, in Lore's voice, inside my head. I did not trust a father who only thought of his daughter in monetary terms.

He continued when no Council Member responded. "We shall need to adjourn to the park." He paused and tilted his head slightly as if he was waiting for their answer. "For the Novus Pack's cooperation, I will reduce my asking price by half."

I felt my eyes widen at the offer. That was surprising and troubling.

Black responded immediately, "Of course, to the park."

Our people circled around us in the park. Conal observed, "Nobody saw that coming."

Issa spoke close to my ear, "Do not worry, Black can defeat any fighter of the Dolans'."

I didn't want this, but I was powerless to stop it. I could only nod in agreement.

We gathered in an open field. Black, Glass, and Onyx stood on a set of risers that overlooked the field, along with the Dolan contingent and the Sargent at Arms from today's hearing. I was surrounded by my guards with Conal behind me. I knew he was near in case I freaked out at the violence. Nobody was sure of how I would react, including me.

The Sargent at Arms spoke loud enough for us to hear, "All right Roy, we have gathered. Issue your challenge."

I watched Black. He had a slight smile on his face as he waited to hear his name. He held no fear. Hell, he lived for this shit.

Roy Dolan paused dramatically waiting for all gazes to rest upon him before he chose to speak. "My best fighter will meet the one who caused us much damage, Theodora Morrissey."

I know my eyes widened, but I don't think I exhibited any other signs of surprise. *So today, I die.* A part of me didn't mind. It would end my misery.

Black's eyes narrowed as I heard the rumble of many voices behind me. I think Issa moved in closer to provide a barrier.

The Sargent at Arms spoke again. "That is impossible. In fact, The Council forbids it."

Before relief could set in, Lore spoke, "I volunteer." He whipped his shirt over his head. "As a member of the Novus Pack, I will fight in the Seer's place."

"Lore…" I lunged for his arm, but Conal pulled me back with an arm around my belly. I didn't fight the huge male. I stood stiffly against him as I watched Lore saunter toward the center of the field.

Conal's breath was hot against my ear. "Let him," he urged. "Any doubts you show will be interpreted as you fear him weak. I know that you do not."

Lorenzo Barducci was not weak. I didn't make a move as he traveled deeper into the circle.

"Allow him to honor you, Novus, and his name," Conal continued.

I made a sound of agreement deep in my chest because I couldn't form any words as I watched my friend walk confidently into battle.

Lore paused in front of the risers and bowed deeply

to Black, and turned in my direction and gave what could only be described as a cheeky grin. He then walked toward the other male like the prince he was, with his head held high, his chest thrust out, not hurrying but also not holding back. He was fuckin' gorgeous and so confident.

It had registered when we first met that he was attractive, but today, his muscles were shredded, and with his swagger, he took my breath away. *He is made for this.* The thought invaded my brain. I quickly offered a small prayer to The Lady, and for good measure, I added Lady Octavia, Lore's mother, asking for them to protect the brave male.

Lore met the Dolan fighter in the center. As the other male made his move, Lore did nothing to shield his body. His chest took the blow and the crowd cheered. Lore only smiled, communicating that he had allowed it to happen.

Solle moved next to Conal, "Why is he doing that?"

I knew. He was allowing the male to feel superior, so that when he struck it would be a crushing blow, physically and mentally. Lore wanted to take away his hope. He not only would inflict pain on the male's body, but also to his psyche.

I swallowed hard as my eyes tried to follow the fight. Lore was accepting blows and following up with punishing strikes that did great damage. I think it was the look of enjoyment on his face that should have scared the Dolan male and the rest of the crowd.

All Lycans were violent. I'd been taught this from the start. I'd accepted it. I'd witnessed Black administer pain. However, Lore... Lore *needed* to do violence. He held it under control, but it was with him, always. He liked to inflict pain.

And I'd never feared him after that first night. He would never turn on me; I knew this to be the truth. But like Black, if I should ever become dangerous to others, he would end my life without a thought. Perhaps that was why I trusted him so much; I was utterly safe with him.

The Dolan male was on the ground, bleeding from multiple wounds with Lore on his knees beside him. He turned his body to face Black and inquired, "Laird?"

Black responded, "Enough."

Lore rose gracefully to his feet and again bowed to his Leader.

Roy Dolan voice sounded like thunder, "What is this? What kind of male is he to let him live?"

Lore paused and gave Roy Dolan a superior look that was befitting a Prince.

"He bested your man. The Lore needs to do no more," Black announced.

I feared that Roy Dolan would attack.

"Twenty-five," Black told the Leader. "Onyx, send the money."

Roy Dolan's mouth opened and closed twice, but I could hear no words.

Lore made his way to where I stood and dropped to his knee. "My Queen."

I stepped away from Conal's body. "You have made me very proud, Lorenzo." I touched the back of his sweaty neck. "Rise and enjoy your victory."

He stood and gave me a huge smile. He turned and was immediately surrounded by females. I hoped that he would have a perfect day and evening. He deserved it.

TWENTY-FIVE

NOVUS

RAIDER BLACK

Good Times, Bad Times by Godsmack

"HE DID IT TO HURT THEO, AND ULTIMATELY NOVUS," I told them as I refilled Conal's glass.

"He had to know the Council wouldn't allow the Seer to fight." Solle was slowly rubbing her stomach.

Conal arched an eyebrow. "I don't think Roy expected Lore to volunteer to be her champion. I'm sure he thought it would be you."

"My question is, how did Lore know?" I paused. "You mentioned twice that he seemed excited about this trip... I mean, Lore, excited?"

"So, you think that none of it was a surprise?" Solle drew her eyebrows together. "Lore was impressive."

My spy had been in control from the moment he'd stepped into the make-shift ring. He'd played with the representative of the Dolan Pack, the head of their guard. I had never doubted that Lorenzo was vicious, but it was his controlled brutality that fascinated me. He truly was a masterful wolf.

"You should be greatly honored that he bows to you," Conal observed.

"What did Theo say during the fight?" At the time, I'd thought it odd that Dolan had requested the conclusion of the meeting transpire outside, but since I'd done damage to his Pack, I didn't object. I would fight.

The agreement had been that once a punitive fine was assessed, we'd be done. The matter settled. But to call for Theo's blood…that would not be forgotten by Novus or me. We now considered Roy Dolan, an enemy.

"She tried to grab his arm to stop him," Conal said. "I pulled her in so that I could control her, but also so that I could interpret what she would see."

"Did she struggle?" I'd worried over how she'd felt being held by another male, even someone she considered a close friend.

"No, but her body shook the entire time. As soon as he stepped forward, I told her that if she tried to stop him, her action would dishonor his name. She then leaned back into me." Conal glanced at Solle.

She nodded and turned to me. "Since the attack, her connection with Lore has grown. I think it's because they share emotional scars." Solle bit down on her lip. "I can't say that I liked Lore much at first, then I didn't *not* like him, but after yesterday, I know he would do anything for her and for you."

"And Novus," Conal added.

Theo had not joined us for breakfast. She was still resting. I hoped that she felt a degree of relief knowing that the Dolan chapter of our lives was decided and over.

I would keep a close eye on our dealings with his Pack. His plan had been foiled by those most loyal to Theo and Novus. He left monetarily richer, but his stature had decreased. I owed Lore much. He'd truly bested the fighter and brought honor to his name.

The Packleader and I did not share a handshake after the battle. It wouldn't be that easy. I could only hope that Dolan would go home and look at his accounting ledgers and realize that our business agreement was profitable to both of our packs. He could hold a grudge against me personally, but not against Theo or Novus.

"I would appreciate it if you would stick close to her today, Solle." Conal and I would be in meetings all afternoon.

"Oh, uhm, okay." She glanced at Conal briefly.

"I told you I didn't want you to go there." Conal's voice had taken on a slight growl. He then looked at me. "Her birth family is close by," he explained.

Solle's lips tightened, but she nodded her head. "I'll hang with Theo, maybe by the pool...?"

Later, my phone vibrated in my pocket for the third time in the last two minutes. I pulled it out and checked the screen.

Theo: I couldn't stop her. So, I'm going with her.

Theo: She wants to visit her mother's grave.

Theo: Don't be mad at the guards. Solle tricked them.

This, we did not need. I interrupted the speaker from Vermont, or another of those cold, small places. "I apologize, sir, but I must deal with an issue." I shot Conal a look, and we packed up our things and left the meeting room.

In the hallway, my Second asked, "What's going on?" He was looking at his own phone.

"Where does Solle's family live?"

His gaze shot up from his screen. "*Fuuuuckk.* I forbade her from traveling there. It isn't safe. How will she explain that she has not aged in almost fifty years?"

TWENTY-SIX

NOVUS

THEODORA MORRISSEY

Highway to Hell by AC/DC

I DIDN'T NEED MY GIFT TO TELL ME THIS WAS A BAD IDEA, but I couldn't let my best-friend go alone. I'd hoped that I could talk her out of it on our way to the garage where vehicles were stored for our use.

I continued arguing as we got on the freeway and headed south while Solle negotiated the heavy traffic with ease. "I thought you weren't allowed to see your family." The dread I felt was increasing with each mile.

With her gaze on the road ahead, Solle grimaced. "They were pissed after I took off with Conal. Javi had wanted me to hook-up with the leader of the Fire Eaters. Since he was the head of the family, and I disobeyed him, they disowned me. When I called to tell my mama that Conal and I were mated, I called it married…she hung up on me."

This was the first time that she had ever shown that mating with Conal wasn't perfect. Giving up her human life had taken a toll. "That was long ago, Solle, and I do understand what that feels like." I tried to empathize with her, but this was a huge risk for so many reasons. "What if somebody sees you or the person from the church mentions your call? How will you explain that you haven't aged?"

"I told Mrs. Moreno I was Solle's daughter and not to tell my family I was going to visit." She flipped her hair over her shoulder. "I want to see her grave to explain to her about Conal and to tell her about the baby."

Black had allowed her to continue her medical studies but, in the end, her vocation had benefitted Novus. She'd walked away from her family and all that she'd known for Conal. "I get it, but we're going to be in so much trouble when we get back."

"I'll handle it," she told me confidently.

I was glad I'd managed to send those texts to Black while she searched for the keys, not that it excused me for disobeying his orders, but now he knew the reason why.

Her old neighborhood was filled with tiny, rundown one-story houses with men gathered on the porch steps or on corners.

"Very different from my house now..." she said quietly.

I agreed. "I imagine it was a huge culture shock, moving from here to Nebraska."

"I'd always wanted out. I hated it here." She stopped and backed into an open space. "That's the church." She pointed across the street to a rundown Catholic church with a small cemetery beside it.

"Do you want me to snap some pictures for you to have?" And I could send them to Black because my inner sense was shouting an even stronger warning.

"That would be nice." We got out of the car and crossed the street. Solle opened the rickety metal gate that wouldn't have kept a toddler out and looked around. "Her grave is under a shade tree in the eastern corner." Solle pointed in the direction of tall stones, many shaped like a cross.

Some of the plots were well tended with bouquets of drying flowers, others seemed to have been long forgotten. I followed her while trying to pay attention to my instincts.

"There!" She pointed at a reddish marble stone. "That's mama's." Solle walked faster, and then stopped in front of her mother's final resting place.

After ten or maybe fifteen minutes a man approached us, and rapid-fire Spanish was exchanged. I caught the word "*puta*" so I knew the discussion wasn't going well.

Solle was furious. Her hands were balled into fists at her sides as she raised her voice. When he folded his arms over his chest, Solle turned and grabbed my arm. "Come on. Let's go."

I didn't argue. I wanted to be on the freeway, far away from here. I was so tense that I could only take in short, shallow breaths. It felt like an iron band was around my chest.

When we started toward the gate, we were suddenly surrounded by more men blocking our way. The cemetery was full of people, and they didn't look friendly.

"Solle?" I whispered as I looked for a path to escape.

"Do not move," a man in his early forties stepped forward, followed by a man wearing a priest's cassock.

"You think you can keep me here?" Solle fired back as she stepped a little bit in front of me.

He gave a wicked laugh that caused the hair on my arms to stand up. "Papa always said you were the smart one," he said, his chin tilting higher in challenge.

"You have no idea what I am." Solle dropped her hand to her hip as she confronted the man who must be related to her. They shared the same cheekbones and eye color.

"You are correct, but I do know that the Devil has touched your soul. You are his tool." He got right in Solle's face. "How dare you desecrate your mother's grave with your evil?"

I felt Solle's anger radiate from her body. I needed to diffuse this now before she did something reckless. "Look, sir…" I stepped around Solle. "My friend said that she wanted to see the grave. I'm sure she meant no disrespect."

He turned his hate-filled eyes on to me. My inner voice screamed, *Killer*. "So, she brought you here with her, did she? That is very unfortunate for you." He looked me up and down.

"What's it going to take for you to let us leave?" Solle asked, her words clipped.

"When Maria-Christina told me that a call came in asking about your mother's grave, I knew it was you. My father, your brother, told us that you gave yourself to a servant of the devil."

This was insane and terrifying because I could see that these people believed what was being said.

The man continued, "I made a call to our friends. They want to see you, to play with you perhaps? The Fire Eaters do not fear evil." Then he flashed a smile that made my heart skip several beats because I'd seen Black use it right before he'd ripped somebody's head off.

"I have money," I told him. "What if I give you money? And you let us get out of here."

"Theo..." Solle said quietly.

"Your friend...she is rich?" he asked Solle.

I answered because I didn't believe Solle understood our situation. I could barely comprehend it myself; this was like some third-rate horror movie. We needed to get away. "To get to our car and to have safe passage off of this block, how much?"

The man looked over his shoulder at our ride, and then back at me.

It was taking too long. I couldn't depend on Black getting my message, and we needed to go now. "Twenty-five? Forty? Fifty?" I lifted my phone started to punch in numbers clumsily. Black had allowed me a phone for this trip because we were going to be apart so much. Issa had shown me how to get to my banking information. "What's it going to take?" I glanced at the man.

"You think you can buy me? I am a servant of God," he roared.

"No, I don't think that, but I'm hoping we can agree on an amount so that we can get out of here."

"I got this," Solle told me, aiming a warning glance my way.

"You can't change," I said, trying to use my gift and send a push with my words, praying it would work this once. "The baby," I reminded her. Pregnant females couldn't change. Changing would abort the fetus. It was why it was incredibly difficult for a Lycan to carry a child to term.

"I won't let them hurt you," she vowed.

I couldn't let her sacrifice her child for me. "No," I said, using my calmest voice. "We are going to agree on a sum, and then we are going to go."

He chuckled. "I like your friend," he told Solle. "She's a little *loco*."

I held up my phone and said recklessly. "Just type in an amount and transfer it." I hated that I sounded breathless, but I was desperate.

I felt another approach from the back and pull me against him. I fought. I didn't know him, and I couldn't stand that he was touching me.

"Just put in a sum and let her go," Solle raised her voice.

"We will see what the Fire Eaters say."

I struggled against the man's hold until I saw a blade glint in the bright sun. I felt a tiny sting at the side of my throat, and I stopped fighting. "Don't." My word was directed at Solle, but my captor thought I meant him because he laughed cruelly.

Then I felt *him*. I knew he was near, and he was enraged. I tried not to move as I looked sharply to my left to see if Solle sensed their approach. She'd gone rigid. "Don't change, Solle," I repeated. I knew what was coming and that her wolf would want to join the fight.

And then all hell broke loose.

For as long as I live, I will never forget the scene of the Lycans leaping in wolf form from rooftop to rooftop. It was as amazingly beautiful as it was utterly terrifying. My captor's hold loosened, and I did as I'd been trained.

I dropped to the ground, landing on my ass. When I rolled away from him, he screamed in terror as a huge black wolf landed in front of him.

I looked for Solle, knowing she would smell blood and feel the need for violence, but she could not participate. I crawled away from the fighting on my hands and knees, and then I got to my feet and ran, bent over, to where I thought I saw her hair.

"Theo," she yelled.

I threw myself on top of her, shielding her from the body parts that were flying by. "Just stay with me. Solle, promise you'll stay with me," I begged my friend. "Don't change, please don't change."

I don't remember much about how we got out of California. I know it was rushed. When Black pulled me off Solle, he was still breathing heavily, and very angry. I glanced around, and Christ, there was blood and gore everywhere. Then everything went dark.

I woke up in Black's huge bed on Novus land. I'd slept almost eighteen hours if the clock and my math were correct. I used the bathroom, brushed my teeth, washed my face, and ran a brush through my hair. There was a bandage the size of a dollar bill on my neck. As I stared at the stark white gauze, yesterday's events rocketed back through my mind.

"You're up." Black stood in the bathroom's doorway.

"Have you slept?" I didn't think I needed to comment on the obvious.

"No. There was quite a bit to clean up." He crossed his arms over his chest.

"How's Solle? Is...is the baby okay?" While I'd been shielding her body, I'd felt her wolf fighting to change.

"According to Conal, she is awake, and both she and the baby are fine."

I knew I needed to get straight to the point. Black was a big believer in admitting your mistakes. "Did anybody get hurt?"

"Do you mean besides the decimation of a city block, Theodora?"

I could hear the fury in his slow delivery. "I couldn't let her go alone."

He opened his mouth to respond but then tipped his head to the side. "Hold that thought." He turned abruptly and left the doorway.

I followed him into the living room as he headed to the door, and then I heard the single knock. I knew who was on the other side because Conal only knocked once.

Black opened the door to his Second. "Didn't expect to see you today."

Conal burst into our quarters. "Need to take care of something."

Black slowly closed the door.

"Need a moment with Theo," Conal told Black, but his gaze was on me.

I felt my heart thud faster. Conal was a big man, taller than Black by two or three inches, and he outweighed him by around thirty pounds. I considered him to be one of my closest friends, and from the beginning, I'd trusted him implicitly. I didn't move as he approached, but he wasn't smiling, and he didn't reach out to offer a hug.

"I think I'll stay," Black continued in that same slow

cadence as he followed Conal into the living room and leaned against the side of the wing chair.

"You don't have to," I told him. I was confused by Conal's tone and the rigidity of his shoulders.

"I think I do," he said, using his kingly tone.

I tried to silently communicate to him that he needed to allow Conal to say whatever was so important that he'd left his mate alone to come here.

Conal glanced over his shoulder at Black, as if he was measuring the distance and how many steps it would take before Black could attack him.

"Would you like to sit down?" I asked our friend.

"No, I would not." He took another step closer. "How could you, Theodora? How could you let her go there?"

I stiffened at his closeness and tone which wasn't friendly. "I couldn't stop her, Conal. She wanted to see her mother's grave...to tell her about the baby..." I didn't move. I knew he was barely holding onto his control.

"She could have died," he shouted, his voice thundering in the quiet room.

I couldn't help myself, as I took a few steps away from him. Trying not to infuriate him or his wolf any further, I made sure that I spoke quietly, calmly. "She was going there with or without me. I thought that—"

"You didn't fucking think." He took another step. I could feel his body's heat, he was so close.

A small whimper escaped my throat as I forced my body not to flinch.

"You didn't stop her; you didn't tell a guard. You let my mate go and did nothing."

I saw Black straighten. He was going to intervene. "Back off, Conal." It was an order.

I needed to take control. I waited for Conal to take a step back and I spoke, "I tried to talk her out of it."

"You didn't do enough. You put my mate and my young in danger," he roared.

I felt Black's rage. I turned to him and gave him a pleading look not to interrupt. I then focused on Conal, "I tried."

He moved in again. "Not hard enough."

I felt his spittle land on my face and neck as he yelled. He was scaring me. I felt my body begin to shake.

"I will never forgive you for this, Theodora."

Black had joined us. His hand was against the small of my back. It was hot and vibrating as he held back his anger.

My chest tightened. "I tried, Conal. She would have gone anyway. I think it has to do with motherhood…" I tried to defend her…our…actions.

His face was red, his features taut. "You didn't fuckin' think. Do you have any idea how much work this caused us? How much you're costing us? It's like you want to ruin Novus." He looked at our leader, and then back at me. "Do you secretly hate Black that much for choosing Siobhan over you?"

What? My jaw sagged a little. I blinked at a sudden stinging in my eyes. He couldn't really mean that. "You know that's not true," I cried.

"If I so much as see you in the same room as my mate, I will kill you." He addressed Black. "I can't trust her. I don't want her anywhere near my family."

"Conal—"

"You are dead to us."

"Conal, please?" I started to beg.

"You almost got my mate and my young killed. *You*, Theodora. We took you in, gave you a home, loved you, and this is how you repay us? If it wasn't for my mate, you would still be in Texas at Charles Burke's mercy."

"Conal..." I needed them...what would I do without them?

"We should have left you there," he said, his voice becoming ragged and low. "We'd all have been better off without you." He turned and headed to the door. When he reached it, he turned one last time. "Remember my words. I will kill you, and I will kill him if he tries to stop me. Stay away from us." He threw open the door and left without closing it.

My knees gave out, and I fell to the floor. My heart was breaking.

Black lifted me from the carpet and carried me to the sofa. "I'll talk to him."

"Don't," I told him in a sob.

"He has the wrong idea."

"I don't want him to turn that anger onto Solle," I said, gripping the front of his T-shirt. "He can't unleash that kind of anger on her, not now."

"He should know the truth, Theo."

"Black, please don't," I implored him. "Let him be mad at me... I don't want there to be problems between them. You know how risky a Lycan pregnancy can be."

"He has to know you would never do anything to hurt them," Black told me slowly. "In time, he'll see reason. He'll calm down and figure it out."

"I don't want Solle to suffer any more stress than she already has. Nothing can happen to this baby, Black." I leaned away from him so that I could clearly see his face. "Please, let him blame me."

"He threatened you…in front of me." His voice had gone scary calm.

"He just had a terrible shock. His mate and baby could have died. He's angry because he felt so helpless." Now, I was making excuses for Conal's reaction and decision.

"He threatened you," Black said with a little more heat.

I didn't want to think about not seeing Solle. We talked every day. "Please allow him to be mad at me… for Solle and the baby." I bit down on my lip. "I don't want them to have problems. They deserve to be happy. If it makes things better between them to…to cut me out," my voice cracked, "then let them."

He didn't answer right away. His frown deepened. "I don't like this."

"Conal will calm down, and he'll figure it out, or maybe Solle will tell him everything." If that happened, then we could go back to being good friends.

"I will not allow this to go on forever."

"Think of the baby." I rushed my words.

"I will, but Theodora, it is my decision."

Seven months wasn't that long, really. I'd miss our friendship and watching Solle's pregnancy progress but it would all work out in the end. It had to.

Another knock sounded on the door. "I am expecting a call. It is important." Black lifted me to my feet and stood.

While he was on his call, I took a shower. Under the hot water, I realized Black hadn't said that the other things Conal had shouted were false. I leaned my back against the tile and lowered my body slowly to the floor as the water fell upon my body. Did he believe his Second's charges? Was I a detriment to the Pack? And to him? The Council had agreed that I should stay with Novus, and yet, I still didn't carry the Novus brand. I held out my scarred right forearm. It would hurt like hell, but it would mean that I belonged.

He doesn't want you anymore. If he did, you'd be wearing his brand. I tried to quiet the voices in my head.

He watched Charles Burke fuck you. You are soiled. Even the doctor couldn't say if you were redeemable. I covered my ears, trying to shut out the voices. "Stop, please stop," I cried while I began to rock back and forth. I didn't want to hear those truths.

If Solle had not implored Black to save me, would he have traveled to Texas?

"Make them stop. Please, make them stop."

TWENTY-SEVEN

NOVUS

RAIDER BLACK

Broken Halos by Chris Stapleton

WEEKS HAD PASSED SINCE WE'D RETURNED FROM California, and I was barely holding it together. I was being pulled in so many different directions and doing a shitty job at everything. Conal and I barely spoke, and when we did, it was in short sentences about Pack business only. I snapped at my people often, and I feared they had begun to avoid me on purpose. Onyx seemed to be enjoying the chaos, and that concerned me. It was those you trusted, who usually made the killing blow.

I leaned back in my office chair and closed my eyes as I rested my head against the padding. Charles Burke was in Northern Canada under the protection of the Red Pack. I was allowing the Council to take the necessary steps. However, the Leader of the Reds was one of the least progressive in the world, and we knew little about their pack or their holdings. It was widely believed they didn't have electricity in the castle they used as their Packhouse. In fact, the few times that it had been necessary, I'd dealt with his Second, his half-brother Bredon. I feared it might be years before they surrendered Charles if we continued to rely upon diplomacy.

We didn't have that time. I was losing Theo. She was wasting away, and I didn't know how to save her.

"Laird," Basil's voice sounded through my phone's intercom, "Dr. Richards and Lore are here."

I sat up and pressed the "talk" button. "Send them in."

They took the chairs in front of my desk. "Thank you for seeing me, Laird." Sophia bowed her head. She'd arrived five weeks ago. She met daily with Theo and then worked various shifts at our hospital.

"What is on your mind?"

"I'm concerned about Theodora." The doctor crossed her legs. "She is not improving or even plateauing."

Theo rarely left our bedroom.

"Although I did study psychology at one time, I fear that Theodora's problems are too extensive. I am not equipped to really help her."

"She likes you and trusts you," I told the doctor, "that has to mean something." I recognized the desperation in my tone. She'd been a witness when Glass had once again placed the Novus brand on Theo's inner forearm. I'd hoped that knowing she was once again a member of my Pack would help her.

"And I like her very much, but she needs more and better help if she is to improve."

"The issue with the MacGregors has hurt her greatly," Lore said in his very matter-of-fact way.

I glanced at Sophia. "Are you suggesting that I speak with Conal?"

"Lore is correct. Losing two of her closest friends and supporters has been a setback, but I think we need to explore other options at this point. The void left by their friendship and support is only one contributor." Sophia's lips tightened into a straight line. "I would never presume to tell you, Laird, what to do."

"We've tried to bring other doctors here. It didn't work out." I grew exasperated. I didn't want her to be subtle or say the right things to stroke my ego. Not now. I wanted her to save Theo.

"Laird..." Lore's gaze locked with mine. "You spend every night with our Seer. Even you must admit that Theo is not herself. She is traumatized, and I fear..."

"What do you fear Lorenzo?" I asked too sharply. I knew he was going to say aloud what scared the shit out of me.

"I fear that she will do harm to herself to end her pain."

I squeezed my eyes closed as the truth was stated. The woman who shared my bed was not the woman I'd met and fallen in love with. This Theo had to be reminded to shower. She was too docile. Too agreeable. She rarely offered an opinion and was so silent, and still...it was as if a part of her soul had disappeared. "I hold that fear also," I admitted and then felt defeated.

Sophia and Lore both were silent. I think that I'd surprised them by agreeing.

Sophia cleared her throat and spoke in a tentative manner, "Has she shared those thoughts with you?"

267

"Several times, Theo has said she doesn't feel that she's contributing to Novus and that she's not being a good partner to me." I swallowed the boulder that had lodged in my throat. "I thought at first she referred to intimacy, but since our return from the west coast, I believe she means in all ways. She has also shared that she believes she'll never recover from the attack."

Sophia didn't speak as she reached into her briefcase. "I have information regarding several options that I think we should discuss before it is too late."

"Go on." I knew I wasn't going to like this, but I needed to help Theo.

She pulled out her tablet then tapped and swiped the screen. "There's a facility in Tennessee that specializes in working with women who've been physically traumatized. The programs start with twelve weeks of therapy, but can last as long as twenty-six."

"She must be accompanied by guards."

She didn't even lift her eyes from the screen. "There is an outpatient program in Northern California..."

"No."

"Laird, she needs intensive therapy. I mean no disrespect, but being surrounded by those who care for her might actually impede her progress." Sophia's tone softened the chastising words. As the independent thinking daughter of a long-time Packleader, she knew how to present her opinions.

"What are you saying?"

Lore surprised me by answering, "We do not push the Seer. I, myself, am guilty of this. If I see that she is having a bad time, I do not encourage her to ready herself for the day." He bowed his head.

I did the same thing. Fuck, she was right. "Tell me," I

said, my voice huskier than before, "tell me what you think would be best for Theo."

"My first choice would be the intensive therapy in Tennessee, but I do understand the safety concerns. She could not bring guards. I admit that with her gift, although it appears to be dormant, I worry about her being there alone."

It had been another blow to Theo's psyche that her gift had disappeared. "We cannot send her there."

Sophia sat back in her chair and rested her tablet on her lap. "I know of a doctor who I think might be able to help Theo. She does intensive work and only sees a few patients at a time."

A thousand objections and questions filled my head, but I did not speak. I had run out of options.

"Her name is Bayla Joseph, and she runs a private counseling practice in Ohio." When I didn't interrupt, she continued. "She is brilliant, and I've heard her speak several times. She approaches each case, not as a research opportunity, but as a chance to help the patient improve and live the best life they can. She doesn't claim to be able to cure, but I think she may be able to help Theodora learn to deal with her feelings."

"Where in Ohio?"

She glanced at her tablet. "Dayton. It appears to be in the middle part of the state."

"That is in the general area where Theo grew up." I wondered if that would bring her comfort or whether the memories of her uncle's act would torment her. "Tell me more about this Dr. Joseph."

"She graduated first in her class. She completed several fellowships with top hospitals, but for the last ten

269

years, she has worked with a very limited practice." Sophia again glanced at her screen.

"What happened ten years ago?"

Sophia's eyes widened for a moment. "She was driving with her husband, and an impaired driver hit them. Her husband died."

"So, she has experienced a personal loss…" My wolf stirred and did not argue with my thought process. "How do you think that has affected her ability to help her patients?"

"I think that because she has experienced and lives with trauma and pain that she would be a better doctor."

"I agree that your Dr. Joseph sounds ideal. So, please tell me what you are thinking, Sophia. I know you came in here with a plan."

She drew a deep breath. "We are talking months, Laird. Theo would need to move to Ohio and probably see Bayla four or five days a week."

Sophia did not disappoint with her plan. I considered what she offered. "We would need permission to stay in the area. I can make that call personally."

Lore shifted forward in his seat. "She would only need a small number of guards.

Although dread filled me at the thought of her going, I said, "Please contact Dr. Joseph, and if need be, make arrangements to travel to meet with her. I want Theo to be given her full attention. Offer her double, and if need be, triple her rate. Once the arrangements are made, we will present this plan to Theo."

Sophia nodded twice. "Yes, Laird. I will update you shortly."

"Thank you," I said, excusing her.

Lore did not follow the doctor, so I knew he had something on his mind. I raised an eyebrow silently inquiring.

"Do you worry that Theo might speak of the Lycan world?"

"No." It would sound like a hallucination. "I will discuss it with her, but I am not concerned." Theo had never tried to run. She had accepted our world and knew that if she did speak of the Lycan world, I would sentence her to death.

My spy did not move to take his leave, so I knew that he had more on his mind.

"I will go with her."

I nodded. I'd expected as much. "As will Issa. Hand-pick who you want." A large group would draw attention, but three or four moving into a house would not seem out of the ordinary.

"And what if...if she begins to..." Lore seemed to be having problems articulating his worry.

Yes. My mind had traveled there as well. I gripped the arms of my chair. "It is my duty to protect our race. If she cannot handle her gift, if and when it returns, then she must be destroyed." I sounded so calm, and yet, my stomach cramped, and my wolf howled in concern.

"And if we cannot wait for your arrival?"

I barely breathed. "Then you must do what needs to be done. She would never want to be a threat to the safety of our world or the humans," I reminded him.

He did not disagree.

"In caring for her, we must bear the responsibility that one day, we might be her executioners."

"The ultimate promise and obligation," he said softly.

"I pray it will never come to that." I would pray to The Lady every day.

"I agree." Lore bowed his head slowly and then stood.

"Theo trusts you, as do I," I told the loner who had changed his life to care for Theo.

"I believe that if she can recover, she will be stronger." He left me, closing my door with a quiet click.

I let out a long breath and closed my eyes again. I hoped that she could heal. I missed my Theo, and I knew that she hated what she was experiencing. I had found her many times in the past few weeks bemoaning that she couldn't face the day. She recognized that she was failing, and it made her hate herself more.

I wished that I could speak to Conal about this or Solle. In the past, they had always offered good counsel, and at times commiseration, but now that was not an option. I was alone.

TWENTY-EIGHT

NOVUS

THEODORA MORRISSEY

In My Blood by Shawn Mendes

I WAS HUDDLED IN THE CORNER OF THE WALK-IN CLOSET. I held my knees tightly to my chest where I'd buried my face. It had been three hours since I'd seen her. Conal had not come to kill me, so a part of me thought he wouldn't act.

I heard Black's low voice rumble as he said some words to Issa, and then excused her. They were very careful to always to speak loud enough so that I could hear them. I felt him standing over me, probably trying to figure out what to say. It had to be exhausting; the need to be so careful around me. I honestly didn't know why he still kept me around. I was a liability.

"I hear you had a rough outing today."

I raised my head to look at him. "I tried to get away," I swore. "I didn't see her until...until it was too late."

Solle had looked so beautiful, healthy and rounded. Her long hair had been pulled back from her face with a clip. She'd been wearing a white wool coat.

"Mind if I join you?" He didn't wait for me to answer before he planted his ass beside me. "Start at the beginning."

"Issa made me go out today. She said that it was sunny, and I needed more shampoo. So, we were shopping, I was walking from the drugstore to the bakery. I wanted to get you those doughnuts you like." I tried to smile at him, but it felt like I'd forgotten how to. He'd given me so much, and the best I could do was fucking fried dough. *Loser,* my inner voice reminded me.

"We haven't had those in a while." His deep voice held a note of warmth.

"I was thinking about getting the doughnuts and maybe some cookies…I was trying to figure out how many to get when I heard her call my name. We were almost face to face, Black. I didn't have anywhere to go," I rushed to explain.

"It was bound to happen. The town's not that big." He wrapped his arm around my shoulders.

I steeled my muscles so that I didn't shudder at his touch. I hated my body's reaction. I liked his touch. In fact, I craved the comfort he gave, but my body didn't understand. I counted backwards slowly from ten. By three, I was more relaxed. "She looked so good. So happy. I think I stared at her for a minute. I was so glad to see her and that she was fine." I didn't mention that a little part of me noted that the loss of our friendship hadn't seemed to have upset her at all. "She finally spoke and said, 'Are you okay?'"

By the concern in her voice, I obviously wasn't. "I

could hear Conal's edict in my head, so I... I started to back away, and she grabbed my arm to stop me." I felt the tears coming. "Issa stepped between us and told her that we needed to go."

"I know it had to be hard seeing her."

"She...she said, 'Why Theo?' like this was my fault." I buried my face against his chest. God, it hurt so bad. "I protected her, and she magically forgets it all?" My chest ached where I knew my heart was beating.

"Did you say any more?"

I shook my head. I'd rushed to our SUV and told Issa that I wanted to go home where I was safe. Very few people visited me anymore. Maybe being my friend, associating with me, was bad for the Novus members. Did they think I wasn't worth their time? How long would it be before Black gave up on me?

For the last two days, I couldn't stop crying. I didn't want anything to eat, and I couldn't sleep. The nightmares came when I closed my eyes. The voices in my head never seemed to stop. I'd tried ignoring the horrible words. I used to know that they were wrong, but now, I saw that they held merit. I was so tired of this, the hurting, the fear, and the isolation. I'd glanced at Black last night, and he'd looked like he hadn't slept in days. I knew he worried about me, the intended mate that couldn't get out of bed. Plus, there were rumors that things were tense at the Novus office. He and Conal rarely spoke, because of me. Everything was falling apart.

It would be better if I was gone. I could go to the kitchen and grab a knife claiming that I wanted to prepare some food. If Issa was suspicious of my hunger, there was a pair of scissors in the vanity's top drawer that had a sharp point. I glanced at the balcony door. I wondered if I jumped over the railing, would my fall to the frozen ground be enough to kill me?

Did I want to die?

It would bring the peace and quiet that I craved. Finally, I would be able to rest.

Today, I was again in the closet. Conal still hadn't come for me. I should feel relief, but instead, I wished that he had. The voices were louder, more insistent. I glanced through the opening toward the bathroom then through the door toward the kitchen, considering which knife to grab in order to do the most damage. I could feel the coolness of the metal in my hand as I pushed the tip into my body. There would be a burning sensation and pain but finally, I would have relief.

"Issa," my voice shook.

She looked up from the magazine she'd been studying for the last hour. "My Lady?"

"I…I need Black."

"He should be back…"

"Issss," I felt the hysteria pour from my body as I hissed her name. "I need him now. Tell him that, and then don't let me out of your sight. Please, Iss, you've got to help me." My eyes filled with tears. This was it, I was done. "If you leave me alone…I think…no I know…that I will…do something final."

TWENTY-NINE

RAIDER BLACK

In the End by Linkin Park

I REACHED FOR MY CELL THAT WAS NOW VIBRATING across my desk. I glanced at the caller i.d. before tapping the screen. "Issa?"

"Laird, she is asking that you come home now."

I was on my feet and moving to my office door. "How bad?" Theo had done little but cry and then apologize for crying in the last few days.

"She ordered me not to let her out of my sight." Issa paused and then lowered her voice, "She fears that she might hurt herself."

"Christ," I growled. "Don't leave her alone for any reason," I ordered.

"No Sir."

"Even if she orders you from the room Issa, Do Not Leave Her Alone." I jogged down the hallway and then took the stairs in great leaps. As soon as I exited the building, I changed and ran towards our home.

I couldn't lose her. I wouldn't.

I changed at the back door to the Packhouse and ran up the stairs. At the door to our rooms, I paused to try to take in a few breaths, hoping to calm myself. She needed me to be strong and in control. When I felt my heart beating steadily, I opened the door. Following her scent to our bedroom, I found Theo sitting in the chair used by her guard and Issa sitting on the floor directly in front of her.

Theo saw me and reached out her hand, gripping mine in a surprisingly strong grasp. "They are too strong, Raid. I can't take it anymore. I can't fight them any longer." No longer able to hold back the tears, she began to sob.

"No...no babe, I won't let you." I pulled her into my arms, crushing her much thinner body to my chest. "Never, Theo."

"I can't...too much," She admitted dejectedly. "Too strong...too loud." She lifted her face to look into my eyes. "I'm so tired, and I'm not getting better. Everything is worse." She again dropped her face to my chest. "I don't know how to make it better, nothing seems to work. I've tried to get better and I keep failing."

"Don't you give up, Theodora, don't you dare," I ordered while mouthing the word, "Sophia," to Issa.

The guard nodded once and pulled her phone from her pocket as she left the room.

"Raid...please..." She cried.

I didn't know if she was begging for my help or for me to give her the relief she craved. "Theo, I need you. I need you to be strong for me, just a little longer."

"I can't make them stop. Why won't they stop?" She gripped my t-shirt in her fists. "God, what they say…it hurts."

I knew that she meant the voices that were constantly whispering recriminations in her head. "Theo, baby, trust me. Stay with me," I implored. I glanced at the doorway. Where was Sophia? I needed her help now. The intensity of Theo's emotions was scaring me.

"I don't know if I can…"

"Trust me. I'm getting you help. Real help. The best. I'm not giving up." I would never give up. If my mate was too weak to fight then I would fight for both of us. For our future because I couldn't imagine my life without her. "I won't give up on you."

I heard rushed footsteps outside of our rooms.

Issa opened the door and said, "In here."

I could only give Sophia a look of pure helplessness. The time had come for Theo to leave me again, to get the help she needed.

THIRTY

NOVUS

THEODORA MORRISSEY

Right Now by Van Halen

THOSE MEMORIES MADE ME BREAKOUT IN A COLD SWEAT. Weeks had passed and I wasn't as vulnerable. I took in and then let out a deep breath. Thankfully, the front door opened and Lore entered followed by Luna halting those thoughts. I looked up from the cross-stitch I was working on. "Did you guys have fun?"

"The snow drifts aren't that high," my guard said with a grin.

"You mean not too high for a Lycan." I knew what that superior smile meant.

He went to the kitchen, and I heard him refilling Luna's water bowl.

Issa cleared her throat. "Does anybody mind if I go for a run now?"

I didn't answer. That was Lore's call.

"No. I will stay up until the morning." He walked around the corner from the kitchen into our living room.

What had transpired after I'd confessed that I was ready to die was still cloudy. Sophia had kept me sedated while Black probably moved heaven and earth to get us here. Issa had traveled ahead and rented this small house in a rural area outside of Dayton. I have murky memories of a few conversations. One being of Black tossing my clothes into a suitcase while telling me that he was leaving most of my belongings in our closet because I would be coming back.

Issa, Lore, and Luna had moved in with me, and we were still trying to make this work. Three other guards took turns patrolling the area, but did not have direct contact with me. Our days were very much the same. I worried that they were bored out of their heads. I saw Dr. Joseph, or Bayla as she'd asked me to call her, five days a week from nine until noon. Then my guard and I went out to lunch and came home. I would nap because my therapy sessions were exhausting, then I would do a craft project until dinnertime. After dinner, we would watch TV or a movie and go to bed. On the days I didn't have therapy, we cleaned the house and went to the grocery store.

It sounded boring, but I loved the structure. I knew what to expect and when it would happen. On Friday night, I would study recipes from the ten books Issa had ordered for me and tried to come up with different menus. The cashiers at the local box store would even comment on the new cooking tools I bought every Saturday.

If Issa or Lore regretted this assignment, they didn't show any signs in my presence. Issa had attended a two-hour class at the craft store on needlecraft, and Lore had shown some interest in the coloring books that had come home with me. They encouraged me by trying to do what I liked. In return, I allowed them to pick the movies we watched.

I knew my nightmares upset them. My screams would wake the entire house. Luna would howl as we followed the steps Bayla had drummed into our heads on how to help calm me afterward. I would reach for my bedside journal and write down what I remembered. If I was still breathing heavily and felt anxious, then we would put on the yoga DVD and follow those exercises. If I was still uneasy, I would bake.

Bayla Joseph was unique. She was confident, and yet at times, I saw her eyes flash with pain. By the end of the first week, she had my trust because she didn't make promises. During our first week, Sophia had accompanied me and had done most of the talking. I had still been reeling from Black's goodbye where he'd almost broken down. My strong alpha had had tears in his eyes as he'd begged me to fight.

I could do no less. So, I listened to Bayla with my ears, and even though my gift had disappeared, I acted as though it worked. During an early session, she'd told me to take a seat at the table in the corner of the room where we met. I had to make a list of what my goals were, specific answers, not just to "get better". What did "better" mean to me? Then we'd discussed a timeline. We would talk about my life first, my education, my job, and finally what had happened that had caused me this traumatic injury. Knowing that I didn't have to discuss the attack immediately lessened the pressure. She'd also explained that I was to have a daily schedule, and for that, Issa and Lore had to attend the meeting to discuss how that would work.

That had been an odd day. It was as if Bayla understood she was in the company of predators. She didn't speak too loudly nor move too quickly. Lore stood the entire time and hadn't spoken. It was as though he'd been memorizing every detail so that he could replay it later in his head. That evening when Issa had brought it up, he'd asked in a cold voice, "Are you questioning me, female?"

His tone had made my blood run cold. It must have struck Issa the same way because she'd dropped her gaze and changed subjects.

But other than disagreements about menus, we all got along well enough. I knew that they watched my every move and gave detailed reports to Black, Sophia, and maybe Bayla. I was improving. Not in huge ways, but I had started to laugh, and that was new. The only part of my new routine that I hadn't embraced was that I could only talk to Black once a week for thirty minutes. I felt cut off from him. I worried about what he was doing. Who was acting as his support system? When it came time for our calls, I didn't know what to say. How do you wrap everything up in a few sentences? Perhaps he was experiencing the same unease because he said little. We spent the majority of our calls asking polite questions of one another and discussing the weather.

It didn't help that Issa had shared that Sophia had not gone back to her Pack. Instead, she planned on staying with Novus for an undetermined length of time. I tried not to worry about Black and the strikingly beautiful doctor. Would loneliness push them together again? He liked her, and she was the daughter of a Packleader.

So compared to me, she was a much better choice for a mate. They'd found one another attractive once before so maybe they would again?

I needed to stop pursuing those thoughts. I did as prescribed, placing my needlework on the end table and stood. "Can I walk down the drive?" I asked Lore. When I started to have negative thoughts, I was to do something physical to change my focus.

Instantly, he stood. "Of course." He walked to the coat closet. "Button up, because the wind is cold." He was wearing a sweatshirt and would be fine.

We headed out, and walked on the plowed driveway. How he had arranged that I had no idea, but Lore was a surprisingly good homeowner, responsible and prepared. I kicked up white, powder-like snow with each step. Luna raced up and down the drive. At the end of the drive, I paused and looked up at the late afternoon sun. "It's beautiful today."

Lore was watching me. "It is."

I smirked. "I meant, out here."

"I meant, seeing you smile. You are improving." He made it sound like a certainty.

"I'm trying." I didn't look at him as I answered.

"Next week will be difficult." *Damn honest wolf.*

It was time to discuss the attack by my uncle when I was a teen, and what Charles Burke had done to me. "I know." Black had shared that story after getting my permission with Issa and Lore. I looked at the golden sun as it drifted down toward the horizon. "I shouldn't feel any shame, but I do."

"The day will come where you will confront him. Then the shame will leave you forever."

"I don't know if I can ever do that, Lore." I knew

that he wouldn't understand. My friend and protector was the most self-aware being that I'd ever met. He knew who he was and made no apologies.

"You will," he said, his deep voice perfectly even and confident.

Christ, he was so sure that if I faced those that had hurt me, it would help. I didn't want to argue. The act would be pointless.

"I saw it," he said emphatically.

"What?" I could see my breath, so I knew my mouth was hanging open. Did he mean he'd had a vision?

"It is true." He motioned with his hand that I should start heading toward the house. "You were standing tall and strong...magnificent. You burned with vengeance."

I started to laugh. I can't explain why, but I felt as though a weight had lifted from my shoulders.

"Why do you laugh?" he asked, his drawn eyebrows reflecting his puzzlement.

I stopped, and Luna sat at my feet. I rested my hand on her head. "I don't know, but it felt like something clicked into place when you said that. I'm...relieved... and maybe, a little... hopeful." It felt good to laugh. Perhaps one day I could take back a little that was stolen from me.

"My queen is bloodthirsty," he said admiringly.

"Hardly." I rolled my eyes because I knew he was plenty vengeful. Then I came up with a great idea. "Have you ever made a snow angel, Lore?"

I swear, he looked defensive, as if I'd found a secret weakness. "No." His eyes studied the landscape warily.

"It's fun. Come on, I swear." Giggles escaped as I grabbed his hand and dropped to my knees, and then to my ass. "Watch." I let go of his hand and stretched out

286

on my back in the snow. I waved my arms up and down, clearing a path in the snow. "See? It's supposed to look like wings." I stilled.

He tilted his head to the side slowly as he studied me. "It does somewhat."

"Come on, try it," I coaxed.

He gave me a superior look that was worthy of a Prince.

"It will make me laugh," I offered, "and that feels really good."

He let out a long-suffering sigh and gracefully knelt nearby.

Luna had fun licking our faces since she didn't understand what we were doing, and not only did I laugh, so did Lore.

THIRTY-ONE

NOVUS

RAIDER BLACK

It Will Rain by Bruno Mars

"How long has she been asleep?" I asked Issa. Today was the second day in which she was discussing the attacks with the doctor.

"She had a bowl of soup and a salad. When we got home, she went to her room. She's been asleep for eighty-two minutes," the guard told me.

I hated that I couldn't talk to Theo every day. If it hadn't been for the guard's afternoon calls, I would probably have lost my shit long ago. "How was she last night?"

"We ordered pizza. Lore did not remember the extra sauce for the breadsticks. I allowed her to select the movie. It was terrible. It had no fights or car chases, however, the clothing was interesting."

It boggled my mind that Lore was picking up dinner.

How Theo managed her guards and their diverse personalities, while working so hard to get better, was a mystery to me. "Did she say anything, Issa?"

"Only that we needed to stop at Target tomorrow to get more moisturizer after her appointment."

I rolled my eyes. Note to self, Issa was great at giving a report but not so good with emotional nuances. "How did she seem? Did she cry after the session? Did she go into her closet? Give me something, Issa." I tried not to let my frustration show.

"She didn't go in the closet. She has not done that in a very long time. It is very small. She was tired and seemed quiet, but she didn't cry."

I thought that was good news. "Did she get my presents?"

"She placed the roses in her bedroom by her bed, and she spent a few minutes studying each book after she took them out of the box. When she found the note, she excused herself and went into her room."

I'd worried about not being there for her, so I'd done the next best thing. I'd sent tokens. I'd wanted her to know that I was thinking about her. Always.

"Laird, I do see it. She is improving. The dreams, they do not come as often. She talks more. This is working."

"Thank you for your report, Issa. I appreciate your observations." I couldn't believe that I needed to turn to Lore, a mass-murderer, for emotional insights into Theo's life.

"I hope it is all right that I tell you this, but she misses you. She wants to hear everything that is going on at Novus."

"We miss her. You and Lore as well."

"We are very good at our jobs," the petite assassin reminded me. "It is an honor to care for the Seer."

"We will talk tomorrow." I lived for these phone calls. I wished that I could find the words when my weekly call with Theo came around. Instead, I tried to listen to her tone and what she wasn't saying and knowing her, I worried that she was being cautious. I wanted to see her, to touch her.

I dropped my cell onto my desk. *She is getting better.* The guard wouldn't tell me that if it weren't true. Dr. Joseph had decided that too much contact might interfere with her therapy, so I'd agreed to the damn rule. Once again, I wished I could head down the hall and share this news with Conal, who I missed very much. As it was, I spent too much time alone, rarely going into the Control Room or visiting the community center for Zumba night to see the kids. Basil had reported there were rumblings that I was making a string of poor decisions and that I wasn't listening to my Board's recommendations.

Irritated, I made a grunting sound. I did listen to them, but I was only on speaking terms with Glass and Tex. At our last meeting, Onyx had tried to convince us that, with Theo's current condition being public knowledge, I should no longer refer to her as my Intended Mate. He'd called her infirm and unworthy.

In anger, I'd banned him from my presence. He couldn't grasp all that she had been through and how traumatized she was. This experience had shown me hidden sides of those closest to me. Some amazed me with their gentleness, like Glass and Tex, while others were unable to empathize. If I couldn't put myself in the shoes of my weakest member, then what kind of leader was I?

Basil knocked once and entered my office. "How is our Seer today?"

"According to Issa, she is showing signs of improvement."

Basil rested his forearms on the back of the chair in front of my desk. "That is good news."

"This is the week when she is to begin discussing the attack," I told him solemnly. "She is tired but not crying or hiding."

"I will ask The Lady to send her strength." Basil cleared his throat. "She has been through so much, and yet, she continues to fight. I cannot begin to fathom how hard this has been for her and you."

"She has the heart of a wolf." I'd told her that the night she'd faced a feral, newly-changed wolf. "She is a warrior."

"She loves you very much."

His comment took me by surprise. We weren't friends. Although I was sure that, in many ways, Basil knew me very well.

He straightened as if he feared a repercussion. "What I meant was…"

"What you said is very true. I do love her. I promised Dr. Joseph that I would stay away." I tried to shrug to lighten the truth of the next statement. "I'm probably making everybody pay for that decision."

"Most of us understand, and those who don't… Well, they were never her supporters."

He meant Onyx and those who felt that humans were beneath our superior race. "We must continue supporting her. When she returns, we will have a celebration."

His eyebrows rose. "Your Mating Ceremony?"

"Theo will be consulted about that date and how we will celebrate."

A huge smile appeared on Basil's face. "I applaud your decision, Laird. She should have equal say. I think it is wrong that so many still follow the tenet that the one who holds the more esteemed position calls the shots."

Since my falling out with Conal, I'd been talking to Basil more, not merely issuing orders. He held progressive opinions. I found that I liked listening to them. "I apologize. Please take a seat." I pointed at the chair. "Are there Pack needs that should be addressed today?"

Even though my personal life had gone to shit, there was always work.

I stood outside pacing. I'd spent the morning running in my wolf form. I held my cell and watched the clock. In two minutes, I would hear her voice.

The cold wind whipped my hair around, so I pulled up the hood on my sweatshirt. I hoped she had enough warm socks. Her feet were always cold, and she'd found many sneaky ways to rest them against me to warm.

I re-checked the screen, pressed the number, and waited impatiently for her to answer. A part of me always worried that she would ignore my call.

"I love the flowers, all of them."

She sounded…happy, lively, like my Theo. "I knew you didn't have one favorite." I'd sent her a different bouquet every day this week.

"I put the roses on my nightstand, the tulips in the

living room. I don't even want to think about how you found lilacs, but they are so pretty, Black. They're in my bedroom on the dresser."

"I wanted you to know I was thinking of you...of everything that you've been going through."

She sighed deeply. "It hasn't been easy. Bayla hasn't watched the video. She said she would later. When I went in on Monday, I told her I wanted to talk about what my uncle did in the barn, and how it came up when we were together."

I knew the incident had contributed to her breakdown. Her uncle had tried to sodomize her when she was a teen. His mother had chosen to keep him on the farm and sent Theo off to college at sixteen. She'd buried the memory. After she'd graduated from Ohio State, she'd never returned to the area, until now, to recover from another sexual assault.

She continued, "I've been thinking about my cousins. I'm an hour away from the farm. I could run into one of them at the store or when we're having lunch. Of course, I might not recognize them..."

"Did you ask Dr. Joseph about that?"

"No. I thought I should talk to you first." She cleared her throat. "I sort of want to see them... I mean...if they wanted to meet me. I know it's been years, but I'm a little curious about their lives."

"As long as you take your guards, I wouldn't be opposed," I answered cautiously, overjoyed that she wanted to take action but concerned about what she would encounter.

"I wasn't asking you as my Leader," she said slowly. "I was discussing it with my partner."

The rebuke was clear in her tone, and I smiled.

294

"Babe, I want what you want. If you want to contact your family, and you discuss it with the doc, then make the calls or shoot the e-mails. You are so close that it would be a shame for you not to reach out."

She drew a deep breath then said softly, "I worry. What if he's still doing it? I feel like I need to see...even if I can't tell, but I feel like maybe I could. Is that crazy?"

"No." I smiled. "You have a big heart."

"If I...uh, find something...what do I do?"

"You call me first," I said, using the tone that always made her roll her eyes when we were alone, "and then you tell Lore."

"Um..." She lowered the volume of her voice, and it sounded a little muffled. I pictured her cupping her hand over the phone. "Would he feel like I was using him because...you know he is willing to kill?"

She left off that he seemed to enjoy it, as opposed to Issa, who would require my order before acting. "I think he would be hurt if you did not give him a choice to act or refuse."

"Thank you. That's what I needed to know."

I could hear her moving. "Where are you?"

"I was sitting on the sofa in my bedroom, but I just climbed up on the bed. Now I'm sitting in the middle of it."

I tried to picture that. Issa had still been buying furniture when I'd left Ohio.

"So, how has your week been? I feel like we talk a lot about me and so little about you."

"Basil says he's tired of sending me home at night."

"You're probably interrupting his plans," she murmured.

295

"We've been exploring some new routes to Oregon and Washington State. There have been some inquiries."

"It might be wise to diversify. California isn't the only state on the west coast." She cleared her throat. "Have you seen or talked with Solle?"

I hated that she sounded tentative, but I hoped the fact that she didn't hide her emotions from me was another positive. "No." It hurt me, too, their absence. "Glass saw her on Tuesday and said that she wasn't feeling sick anymore. She asked a lot of questions about you."

"Oh, that's good...I guess," she whispered.

"It will get straightened out," I promised.

"This has affected so many things for you and for Novus," she said, her tone tentative. "I didn't consider all of the ramifications at the time...especially for you."

"We are in this together."

"I like it when you say 'together'." She sounded very sure.

"Don't you ever doubt it, and if you start to...I don't give a shit about what your doctor's rule is. You call me, and I'll set you straight." My hand cramped I was gripping my phone so tightly.

"I never stopped loving you, Raid. Even when...even if I can't...I won't," she said, her voice cracking.

I squeezed my eyes shut. "There have been times I've wondered if you blame me...and if you do, it's okay, I'd understand. I let you go—"

"*No!*" she cut me off. "Never." She sounded ferocious. My wolf was thrilled to hear so much emotion in her voice. "You are not responsible for any of this. You...honey, when I needed you most, you got me help.

I wouldn't be alive right now, if you hadn't arranged for me to be here."

"Don't say that," I told her. I didn't care if it was true. The thought of losing her was too close and too real. I didn't want to think about it.

"Will it upset you if I tell you about what I said this week? I get it if you don't want to hear it."

She was worrying about me. "Babe, I want to hear everything. If we go over the minutes, I won't tell if you won't."

She giggled. "A bad boy and a biker...it's every romance reader's dream." Then she turned serious. "I didn't have to give Bayla a play by play. Well, there are parts that I don't remember, and I was unconscious. She made me... I mean, I was to talk about my feelings throughout."

"That had to be overwhelming." I was surprised and encouraged that she didn't sound as defeated today as she usually did when referred to the attack.

"What I realized was that I always knew Charles was off. I mean, he always felt wrong to me." She paused. "So, when he kicked in my door, I knew he was there to hurt me. He's the type who gets off on fear. I think...I think I fought him, hoping in a way that I would make him angry enough to kill me rather than all of the other...stuff."

I let out my breath slowly, preparing to speak. "You have never been afraid to face death, my Theo."

"I wasn't happy there," she said, her voice rough. "A part of me was slowly dying. My gift was abandoning me and...and without you, I wasn't really alive."

She killed me with her honesty. "Honey, I...love you."

"Has Bayla or anybody said how long until you can visit?"

I didn't want to admit that I was afraid to ask. I thought that when I couldn't stand it any longer, I'd take the jet or maybe my bike and head east, to her. "I haven't spoken to your doctor."

"Oh, okay." She sounded puzzled by that.

"I don't contact your doctor because I felt, and Sophia advised, that I am to put my trust in Dr. Joseph and the process." I felt like I'd let Theo down. "I want to be there with you. Theo, you have to know that, but… but I'm trying to do as she advised. I have to say, honey, you sound good."

She sniffed loudly. "Thank you for telling me all of that, and I understand. It's just that I miss being with you. I see something, and I turn to tell you because I forget that you're in Nebraska."

"I get it." I did the same thing.

"Most of it is kind of dumb," she said, downplaying the urge.

"I seem to recall I enjoyed the dumb stuff." I smiled because we'd both laughed at silly things.

"I'm trying really hard."

"I know baby. When have you not given one hundred percent?"

"Well, there might have been a few times when Glass was kicking my ass."

I chuckled. "That doesn't count."

"Oh, I almost forgot." She made some more shuffling sounds. "I think Issa and Asher are talking."

"Hmmm." This was new… She was gossiping.

"I mean talking-talking," she whispered and emphasized the last word.

"That's good, right?"

"She's afraid he'll make her give up what she loves," she confided.

"Like anyone could stop Issa?" I drawled. "Her father forced her out of her Pack because she wouldn't submit, and nobody stood up for her, so I can see why she's worried."

"I didn't know that." When she had applied to Novus, we were thrilled that someone with her skills had wanted to join us. "Now it makes sense why she is so proud of her position in Novus. She earned it."

"So, maybe you could talk to Asher...explain that independence is important...?"

"Are we matchmaking, Theodora?" I used an overly stern tone so she'd know I was teasing.

"Maybe?" She giggled. "If you want to? We could help them or at least give them some good advice. I mean, God only knows what his buddies tell him."

"I don't think he's asking the other guards for advice." Asher was driven. Although he appeared easy-going, I knew he was methodical and calculating. He'd study the situation, er, Issa, before drawing conclusions about the best way to approach her.

"If you run into him, maybe you could work the topic of Issa into a conversation and see what he says...?"

"I'll try," I promised. I would do anything she asked because, even though she was going through hell and miles away, I wanted to hear the pleasure in her voice again.

THIRTY-TWO

THEODORA MORRISSEY

Million Years by Adele

I WAS SWEATING. THE DROPS WERE SLIDING DOWN MY back. It was one of those dark, rainy, March days. Even though my feet and hands were freezing, the rest of my body was burning up, all due to the stress caused by what we were discussing.

I glanced around the room. Bayla's gorgeous cashmere sweater that matched the caramel highlights in her hair caught my attention. I wondered if it would be odd for me to ask if I could stroke her arm; the sweater looked so soft.

"I know this period is very difficult to relive, but I'd like to hear more about your conversation on the plane ride from Texas."

"I didn't know it at the time, but Black had watched the video over and over."

"What does that mean to you?"

"It means he saw that man do those things to me. He watched him fuck me." I took in a shaky breath and pulled my leg to my chest. I could barely force the word out because my jaw was clenched so tightly, "Everywhere."

"Take a breath. Draw it in slowly, hold it, and let it out." Bayla's voice was rich and calming.

It took a few minutes before I could continue. "So, yeah, it bugs me. He was there with me, being so calm and caring, and he'd watched that man do all of that to me." I sounded angry. I flexed the fingers gripping the arm of the sofa tightly. "On the plane, I asked him to sit down on the edge of the bed. I couldn't stand thinking about that with him standing over me. He was gentle and…compassionate." I swallowed hard. "I don't know what he was thinking."

"Elaborate a little more on that. What do you think was going through his head?"

I blinked a couple of times while my mind raced, trying to figure out what I thought. "I guess, I kind of wondered if he wasn't angry that it hadn't been him." I rushed to explain after I heard what I'd had just shared. "Not that Black would rape me. I liked what we did together. We, he…it was good and hot. But it got physical, and he pushed my limits sometimes…but when I gave him a 'hard no,' he'd always stopped."

Bayla smiled a little. "Then good for you to have found a partner that can share all of those things with."

"I guess, I worried that he might think that somehow…I gave that to Charles when I'd withheld it from him." My chest was heaving up and down like I'd just run a marathon.

"Think about that for a moment."

I combed my fingers through my hair. It was too long, and I'd started to throw it up in a high ponytail to forget about it. "That doesn't make any sense really." I bit down on my lip so hard that it stung. "He'd never believe I'd do anything willingly with Charles."

"And because he did see the video, he knew you were taken against your will."

"Then why did I think he might blame me? Be mad at me?" I was so confused. Why would I think that? I stared at her, willing her to give me an answer.

"You had been through a severe trauma, Theo. When you spoke with Black, you were sedated. I think we can agree you weren't completely rational."

"But I believed it."

"There is always guilt associated with rape. It's something we've been conditioned to believe. Even after all of these years and miles of research to tell us that rape is about control and violence, the victim still thinks it's her fault and carries the blame."

"I know it wasn't my fault," I said slowly. "I did everything in my power to avoid Charles from the start." I couldn't tell my doctor about the Lycans, so we'd fabricated a story as close to the truth as we could. I'd said that I'd been involved with my boss, but he'd been engaged to another. I'd chosen to be loaned to another company, and while there, I'd been attacked by the CEO's son.

"And yet, you worried that your lover, who dropped everything to come to your rescue, would doubt your word?"

My shoulders relaxed. The tightness that had been

there forever lessened a little. "I don't understand." I shook my head in confusion and understanding.

"You thought that about yourself, Theodora. You allowed a little bit of that evil virus of recrimination to get into your head, and once it took hold, it grew."

"Do you think I've been worried that Black thought that all of this time?" My hands were balled into fists with my nails biting into my palms.

"Maybe."

"Have I been blaming myself for something I made up?" Swallowing was so difficult that I felt like I might choke. "He's never done or said anything to make me believe it was my fault."

"I think you've felt guilty for many things for a long time."

She was right. The guilt and my uncertainty about my future were all tied together in my head.

"Theodora, you were the victim of brutal attacks twice in your life. Those kinds of events are life-altering. After the first, you were basically disowned, relocated, and yet you forged a new life."

"I always felt that my grandmother chose my uncle over me."

"She did." Bayla frowned. "That choice was hers. I'm sure it was very difficult. Her decision allowed you to start over, and you seemed to prosper."

I thought about her summary. "That is true."

"This most recent attack... I've read multiple reports, listened to your version, and last night I reviewed the video. I can say with total certainty that you, Theodora, did nothing to deserve that."

I played with the edge of the blanket for a few moments as I thought about what she'd said. Another thing that I liked about Bayla was that she allowed me time to absorb the information and I didn't have to rush to answer. "I do know that I didn't deserve to be raped or touched by my uncle. I can't explain why I listened to the voices."

"What you just said is a great start."

"I hate it that I can't stop them." My eyes filled with tears.

"You will in time. They will cease to matter, and then they'll stop," she assured.

"I want that," I told her in a sob.

She gave me time to compose myself once again. "Now, we got a little off track, so I'd like to go back to what happened on the flight."

I didn't speak for a few beats as I searched for my center and calm. "I told him that I loved him." Then I remembered something else. "I didn't say it, but I wondered if he thought I was soiled, and if he would want me again." I reached for the bottle of water because I was suddenly very thirsty. I downed half of the bottle. "Charles spat on me, and he… They said he peed on me." I wanted to run my hands over my arms as if I still carried his fluids.

"Those were things you washed away. They are gone. The only way Charles can touch your heart and your soul, Theo, is if you allow it."

"I let him." I bowed my head. "This anger and guilt, it keeps him with me." I wanted to scream. "I did this to myself?"

"No." She shook her head so hard that her bobbed hair swung touching her cheekbones. "Your brain picks and chooses what to hold onto in times of trauma. Then when you try to put it all together, the pieces don't fit.

We might assign emotions, ghosts of the past creep in, society creeps in, a snippet of conversation creeps in, and it suddenly means something different."

"None of it makes sense," I said, my voice very loud in the quiet room.

She nodded approvingly. "Say it again."

"It doesn't make sense. I believed the worst." I tried to wrap my head around it. "Why did I do that? I'm really not a bad person."

"I'm sure that you are not. I can give you terms and a lot of research, but the bottom line, and this is more opinion than databased, I think you never worked through your feelings about some of the things that had already happened to you. The life with your mom, basically living on the street, not feeling safe, then what your uncle did proved that you were not. You were in love with a man who was with another woman, and you left. That meant a new town where you couldn't find your place. You didn't have a strong foundation when this attack happened. I think that once you started down this path of self-recrimination, you ran. You went back to Nebraska, but you still weren't sure of your place, and since then, you've lost the support of two of your best friends. You've been through a lot."

Christ, no wonder I was a mess. "Can I get better? I mean, can I go back home and function?"

Her expression softened. "Of course, you can."

Now, I asked the hardest question. "Am I going to be able to have sex?"

She paused.

She. Fucking. Paused.

"Oh, God," I started to sob. I think I crossed over into wailing territory. My throat burned, and my nails

306

dug into my hands so hard they might have broken the skin. I fell to the side and buried my face into the arm of the leather sofa.

"Theo. Theo. Theodora!" Bayla said my name sharply.

"I'm never going to be able to keep him, am I?" How was I going to live without him?

"I didn't say that. I didn't say any of that."

I wiped my wet cheeks and my nose on my sleeve. I prepared to listen.

"You have been through a terrible trauma. Your body might remember some of it, but I'm darn sure that your mind will. There could be times when you freeze up for what seems to be no apparent reason. You might be in the middle of the hottest sexual moment ever, and you could start fighting your partner. You might scream 'no'. You could have a flashback. So, sex could change."

"Oh."

"You must disclose your history to your partners."

"There's only Black," I said through gritted teeth. Why couldn't she accept that?

"You must be honest with Black. You're going to have to trust that he'll understand. You can no longer tell yourself, just do this once, and it'll be okay."

That went against some of the games we'd enjoyed where he would test my boundaries, and except for one, I'd given way to him. "He wouldn't hurt me."

"No, he wouldn't intentionally," she said slowly. "However, your responses might not make sense. You both have to be prepared for that."

I tapped my heel on the floor. I didn't know if he could change. Would he want to?

"This is something I should discuss with the both of you, and perhaps, him alone."

I nodded. I had a lot to think about.

Lore and I were sitting in a booth at the cafe that was about four blocks from Bayla's office. My session had run long. We were the only people in the place.

"You are very quiet," he observed.

"Today was hard. She gave me a lot to consider," I told him slowly as I played with my fork.

"You do know there will be moments you can't prepare for." His dark brown eyes stared intensely into mine.

"Yes," I answered slowly.

"So, no matter how much you plan, there will always be the chance of a surprise." He leaned back in his chair as if he had just imparted the secret to the universe.

I started to laugh. "Oh, my God! I find that so rich, coming from you, the one who made me practice with knives over and over so that I would be prepared." I'd endured hours upon hours of drills. I used my hand to thrust up and twist as he'd taught me.

He nodded. "Very good, Theodora."

"Maybe when the weather gets a little warmer, we could do something again…?"

He tilted his head slightly. "That can be arranged."

Then it hit me. I wanted to work out. I wanted to be active. I stretched my legs out in front of me, enjoying the moment. "Wow."

"Wow, indeed, my Lady." Lore flashed one of his rare smiles.

THIRTY-THREE

RAIDER BLACK

Fire and Rain by the Glee Cast

I FELT THE MUD KICK UP BEHIND ME AS I LOPED THROUGH the field. Overnight, it had rained, but the day was sunny. I'd set out with no set destination in mind. A half mile back, I'd realized that I was going to pass by the MacGregors' house. Perhaps subconsciously, I wanted to speak with them, to share the good news and to right the wrong. My wolf snarled, *Do it.* He was correct. This breach in our friendship had gone on long enough. It was hurting me, Novus, and most importantly, Theo.

I stopped at the corner of their property and changed. I then cut across their yard and listened intensely for any signs they were home. They were. I climbed the steps to their porch and rang the doorbell.

From deep inside the house, I heard Conal's footsteps on the hardwood floor. He opened the door, "Laird." He, however, did not open the glass storm door.

Solle approached the door with a smile. "Black, this is a wonderful surprise." She stepped forward and opened the heavy glass door. "Come in. Were you out running?"

"Thank you. I apologize for stopping in unannounced."

"You honor us, Laird." Conal made it clear by using my title for the second time and the formal greeting that he was not pleased by my unscheduled visit.

"Solle, you look beautiful," I said as I crossed their threshold. "How are you feeling?"

"Much better. Morning sickness was the worst, but now, I'm only growing bigger." She rested her hand on her belly.

We all sat in their living room, and then nobody spoke.

Solle broke the silence. "Laird, I am truly sorry for what I did in California. I was selfish. I knew that visiting my mother's grave could be a problem. I...I wanted to see it...to tell her that I was well and happy, and to share our news. It might not make sense, but we were close at one time, and I don't know if I'll ever return." She bowed her head.

"I understand." Theo had stressed that Solle had needed to see her mother or the site of her final resting place to close the human chapter of her life. When she'd mated with Conal, she'd turned her back on her human life. I'd never given her the option to return to say her good-byes. I had not considered that she might want or need that.

Solle raised her head and gave me a shy smile. She

leaned further back into the sofa and flipped her hair over her shoulder slowly before asking, "Do you think Theo will ever forgive me for putting her life in danger?"

I glanced at Conal. This was the appropriate time for him to speak up.

I waited a solid minute for my Second to speak. When he chose not to, I began, "Is that what you believe happened?"

"Well, yes," she gave her mate a questioning look. "Conal told me that she was angry and you deemed that I was to have nothing to do with Theo while she was upset."

"Did *I* decide that?" I asked her quietly. That wasn't my style. I would have put the two friends in a room and let them fight it out with certain rules in this case, like no changing.

She turned her body toward the male sitting at the other end of the sofa. "Conal, isn't that what you told me?"

My Second glared at me, but added nothing.

I was reminded of the many times Theo had complained about our "damn Lycan pride." I modulated my voice so that it was low and non-threatening, "Why don't you tell us what happened that afternoon, Solle? I don't believe I've ever heard you tell your side." Conal had been enraged and wouldn't allow anyone near his mate for several weeks after our return for another doctor.

She licked her lips before starting. "I told Theo I was going to sneak out to see my mother's grave. I'd called the day before to verify the location. It was in the cemetery in my old neighborhood. I'd been giving it a lot of thought, and I knew how to get away. You all were in a meeting, and Conal had said it would last all afternoon."

I nodded once.

She glanced at her mate. "We'd discussed it before we flew to California. He'd told me not to go. He thought it too dangerous. You see, my brother, he…he knew of Lycans. The Fire Eaters, they…" she was fumbling for the shortest and most clear explanation.

"They have done work for the De La Cruz pack." We had learned of this association when Conal first met Solle.

She swallowed loudly and continued, "Theo tried to talk me out of it, and then she wanted to bring her guards with us." Solle rolled her eyes. "I didn't want to draw any attention to my visit. My plan was to take a car, visit, and then leave. I'd be gone about three hours if traffic cooperated."

Conal grumbled under his breathe.

"She wouldn't let me go alone. Even when we were sneaking down the back steps, she was trying to talk me out of it, but she stuck with me."

"She didn't do a very good job of dissuading you," Conal snapped.

Solle shot him an angry look. "I was going no matter what. I needed to, okay? I…needed…to do it. She was my mother."

I cleared my throat. "Did either of you ever wonder how I knew where you had gone or that you had left?"

That had both of them staring at me.

Solle's eyebrows drew together. "I hadn't really thought about it. I guess I thought you had some kind of tracker on the car…?"

"How did you know?" Conal asked suspiciously. Then his eyes widened. "Those texts?"

"Theo sent me a few short texts, telling me what was going on. She was worried about your mate." I scowled at Conal. "She wanted me to follow, in case things didn't go well."

"She did that?" Solle asked slowly.

"She said she couldn't stop you, so she was going as your back-up."

Solle frowned. "Even when we got off the interstate, she wanted us to turnaround."

"And when you were intercepted, didn't she also ask you to fight your instinct? Begging you not to change to protect your young? Reminding you of what would happen?"

Solle's voice shook as she recounted, "When she got free...she shielded me from the fighting. She ran to me." She began to cry.

"That sounds like something a good friend would do." I settled back into the chair.

She wiped her damp cheeks and choked out. "The best."

Conal's eyes narrowed. "Why didn't you tell me that *she* had sent you a text? I thought someone had seen them leave. You let me think that."

"There wasn't time," I bit out. "When you came to the house and...made your proclamation, Theo made me promise not to tell."

He leaned forward on the sofa and spoke slowly, "I don't understand."

"You were angry, Conal, furious. Theo didn't want to expose your mate to that wrath. So, she allowed you to

313

blame her for everything." I tried not to let my own anger and disappointment show.

"What is he talking about, Conal?" Solle cried. "Did you do something to Theo?" Her brown eyes were wide with worry.

I studied my Second. I had always believed that Conal was a truthful man. The one I could trust with my life, but at that moment he wanted to lie to his mate.

"Tell me the truth, Mate," Solle ordered in a firm voice.

His expression must have given him away before he uttered a word.

"Oh God, Conal, what did you do?" Solle got to her feet and started to pace. "When I saw her on the street, she was so scared. I didn't understand it at the time. I thought she was worried that she would be in trouble with you." She glanced at me for a moment and then continued. "She wasn't angry, which I had expected, because you led me to believe that she was so mad she didn't want to talk to me." She continued walking back and forth, "Conal, it doesn't matter what you did, but we have to fix it." She stopped to the spot in front of me. "What can I do to make it right, Laird? Theo...she delayed things. She kept my nephew talking. I was ready to change, but she kept stalling, offering money for our safe passage." She turned on her heel and faced her mate. "Tell me right now what you did because, Conal, you have to fix it. Theo didn't deserve this."

"She could have told me," he started defensively.

Solle shouted, "Really? You are going to try to blame her again?"

He got to his feet, towering over his mate. "I admit that I have..." He let out a ragged sigh. "I thought she encouraged you. It seemed to be a very human urge to go back to see the grave. Theo has a way of walking into danger. I thought she'd allowed you to do the same." He dropped his gaze. He knew how ridiculous it sounded as soon as he spoke his belief. His cheeks reddened, and his wide shoulders slunk.

"Conal, you have to make this right." Solle took his wrist. He turned his hand so that their fingers threaded together. She turned to me. "I am so sorry for not telling him everything. I need to apologize to Theo."

"She is away."

"I'd heard that. I should have been there for you, Black. I thought," she glared at her mate, "*you* let me think that I was unwelcome, Conal." She started to cry again. "She needed me. Now she's not here, and I'm going to have a baby... I miss my friend."

"Shh..." Conal pulled her into his arms. "I was wrong. I promise I will make it right. Don't cry, please don't cry."

Why do we tell our women not to cry? It never seems to make them stop. I liked it when Theo turned to me for comfort.

A few moments later, Conal said quietly, "You need to lie down." He took her hand and started to lead Solle from the room. "Laird, I will be right back. Please make yourself at home. We have much to discuss."

I nodded my head once. It was a start.

I heard him descend from the stairs. "Beer, whiskey, water, or what?" He asked as he returned to the living room.

"Beer."

He continued to the kitchen. A few minutes later, he sat on the sofa after handing me the ice cold bottle.

"Why does it seem that your beer is always the coldest in the land?" I asked with a wry smile.

"Luck?" He took a drink then turned serious. "Being protective is ingrained in my nature," he began. "When I found Solle, I didn't want to let her out of my sight."

"You always believed that you would find your mate."

"With her carrying our young...it's so difficult...I fear so many things."

I nodded in understanding.

"I needed to blame someone. Solle and our child could have died. I didn't want to blame my mate. I am sorry I blamed your woman." He lowered his chin.

"You blamed your good friend, Conal. Theo trusted you and held you in the highest regard."

He silently finished his beer. "Did I...contribute to her decline?"

I waited until he looked me squarely in the eye. "Yes."

He closed his eyes and let out a deep breath.

"I believe that by losing the support of you and Solle, she felt cut off and more alone. Your threats terrified her."

He nodded once slowly.

"The day she ran into Solle, I found her hiding in our closet. She feared you would come for her. We finally convinced her three days later that you weren't going to attack."

"You would have stopped me."

"And that increased her concern and stress. She knows to what lengths we both are prepared to go to protect those we love." If Conal had made an attempt on her life, I would have killed my Second and oldest friend.

He dropped his head back and stared at the ceiling. "I fucked up." After a long moment, he sat up straighter and asked, "How bad was she? I've heard things, but I want the truth."

"She told me that she feared she couldn't fight the voices in her head that urged her to end her life." I still flinched inwardly every time I thought about that afternoon. I had smelled her desperation, exhaustion, and surrender. "She had made three different plans to kill herself. She begged Issa not to leave her alone."

"I didn't know it was that bad."

"We weren't talking," I said shortly.

"If Solle had known, she would have...she wouldn't have..." He covered his face with his hand. "This is going to hurt her deeply."

"Being separated from my Intended and my closest friends has been difficult for me as well," I admitted.

"Fuck, Black, I should have asked, I should have known." Conal shook his head in frustration and embarrassment.

Adding more recriminations would do no one any good. Conal would carry this with him for the rest of his days. "There is good news."

He lifted his head and tilted his head inquiringly.

"Her time in Ohio has helped. Theo called last night to say that the doctor believes that she is ready to come home very soon."

"That's great news," Conal smiled.

"I must travel to meet with the therapist for a few days. I am sure we will have much to discuss."

"What can I do to help? Do you want me to travel with you?"

"No, your place is here with your mate." I would not force him to travel out of state at this time. "However, I do expect you to talk to Theo when we return. She will accept your apology because she loves you and Solle, but I expect you to make this up to her Conal." I stared at him for a few beats. "And never again." If there was a next time, I would kill him.

"She shouldn't forgive me." He bowed his head.

"Her plan was to wait until after the babe was born, and then she would attempt to speak with you."

"How do I make it up to you?"

I didn't have a plan. "We have many, many years of friendship ahead of us. A few months of turmoil will not do any lasting damage."

"That is very magnanimous of you, Laird," he stated solemnly and bowed his head.

"And Theo made me promise." I grinned at my oldest friend.

He started to laugh. "Want another beer?"

"Yeah, if you've got the time...?"

"I'll always have time for you, Black."

THIRTY-FOUR

NOVUS

THEODORA MORRISSEY

Shallow by Bradley Cooper and Lady Gaga

I KICKED OFF MY COVERS AND SAT ON THE SIDE OF MY bed. "I give up, Luna. I can't sleep." Yes, I talked to the wolf as if she were a person. She seemed to understand, and she was a good listener, never arguing with words. Four weeks ago, Issa had stopped sleeping, or rather sitting on the sofa and watching over me while I slept. I kept the door open, and Luna stayed with me stretched across the doorway or beside the bed. The nightmares still came but not every night. Very few were so severe that I woke. I glanced down to see whether my sleep shorts and navy camisole adequately covered my body then walked out into the living room.

"My Lady?" Lore looked up from his laptop.

"I can't sleep." I perched on the arm of the sofa.

"Dreams?"

"No." I hadn't had a bad dream in over a week. "I think I'm nervous about tomorrow."

"Why would you be nervous?" He closed his laptop and placed it on the coffee table.

"Because…" Why the fuck wouldn't I be nervous? I missed Solle so much. She would have understood immediately. "Because Black is coming…we haven't seen each other in months and what if he…" I couldn't finish that sentence.

Lore's lips tightened into a line. "You are thinking like a human."

I wrinkled my nose. "I am a human."

"You are his mate."

"But I'm not like I was…I can't…"

"Your powers will return when The Lady deems that you are ready."

Christ, he sounded so sure. I adored Lore, but he wasn't always able to comprehend my reasoning or fears, and yet, he'd stayed with me through all of this. He should be given a medal or a cash bonus. I let out a loud puff of air. "Are you sick of me?"

"No."

"I don't think I ever asked if you'd rather be somewhere else, attending to your other concerns." I didn't want to say spying and killing.

"My duty is to you, Theodora."

"But if you wanted to take a break, I'd understand." I slid down to the sofa cushion. "I know I've been tiresome. You've had to deal with…with stuff that you probably aren't used to." The male had been a wolf without a Pack for centuries. He'd joined Novus, but from all that I'd learned, he was still a lone wolf. Then he'd met me and—boom! Inseparable through my crazies.

"It is a pleasure to know you, Theodora Morrissey, to watch you fight so bravely, to give so generously. It is an honor to serve you."

His speech touched my heart. I didn't want to cry, so I tried to joke. "Well, if you get an urge to go off and cause mayhem, you have my blessing."

"When you are once again settled with the Laird, I will hunt Charles Burke."

He would find him, of that I was sure. Everyone said that Lore was very good at his job, and this was personal. Hopefully, the Pack that was sheltering him would turn Burke over, or I feared that Lore would kill everyone in his path.

I didn't feel bad about that happening.

"What else worries you?"

"I don't want it to be weird, and it will be. I don't know how to make it not." Christ, was I really discussing this with Lore? He would intimidate the other guards by simply staying silent for hours and watching them. "I haven't been good for so long…"

"You are thinking too much. The Laird will arrive with his entourage. Everything will be fine."

I hope. I noticed there was dust on the end table. "I'm going to dust unless it will interrupt whatever you were doing…?" I had no idea what Lore did when he was on his laptop or when he and Luna were off duty.

"You can do whatever you like as long as I do not have to help."

I chuckled. Lorenzo Barducci did not do housework. I didn't mind. He and Issa had uprooted their lives to come with me and help me get better.

The house we'd rented wasn't large—three small bedrooms, a kitchen, a living room, and a small front porch. Our location was rather rural, as in no sidewalks. We were located off a highway and shielded by trees. Issa and I had cleaned the kitchen yesterday, so it didn't take me long to dust and vacuum the living room. I made the dusting a much more elaborate task than it needed to be. By the time I finished, I was hot and sweaty. I wrapped the blanket that hung over the back of the huge recliner Lore usually favored around my body and headed to the front door. "I'm going outside to cool off," I called over my shoulder. "Luna, come."

The wolf trotted to me, and Lore nodded once. He knew I wouldn't leave the porch. I followed the rules he had set in place without question.

I sat on the steps with Luna sprawled out beside me and started to scratch her back. She was giving me a wolfy grin when all of a sudden she jumped off of the porch and ran to the edge of our yard.

I couldn't see anything. Our outside lights didn't illuminate that far. "Lore," I called as I got to my feet, preparing to hurry back inside, but I heard something running. I strained to see in the dark.

A large black wolf ran toward our porch with Luna trailing behind him.

I didn't check with Lore to see if it was all right before I started to sprint toward the wolf.

He changed as I threw myself into his arms.

"You came." I was out of breath from laughing and crying at the same time.

"My beautiful girl," he said, his voice rumbling.

I buried my face in his neck and held onto his shoulders. It felt so good to be in his arms.

He carried me to the porch and slowly allowed me to

slide down his body until my slippered feet touched the ground.

"Welcome, Laird," Lore said from the porch. He leaned against the column looking relaxed as if this was an expected visit.

"Thank you." Black flashed a smile.

"What are you doing here? You weren't supposed to arrive until tomorrow afternoon." I sounded whiny and immediately shut up. I was surprised, not upset.

"We were ready, and I had nothing important on my schedule, so I decided that we should get on the road."

I leaned into his side. "I'm glad you're here."

"I thought that you'd be sleeping."

"She began cleaning at midnight. Please, come in." Lore led the way up the stairs and into the house.

"It probably looks different with furniture." Suddenly, I was very nervous.

"You have been comfortable here?"

"Yes. I think so." I pointed to the sofa. "Please, sit down. Would you like something to eat or to drink?" Automatically, I went into hostess mode.

My guard shook his head. "Theo, please sit. I will get the drinks and then check on Luna."

I blinked. Lore surprised me by taking over the host duties.

Black had a beer and, I, a bottle of water, and then we were alone.

"Were you going to make yourself known tonight?" I asked.

He seemed to be thinking about his answer. "Perhaps." He took another drink before answering. "I needed to run after driving straight through. I wanted to check on you, but I didn't want to wake you."

I didn't know what to make of that answer. "I guess it was a good thing I was up and outside." I tried to smile, but it felt strained. I gave him a sideways glance. "When did you grow the beard?"

"I hear that in some places men grow beards during the winter."

I liked the beard on him very much. It made him appear even more dangerous.

His gaze raked over me. "You cut your hair."

I touched my now shorter hair. "It needed it. I think the last time I'd been to a salon was before I went to Texas."

"I like it."

"I found out that my cousin…well, one of my cousins, owns a salon, so I went there."

"You're enjoying getting to know your family?"

I gave him a little smile. "Aly, who owns a salon, cut it. She was the second to respond to my call, Meg was the first to answer. She's the oldest and works at the high school and we've met for coffee a few times. There's a younger cousin, Ken, and his wife, Polly, I haven't seen them yet." I realized I was yammering. I'd mentioned all of this to him this during our calls.

"Do you find them enjoyable?"

"They're very nice and curious about my life." I rushed to add, "I mean, that I moved around and now work for a security company." I didn't want him to think I'd ever strayed from the cover story. "We live different lives. I remember them as kids, but many years have passed."

"You are happy to reconnect? It is not wrong to wonder about your family."

"Novus is my family." Isn't it? Had something changed?

He nodded once. "I mean your human family."

"It was nice to see them, but I don't feel any deep ties." I yawned and covered my mouth. I think the fact that it was after two had finally caught up with me.

Lore and Luna returned a second later. "We will be in my room," Lore announced and headed to the hallway.

"I should let you go to bed." Black looked at the front door.

"You...you aren't going to stay?" What was happening?

I read surprise in his eyes. "You want me to?"

"Well, yeah," I choked out the words.

He glanced at the hallway, then back at the front door.

"You didn't kiss me," I said quietly.

"What?"

"When you got here, you didn't kiss me, and you still haven't," I accused. I'd been the one to throw myself at him. I'd leaned into his body, giving him every opportunity. I felt my anxiety shoot up, "Do you not want me anymore?"

"No," he answered quickly.

"Then why?" My voice shook. None of this made any sense unless he was here to break up with me.

"Honey, I don't know what to do." He said the words really fast as if he wanted them to calm me.

"You do what you always do. You always sleep with me." Then I added, "That is if you still want me...?" I tried to meet his eyes. I needed to know. All of my plans for the future included Black and our life with Novus.

He grabbed my wrist gently and pulled me into his body. "Of course, I want you, Theo. We want you. You are our mate."

I swallowed hard and closed my eyes, feeling the relief wash over me. "Then why?"

"I'm not sure what the rules are. You've come so far. I don't want to do anything to fuck that up."

I knew he was speaking the truth. "You won't." He was the reason I'd hung on and fought for so long. I ran my hands over his chest and gripped his shoulders. "I want you to stay. I've missed you so much."

"But what... I don't know what I can and can't do," he ended weakly.

"You'll know, we'll know." I turned and led him to my bedroom.

THIRTY-FIVE

NOVUS

RAIDER BLACK

Still They Ride by Journey

I SHOULD BE TELLING HER NO. I SHOULD WAIT TO SPEAK with her therapist, but my wolf wanted to be with Theo. We would sleep. That would be all, after I kissed her, because I wanted to kiss her so very badly.

My plan had been to run past the rental, perhaps look in a window, speak with her guard, and go back to the hotel. However, I hadn't been able to resist the pull of my mate being so near. Seeing her sitting on the steps, looking so much like she had before the attack, petting that damn pet wolf, I couldn't stay away.

She appeared to be healthier. She'd gained much of the weight that she'd lost. Her blue eyes were bright and expressive, not the dead and hurt-filled gaze I'd stared into for so long. The pliant woman was gone and in her place was the Theo I remembered, the one who spoke up. I felt like a huge weight had lifted from my shoulders. *We will protect her.* My wolf spoke as if I needed a reminder that she'd still have triggers and reactions. I'd spent hours every night reading about PTSD and accounts from rape survivors about the after-effects. When Solle and Conal had joined me for dinner last Saturday, I'd instructed her to institute a monthly mandatory information session for the Novus Guards, so that they could be educated about this disorder and so would my Pack.

She led me into her small bedroom. "My bed isn't as big as yours."

"There's room on the floor." I'd slept in my wolf form, either beside her bed or at the foot, when she'd returned from Texas.

"No." Her response was sharp. "I don't want that. I want you with me," she motioned up and down with her hand, "in this form."

I refused to second guess her. I pulled my shirt over my head, and as soon as the cotton fabric uncovered my eyes, I could see her smiling.

I sat on the edge of the bed to take off my boots and socks. Then I stood again. "Climb in." The bed rested against the wall so I would sleep on the outside.

She kicked off her slippers. As she moved on all fours, she paused to shoot me a sly look over her shoulder before she settled on the mattress.

I prepared to get in.

"Why are you wearing your jeans?" She scrunched her nose and looked adorable. Tasty.

And that was why I was wearing my jeans. "Thought

it would be a good idea." I stretched out on the soft mattress.

She rolled onto her side, facing me. "Black, don't be silly. Take them off."

Her scent wasn't nervous or apprehensive. So, I did as she bid. Once again, I was back in bed, and she wrapped her arm around my belly.

"Better?"

"Yes." I was hard. I wanted her hand to travel lower as I... No. I couldn't do that.

She was using her fingernails to lightly brush over my side. "Do you want to kiss me?"

"*Yessss.*" I wanted to do so much more.

"Good." She pushed up on her forearms, leaned over me, and kissed my lips.

I allowed her to explore. This was about her and her comfort. When she used the tip of her tongue to trace the seam where my lips joined, I opened for her.

"You can touch me," she urged against my lips.

I didn't know if I should. I wasn't sure I could stop. I rested my hands lightly on her shoulders.

"I won't break."

"I'm not sure about this."

She lifted her head. "What aren't you sure about, Black?" Her tone was angry.

I'd upset her. "I want you. It's been a long time, Theo, and you, like this, soft, and enticing...you know you're sexy as hell." I ran one hand down her spine. "I would want more."

"And you think I don't?"

I could smell her arousal. "I think that right now you do, but if something should change...I want to know the right way to handle it."

She rolled off me, dropped onto her back, and covered her eyes with her forearm. "Jesus, fuck." Her voice shook. "I don't want it to be like this."

I could see her breasts rising and falling with each breath. "It won't always be like this," I promised. "I'm sure I'm breaking one of your doctor's rules by being here." I grinned, since when did I care about other people's rules? However, for this woman, I would do anything.

She uncovered her eyes and turned her face toward me, studying my expression.

"You two, together, have done amazing work. I almost lost you. To see you like this, it's better than I'd hoped."

Her forehead creased as she drew her eyebrows together.

I continued, "I knew you were better. I could tell from our weekly calls, but to find you looking healthy and being demanding. I want to listen to what Dr. Joseph says. She has proved she knows what she is doing."

"I'm not demanding," she said with a tiny smirk.

"A little," I countered and smiled in answer, "and I like it."

She rolled onto her side and once again placed her arm over me. "I like you."

"That's good, babe, real good."

She rested her cheek against my pec.

I dropped a kiss onto her hair. I sent a silent thank you to The Lady. My Theo was back in my arms.

I woke before Theo. She had not had any bad dreams and was resting peacefully. I slid out of bed, pulled on my jeans, then walked down the hallway to the kitchen.

Issa was pouring a cup of coffee. "This is for you, Laird."

"Thank you." I accepted the mug from the guard.

She poured her own, walked to the refrigerator and opened the door. "Lore will be back in time to drive us to the doctor's office."

She had not made eye contact. "It wasn't my decision, Issa."

She finally looked at me. "You could have ordered him to attend to you on this trip."

"Is that what you want?" Their courtship seemed to consist of fleeting moments of understanding, followed by physical and verbal fights, then times when she would not speak to the poor male for weeks.

She pulled out two cartons of eggs and meat wrapped in brown paper. "I don't know what I want." She slammed the meat package on the counter by the stove. "Is that okay with you?"

"Don't snap at him." Theo leaned against the doorway. "None of us knows what's going on with the two of you. If you're mad that Asher didn't make the trip, then call him and have it out." She took two more steps inside and stopped beside me, presenting her Novus brand then continuing to the coffee maker. "Tell him to get his ass here or to go to hell, but for God's sake, tell him something. You've kept him waiting for too long."

Issa, who was in the process of lining up strips of thick cut bacon on a baking pan, turned quickly and snarled at the Seer. "Everybody wants to tell me what to do, but nobody ever asks me what I want."

Theo glanced at me. I wouldn't intervene, yet. Issa was her personal guard. It was her responsibility to deal with the outburst.

"Why don't you go get the paper at the end of the driveway? Just give us a minute," she suggested.

"Sure thing." I left my now empty mug on the edge of the counter and decided to do as she asked.

"Iss, nobody says this mating and relationship thing is easy," I heard Theo begin. "But you haven't been exactly forthcoming about what's going on."

"That's because I don't know what's happening. It's so confusing. I do not like feeling..."

Theo chuckled. "Out of control, full of need, warm and fuzzy? You can stop me if I'm wrong."

I had slowed so I could hear her very interesting thoughts. Now, I felt a grin spread across my face. Theo had this handled.

"The paper, Black," she yelled.

I'd grabbed a quick shower after Theo had finished hers. We were now sitting in Dr. Joseph's waiting room. Theo had been nervous during the ride, and now she couldn't sit still. I was unsettled, but I was doing a better job of hiding it. It was Lore's behavior that had my attention.

He seemed to be on full alert, and I detected no threat. Dr. Joseph was on the other side of the wall, but the human was alone. There was activity on the floor below us, but that was expected. It was an accounting office with many employees. The wolf seemed totally focused on what was going on inside Dr. Joseph's office.

I heard her walk toward the door and open it.

Theo stood, and I followed.

Bayla Joseph froze mid-step. Her gaze swept from Lore to Theo and then stayed on me. Two points of color appeared on her cheeks as her eyes widened in surprise. "You honor me, Sire." She bowed her head.

I felt Theo's body jerk, but she said nothing.

"It is I who owes you much, Sister."

Bayla Joseph was an attractive woman with dark blonde hair. She was dressed conservatively in a navy skirt and a pale peach silky blouse. She wore little jewelry, only a thin gold chain around her neck that I would bet carried a pentagram charm most likely hidden at the back. She had already proven herself competent. I believed that we shared a no-nonsense temperament. I liked her immediately.

"Now, many things make sense." She moved closer.

"I don't understand." Theo had taken my hand as we stood. Now she added pressure to our joined hands.

"Dr. Joseph recognized me by my aura." I glanced at her for confirmation.

The doctor inclined her head. "That is correct."

"And I knew by her scent," I explained.

Theo was studying her therapist openly. "What is she?"

I wondered if the doctor had noticed that Theo had turned to me for the answer. "I call her Witch."

"You mean, like me?" Theo glanced at the doctor.

I shook my head. "There is no other like you." That was the truth.

Dr. Richard smiled. "I am Wiccan. I descend from a long line of female practitioners, born with certain talents."

"You can read auras?" Theo asked slowly.

"Yes." Dr. Joseph was not relaxed, but she was not uncomfortable in the company of two Lycans. "Your

Leader's aura carries strong colors because of his station, and earth tones because you are near."

Theo was staring at me, trying to see what the witch saw. "What about Lorenzo?"

The woman's demeanor changed. She was flustered but recovered quickly. She slowly turned to the guard.

He spoke first. "It is of no matter."

Theo didn't insist on her reading Lore. Instead, she asked, "And me?"

"Today, you are very content."

"So, what you see is emotion driven?" she asked.

"Not exactly," the therapist hedged. "I've never seen an aura like yours, Theodora. I don't know how to label you."

"A true gift," Lore said in his deep voice.

The therapist didn't turn her body to face Lore, only her head. "Really?" Her tone was almost a challenge, and yet I didn't sense any anger in the room.

There was a strange energy between the two. Clearly, the Witch was dismissive to the Guard. I'd never seen any being react to Lore in this manner.

Theo defused the tenseness of the moment. "You didn't think that when you had to go with me to shop for new make-up."

One side of his mouth tipped up. "That was trying."

The doctor took over. "I think it would be best if I spoke with Theodora first, then you, Sire, and finally the two of you together."

I returned to my seat as Theo flashed me a small smile and followed the doctor into her office.

One hour later, Theo returned and seemed tired, but no longer nervous. Lore had warned that this would happen. I didn't want to leave her. She gave my hand a reassuring squeeze and said softly, "Have fun."

I entered the smaller room. The space had large windows, a sofa, and two chairs. I chose the fabric-covered wing chair that sat opposite the dark brown leather chair belonging to the doctor.

"Now, I understand," she began.

"Sophia spoke highly of you, but she did not mention your lineage. My advisors and I devised Theo's story before the first therapist arrived."

"Glossing over the supernatural elements..." She glanced at her leather-bound notebook, "Otherwise, to an outsider she would seem delusional."

"The violation she experienced in Texas was by a male. Does it really matter if he was of human or of Lycan origin?"

"No."

"You recognized her guards for what they are?"

"Yes, but I believed that Theodora did not know."

"She was instructed not to disclose that information."

"Do you always speak of her in such a cold tone?"

"No. I am addressing my order that Theo was not to disclose her ties to our world." I leaned back into the chair. Dr. Joseph was intelligent. I enjoyed parrying with intelligence.

"She apologized a number of times to me."

"Theo is truthful. She would consider not being fully transparent with you as being untruthful, and that does bother her greatly." She understood the ramifications, but I knew her heart.

"You care for her," she observed.

"I love her. She is mine."

"You do understand that the traumatic event and its aftermath has affected her greatly."

I cut her off. "I accept that it has changed her. She will behave differently, and in certain situations, she might shut down. I am prepared to face these changes." I stared evenly at the doctor.

She smiled ruefully. "I suppose it is a benefit that you have lived many years and made many changes in order to survive and succeed."

Our session continued for another fifty minutes. Not much was accomplished. We were measuring one another, each giving only a little after considering each word.

Theo had joined us. I sat beside her on the sofa. She was tense, and I wished that I could put her at ease.

"I told your Leader that you've made remarkable progress and that I believe the next step is for you to return to your home."

Dr. Joseph might not fully comprehend the depth of my feelings for Theo. I did not have to prove that to her. Theo knew, and that was all that mattered.

Theo smiled and relaxed a little.

"I mentioned to Dr. Joseph that she is welcome to visit if need be. We can also set up videoconferencing."

"How often?" Theo asked the doctor.

"At first, daily, and then as you settle in and progress, weekly."

"I have assured Dr. Joseph that I will give you whatever you need." It was my duty as her mate.

Theo's smile warmed my heart as she looked up at me. "I know that. You always have." She continued smiling at me.

"At this time, how would you describe your relationship?" Bayla's question seemed intrusive, but I reminded my wolf that this was part of Theo's healing process.

Theo shifted, tucking her left leg under her right. "I love him. I think I always have. I left Nebraska because I knew I couldn't stand to see him with another female." She paused to take a drink of water. "When...when word got to him about what had happened, he came immediately. When I woke up in the hospital, I knew that he still loved me."

"And now?"

Theo glanced at the doctor then at me in concern. "We are together." However, she did not sound sure. She looked at me once again.

"We are. I believe the doctor is unsure of our bond. Perhaps there are concerns that you will be unhappy living amongst our race? Allowing me, a Lycan male, to touch you."

The doctor gave a slow nod.

"It didn't matter last night when I asked you to kiss me," Theo said directly to me.

"Did things progress farther?" Dr. Joseph asked.

I answered, "No."

Theo continued, "Because he wouldn't let them."

"Lycans are known for their sex drive." The doctor made the statement sound like a challenge.

"I was with Black before, and we did just fine." Theo's eyes flashed a challenge.

I wanted to laugh, but there was a tightening in my gut, warning me that the Doctor was pushing for something else.

"Were you celibate during your time in Texas, Theodora?"

She frowned. "Of course."

"Because you were still in love with him?"

Theo shifted again and dropped her leg so that both feet rested on the floor. "Okay, let's get this straight. I was thrown in with a new Pack." She looked at me to see if she should continue speaking about our race.

I nodded once.

"All the reports that I'd read weren't giving them gold stars, so I was trying to figure all of that out. Then, I was basically locked away for days at a time. I had to ask to go outside. I didn't have a schedule or a regular job. I had little interaction except for one female, so it wasn't like I had the opportunity to check anybody out." She rolled her eyes. "I will say it again. I knew about his contract. I knew about Siobhan—that was never a secret. I loved him, but he was promised to another. It hurt, leaving those I'd come to think of as family. It broke my heart, but it was my choice." She began to tap her heel on the floor. "Would I have started looking for another? I don't know." She shrugged. "But during my time in Texas, I didn't want another for sex or for any kind of relationship."

"Were your feelings the same, Sire?"

Theo rushed to my defense. "He was in a completely different situation."

I took her hand in mine. "My answer is that I loved and do love, Theo. However, it was my duty to my pack and myself to try with Siobhan."

"Elaborate on what you did to try." The doctor made it sound like an order.

"We shared meals, conversations."

"And sex?" the doctor pushed.

"Yes."

I felt Theo's pain immediately. I studied her reaction.

She blinked several times, and her forehead was creased in worry.

"How does that make you feel, Theodora?"

She dropped my hand and pulled her bent knee to her chest. "Well, not very good." Then she let out a long breath. "A part of me knew that was a very good possibility." She looked at me and back at the doctor. "It stings to hear it, but I'm okay with it. How could I not be? She was to be his mate for eternity. It only makes sense." She licked her lips before she continued. "I made him promise that he would try with her. Forever is a very long time." She rolled her eyes. "I didn't want him to be hung up on me if he could be happy with her."

The doctor made a notation in her notebook. "You seem very comfortable with his world."

"Our world," Theo said with certainty.

I wanted to kiss her.

"If she had ever asked, I would have told her the truth. I don't lie to her." I gave the doctor a long stare.

"I must say that I find your relationship fascinating," the doctor admitted. A chime sounded, and she checked her watch. "I would like to see you be if your schedule is…accommodating…?" She directed the statement to me.

I waited for Theo to nod even though we both knew her schedule for her daily appointments. "I will be available."

We'd picked up sandwiches for lunch and had eaten at her rental house. I knew that she usually napped in the early afternoon. So, she was in bed, and I was sitting beside her. "Are you sure you want to go?"

"I feel like I have to. Did you see how excited she got?" We had run into one of Theo's cousins at the sandwich place, and she'd invited us to dinner.

"I don't want you to be upset," I said, frowning.

"This will be the last time I'll have a chance to see them, so I think I should go." She snuggled into her pillow. "I'm sorry you got roped into it."

"I'm going with you. I might learn more about you as a child."

She scrunched her nose. "They'll tell you I was a weirdo."

"Good to know that nothing has changed," I teased.

"I hope the food will be good." She closed her eyes.

"I need to make some calls, but I'll be in the living room if you need anything." I stood and smoothed the light blanket over her.

"'Kay."

Meg had been busy during the intervening hours. She'd invited her sister Aly and her husband, Mitch, and Ken and Polly. We were sitting around the antique cherry, dining room table. The conversations had come in stops and starts. Aly was still giving me curious looks, although Theo had introduced me as her boss and friend.

"So, what line of work are you in, Black?" Ken asked.

I thought the man was a bit of a blowhard, but I didn't let it bother me. "Security."

"Like a bodyguard?" his wife Polly joined in.

"Not personally. My company focuses on cyber and logistics."

"I don't think you ever said what you do there,

Theodora. Last I heard you were in school, taking some silly classes." Polly used a sweet tone, but her tongue was venomous.

"It's hard to explain," Theo smiled. "I try to identify threats before they happen."

Aly leaned forward. "That's so cool. How did you learn to do that?"

"I was dumped on the company." She winked at me. "I showed up, and then we had to figure out what I could do."

I wanted to kiss her. "She is very good at her job and vital to our people."

"For being in the security business, I'm surprised that she got hurt," Aly's husband murmured.

I broke the uncomfortable silence at the table. "That was very unfortunate. I've told Theo that it will be my mission to see that nothing like that ever happens again."

"It wasn't your fault," she said vehemently.

"It doesn't change the fact that you were injured."

"I think the world is going to hell," Polly complained. "Every day, I hear about people doing something awful to their neighbors. It was just two or three weeks ago in the next county over, Mr. Black, that a son killed his father and sister because they weren't willing to sell their farmland." She shook her head sorrowfully.

Ken leaned back in his chair. "I'm glad you brought that up." He turned to Theo. "I was surprised that you didn't agree to sell that acreage over on the creek side. With you moving away, I wouldn't think you'd care, Theodora."

She tilted her head a little before she answered. "I don't know what you're talking about."

"The lawyer said you sided with Uncle Doug, so we couldn't sell," Aly said.

Theo bit down on her bottom lip and said softly, "Uncle Doug?"

Thankfully, Meg took over. "When Grandma died, she left each of her children an equal portion of the farm. Since you momma's dead, hers went to you."

Theo slowly shook her head.

Meg asked gently, "You don't know anything about this, do you?" When Theo continued to give her a puzzled look, the woman continued, "That Goddamn son of a bitch." She glanced at her sister. "I told you and daddy that something was funny."

"I found out that grandmother had passed when I didn't hear from her at Christmas. I saw her obituary online, but by then, so many months had passed…" She looked around the table helplessly. "Oh dear, what must you all have thought about me?"

Aly spoke first, "I think we figured you were in school and didn't have the money to get back."

"I thought you should have called us for a bus ticket," Ken grumbled.

"She didn't know," Meg's voice was hard. "He lied about calling her." She then glanced at me. "Doug said that he'd left messages. The lawyer always acted like he was in contact with you."

"Never," Theo told her cousins.

"So, who's been cashing the checks?" Ken asked.

"Checks?" I wanted to keep this on track with getting information, instead of amplifying hurt family feelings.

"Every year, the family trust makes a disbursement."

"And Theo should have been getting this money?" I

pulled out my phone and started to compose a message to Tex.

"Well, somebody's been cashing those checks." Meg pushed her chair back and stood. "I'll get my laptop and show you the latest financial report."

"I bet Doug and that lawyer are taking the money," Polly spat.

"Now, cousin, are you sure you didn't make some side deal with Doug, and you don't want to admit to it?" Ken was giving her a sneer. "Your mama wasn't right in her head, so maybe you did something and forgot about it."

"Ken!" Meg slammed her laptop on the table. "That is no way to talk to a guest in my house." She turned to Theo. "I apologize. Money makes him stupid."

"Getting robbed would make anybody mad," Polly told the table.

"But Theo is the victim," I reminded the couple.

"Because she sided with Doug, we lost out on a couple million dollars," Ken raised his voice.

"I didn't know," Theo said quietly. "I haven't seen or talked to Doug in over twenty years. Everything you're saying is a complete surprise to me."

I felt the push in her voice, the slight vibration of the electrical buzz of her magic against my skin. My wolf stirred, waited, and watched.

The others nodded. Meg resumed booting up the computer.

"I would like the name of the attorney you mentioned." My people would get to the bottom of this. Doug was already a dead man. I'd been waiting until we were about to leave for Nebraska before taking revenge for his past transgression.

"I'll send you the file where I keep all the financials and everything that I have. I need the e-mail address," Meg said.

I pulled my card from my back pocket and slid it to her. "I appreciate it."

She glanced up and met my gaze. "I figure a man like you will know what to do."

I liked Meg very much.

Theo was talking in the corner of the living room with Aly. I took the last of the crystal glassware to Meg in the kitchen.

"Thank you for including me in your invitation," I said. "Dinner was delicious."

She glanced over her shoulder. "I didn't think Theodora would come alone." She shrugged. "I don't know much about what happened to her, but I've been around animals all of my life, and I can tell when one's been traumatized."

I didn't answer.

"I'm glad to see that she's a fighter. She'll learn to deal with her pain and prosper." Meg turned off the water in the sink and reached for the dishtowel to dry her hands. "Her mother, I used to stare at her because she was so pretty, but she was lost. I was just a kid, but I could tell."

"Her mother's story is very unfortunate," I answered.

"I'm glad that Theodora has somebody like you to care for her." Meg looked me straight in the eye.

"I take that responsibility very seriously."

"Well, I hope there's room for a little bit of fun," She then bumped my arm with her shoulder and chuckled. "You look like you want to have some fun with my cousin." She then shook her head. "Friends, friendly lovers is more like it, right?"

"I do love her," I admitted to the straight-forward woman.

She nodded. "Glad to hear it. I think she deserves a good man."

THIRTY-SIX

NOVUS

THEODORA MORRISSEY

Come to Me by the Goo Goo Dolls

BLACK HAD INSISTED THAT WE DRIVE ALONE TO MEG'S. I was sure our guards were around but out of sight. I was glad we had this time alone. "I can't say that I'm surprised," I said, speaking my thoughts aloud. "I mean, Uncle Doug was always sneaky." I glanced at Black's profile.

"He stole from you." His voice was hard.

"And the rest of the family."

"He will die."

I wasn't surprised that the Leader of the Novus Pack had made that declaration. A part of me was a little surprised that Doug was still alive. I had asked Black not to kill or have Doug killed after I'd shared what had happened in the barn when I was fifteen, but Black dealt with those who attacked Pack members with finality.

347

"You have no comment?"

I could barely make out his expression by the dashboard lights, but one side of his mouth was hitched upward. "I wear the Novus brand. A member of your Pack has been wronged, so it's your right to decide how he will pay."

"My Intended Mate was wronged," he corrected me, his voice taking on a tiny bit of a growl. "He harmed you when you were young. For that alone, he earned death."

"And then I told you I didn't want you to have more blood on your hands. I didn't want to add to that," I reminded him with heat. "I never said you couldn't kill him; I just didn't want it to happen right then."

He started to laugh. I didn't understand why. I replayed my words and still didn't see the joke. "Why are you laughing?"

"Because My Queen, it always thrills my wolf when your thirst for blood emerges. You may have been born human, but you have the spirit of a wolf, my love."

I felt the long-dormant heat start to build low in my belly. It increased with each beat of my heart. My nipples were so hard they hurt, and my thigh muscles tensed with anticipation. "Stop the car," I ordered.

"What?" He looked at me but was already applying the brake. "Babe, what's wrong?

I unhooked my seatbelt and scrambled to my knees on my seat and leaned across the SUV's center console, grabbing onto his strong shoulders. I kissed him.

I wanted him.

As his tongue invaded my mouth, I wound my hand in his long hair. I think the ring he'd given me tore a few strands as I grasped the back of his skull. I finally had to

348

break away to breathe. My lungs were burning because I forgot how to take in air.

"Baby, what the fuck was that?" His voice was rough as his hands gripped my waist.

"You." I sounded out of breath "I want you." My smile was so big my cheeks hurt.

"Not here."

I considered that for a moment. I knew he could be convinced, but Black was a big male, and I liked room to move. "Then let's go home." I started to push away from him. He stopped me with another sensuous kiss. This one was full of promise.

I think I fanned myself for a few moments. The drive seemed to take forever. This was how it had always been between us, once we'd given into our feelings. A look, a touch, or a single kiss, and I was ready to give him whatever he demanded.

He parked in the driveway, and Issa opened the door as we walked up the porch steps.

"It sounded like your family is nice." She was bouncing on the balls of her feet.

"Did you eavesdrop?" I teased. Of course, she had. Issa was fascinated by the human world and my old life here.

She shrugged carelessly. "I needed to know what was going on."

"Thank you for your service, and now, you are excused for the night," Black followed me into the house.

"Lore is not back, so I will stay," she said.

"Issa...go," Black told her slowly.

She glanced at our Leader, and then at me with a question in her eyes. She wanted to make sure that was what I wanted.

"Go enjoy the rest of the night." I smiled at my guard. "I know I will."

"Thank you, Seer and Laird." She bowed her head and changed into her wolf form by the time she leaped from the top step.

Black closed the door and locked it. "We need to set some ground rules."

I grinned saucily. "That sounds fun." The memory of the night he'd given me a spanking flashed into my head. "Lay them on me, Sir."

I knew he was trying to fight a smile by the way his gray eyes turned warm. "You have to tell me what you want, and you can change your mind at any time. I'm good with holding you all night. We don't have to rush."

"I'm not good with that." I stood tall.

One brow rose. "Then, tell me what you want."

I walked to where he stood and wrapped my arms around his waist. "I want you, naked."

"I need a shower." He wrapped his arm around my waist, and we headed down the hall.

He'd undressed, dropping his clothes on the floor in a pile, and headed into my bathroom. I heard the shower come on. I undressed more slowly.

Black must have noticed, because he pulled back the curtain and called, "Babe, you comin'?"

"Hopefully, I will be," I said under my breath. I stopped at the laundry hamper and took off my bra and panties.

He continued to hold back the white curtain as I climbed in. It wasn't as spacious as the shower in Black's home. This was a regular human tub/shower combo, so we were standing close. Black took up a lot of room. His slick hands started at my shoulders and stroked down my arms.

I closed my eyes and stretched my neck so that my hair was under the warm spray. My hands ran over his strong chest.

His were now on my back, tracing the vertebrae of my spine.

I spoke quietly, "I have so many scars." I'd worn the marks over my hips from his claws with pride. I had considered them another mark of his ownership and of what we'd shared. However, my ribs, back, and thighs carried marks from another. Every time I looked at them, I remembered the pain.

"All true Warriors do." He pulled me closer and hugged me to his chest. "They are a history of what you have overcome and survived."

"They don't bother you?"

"The more important question is, do they bother you?"

"They do. I hate them." His chest muffled my answer.

"Then we will do something about them. When you are ready, we will find a doctor who can remove them."

The sureness of his tone and his words made something inside my belly unwind. "Thank you." I kissed the skin over his heart.

He gently palmed my cheeks and lifted my head so that he could kiss my lips. "You are my heart."

I loved this male. My hand traveled down his right side, and then to his center. I stroked his hardness, and he grew bigger in my hand.

I tightened my grip, measuring his thickness. With my other hand, I used his strong thigh to help me balance as I lowered to my knees. My mouth watered in anticipation of his taste.

Once I was settled on my knees, Black widened his stance and rested his fingertips on my shoulder blades. I took him into my mouth, sucking lightly as he filled my senses. His cinnamon taste, the mystery of the softness of his skin and his scent, as I buried my nose in his wiry hair at the base. I used my tongue on the sensitive underside of the head, and I felt the fingers resting on my shoulders flex.

I've missed this. The second the recognition registered in my mind, another bit of the tightness deep inside me lessened. I made an appreciative sound deep in my throat. This felt so right. I wanted...no...I *needed* more.

He read my mind, or maybe he felt the same. His hands shifted to under my arms, and he lifted me to cradle me close to his chest. He climbed over the tub's side and carried me to the bed. He climbed onto the mattress, and then twisted his body so that I was resting on top of him.

"I missed this." I sounded breathless.

"I missed you, Theo." He kissed me. It was wet and messy—more teasing than passionate. "Sit up. I want to taste your tits."

I pushed off his shoulders and sat up, feeling his cock against my ass. His hands were on my breasts, and he sat up. His mouth was so hot as he took my nipple inside that I kneaded his shoulders with my nails and threw back my head.

He rested his hand against my mound. He wasn't demanding entrance; he waited for me to shift my body. Slowly, his thick finger followed the contours of my outer lips.

I moaned, wishing to be filled. "Please, Raid."

His finger continued playing with me, teasing, making me crazy with need.

"Baby, please," I cried, but I was loving this. Feeling the need and our bond, it was like we had never been apart.

"What do you need, Theo?"

I laughed low and deep. "You." Wasn't that obvious? He was my everything. I had sacrificed my happiness for his, and when I'd given up, unable to feel hope, it had been his urging that had kept me fighting to live.

He kissed me again.

I pressed against his chest so that he lay flat. I then gripped his cock and positioned it at my entrance. I paused and met his gaze as I slowly lowered my body. I could feel him stretching my channel.

When I was full, I didn't move. I took in a deep breath, memorizing this feeling of Black buried deep inside of me.

"Shit, Theo," Black's hands were clutching my hips. "Don't move, babe, just give it a minute. Let me have this."

When I could wait no longer, I started to roll my hips. Very soon, we found our rhythm. In the past, our lovemaking had been tender, and at other times, wild and physical. I would call tonight's tentative.

He started to circle my clit, and I felt the fire spread up my spine. "*Yesssss.*" I was close. I sped up my movements. I was reaching for my release, chasing the feeling.

He rolled us so that he was over me, resting his weight on his forearms. "Easy, Theo."

I lifted my head and kissed him as I tried to wrap my arms around his upper arms.

"You okay?"

"More," I urged.

He set a faster pace and mumbled an occasional word in a language I didn't understand.

I closed my eyes and enjoyed how good it felt as his cock moved inside of me. How our bodies seemed to fit together perfectly, how easily my leg looped over his thigh.

And how amazing it was when he touched that special place. "Ahhhhhh." My release was as if my muscles tensed in synchronicity, and then all relaxed at once. I felt...complete.

Black lifted my thighs so that they were higher on his body and pumped into me. He tensed and growled as he emptied his cum inside me.

He was breathing heavily. "Theo, babe, you okay?"

I nodded because I couldn't find my voice.

He slowly pulled out of me and rolled to his side.

So many thoughts flooded my head. I think a sob escaped.

"What's wrong?" He sat up. "Baby, did I hurt you?"

I slid up until my back was resting against the headboard. "No." I managed to get the word out. I reached for the pillow beside me to use the pillowcase's edge to wipe my tears.

Black shifted on his knees to face me. "Theo?" he asked softly.

I needed to reassure him. "I-I'm okay. Really."

"Then why are you crying?"

I was trying to control my breathing. I rested my head against the wood. "It's silly."

"I could use some silly about now." He sat back on his heels, but his gaze never left mine.

"I guess it's because I'm relieved." I shrugged because that was too simple of an explanation for what I felt.

He moved so that he was sitting beside me and took my hand. "I think I'm going to need a little bit more to understand."

"I did it. Well, I mean, *we* did it…but I did it." I smiled because I felt so joyous. I glanced at Black. He was still confused. "Since the, uhm, the attack, I haven't done anything sexual," I admitted.

"Not even alone?"

"What I mean is that I didn't feel anything."

He spoke slowly as if he was trying to comprehend what I was and wasn't saying. "Like you were numb?"

"At first, I hurt constantly. Once I had healed, I didn't have any urges. I didn't feel sexy at all. I didn't really want to be touched."

"But you let me hold you…"

"I wanted comfort and security, but the thought of anything sexual… I felt nothing, and that scared me."

He let me talk. That was another thing I loved about him. Black could be demanding and low on patience, but with me, he was a really good listener. He always made me feel safe so that I could speak my truths.

"I haven't touched myself since that night. I haven't wanted to." I shifted closer to him. "From the moment I saw you in the yard, I felt…more, and tonight, I wanted you inside of me."

He cradled my jaw with his hand. "Just when I think I couldn't love you more, you blow me away, Theo."

THIRTY-SEVEN

RAIDER BLACK

I Go Through by O.A.R.

I heard the older model truck pull into the driveway. Lore was outside with his wolf and would be watching. Two minutes later, the doorbell rang once.

Theo stirred. "Was that the door?" She started to sit up. "It's seven, who comes to the door at seven?"

The bell sounded again, this time followed by knocking.

She pulled on a pair of yoga pants and a T-shirt with no bra. "Are you coming with me?" She glanced at me.

I'd pulled on my jeans. "You answer the door." I knew I should warn her, but I wanted her to face him. She needed to believe in her inner strength.

She hurried to the door. I trailed after her, staying in the shadowed hallway. I watched as she opened it then blocked the entrance. I couldn't see the man, but I knew exactly who he was.

"Theodora? Is that you?"

"Yes." Her one word sounded short and angry. "What do you want?"

"Is that any way to greet your blood?" the man drawled in a slightly whiny voice.

"Why are you here?"

"I heard you were in town. Last night my phone rang off the hook."

"You have five minutes, Doug." She opened the door.

An older man entered the house. He was muscular and barrel-chested. I smelled a mixture of aggression and tobacco. My wolf urged, *Kill him.*

"I thought you were too high and mighty to come to these parts." His tone was angry.

"It's a visit." Theo leaned against the armchair's back, putting plenty of room between them.

Doug shook his head while his gaze narrowed on Theo. "You stirred up the hornet's nest. Got Meg and Aly all upset, and that Polly was screeching into the phone."

"They seem to think that you cheated me out of my inheritance," she told him calmly.

"You weren't around, just like your mama."

"I was sent away because you sexually assaulted me."

Kill him now, my wolf growled in frustration.

"You were askin' for it, just like your mama," he sneered.

"What do you mean?" she asked quietly, too calmly.

"She wanted it, always coming back to the farm, wantin' me."

"Did you hurt her?" Theo advanced on the man. "You, pig!"

He started to swing at her, but I was there, shoving him to the ground. He would not touch her. I stood over the man.

"What did you do to her?" Theo yelled.

The man slowly got to his feet and studied me. "Just like your mother, a whore."

"Fuck you," Theo screamed trying to get around my body.

"We ain't done, girlie." He spat on her floor.

"I think we are." I glared at the human. He would be dead by nightfall.

He moved slowly to the door, stepping sideways so that he didn't take his gaze off me. "Crazy whore." He stomped off the porch.

Theo wrapped her arms around my middle and rested her cheek against my back. "He's so old."

"He will never touch you," I promised her as I gently pulled on her arm so that she would face me.

"I know," she stepped around my side so I could see her face. "A part of me wanted him to hit me. I could have him arrested."

"Our way is better."

I heard her snort. "I'm surprised that you let him leave...alive."

Cleaning up was time-consuming, and I didn't want that to happen in Theo's home. I would handle things later, I vowed to my wolf. "Over the years, I have learned patience."

"But he will die." It wasn't a question.

"Yes, My Queen." I lifted her chin and kissed her.

. . .

359

We again sat on the sofa in Dr. Joseph's office. I'd watched Theo closely this morning, and she did not appear to be upset by her uncle's visit or my promise to end his life. The doctor had spoken with Theo alone for a little over an hour, and then asked that I join them.

"Theodora has shared that you were intimate last night." She looked from Theo to me.

"We were." I answered for us both.

"Any concerns or observations that you'd like to share?"

"Theo initiated it," I started, "she set the pace."

"And how do you think it went?"

"I think the more important question is what she thinks." I stared at the doctor.

Theo stretched her legs out in front of her. "I think it went great." Then she smiled at me.

"No worries?"

"A few before, but it all worked out." She blushed, and I wanted to kiss her because she was so cute.

"Like riding a horse," I teased.

She elbowed me. "Are you comparing yourself to a horse?"

I shrugged one shoulder and smirked.

She turned to the doctor. "I think things will be fine. I can talk to him. He listens."

"I noticed that you diffused what could have been an uncomfortable moment with humor." The doctor spoke to me.

"She likes to laugh and to make me laugh."

"I shared with Theodora that, when she returns to Nebraska, I will be available if an emergency arises for either or both of you."

"You are welcome to visit. You will be an honored guest," I told her.

"Thank you." She nodded her head.

The chime sounded, ending our session. We all got to our feet.

Theo hugged Dr. Joseph. "Thank you."

"You put in the work, Theodora. You should be very proud of what you've accomplished."

Theo hugged her again. "I am, but I couldn't have done it without your guidance."

I nodded my head at the doctor. "I am in your debt. Remember that, doctor."

"I wish you would call me, Bayla."

I grinned. "Bayla, we look forward to your visit."

I climbed into the SUV after Theo and closed the door.

"The diner?" Lore asked from the driver's seat.

"I'm starving," she told us.

Theo ate a salad with chicken. Lore and I ordered four burgers each.

"I told you she would get used to your order," Theo told Lore. "The first time, the waitress stared at him for a full minute because he ordered so much food."

Issa joined us. "Am I late?"

"No." I waited until she had placed her order, which matched ours, and then I continued. "We should discuss how soon you wish to leave, Theodora."

"Tomorrow," Theo said instantly.

"So, you are cured?" Issa asked.

"No, I'll never be cured, but I am better. Bayla taught me coping strategies. There are signs to watch for so that I don't slip into depression like last time." She glanced at me. "Maybe Sophia can hold a class for everybody?"

I nodded. "That has been arranged."

Theo started to shred her paper napkin in her lap. I wanted to cover her hands to still them, but I knew it was important that she explain her condition. "There will be times when things frighten me. They might not make sense, but the way Bayla explained it is that my brain and my body remember things. Something might remind them of the attack, so they signal danger. Remember a week ago, when that thunderstorm freaked me out a little?"

"You paced," Issa recalled.

"I've never been afraid of thunder, but that night, my anxiety was through the roof for a little bit." She took a sip of her water. "Instead of trying to figure out why something like the rumble of thunder is making me uneasy, I will accept that it's my body's reaction. I'll try one of the relaxation techniques I've learned."

"And you'll teach them to me," I told her.

"You will adjust," Lore added.

Theo gave her guards a warm smile as she leaned into my side. "My grandmother used to say that 'you can't argue with crazy,' so I'm going to try to work with it."

"We will need to pack up the house," Issa announced.

"That shouldn't take long." Theo reached for another napkin from the metal container on the table. "Are we taking back all of the furniture and kitchen things?"

"What do you suggest that we do with them?"

She glanced out the window for a moment, and I felt

her use her gift. She was trying to sense my reaction. "I was thinking that I would call Meg and see if she knew anybody who might need them."

"I could leave someone here to oversee, and that way, we could be on the road faster," I said.

"We can stop and buy boxes. It shouldn't take us more than three hours, Laird," Issa estimated.

"We need to stop at the hotel. I will explain the timeline to my people."

"I will need some time to take care of a few things," Lore said quietly.

Theo's gaze went to me immediately. "I'm sure Issa and I will be fine on our own."

"That's settled then," I said.

Issa drove us to the hotel. As she pulled into the drive, I instructed, "Let us out, and then come to room four-sixty-five." We had already drawn enough attention to ourselves. Apparently, this hotel wasn't accustomed to having an entire floor reserved and not every room filled. I didn't want to add to their curiosity by bringing more people through the front door with me.

Theo was walking beside me as we entered through the lobby's front doors. I saw the two soldiers immediately. They were sitting in two wing chairs facing us. I reached into my pocket and handed her my phone. "Call the Control Room, now."

She took the phone and headed to the right as if she was going to the reception desk. When I saw her swipe her finger over the screen, I continued deeper into the lobby.

THIRTY-EIGHT

THEODORA MORRISSEY

Paradise City by Guns N' Roses

THE TWO MALES SITTING IN THE LOBBY WERE LYCANS. When Black thrust his cell into my hands, I knew he was unsure of the reason for their visit. I tapped the number associated with the Control Room at Novus. While I waited for somebody to pick up, I tried to count how many humans were in the lobby. There were two behind the desk, and a family organizing their suitcases in the far corner.

"Control Room," a male's voice sounded in my ear.

"It's Theodora. I'm with Black in the lobby of his hotel. There are two males here. I think they're waiting for him. He didn't know them."

"You sound good, Theo, like your old self."

Conal's warm tone surprised me for a moment. "Thank you, sir," I answered automatically. "They're now on their feet, talking to Black. He looks calm, but he sent me away to call," I told his Second. I studied them closely. "I'm going to try to take photos and send them to you."

"I've alerted his guards," Conal told me calmly.

I clicked and hoped that Conal would recognize them. "I'm sending you the photos." I wished I could use my gift to learn their intent. My common sense said that since we weren't already in the middle of a bloodbath, that this was a friendly talk.

"They are two high-ranking guards from the local Pack."

I let out the breath I'd been holding. "They look to be talking, only."

"Where is your guard, Theo?"

"Black thinks his party has drawn too much attention."

Conal swore under his breath.

"I thank you for your help, Second." I missed Conal and our friendship. I wanted to ask about Solle and the pregnancy, but I couldn't.

"When you return, Theo, we need to talk."

I felt my heart begin to beat even faster. "As you wish, Second."

Black turned to me and held out his hand. "Theodora."

"He's calling for me," I told Conal, grateful for a way to end this strained call.

"Be safe."

I walked to Black and took his hand, but I released it once I was beside him, in case he needed to fight.

"This is my Intended Mate, Theodora Morrissey."

He introduced me to the two men. "Jenkins and Skiles are with the Lincoln Pack."

I nodded my greeting.

"They are here to issue an invitation from their Leader. We are invited to dinner tonight."

My mouth fell open a little. I didn't know what Black expected from me. My first reaction was that I didn't want to spend the evening with Lycans I didn't know. "That is very kind."

"I have explained that our time here is limited. We planned on being on the road tonight." He was feeding me the information so that I'd respond appropriately.

"I've been away from home for many months, as I'm sure you know. I very much miss our land and Novus."

"We would like to stop by and pay our respects and express our gratitude for allowing the Seer to stay here," Black told them and me.

"I will inform our Leader. Shall we say around five?" the wolf on the right asked.

"I will give you my card. If you would text the address, we will be there at five." Black slowly reached into his pocket and pulled out a business card.

Both wolves watched his hand.

After he handed over the card, he took my hand and said, "Thank you." He led me toward the elevator bank.

I didn't say a word or even glance to my left or right as two Novus guards appeared and followed us into the elevator car.

When the elevator beeped, signaling a stop on our floor, Black spoke, "Meeting in fifteen."

One of the guards handed Black a key card, and then he stationed himself outside the door Black unlocked. I followed him inside. I placed his cell on the desk, and sat on the corner of the bed.

His phone buzzed, and he answered it. "Keep your bitchin' to a minimum."

I assumed it was Conal. He would be livid that Black had walked around on another's land unguarded. I felt the stab of pain that appeared whenever I thought of the Second, and I wondered what our next conversation would cover.

"A drink, I told them. It's only right, and Ephraim isn't one for a lot of small talk if you remember." Black winked at me. "He probably just wants to say that he met a Marked and was too lazy to ask permission to call."

I leaned back on my elbows. This sounded like one of their regular calls, nothing concerning.

"We'll take Lore. That should shake them up," he continued. "Okay, maybe not, but I'll bring plenty of guards."

I stopped listening to his words and focused my attention to his tone. He was relaxed and teasing his friend.

He finished his call and dropped the phone on the table. "You need a nap?"

I dropped so that I was lying on my back. "No, I was just thinking about Conal and Solle."

"I spoke with them."

"What?" I sat up in surprise. "What happened?"

"Now, I don't want you to be mad, but it was time."

I'd thought about Conal and Black many nights as I'd tried to fall asleep. When I'd left Wolfsbane, things had been very tense between the two friends. "I worried

368

about you… I wished you could turn to Conal while you were going through everything with me."

"He could have come to me," he said, his words bitten.

"That is true." I blinked slowly. "At the time, I thought I was doing the right thing. Lessening the stress on their relationship, but it hurt you, adding to your stress. I never intended for that to happen."

"You chose to shield your friend from her mate's anger. It was unfortunate timing. I should have stepped in earlier and corrected Conal's interpretation of events. He threatened you when you were weakened. As well, Solle could have checked in with me at any time. We all share in the blame for this. I decided that I'd had enough. They were home, so I rang their bell."

"Holy Moly, you are the boss," I said under my breath.

The corners of his eyes crinkled, so I knew that he was enjoying this. "I didn't have to point fingers or lay blame. Once I asked them to think and look beyond the easiest answer, Solle figured it out."

"Was she angry?"

"At Conal and herself, and before I left, at me for not setting the record straight sooner." He smirked. "She ordered me to bring you around when we get back."

"Is she doing okay?" I asked wistfully. "The baby?"

"She is fine, and the young will be born within a month."

I shook my head. "I thought it odd that Conal was friendly when I called the Control Room."

"He has much to apologize for." His mouth tightened.

"I've missed him," I said softly.

He sat beside me on the bed and wrapped his arm around my waist to pull me into his side. "And he, you."

"I want to move on." I rested my head against his chest.

"Our way is that he must pay for wronging you."

I closed my eyes. "I hope we can go back to what it was like before."

"We will, because that is what you want."

Could it really be that simple?

A knock sounded at the door. Black and I broke apart. "Time for the meeting."

I scurried to the mirror to check my hair. I finger-combed it, then followed the Laird down the hotel's hallway.

Two hours later, we were in a convoy of four SUVs heading to the local Packhouse. After the very brief meeting, Issa and I packed up my clothing, along with the personal items I wanted to take to Nebraska. I'd called Meg, and she'd agreed to meet with Issa, who along with Lore, was staying behind to tie up loose ends here.

While I had dressed, Lore gave me a short etiquette lesson. I hoped that I remembered what to do. According to my guard, the Ohio Packleader was not considered as powerful as Black. His land was larger, so in some ways, they were considered equals. I hoped I could sit beside Black and simply nod at the correct times.

"You look beautiful," Black said against my ear.

Issa had helped me choose a new dress. It was an impulse buy while we'd been out one day in the mall. The dress was royal blue, with a V in the front and back and a full skirt. My make-up played up my eyes, and my lips were glossy.

Our driver, Seth, pulled into a long drive that led to a large, red brick house. I felt my gift stir. "There are a lot of people in there," I told Black.

"Thank you, Seer." He didn't act like he was surprised that I'd intuited that.

Now, I understood why so many accompanied us. He helped me from the SUV. I made sure to stay one step behind him, on his left. I did this so that he could maneuver easily if threatened.

"One drink," he said, placing a hand on the small of my back as we climbed the steps to the ornate front door.

The door was opened immediately by a Lycan in a dark suit. "Sire," he greeted Black solemnly.

Black was dressed in his usual jeans, but he'd changed into a button-down shirt. "Good evening. Raider Black and Theodora Morrissey."

"You are expected." The male stepped out of the way and opened the door wider. "Your men may stop in the cloakroom." He glanced to his right.

We then followed the male down a well-lit hallway. The walls were white, and there were crystal chandeliers everywhere. We entered a large drawing room filled with ten, no, twelve Lycans. "Ah, Black, you made it." A male placed his glass on the edge of a table and headed toward us. He looked to be in his early fifties, although I knew that he was much, much older. He might pass for a mild-mannered suburban homeowner, but I knew he'd ruled this land for over two hundred years.

"Ephraim, it is good to see you again. This is Theodora Morrissey."

I felt the Packleader try to measure my strength. I nodded and gave a closed-lipped smile.

He held out his had in the human custom. "It is a pleasure to meet a Marked."

I placed my hand in his and was surprised that he did not squeeze too hard. "Thank you for allowing me to stay on your land, Sire."

"You were no problem, just as Black promised."

A rounded woman who appeared to be older than the leader approached us.

"My mate, Katherine," Ephraim said.

The woman gave me a friendly look. "We shall leave the men to discuss business. Please, follow me." It wasn't a request.

I glanced at Black in confusion. Being separated had not been discussed.

Katherine sensed my misgivings. "We will be across the hall. I will leave the door open." This time her smile was kinder.

"Thank you." I lowered my chin.

"Shall we?" she asked the room, and several women followed us across the hall. It was decorated in soft pinks and blues, truly a ladies' parlor. I took the chair my hostess offered. "I think we can accommodate your drink request. Jeannette spends quite a bit of time watching cooking shows, keeping up with the times."

I glanced at the tall female behind a small pale wood bar. "A vodka tonic, please."

I accepted the drink from a maid and took a sip, and then placed it on the tiny table to my left. "This is a lovely room."

"Thank you. We have lived here a long time."

A younger woman with red hair rushed into the

room. "I do apologize, Mama. The traffic was terrible. I told my guard to hurry, but he still drove the speed limit."

"Loreen, we have a guest." Katherine's tone was sharp.

"I thought I smelled a human." She did not sound pleased.

"This is Theodora, the Seer to the Novus Pack, and Intended Mate to their leader," Katherine said, giving the female a warning glare as she introduced me. "This is my son's mate, Loreen."

"I've heard about you." The redhead moved toward me. "They say you are a witch."

"Loreen," Katherine chastised the female.

"They say she has put a spell on the Black. That is why he claims to care for her." The woman looked down at me.

I felt my gift awaken and stir deep in my belly. "I can assure you, there was no spell." I smiled, but it was cold. I did not like this female's demeanor.

"But you are human. What could you give him that a Dolan could not?" the female taunted.

I stood and tipped my chin like I'd seen Black do when he thought someone's question was out of line. "Are you stating that a *mere* human could trick the powerful leader of the Novus Pack? That Raider Black is not in control of his own mind?" My anger increased, and I felt my gift add to the power of each word. "Are you disparaging my Laird, female?"

The woman cowered onto the floor and started to cry as I stood over her. The others were staring at me wide-eyed, afraid and unsure.

"Theo?" Black's voice calmed me.

I turned and gave him a real smile. "I think it is time to go."

He held out his hand to me.

Katherine sputtered, "I apologize Miss Morrissey. Loreen, she is impetuous and does not think."

I stopped then turned so that we were almost nose to nose. "I belong to Raider Black, Leader of the Novus Pack. I carry The Lady's Mark. I will not be disrespected by any male or impetuous female." I felt energy flow behind my words. The power lightly burned against my skin.

"You have my sincere apologies, Black, Seer." Ephraim stood behind his wife.

"Accepted," Black told the Leader.

Once again in the SUV, Wale, my senior guard, leaned into the space between the front seats and asked, "What the fuck was that?"

THIRTY-NINE

NOVUS

RAIDER BLACK

Better Man (Live) by Pearl Jam

I'D FELT THE FAMILIAR BUZZING AGAINST MY SKIN THAT signified that Theo was using her gift. Ephraim had been making polite small talk. I knew he wanted to know whether Theo's family ties to the area would signify my return. He would try to find a way for me to pay for the privilege. I was not happy that Theo was in another room, so I cut to the chase. "I'm going to need your help."

"Go on."

I had the Packleader's full attention. "We have reason to believe that Theo's uncle has tried to cut her out of a family business. I'd like to use your legal team to investigate."

"Of course," the Leader agreed. He lightly cleared

his throat. "I assume that means you will be making more trips to this area?"

"I'm not sure. Theo is not close to her family here, but if she should wish to reestablish ties, then we would ask for permission to make a short visit."

"You and your Intended are welcome. Your people have caused no problems during their stay. I was concerned about the crazy wolf, but he did not damage while here."

I heard a female's footsteps in the hallway, and a few moments later, raised voices. Suddenly, I felt the pull deep in my belly. It was as if my magic was being ripped from my body. Instantly, I was on my feet and moving toward her.

She was angry. Her blue eyes flashed as she shouted at the woman. "Are you disparaging...?" Each word was filled with a combination of her fury with my magic's strength.

She needed to calm down immediately. "Theo?"

She turned me to in surprise, and I felt the pulling sensation cease.

We needed to go. I didn't want to face questions when I had no answers and I wasn't sure that Theo knew what she had done.

Wale's eyes were wide as he glanced in the rearview mirror at us.

"Get us on the road," I ordered.

"I didn't know," she said quietly.

"That you could do that?" I wrapped my arm around her shoulders. Her body felt cold to me.

"That female, she was being critical...of you. I won't listen to anybody talk about you that way."

"Well, you showed her," I teased lightly.

"But I didn't know," she told me testily.

"Your gift has returned."

"A bit of it...Are you...?"

"What?" As far as I was concerned this discussion was over.

"Worried? Won't they tell others that...that I can, I don't even know what to call it...scare the crap out of a Lycan?" She sounded afraid, and my wolf did not like that.

"You were defending your mate, your Laird, me." I took in a slow breath. I'd sounded angry, but my anger wasn't directed at her. "I do not see a problem with you demonstrating that you are not to be trifled with." Especially after everything she had been through.

She stared at me, and I felt her use her gift as she tried to read my reaction. "You aren't mad at me?"

"No," I told her. "Yes, I wish your gift hadn't reappeared during a visit with Ephraim and his high ranking pack members, but we don't have a clear understanding of your talents, so regret is a waste of time. I have no more control over your gift, or when a new skill manifests than I do the wind."

"I fear I'm causing another problem for you," she whispered.

"No need." I kissed her lightly on the lips. "Now, the plan is that we will stop by your house for you to change and do a final walk through. Then Wale will drive you to the hotel, and we will prepare to depart." I estimated that Lore and I would need about an hour to make our visit to Doug's home.

"I don't have that much left to do..."

I followed her into her room, admiring the expanse

of her back. I stopped her by grasping her hips and pulling her back into me. I licked a line up her spine.

She giggled. "That tickles." She dropped her head forward giving me better access to her sensitive neck while thrusting her ass back against my groin.

"Mine," I growled.

"Can we? I mean, is there time?" She turned in my arms, her hands went to the button on my jeans.

"Always." I couldn't refuse her. "There will always be time for you."

"Well, I did just take on a room full of she-wolves defending your mental capacity." She unzipped my fly and freed my hard cock.

"They might be right. I am crazy about you."

"Show me."

I helped her out of the dress and peeled the pale blue panties from her body. I didn't undress, and she kept her keep her bra on. I pushed her back against the wall and picked her up. She wrapped her legs around my hips.

I slowly entered her as I kissed her lips. Her hand was in my hair, and the other was looped around my neck.

She buried her face against my neck, saying, "So good."

I set a medium pace, making sure to add a twist to my hips.

Her teeth closed on the skin at the base of my neck. My wolf howled in delight.

As my hips moved faster, she shifted so that she could see my face. Her eyes were huge and so dark. "I love you."

"Love you, babe." I pushed into her and came as I felt her inner muscles tighten around my cock.

I carried her to the bed and twisted so that when we fell, she was on top of me. She rained kisses over my cheeks.

I rolled us over and looked into her eyes. "You are mine, Theodora. Forever, no matter what. Mine." I'd added a push to my words.

She raised her right arm and showed me her Novus brand. "Forever."

As I left the house, I told Wale to let her sleep for an hour. She didn't need to be thinking about where I was going.

FORTY

NOVUS

BAYLA JOSEPH

Stitches by Shawn Mendes

I CARRIED THE CRYSTAL GLASS WITH A SINGLE ICE CUBE, the half-full bottle of Jack, and the cashmere blanket onto my screened-in porch. The night was cool, but I would stay out here until the ice melted. Recently, I'd made that new deal with myself concerning my drinking. I knew I was imbibing too often, but it helped numb the pain so I could sleep.

I felt my body unwind while the anticipation for the first rich taste of the wood-aged liquor warmed my belly. I'd done good work with Theodora. I felt justified in giving myself a reward. After the third sip, I relaxed back in the lounger and wrapped the throw over my legs. I stared out at the field across the road from my farm-house, not really seeing anything, trying to clear my mind.

My body took in an involuntary breath. Suddenly, I knew that he was near. My gaze roved to the left and then to the right. I fought not to move my head, sensing more than seeing movement by the moon's light. I was surprised that he didn't try to hide as he'd done several times before.

"Wolf," I called the neutral greeting.

He did not increase his pace, and by doing so, he allowed me time to admire his grace. He crossed into my yard, stopping a few yards from my porch. His familiar sat at his feet. "Bayla." He bowed at the waist.

I couldn't tell his age by reading his aura. It was his manners that gave him away as an ancient. Although he stood patiently, he was surrounded by streaks of deep crimson and black. "You've been busy tonight," I commented blandly.

"I helped right a wrong."

His voice was amazing. I always wanted to lean closer to absorb its warm tone and the hint of an accent that I couldn't place but wanted to spend hours listening to. I gave myself a stern reminder. He was dangerous. "So you claim."

"It was my duty to my Pack and to My Queen."

"Do you love her?" I wished I could take back the words. I placed my glass on the floor beside my chair. *No more, tonight.*

His smile made him truly beautiful. "No. Theodora is not meant for me. I care for her, I admire her, but I do not yearn for her."

I'd spent too many hours wondering. The few times my patient had mentioned her bodyguard, it had always been with respect and fondness. He was very handsome, and his body could have been sculpted by an artist. I'd known immediately that he was Lycan. A beautiful woman and a sexy male who shared a high degree of closeness and proximity... My imagination had run wild while I lay alone in my bed.

"Why are you here?" I didn't know what to do about my curiosity concerning the dangerous male.

"Would you like it if I said to see you?"

"No," I answered too quickly.

"Theodora is leaving tonight."

"So, this is good-bye." I felt the loneliness seep into my soul. I would miss him, although I didn't understand why. We had exchanged no more than a few sentences, words really.

"I did not say that I was going."

My smile gave me away.

I needed to reassert control over my emotions. My interest, this flirtation, was dangerous and pointless. It should end now so that he would leave me alone. "Did you kill tonight?" I asked boldly.

He didn't answer right away, so I freed my hand from under the blanket in case I needed to cast a spell.

"I believe that it would qualify as more of an assist, but yes."

"You admit that so easily." I pressed, wanting to make him show an emotion...to hate me.

"I am a murderer, a legend amongst my people."

"So cavalier," I taunted.

"What about you, Bayla? Have you killed tonight?"

I sucked in a deep breath, feeling the pain directly in my chest. "How dare you?"

He spoke over me. His eyes seemed to glow by the light of the moon. "You choose to slowly kill yourself every night for something that was not your fault."

"How?" I whispered the word. My hand went up as if to shield myself from his words. "Don't."

"Don't what? Speak the truth?" He didn't raise his voice, but it seemed like it vibrated through my body. "You hold yourself responsible for an accident."

"It was my fault. I shouldn't have taken that road. Everybody knows that it's dangerous when it's slick," I cried reliving that night, the sound of metal crunching and the sirens.

"When you learn to forgive yourself, you shall be ready for me."

"What?" I bolted up from my chair.

"Your heart must be ready to accept." He covered his heart with his large hand. "It is closed now, but one day it will open, and then I will fill it." He moved so quickly it was like he disappeared.

What the hell?

FORTY-ONE

RAIDER BLACK

Give It Away by the Red Hot Chili Peppers

LORE HAD FOLLOWED MY ORDERS AND ALLOWED ME TO make the kill. The old man's heart had begun to pound when he'd caught sight of me as he'd rounded the corner of the barn. He knew why I was there.

My wolf chuckled evilly. *Not much of a fighter.*

I'd left Lore to handle the clean-up and returned to the rental home to shower. I gave Issa my final instructions and headed back to the hotel. As I pulled into the parking lot, I noticed that Wale was standing beside one of our SUVs with Theo sitting on the hood. I parked beside them and got out.

She slid down and rushed to me, hugging me tightly. "I messed up."

"Shh." I returned her hug and glanced at Wale, who

gave one shake of his head, which told me what she'd done wasn't a big deal.

She pulled away. "I wasn't prepared...I hadn't really thought about it. There were so many...I didn't recognize some of them, and I couldn't, I mean, it was..."

"Babe, slow down." I'd gotten the gist.

"The others were waiting in the suite when we arrived," Wale clarified.

Eleven males in one room. It would be intimidating to her.

She smiled bravely at me. "I can do it. I just needed a minute and some fresh air."

I stared into her eyes. "You're sure?"

"I want to try." She held my gaze. "Plus, you'll be there."

I didn't try to talk her out of it or question her. This fear would be something we would deal with, possibly forever, our new normal. I took her hand and headed toward the door. Riding in the elevator, I told my guards, "This will take about ten minutes. Then, we'll break for food and after...be ready to leave for home."

"Yes, Laird," they said in unison.

My woman was so brave. As Wale opened the door, I felt her hand rest against the center of my back. I'd learned that she did this to anchor herself when she felt unnerved. I turned my head to say over my shoulder. "You've got this."

She flashed a tense smile.

I would keep it brief. Everybody stopped talking and got to their feet as I entered. I waited for Wale to close the door behind us and motioned for those who wished to take seats to do so. Theo leaned against the wall to my left a few feet from Wale.

"Here's the plan." I recited what I'd gone over in the elevator, ending with, "Questions?"

Brogan Simms, who was new to my squad of personal guards, raised his hand. "Are we doing this straight through, again?"

He had the pretty boy looks of a clean-cut college student, but he was nearly four hundred years old. He'd come to Novus from Alabama. "That might change, but I'd like to get back as quickly as possible."

There were no more questions, so I reminded them unnecessarily, "One hour."

Theo was already moving to me as I held out my hand to take hers. Wale held the door for us, and we headed to my room. I sent Wale to pick up pizzas for us and closed the door behind him. "You okay?"

"It helped having you there." She took a seat on the corner of my bed.

"On the ride back, if you get hungry, thirsty, need to pee—anything—we'll stop." I didn't want her to be uncomfortable.

"I can barely believe it. I'm going home." She kicked off her shoes. "It hasn't really hit me yet."

I sat beside her and reclined so that I was flat on my back. "Not while you were packing or saying goodbye to Issa and Lore and that wolf?"

"I'm sure they'll be glad to have a break from me." She snuggled against me. "It hasn't been a fun job."

"They never complained." I shifted my arm so that it supported her head. "They had opportunities, but neither one of them said a word."

"They wouldn't. Lore thinks of me as his family, a responsibility, because I share his mother's talent and

Issa… Well, she needed time away to make some decisions."

"We need to discuss a few things."

She ran her hand over my abs. "Like we won't have hours trapped inside a car to talk?"

"I figured you would sleep and sing to the radio." I had missed this. The quiet moments when we didn't have to solve a major problem, and we could simply be.

"I guess there will be a lot to do when we get back…?" Her hand moved lower on my belly.

"For the both of us." I couldn't stop thinking about her hand…

"Will we ever….? No, it's selfish." She cut the question off.

"You can be selfish." I covered her hand, lifted it to my lips, and kissed her palm.

"I wish we could have some more time, just the two of us before we go back."

I rolled to my side and studied her. "We could steal a few hours."

Her smile was huge, and then she pulled it back to a smaller version. "I don't want to interfere with your, er, *our* responsibilities."

"Let's get something clear. I want you to tell me what you want or what you need. Don't ever hesitate or second guess." I kissed her.

She started to giggle. "I would ask the same of you, but you're good at making your needs known." She ran her hand over my hard cock. "Like now."

"If you are willing…?" I kissed her again.

"God, yes." She untied the drawstring at her waist. "You have no idea how happy this makes me."

The chuckle started low in my gut, "I have an idea."

"I wasn't sure that I could do this."

"I know," my voice was soft. That she was willing to accept my touch was a miracle and now that she felt brave enough to initiate sex...that was better than my wildest hope.

We were in the middle of Illinois. The road was flat and boring, but I had my beautiful woman beside me. Wale was behind me on his bike, and we were making good time. Theo had her bare feet propped on the dash with a pillow behind her head against the window.

"I think we should wait until after Solle has the baby." She pulled on the seatbelt strap over her chest. "That is if we are still friends."

"You most definitely are still friends. If there had been any way for her to come with me, she would have."

"I think it all hinges on how things go with Conal."

"Things will go fine with him." I expected his apology to be filled with groveling and an expensive gift.

She grimaced. "I don't want him to make up with me because you ordered it."

"They both missed you. He told me that."

"I always thought he'd give me the final pep talk before the ceremony." She brought her feet down and turned her body towards me, pulling her knees to her chest.

"Do you understand what the Mating Ceremony entails?"

"Since I'm not Lycan, I have to be dumped out in the wilderness, and I wander around until you get tired of stalking me."

"That part is true for a Pack member's mate, but

because of my position, things become a little more involved."

"Of course, they do." She poked my thigh with her bare foot. "Is there going to be a roving party around the lands with a ball afterward?"

"Typically, all of Novus will be invited, as well as many dignitaries. They will gather in the public grounds, and there will be food and drink."

"A Lycan party."

I cleared my throat. "You will be freed. It is my job to track you, then claim you."

"Why did you say it like that? You used your 'you aren't going to like this' voice." She narrowed her eyes at me.

I grasped her foot. It was cool, and I considered turning on the heat.

"Black, what happens during the claiming?"

I had made it a practice not to hide things from her. In the beginning, I'd done that because I'd hoped to find fault with her if she fought us, but then I looked forward to her reactions. She might be fearful, but she always faced things head-on. However, after everything that had happened, I paused.

"You have to tell me. I can do it if I know." She sounded like she was trying to convince herself and me.

"I am to take you in front of the gathering,"

"Oh." The one word came in a breathy whoosh.

"In my wolf form." I sniffed the air for a clue what she was thinking.

She said nothing for two minutes.

"It is our way," I said in an apologetic tone.

"Will...will your wolf talk to me while we are

mating? I will need his reassurance if...if others are to watch."

I reached for her hand as my wolf pondered the question. She didn't fear my wolf, just the others watching.

"I think...I can do it if...if he talks to me..." she said in a small, quiet voice.

I will do whatever our mate wishes. She need only ask. "He will. He promises."

"So, what do the people do? Cheer you on or offer suggestions?" She squeezed my hand.

"You think I can do better pleasing you?" I smiled because she had been screaming my name during her orgasm in the hotel room.

"God, no!" She giggled. "You've ruined me for every other man on this Earth."

"That's better."

"So then, what happens?"

"I ask The Lady to bless our union, or maybe you should...? We might want to check with Lore."

"Oh, God, I hadn't thought about that." She covered her face with her hand. "He's like my older brother. He's going to watch? *Yuuuuckkk.*"

"He is our best resource."

"Can I tell him that he can't watch?" she asked quickly.

"To a Lycan, a mating is a reason to celebrate. For a Packleader to find his mate, it is very important for a number of reasons: his happiness, the addition of a Queen-like figure, and many believe that a mated Lycan is more even-tempered." I let that sink in. "For Novus, this is about you, Theodora. You are loved."

"Even though I lost my mind?" she whispered.

"You were brave enough to seek help and work to recover," I said, my voice going hard. I hated that she worried about that. "You are a gift from our Goddess, to Novus and me. What you have endured, it is reprehensible, and yet…you rise. You smile, you ask about your friends, you laugh, and you make others join in. That, my darling, is who you are and what you are to us, my beautiful Queen."

She used her other hand to wipe tears from her cheek. "How do you do that? Turn so sweet." She sighed. "I'll cooperate, but don't be mad if I send Lore on an errand that night."

I chuckled. "He'll probably track you the entire time to make sure you're safe."

"I want to do this right since it is such a big deal. I didn't know that there would be so much to plan."

"We do this on your timeline, babe. I'm sure there will be many who will want to help plan the event. You will have your say and get whatever you wish."

"I only want you."

That pleased my wolf and me very much. "And I, you."

"Basil will be in heaven." She relaxed the grip around her legs.

"He has been collecting ideas for the house."

"What house?"

"While we were talking with the doctor earlier, it occurred to me that you might want to design our home to suit your needs and tastes."

"Won't we still live in the Packhouse?"

"We can, but if you would like to build a home for us, away from the Packhouse, we can." I would build her one hundred houses.

"Are you doing this for another reason?"

"No." I glanced at her and saw that she was chewing on her bottom lip. "What are you wondering…just ask me, Theo."

"Are you sure you didn't have sex with Siobhan in your rooms? In your bed?"

I knew the admission that we'd had sex had hurt her. "I did not. If things had progressed in a favorable way, we would have, eventually, but no, that never happened. We had three encounters, and none were satisfying for either of us."

"I know you wouldn't lie." She dropped her head back and stared upward. "What would it mean to Novus if I wanted us to live in our own place?"

"We would still use the Packhouse for entertaining and for lodging for our guests." I started to consider the positives. "We live in only three rooms there."

"It is a beautiful place." She didn't sound enthused.

"It is a showplace, and you want a home," I stated.

"I can live anywhere, but I'd like for us to have a place where we are comfortable rather than staying in only three rooms because the rest of the house is so fancy."

She smiled at me, and I knew the answer. "Then we shall."

FORTY-TWO

THEODORA MORRISSEY

XO by Beyonce

A PART OF MY BRAIN MUST HAVE FELT BLACK DECREASE
his speed. I stretched as best I could in the SUVs seat.
"Where are we?"
"Iowa."
I glanced at the clock, which read 4:17. He had
driven hours without a break.
"This is the only place for miles that's open." He
pointed his index finger at the large, brightly-lit truck
plaza ahead on our left.
"As long as there isn't a wait for the bathroom, I'll be
good." I slid my feet into my ballet flats.
"We'll grab some food and take a break for half an
hour before continuing."
"Are you going to keep driving?" I knew he could go
without sleep longer than two days.

"No. Somebody will take over."

After taking a trip to the ladies' room and spending time splashing water on my face and brushing my teeth, I felt better. I dined on freshly made doughnuts and hot coffee. Black ate five breakfast sandwiches and then paced up and down the parking area. When it was time to go, he sat in the back seat with me rather than in the front with a red-headed guard named Seth, who had spent the last year driving escorts.

"Can you sleep?" I asked as I buckled my seatbelt.

"I need to answer some e-mails." He pulled a tablet from the seat pocket.

"I'll read then." I felt like I should try to stay awake to be with him.

"Sleep, babe, it'll be fine."

I tried to keep my eyes open for a few miles, but very soon, I was asleep.

When I next opened my eyes, the sun was shining, and Black was tapping on his tablet. I was always amazed at how fast his huge fingers could move over the keyboard.

"You're up."

"What did I miss?" I stretched and wondered how long I would need to stand under the hot spray from Black's giant shower to work the stiffness from my muscles.

"Nothing but fields and cows."

One of the guards pulled up beside our SUV on his bike. His long hair flew behind him, and he smiled wildly at us.

I caught the look Black gave the man.

"Do you want to be out there?" I knew Black would

never allow me on the back of his bike at the speed we were traveling.

"Nah," he answered, but he continued watching the biker.

"It would be okay if you wanted to ride your bike." He wouldn't be far.

His glance cut to me. "You're sure?"

"Yeah." I knew by the size of his smile that I'd said the right thing.

We'd stopped for another short break. I now was in the backseat with a bag of chips, two candy bars, a medium diet soda, and my e-reader. Brogan was at the wheel, and the male had finally given up trying to make conversation. Everything was fine for the first fifteen minutes, but with each question that he asked, I became more anxious. Finally, I told him I needed some quiet time.

I tried to concentrate on the page in front of me. I then closed my eyes and tried counting backwards and controlling my breathing. My inner alarm system was sounding, warning me to be careful, but of what, I didn't know. These feelings could be valid, or they could be caused by a ghost from the past.

I checked the time at least every three minutes, hoping that, somehow, we would have crossed the state line, but Iowa seemed to go on forever. Sixty-eight minutes had passed when Black pulled up beside our SUV.

I placed my open palm against the window, wishing that I could touch him.

He immediately motioned for Brogan to pull over.

The minute we stopped on the side of the interstate, the male got out. "I didn't do anything."

I got out on the non-traffic side and stood beside the SUV. Black approached and pulled me into his arms. "I fucked up," he said into my hair.

"I don't know him," I told myself that was the reason for my anxiety.

"Brogan, take the bike." He opened the door for me to get into the front seat. "Can't talk out here, or they will turn around and head back." He waited for an opening in the traffic and slipped in. Once we were on the road again, he spoke. "I thought because he is quiet that you'd be okay. I shouldn't have put you with him."

I sighed. "He didn't do anything, but he wasn't exactly quiet."

"Doesn't matter. He's new to you. Although he looks like a choir boy, he's vicious with his fists."

"I'm sorry you had to cut short your ride." I frowned because I couldn't help my reaction.

He shrugged and offered me a smile. "Felt like something was missing, and it was you."

Two hours later, I still couldn't relax. I was tired of being cooped up. My body wanted to move.

Black must have noticed. He slowed and took the exit. "Got an idea."

"I need five minutes to walk around. Then I'll be fine," I assured him. It was still three hours until we were home.

"Got something better in mind." He pulled out his phone and scrolled through until he found the number. "Garrett, it's Raider Black."

I couldn't make out the response, but I knew the man was excited for the Laird to call by Black's eye roll.

"I wondered if you had a few rooms available?" The male must have answered affirmatively because Black continued, "Some of the guys will want to run, but I'll need your best set-up."

When he finished the call, I asked, "What do you have in mind?"

"Garrett's family owns a motel. It's about ten minutes from here. We'll crash for a few hours then get home and be ready for tomorrow."

I looked around at the land. "There's a motel out here?" I hadn't seen a house for miles.

"Just wait. I think you'll be surprised."

Fifteen minutes later, I turned in a complete circle and tried to talk as I laughed from the sheer joy of the moment. "I freakin' love it."

"Thought you might." Black took my hand and led me to the male and female who were walking down the steps from a cabin with a sign out front reading, "Office."

They smiled at us. "Welcome, Laird, Lady," the male spoke.

"Garrett, Miranda," Black greeted them. "Thank you for accommodating us on such short notice. This is Theodora."

"It is our pleasure." The male glanced behind us, counting the number of guards. "How many rooms are you wanting?"

"Six for the men, if you have them, and then something for us."

"We have enough vacancies this early in the season for your guards, and I think," the male glanced at the female, "we will put you in the private cabin."

"Very private, with a hot tub and deck," the female told us.

"That sounds lovely," I told them.

"I'll get our bags." Black turned to head to the SUV, which left me alone with the couple.

"It is an honor to meet you, Seer," Garrett told me. "We don't make it to Wolfsbane very often."

"I'm sure this place keeps you very busy. It's amazing." The motel was comprised of individual cabins. Each was themed and had appropriate lawn ornaments in their tiny front lawns.

The female smiled at my compliment. "I will show you to your private cabin."

Black motioned for me to go first as he followed with my tote bag and his duffle. "How are things?" he asked the couple.

"Essinia has been accepted to six schools."

I could hear the pride in Garrett's voice. "She wants to go somewhere east, but I worry that she will be homesick."

Miranda said, "She is human, from my family's line. Her mother died during her birth, and we adopted her. Our boys have been grown for centuries, and I always wanted a daughter."

"She sounds amazing," I told them.

"Theo went to college when she was sixteen," Black told them. "If you would like for her to talk to your daughter, that can be arranged."

"Or if I can answer any questions that you have…? I think you might classify me as a professional student. I love learning."

"Thank you, Seer," Garrett said, smiling.

"I'd like for her to stay with Novus, but that is her decision." Miranda sounded resigned.

"She is young. Many things will change before she reaches full adulthood. She has time to explore and decide," Black told the couple. "She will always be welcome on Novus land."

I saw the cabin ahead. There were dogs made of logs in front and two rocking chairs on the porch. "This is great."

The tour was over, and the hot tub was heating. Plans for dinner had been made, and we were finally alone. I was sure the guards were in the woods nearby, but I felt like it was just the two of us. "This is the best place ever." I wondered if we could build a fire in the fireplace in the bedroom.

"You know it is customary for a newly mated couple to take a trip after the ceremony." He pulled off his shirt.

"Even the very important leader of Novus?"

"Yes, even him."

"We'd still be on Novus land, right?" I waited for his nod. "So, technically, you would be available, if needed."

"Shall we reserve this place?"

"That would be perfect." Plenty of woods for Black to run. It was out of the way, so not too many strangers. Maybe by then, Conal, Solle, and the baby could come as part of our entourage...

He walked to the deck and tested the temperature of the hot tub. "Get naked, Theo."

FORTY-THREE

RAIDER BLACK

Slide by the Goo Goo Dolls

WE DIDN'T GET MUCH REST, BUT I WAS RELAXED. THEO was digging in her bag, looking for something to wear to dinner. "I can send somebody to grab a box of your clothes from the truck."

"Think this top will be okay?" She shook out a blue shirt that almost matched her eyes. "I hope they didn't go to a lot of trouble to feed us."

"I told them to keep it casual."

"And to you all, that could mean a quartet in powdered wigs, fine china, and crystal." She pulled the shirt over her head.

I couldn't argue, because that might be true.

"What do you know about their daughter?"

"I've seen her once or twice. She wears my brand, so she is protected."

"And you trust her to go out into the human world and not tell any secrets?"

"She will be called before me before she is to leave. I will remind her of her vow, and the responsibility that she carries by wearing my mark."

"Was she old enough to understand the vow when you branded her?"

"What are you getting at?"

Her eyes widened, and her body froze for an instant. I instantly regretted my tone.

Her gaze lowered. "How old are Articles when they are branded? I wasn't criticizing. I was curious," she told me as she brushed her hair and studied me in the mirror.

"They are branded during their thirteenth yeas. Some packs require it soon after birth."

"Have any refused?"

"Not to my memory. Why would they?" I had not really thought about it.

"I mean no disrespect. I just need to understand... There's so much I still don't know." She let out a loud sigh.

"There is plenty of time to learn. You can always ask us. I don't expect for you to have all of the answers," I reminded her.

Wale knocked on our door then entered. "Laird, they are ready."

Dinner was held in a large building that was used for banquets. The tables were covered in white clothes, with candles in the center but no crystal or powdered wigs. Theo charmed the owners, their sons, and their mates. She was now in the corner talking to Essinia. I watched her hold out her arms to the teen who hugged her. I could just make out Theo's words. "Call Novus, and we will get together."

Essinia nodded and smiled shyly.

When she returned to my side, she told our hosts, "I am totally in love with this place. It's perfect."

"Then we will see you two soon?" Miranda pressed.

I had already discussed our post-ceremony trip idea with them.

"We will try our best to attend the Mating Ceremony," Garrett announced. "The entire family."

"Essinia shouldn't attend," Theo blurted.

Miranda switched into protective mother mode. "Why, Seer? Do you know something?"

Theo shook her head. "I...no. I have offered your daughter my friendship. I'm not sure that seeing...experiencing the ceremony wouldn't cause her distress."

Garrett nodded. "I see your point. Thank you for thinking of her."

We said our goodbyes, and once we were on the road, I spoke, "That was not the complete truth, Theodora. Why can't their daughter attend our Mating Ceremony?"

"Sin, that's what she asked me to call her." She grinned a little. "She is the mate to one of the Novus males."

I turned my head. "You know that?"

"Watch the road," she cautioned me unnecessarily, "and yes, I do."

"You had a vision tonight?" She had not passed out or thrown up.

"It was different." She spoke slowly, "I shook her hand because she offered it, and when we touched, I felt it."

"But you didn't get sick."

"It wasn't like a movie unfolding, it was more of a thought in my head. Does that make any sense?"

"So, your powers are returning?"

"It seems that way. I don't know what to expect in the future, but I'd be happy if I never threw up again," she grumbled.

We would be calling to The Lady very soon. "Which male?"

"Are you asking me or ordering me to tell you?" She turned toward me.

"Why don't you want to say?" I could order her so easily to ease my curiosity.

"She is so young. She's never left Nebraska."

"You think she needs life experience before mating?"

"I think she needs experience in order to deal with her male, or he will run over her."

Hmmm, so he was strong-willed. "She has grown up in a Lycan family. She knows how her life would be."

"We won't be sending her a ticket to Africa, so there won't be millions of miles between them. If they cross paths, then it is The Lady's will," she spoke heatedly.

"But you don't want her at our mating."

"Well, first of all, I don't really want a seventeen-year-old, seeing us doing it." She blushed as she stumbled over the words. "And since there will be The Lady's magic in the air, if her mate saw her, he would take her then and there."

"How do you know that?"

"Issa told me. She plans on being miles away from Asher or armed with a flame thrower."

I considered all that she had said. "I think your decision was wise."

"Thank you, Laird," she said cheekily.

We were quiet for a bit. I liked that about Theo. She didn't mind silence.

"Sin wants to study computers and technology. She games and wants to create a game where the females are the heroes."

I grinned. I understood her hint. "Then Tex will share many interests with her and cherish his life with her." I was happy for my friend.

"I made it too easy for you to guess." She placed her hand palm up on my thigh. "So, you understand my concern."

I took her hand. "I do."

"Are you angry?"

"That you care about our Pack members, never."

"You know I'll continue to make mistakes," she said quietly.

"And you will think that I have done so, too."

She laughed. "Spoken like the most powerful male in the land."

I squeezed her hand. "Just the land?"

"In my world."

It seemed like the last ninety miles took forever. Theo stared intently at the windshield as though she was looking for changes since she'd last been here.

"The grass has changed to green, so Spring has arrived," she mumbled.

"Soon, they will be planting the fields, and Conal will open the pool."

"That might change with the baby and all," she reminded me.

"Then would you like to move the party to the Pack-house?" I knew she enjoyed the weekly summer gatherings with our close friends.

"Would that interfere with your Sunday teleconferences?"

I grinned. "It would give me a reason to keep the calls short."

"Okay, if the MacGregors are too busy, then we'll move it to our house."

Warmth spread across my chest whenever she referred to things as "ours." "Somebody's up." I pointed to the lights at the main entrance.

"You said we would sneak in," she accused.

"Looks like the staff has a different idea." They did like the pomp of the old ways.

"Then you had better go over what I'm supposed to do." She didn't complain. She accepted her position and dealt.

She was perfect for Novus and for me.

My phone vibrated on the nightstand, so it had to be important. I'd left instructions to hold all calls. I rolled away from Theo and reached for the damn device. I answered with a gruff, "What?"

"How soon can I meet with the Seer?" Conal asked.

"Conal, we were sleeping." I glanced at the clock.

"Solle wants this to happen. She has been bugging me since I got the text that you had arrived." Conal didn't sound angry, but I knew he was frustrated.

A small hand tapped my back. "I need to shower and eat something." Theo's voice was still slurring from her deep slumber.

"Did you hear that?" I asked my Second.

"I'll be there in two hours."

"You will meet with me first," I instructed.

"Yes, Laird."

He would not upset her. If she agreed, he could be alone with her, but he needed to be clear on the rules: no scaring her, threats, or raised voices.

"Bossy," she told me as she lifted her leg and straddled my body. "Good morning, Laird." She presented her brand, naked, with my cock resting along the crack of her ass.

FORTY-FOUR

NOVUS

THEODORA MORRISSEY

Sweet Child of Mine by Guns N' Roses

"Conal's here," Black announced.

It used to bug me that I couldn't hear what a Lycan could. Now, I'd come to rely on their early detection of sounds and presences. "Be nice," I warned him. "This is for Conal and I to work out."

"You are mine, so it is also my concern," the Laird said.

"Don't beat him up too much," I urged gently. I wanted Conal and I to find our way back. If things continued to be tense between us, Solle and I could never be close again. These past months had proved to me that I needed and would continue to need, a strong support system in place if I was going to survive and hopefully thrive in this life.

Black pushed his chair back from the table and

walked around to me. He brushed a kiss over my lips and said, "Come to my office in ten minutes."

I pushed my plate to the side and rested my forehead in my hands. This was a test for me. How I handled this moment would be talked about by the Pack. I was no longer the Seer who was guarded closely. Now, I was to be the Laird's Mate, the one closest to their leader with even more influence than I'd had before.

I carried our plates to the sink and washed my hands. Glancing in the mirror by the door, I saw a woman who wasn't afraid. That woman looked ready to face her future.

I knocked twice lightly on the door to Black's office after nodding once at the guard sitting at the desk in the outer office.

"Enter."

I walked through the door and saw Conal standing almost in front of me.

He checked me out, looking me up and down three times. "You look good, My Lady."

The use of the formal title versus something more casual didn't throw me off. "Thank you, Second."

Thankfully, Black didn't allow the ensuing silence to go on too long. "With your permission," he glanced at me briefly, "I'll leave the two of you to talk."

I nodded my head once slowly.

"Thank you, Laird," Conal said.

As Black passed me, he grasped my hand and kissed my cheek.

I watched the door close, then turned back to Conal. He was a proud and respected alpha male. I was not going to wait for him to figure out how to start this conversation. "I missed you very much Conal. There have been so many times these past months when I've needed you." I paused to wet my suddenly dry lips. "In Ohio, there were moments when I wanted to ask for the phone just to hear your voice."

His chest rose and fell with each deep breath, and yet he said nothing.

"I love your mate. I would do anything for her. That day, I would have done anything to protect her and your young." I could feel beads of sweat run down my back.

"I know that you care for Solle," he said quietly.

"If I could do it over, I would have told my guards."

"Why didn't you?"

I'd asked myself that question a million times. "A part of me kept thinking that we'd get stopped, or that Solle would change her mind, or that your meeting would end ahead of schedule, and you'd stop her…" I shrugged. "But I think, the real truth was that I didn't want to upset or embarrass her and you, by telling on her."

He made a sound that was a little like a grunt.

"Solle has her own life. She has freedom, and I didn't want that taken away from her."

"Is your life so bad?" he asked slowly.

"No." I shook my head. "But knowing that your every move is reported and every conversation documented is at times daunting." I met his gaze. "I have very little that is my own."

"I misjudged you." He bowed his head.

"You were angry and frightened. You needed somebody to blame. I didn't want you to blame Solle or for her to be placed on lockdown." I started to wring my sweaty hands in front of me as I remembered the intensity of his anger.

Conal blew out a breath that billowed his cheeks. "Let's go for a ride. I think better on my bike, and I know that you do, too."

"I'll have to ask Black," I sputtered. He spoke of a time when I relied on him for so much. Before Black and I got together, when I was overwhelmed, Conal would take me for a ride.

Black was accommodating and told us, "I'll meet you at your home in one hour. I'm sure that Solle will be going crazy by then."

Riding behind Conal was different than with Black. I lightly rested my hands on his waist, but I did not mold my body to his. We rode for about twenty minutes before Conal pulled into the elementary school parking lot and stopped. "Time to talk."

I climbed off and removed my helmet. After placing it beside the bike, I walked to the nearby swings. I chose the one on the right and waited for Conal to speak.

He stood in front of me and looked over my head. "I must ask for your forgiveness—"

"That isn't exactly true. You don't have to do anything. We all were wrong. I should have called the guards. Solle should never have gone after you expressly told her not to. You should have known that I would never have done anything to hurt Solle, because I love you, Conal. You…you were the one I trusted first." My voice cracked. "I put Black in a terrible situation by making him promise not to interfere. I put a wedge between the two of you."

His troubled gaze met mine. "I was not a good friend to either of you."

I wiped a tear from my cheek.

"I wanted to kill you that day," he admitted in a rough voice.

"I know." I nodded quickly. "That is why I stayed away. You would've followed through on your threat, and then Black would have had to ..." I couldn't finish the thought. "That would have killed Solle."

"What we did, it contributed to...what happened... didn't it?" He ran his hand over his face and looked away.

"To my breakdown?" I paused to think about my answer. I sat up straighter and met his gaze. He needed the truth. "Yes."

He closed his eyes tightly and frowned as if he felt a moment of pain.

"The attack...it has changed me. Some of those scars will never go away. When you threatened me, I was already traumatized. Everything scared me, Conal. Then losing my two best friends, the people I trusted with my life, who had saved me...it was horrible. I felt abandoned, and the voices in my head told me that I was worthless, and it would be better for everyone if I was dead."

"No." He shook his head and stepped closer to me. "Never... Don't ever say that." He dropped to a knee in front of me. "Theodora Morrissey, I have wronged you. I have done great injury to you. I am so very sorry." He lifted his head, and I saw tears in his eyes. "You have brought joy to our lives. Please don't ever say those things again." He took in a shaky breath. "I, Conal MacGregor, Second to the Leader of the Novus Pack beg your forgiveness this day."

I cried. How could I not? To see such a strong,

honorable male humble himself, I had only one answer. "I forgive you, Conal."

My eyes couldn't track his movement. Suddenly, he was on his feet, pulling me from the swing, to his chest in a tight hug. "Thank you."

I sobbed against his chest. "I missed you so much."

"Me too, baby."

I felt his phone vibrate, so I stepped away from him.

He pulled it out and chuckled at what he read. He showed me the screen.

Solle: You have ten minutes to fall on your sword. Get over yourself and do it.'"

"You'll never hear the end of it if you make her wait much longer." I began walking toward his bike.

Black met us in the driveway. He helped me off the bike and waited while I removed my helmet. "You've been crying." He didn't sound pleased.

"Good tears, I promise." I tried to smile.

"You'd better hurry before Solle comes barreling through the doorway." He took my hand and led me to the front door.

I was nervous, and then I saw her. I don't know why I'd ever felt that way. We were hugging and crying and even jumping up and down a little until Conal barked for us to stop.

Solle cried and said over and over, "Oh, God, honey."

I think I was saying a garbled mix of "Solle" and "missed you so much."

I felt Black's hand on my bicep. "Babe, let her breathe."

I released her slowly and took a good look at her.

"You are glowing." Her belly was big, and she was carrying low.

Solle placed her hands on her belly. "Only a few more weeks."

I took her hand and pulled her toward the sofa. "Tell me everything."

We got comfortable. Conal delivered drinks—beers for the males and water for us.

"First, I must say. I am so very sorry," Solle told me. "I was not a good friend to you when you sacrificed everything for me."

"Solle, no," I told her. "It wasn't like that."

"I should have told Conal."

"It doesn't matter now."

"But when I saw you that day...you were so...so not there."

"I was very near the end of my rope. I was constantly battling suicidal thoughts." Bayla had agreed with my decision to talk about what I went through.

"I'm sorry," she whispered and reached for my hand. "It must have been awful for the both of you." She glanced at Black.

"It was," I answered for us both.

Solle studied me. "You seem very well."

"I'm better," I told them all, "but you know that I'm never going to be cured."

Conal murmured, "Don't say that."

Black's voice was strong as he explained, "She doesn't mean that she won't fight to get better. We all know Theo, and she will. However, there will be times where the ghosts of the past may reappear. We all have to be prepared for that."

I smiled at my lover. "My reactions might not make

sense. Something might spook me that, at any other time, I wouldn't even notice. My therapist, Bayla, encouraged me to not spend a lot of time trying to figure out why a shadow would make me flinch when I knew it was Luna walking onto the porch."

Solle looked at Conal. "You must tell everyone."

"Yes, my love." He smiled at his mate.

She turned serious. "I didn't mean for all of that to happen."

I gave her a sad smile. "You just wanted to see your mom. To know that she was at rest, I understand. I think that I felt a little of that in Ohio. I saw a few of my cousins, and they met Black." I smiled at him.

Solle's gaze went to the Laird. "How did that go?"

"Meg figured out right away that Theo was more than a talented employee to me," he grinned. "I think she gave me her approval."

"Nobody called the next day to express concerns," I told them.

"What I did was dangerous. It put us all in a terrible position," Solle continued reciting her list of sins.

I patted her hand. "We survived."

"But…Conal, what he did…"

"Solle, Conal and I are good." I glanced at him. "We both made mistakes, but we did so because we love you so much."

"I should have asked more questions. I should have visited you, no matter what he'd said."

I talked over her again. "It doesn't matter now. The only thing that matters is that you stay healthy." I looked to Black to help wrap this up. I didn't want her to be so upset.

"Solle, why don't you and Conal share what you told me earlier?" The Laird said with authority.

Conal somehow moved Solle and slid in behind her with his back resting against the corner of the sofa. "You were instrumental in keeping my mate and our babe safe, so we wish to honor you by naming her Theodora."

What? My mouth fell open.

Solle continued. "We are going to call her Tay so there won't be any confusion."

"That is a great honor," Black told the couple.

I felt my throat tighten. "I'm speechless. I'm so happy." I took in air through my nose. "Does this make us something like godparents?" I asked Solle.

"Like there was a chance you wouldn't be in our daughter's life?" Solle stroked the side of her belly.

"I'm so touched, flattered... Honestly, I don't know what to say."

Later that night, I lay wrapped in Black's arms, feeling warm and secure. "Did you know about the naming?"

"Solle told me while we waited for you and Conal to arrive." He brushed a kiss against my shoulder. "She was blown away by how good you look. Seeing you that day on the street, it really upset her."

"With her training and all that she knew about what had happened, I'm sure it was clear what I was dealing with."

"And now?" He ran one hand over my hip.

"She'll watch me closely when she isn't focused on Tay." I smiled as I said the baby's name. "They are so happy." I sighed and closed my eyes.

His hand made large circles on my stomach. "Have you thought about our young?"

I knew my response would be very important by the way he casually brought up the subject as if he didn't want to press too hard. "Did you catch a little case of baby-fever, Laird?"

"There are many decisions to be made."

I turned over so that I faced him. I could make out his features in the dim lighting of the bedroom. I raised my eyebrows. "Is this going to be a discussion, or are you going to tell me how the future will be?"

"To me, the choice to bring you fully into our Lycan world is clear, but it is your life, so I will do as you wish."

"Raid," I breathed the word. I was shocked. Lore's father had refused to change his Seer because he did not want to lose access to her talent. If she had not been murdered, she would have died from old age as humans do. "You would allow…" I ran out of breath, so I started over. "We don't know what will happen…"

"Are you considering it? Being made Lycan?"

"It would mean I could be with you forever…" This was overwhelming.

"It is a huge decision. Not one to be taken lightly," he cautioned, using his "Laird" voice.

"I don't know what to say…what it would mean to my gift." I sighed. I didn't know what my gift now encompassed.

FORTY-FIVE

NOVUS

RAIDER BLACK

Hallelujah by Pentatonix

THE CALL CAME THROUGH MID-AFTERNOON WHILE I WAS
at my desk at Novus. I rushed home to pick up Theo,
then we headed to the hospital. Theo did not use her
office in Novus. There were too many people. However,
she had taken to stopping in a few times a week. Lore
accompanied us but left Luna outside to run free.

We were escorted by our guards to the Maternity
Unit where we found Conal pacing.

Theo rushed to him, hugging him closely. "Why are
you out here?"

"She said I was hovering too close, so the nurse
suggested that I take a break." His blond eyebrows
almost touched his hairline, communicating his
confusion.

Theo patted his arm soothingly. "It will be fine,

Conal. She's in pain and under stress. She probably needed a moment to regroup and focus."

A female dressed in pale blue scrubs approached our group. She bowed her head to me. "Laird, Dr. MacGregor wishes to speak with the Seer."

Theo gave me a look that said I was to take good care of Conal. "Take me to the mama."

Conal tracked Theo and the nurse until they were out of sight. "What's that about?"

"I'd guess that Solle feels bad for snapping at you and wants Theo to tell her that everything will be fine." Theo was good at smoothing over hurt feelings. The women were close friends again. Theo had spent a few hours each morning with Solle since our return.

"So much could go wrong." Conal resumed his pacing.

"But it won't. Not today. Theo said it was so."

"What do you mean?" Conal ran hand through his hair.

"We've been outside almost every night. She…she believes that she can once again feel a connection."

"The Lady hasn't summoned her?"

"No." That was troubling me a bit, but who was I to question a Goddess?

"But Theo's sure about the baby and Solle?" He spoke so quickly the words almost ran together.

"She woke in the middle of the night and told me that she'd seen the three of you sitting by your pool." I did not miss the seizures and the vomiting that her visions had caused in the past.

Six hours later, Theodora Maria MacGregor made her entrance into the world. The entire family was doing well. Conal couldn't stop smiling as he watched his mate feed their child.

"Was that the first baby you've held?" Theo was resting against the headboard with the sheet pulled high, covering her breasts.

"The youngest," I said as I settled beside her.

"Her hands are so tiny, but her grip was strong."

"She smiled at me," I told her proudly.

"Hate to burst your bubble, but it was gas." She scooted closer to me.

I grunted. "She recognized her Laird," I told her as I pulled the sheet lower so that I could see her hard nipples.

She giggled.

"I saw intelligence in her eyes. She will be very important to our people." I leaned over to take her nipple into my mouth.

"Was that ever in doubt?" She combed her fingers through my hair as I pulled hard on the peak.

"I find I like babies very much." I moved to her other breast.

She stretched under my mouth's attention, pushing her chest higher.

"I think we should practice making one so that when the time comes, he will be perfect." I used my arms to move so that I rested over her body.

"I love you." She opened her legs and wrapped them around my thighs. "Thank you for believing in me when I didn't believe in myself. Even when I had given up... you didn't."

I entered her slowly and kissed the woman who meant everything to me.

"Yours," she whispered against my lips.

"Mine."

The End for Now.

Coming in the Fall of 2019: Impressions -Lore
Impressions- Solle
Impressions-Conal

ABOUT THE AUTHOR

M. Jayne doesn't know what she wants to be when and if she ever grows up. She's worked retail, recorded hearings in a Federal Courtroom, worked behind the scenes with security at a casino and currently she is living her dream writing Romance.

She plots and plans from her farm in central Indiana that she shares with her husband and two mastiffs, Ginger and Duncan Keith. When she isn't creating she can be found watching sports, searching for the perfect mascara and reading. She also loves questionable TV- Any Real Housewives, The Steve Wilkos Show and Live PD. Plus she is addicted to the TMZ app on her phone.

M. Jayne loves to meet readers. She attends many conferences and signings. Please take a moment and introduce yourself and tell her what you are reading.

facebook.com/ReadMelanieJayne

twitter.com/1MelanieJayne

instagram.com/ReadMelanieJayne

goodreads.com/ReadMelanieJayne

bookbub.com/profile/m-jayne

amazon.com/author/ReadMelanieJayne

ALSO BY M. JAYNE

The Novus Pack Series
See Me

Made in the USA
Coppell, TX
16 January 2021